THOSE *Scandalous* RAVENHURSTS

VOLUME 1

THOSE
Scandalous
RAVENHURSTS
COLLECTION

February 2016   May 2016

THOSE *Scandalous* RAVENHURSTS

VOLUME 1

LOUISE ALLEN

MILLS & BOON

First Published in Great Britain 2016
By Mills & Boon, an imprint of HarperCollins*Publishers*
1 London Bridge Street, London, SE1 9GF

THOSE SCANDALOUS RAVENHURSTS VOLUME ONE

The Dangerous Mr Ryder © 2008 Louise Allen
The Outrageous Lady Felsham © 2008 Louise Allen

ISBN: 978-0-263-92156-4

09-0216

Our policy is to use papers that are natural, renewable and recyclable products and made from wood grown in sustainable forests.The logging and manufacturing processes conform to the legal environmental regulations of the country of origin.

Printed and bound
by CPI Group (UK) Ltd, Croydon, CRO 4YY

THE DANGEROUS MR RYDER

RYDER

LOUISE ALLEN

Louise Allen loves immersing herself in history. She finds landscapes and places evoke the past powerfully. Venice, Burgundy and the Greek islands are favourite destinations. Louise lives on the Norfolk coast and spends her spare time gardening, researching family history or travelling in search of inspiration. Visit her at louiseallenregency.co.uk, @LouiseRegency and janeaustenslondon.com

Author Note

Jack Ryder first appeared—of his own volition—in *No Place for a Lady*, and took on a life of his own. I found myself wondering about him, what his background was, where he had come from, and I realised I needed to tell his story.

Then I discovered that Jack is not alone—he has siblings, he has cousins, and some of them have a story to tell as well. So this is Jack Ryder's tale, but it is also the first of the stories of THOSE SCANDALOUS RAVENHURSTS, and of how they, like Jack, find the loves of their lives.

It is the start of a journey for me, and I hope you will come along and discover with me what befalls the Ravenhurst cousins.

Chapter One

The evening of 7 June 1815

No one had told him that she was beautiful. Jack Ryder crouched precariously in a stone window embrasure two hundred feet above the ravine river bed and stared into the candlelit room. Inside, the woman he had been sent to find paced to and fro like an angry cat.

He kept his eyes fixed on the image beyond the glass as he wedged himself more securely into his slippery niche. Below, the void beneath the castle was shrouded in merciful darkness, the faint sound of the river floating upwards. Although his whole body was aware of it, he ignored the cold fingers of fear playing up and down his spine, knowing full well that if he let his imagination have full rein he would never be able to move at all. His studded boots ground on the stone, and he froze for a moment, but the sound did not seem to reach her.

Jack gave himself a mental shake and began to work on the

knot that secured the end of the long coil of rope around his waist. As it came free he gave it a jerk, flicking it outwards, and the whole length detached itself from the battlement high above and fell out of sight into the void.

Now his only way down was through that window. Despite his perilous position, Jack had no intention of going through it until he had a chance to size up the woman inside. The woman he had been sent to bring back to England by whatever means he found necessary, including force.

It was for her own good, as well as in the interests of both countries, they had explained at Whitehall. The officials had spoken with the air of men who were glad it was not they who had to attempt to convince the lady of this. They had told him a number of things about her Serene Highness the Dowager Grand Duchess Eva de Maubourg. *Intelligent, stubborn, anti-Napoleonic, haughty, independent, difficult and demanding* was how she had been summed up by the various men who had gathered to deliver the hasty briefing, fifteen days before. *Half-French,* they had added gloomily, as though that summed up the problem.

She had not left the Duchy since her marriage and was likely to be near impossible to move now, the officials added. That was all right; he was used to being asked to do the near impossible.

But there had been no mention of darkly vivid looks, of a curvaceous figure or the lithe grace of a caged panther. And Jack was having trouble believing she could possibly be the mother of a nine-year-old son. It had to be the thick glass in the window panes.

She was alone in the room; he had waited long enough to

be convinced of that. Jack shifted his position, focusing his mind on opening the window and not on what would happen if he lost his balance. The flat of a slim blade slid easily enough between the casement and the frame. Thankfully the window opened inwards, for its height above the floor would make it impossible to use otherwise. He eased it ajar by inches, waiting long minutes between each adjustment so there would be no sudden drop of temperature or gust of wind to alarm her. If she screamed this would likely end in bloodshed—he did not intend that it would be his.

Grand Duchess Eva ceased to pace and sank down in front of a writing desk, her back to the window, her head in her hands. Jack wondered if she was crying, then started, with potentially lethal result, when she banged her fist down on the leather desk top and swore colourfully in English. He could only admire her vocabulary—he was tempted to echo it.

It was definitely time to get off this window ledge. He grasped the frame, put his feet through and swung himself down into the room. There was no way he could land silently, not dropping eight foot on to a stone-flagged floor in nailed boots. She spun round on her chair, gripping the back of it, her face reflecting the gamut of emotions from shock, puzzlement, fear and finally, he was impressed to see, imperious anger masking all else. They had not told him about her courage.

'Who the devil are you?' she demanded in unaccented English, getting to her feet with perfect deportment, as though rising from a throne. Her right hand, Jack noted, was behind her; he searched his memory for his survey of the room. Ah, yes, the paperknife. A resourceful lady.

'You speak English excellently,' he commented. He knew

from his briefing that she was half-English, so it was only to be expected, but it was a more tactful beginning to their conversation than *Put down that knife before I make you!* might be. 'But how did you know I would understand you?'

She looked down her nose at him. Jack registered dark eyes, thinly elegant eyebrows arched in disdain, a red mouth with a fullness that betrayed more passion than she was perhaps comfortable with and one deep brown curl, disturbed from her coiffure and lying tantalisingly against her white shoulder. He focused on those eyes and banished the fleeting speculation about just how the skin under that curl would feel.

'You will address me as your Serene Highness,' she said coolly. 'I was thinking in English,' she added, almost as an afterthought.

'Your Serene Highness.' He swept her a bow, conscious of his clothing as he did so. He was dressed for the purpose of shinning down castle walls, not making court bows, but he managed it with a grace that had one of those dark brows lifting in surprise. 'My name is Jack Ryder.' He had wrestled with whether or not to tell her his real name and decided against it. His *nom de guerre* would be safer in the event they were captured.

'Then you are English, Mr Ryder?'

'Yes, ma'am.'

'So you have not come to kill me?'

That has taken the wind out of his sails, Eva thought, watching the narrowing of the deep grey eyes that had been studying her with what she could only describe as respectful insolence. There was absolutely nothing in this Jack Ryder's expression to which she could take exception, yet somehow he managed to leave her with a distinct awareness of her own femininity and his appreciation of it. It seemed a very long time since anyone had looked at her quite like that and longer still since she had felt her pulse quickening in response.

She managed to keep her breathing under control with an effort, and flexed the fingers cramped around the paperknife. If he was English it was highly unlikely that he was a danger, but she could not afford to take the risk, not after what had happened yesterday. And his unconventional entry through the window had to mean trouble.

'No, ma'am, I have not come to kill you.' A smooth recovery. Why had he not asked her what she meant? Eva studied him while she pondered the disturbing implications of that thought. Some years older than her own twenty-six, but far from middle aged. Slim, dark haired and grey eyed and in obvious control both of his body—given the way he had gained entry to her room—and his face. She had a vivid mental image of him with a sword in his hand; he had a duellist's balance. He was showing no emotion now, after that first fleeting reaction to her statement.

'Convince me,' she said, hoping he had not noticed the tremor that vibrated the hem of her evening gown. 'If you do not, I will scream and there will be two guards in here within seconds.'

He produced a pistol from one pocket. 'And one of them will be dead in as short a time. There is no need for this, ma'am.' The sinister black shape slid back into his coat. 'I am here at the behest of the British government. Your son's god-father is of the opinion that it would be better for the young Grand Duke if you were with him.'

'The Prince Regent? He has hardly shown any interest in Fréderic since he wrote to send the christening gift.' She wished she could move, but the necessity to keep the knife out of his sight kept her pinned against the desk.

'Nevertheless, ma'am, the British government keeps an eye on the Duchy of Maubourg and its affairs, and has done ever since the outbreak of war. To have a neutral country embedded within France can only be a diplomatic asset, however small it is.'

'Of course.' Eva shrugged negligently. He was telling her nothing she did not know all too well. 'Presumably you are aware that my late husband did what he could to mitigate the situation by acting as a go-between. He opposed the French, naturally, but he was too much of a realist to think we could resist in any way.'

'I believe you first met the late Grand Duke in England.' Ryder shifted position, his eyes skimming over the furnishings, searching the corners of the room. She felt it was more an habitual wariness than a search for anything in particular. His knowledge of her history did not prove he had received a government briefing; anyone with an interest in her affairs could have discovered that easily enough, it had made a big enough stir in the news sheets.

She inclined her head. 'We were in exile at the time. My father had died in the Terror, Mama returned home to her father, the Earl of Allgrave. I had my come-out in London and I met the Grand Duke at my very first ball.'

It had seemed like a fairy tale, looking back now. Louis Fréderic, tall, darkly handsome, sophisticated far beyond her experience, an exotic presence on the English social scene, was a catch outside her wildest dreams. The fact that he had been thirty years her senior and that she was barely seventeen had weighed neither with her mother, nor with her.

The Grand Duke carried out his mission by negotiating for an exchange of prisoners, enjoyed a whirlwind courtship and returned to Maubourg with his future Grand Duchess at his side. Eva stared back down the years of memory at herself. Had she ever been that young and innocent?

'And since your husband's death almost two years ago, his brother Prince Philippe has acted as Regent and you and he are joint guardians of your son.' Ryder was not so much asking, as establishing to her that he knew the facts. It seemed he was not completely up to date, but she did not hasten to inform him that Philippe had been confined to his room with some mysterious illness ever since the news about Napoleon's escape from Elba had reached them. That was almost three months ago and she was beginning to despair of his recovery.

'Yes.' Her legs had stopped trembling. Eva shifted her position slightly, resting her left hand casually on the chair back. She could swing it across his path if he lunged for her. 'I have not seen my son for four years. My husband judged it best that he should be educated in England.'

The pain of that, the sense of betrayal, still stabbed like a knife. Louis had not even given her the opportunity to say goodbye, justifying it by saying her tears would weaken the boy. First a private tutor, shared with the sons of a ducal family, then Eton. *Little Freddie, will he even recognise me now?*

'There is no easy way to say this…' Ryder began, and Eva felt the blood begin to drain from her face. *No…no…they have sent him to tell me he is dead…* 'Your son has been the victim of a series of accidents in the last month— No! Ma'am, he is quite well, I assure you!' She felt herself sway and he was at her side supporting her even faster than her own disciplined recovery.

'I am quite all right,' she began, then, as his solicitous fingers closed around the paperknife and whipped it from her hand, 'Give me that back!'

He lobbed it through the open window with scarcely a sideways glance to take aim, but stayed at her side. 'I prefer to remain unpunctured, should I happen to displease you, ma'am. Your son is alive, despite his run of bad luck, and even now, I am certain, is ploughing through his Classical studies.'

'What accidents?' Eva demanded, moving away. Mr Ryder's proximity was strangely disturbing. If she had not been a sensible widow she would have put it down to the close presence of a handsome, dangerous man. But it could not be that. It must be the relief at hearing that Freddie was all right.

He made no move to follow her, simply shifting his position to keep her in view. 'First, in the middle of May, there was a fall down a stone staircase, which was fortunately interrupted by a number of youngsters on their way up. They shared a number of interesting bruises I gather, but that is all. Then on the eighteenth, there was a runaway carriage in the High Street, which only missed the Grand Duke because he was pushed to safety by a passer-by. The carriage and its driver could not be traced afterwards. Then—'

'Hoffmeister should have been taking better care of him,' Eva interrupted angrily.

'His personal secretary and tutor can hardly be expected to keep a lively nine-year-old in leading strings, ma'am. And to his credit Hoffmeister became suspicious enough after the third incident to make contact with Whitehall.'

'Third incident?'

'The inexplicable appearance of one poisonous toadstool in a fricassee of mushrooms that was set before Fréderic for dinner on the twentieth.'

'How…' Eva swallowed, fighting to keep her composure '…how did he escape that?'

'By being immediately and very thoroughly sick. His personal physician tells me that his Serene Highness has a very sensitive stomach.' She nodded, dumbly. 'On this occasion it probably saved his life. He has additional security now, believe me.'

This time she made no pretext of hiding her shaking limbs. Eva sank down on to the chair and tried to tell herself that Fréderic was safe, that all his servants, and especially Hoffmeister, would be guarding him closely now.

'I realise this may be hard to accept, ma'am—' Jack Ryder began, then broke off as she lifted her head to look at him.

'No, Mr Ryder, it is not at all strange. I am fortunate, it seems, that Fréderic gets his sensitive digestion from me, for I spent a miserable few hours with a badly upset stomach two nights ago. At the time I put it down to shock after the accident when the wheel came off my carriage as we were crossing a narrow bridge. Only the parapet stopped it tipping into the gorge. And then yesterday I slipped on the top step of the stairs outside my room; it seems someone had carelessly stood there with a dripping candle for some time. The stone was quite encrusted with wax.'

'Were you hurt?' His instant concern sent a flash of warmth

through her and she found her cold lips were curving into a small smile for the first time in days.

'No, I thank you. But the tapestry hanging beside the staircase is the worse for being torn from its hooks as I clung to it.'

'And how did Prince Philippe react to this chapter of accidents?' Jack Ryder took a chair, swung it round and straddled it, his arms along the back. He had stopped calling her *ma'am,* his behaviour was shockingly casual, but somehow none of that mattered just at the moment.

'My brother-in-law has been indisposed—in fact, in a state of mental and physical collapse—since the news of Napoleon's escape from Elba reached us. We assumed at first it was a stroke. He has been in that condition now for three months. My personal physician and a bodyguard are with him around the clock.' She stared at him, seeing her own scepticism reflected in the steady grey eyes. He looked like an austere priest hearing a confession, with his straight nose and his tightly closed lips.

'You suspect poison. And who rules Maubourg now?'

'My younger brother-in-law, Prince Antoine.'

It was obvious that had been a rhetorical question—this Englishman knew exactly who would be holding the keys of the Duchy. 'Ah, yes, the gentleman who was so anxious to persuade Price Philippe to end your neutrality and join forces with Napoleon after the death of your husband?' Eva nodded. 'And the man who would become Grand Duke should your son and Prince Philippe die?'

'Yes. That is why Philippe is protected as he is. I had not thought Antoine's arm would reach as far as England,' she added bleakly. It had never occurred to her that Freddie would be in danger; she had believed up until now that it was a struggle for power between two brothers.

'It is very likely that an enemy from here could strike at the young Grand Duke, and they could certainly reach far enough to remove the one person who has the authority to protect the Regent,' Ryder pointed out, resting his chin on his clasped hands. It was a well-sculptured feature, she noted absently.

'Myself. Yes, I had thought of that. And I have had time to realise that Philippe's illness happening as Napoleon lands in France is too much of a coincidence. Antoine worships the Emperor—he will throw Maubourg on to the French side in the hope of patronage from Napoleon.'

'Forgive me, I do not wish to insult your country, but while a neutral Maubourg has proved very useful to the Allies in the past, why should Napoleon be bothered with it now, one way or the other?'

'In the past, he was not, or we would never have stayed untouched as we have. But now, I think we may have something he would want.' Jack raised a sceptical eyebrow, but she shook her head. 'I am not certain, it is only a suspicion. What do you know about explosives?'

Instead of answering, Ryder got to his feet and walked quietly to the massive panelled door. He eased the key round, cracked the door open and looked out, then, apparently satisfied, locked it again and came back to her side. 'There are guards at the end of the passage—are they loyal to you?'

'I…I think so.'

'Hmm. I know less about explosives than I suspect I am about to need to. What is going on?'

Eva so far forgot herself as to begin to run her hands

through her hair, then caught herself. A Grand Duchess did not give way to displays of weakness, nor was she ever anything but coolly immaculate under all circumstances. She folded them elegantly in her lap.

'The main industry of the Duchy is perfume.' Ryder nodded. It seemed he knew that, too. 'The State perfumery employs a number of chemists, for it is very much a process of distillation and blending. I take an interest in the enterprise and I was looking through its books last week. Antoine has taken on a number of new men without asking myself or Philippe—professional men by the size of their salaries, not workers or craftsmen.

'And then there have been explosions up in the mountains. That is where I was driving on the day of the accident. We found deep craters, signs of burning, but that is all, although I had the feeling we were being watched. The wheel came off on the way back.'

'So, Prince Antoine is possibly experimenting with some new form of armament, just when the greatest general of his generation lands on the doorstep. And everyone who stands between him and the title suddenly becomes ill or has accidents.'

'Yes.' They stared at each other, Eva wondering suddenly why she had found it so easy to blurt all that out to a complete stranger. He might be a spy of Antoine's, he might be a free-lance, after some end of his own. She had been completely naïve to have trusted him. 'Have you any credentials, Mr Ryder?'

'A little late to think of that, ma'am,' he said, echoing her thoughts. The way his lips twitched with amusement had her eyes flashing.

'Better late than never, sir.'

He raised a hand, its long fingers unadorned by rings, and flipped back his lapel to reveal a small silver greyhound pinned there. 'I am a King's Messenger, ma'am.'

'A glorified postman?' She was feeling chills running up and down her spine as the extent of her indiscretion grew on her. If she could only be certain he was just what he said.

'We do rather more than deliver the diplomatic post,' he said mildly.

'How do I know you haven't murdered the real King's Messenger?'

'You do not. What did you intend to do about all this before I came through your window?'

Eva found her thoughts were suddenly running very fast, very cold. He wanted to know too much. She got up and began to walk up and down the chamber, her crimson skirts brushing against the bed hangings. It did not take much skill to pretend agitation. 'I was thinking how I could get out of the castle and raise the population against Antoine.'

'Madness,' Ryder said flatly, just as she reached her bedside nightstand.

'Oh!' Eva raised one hand to her face and feigned a sob, then opened the drawer and began to fumble in it as though looking for a handkerchief. It was in her hand as she straightened up. 'I think it would be *madness* to trust you any further with the scant identification you have, sir. I am going to ring this bell and when my maid comes I shall send her to fetch my private secretary and my personal bodyguard. Then we shall see.'

'No.' Ryder took two long strides across the room and had his hand outstretched to intercept hers on the bell pull as she flicked aside the handkerchief and revealed the little pistol beneath it.

'Thank you for coming so close, sir. This is not much use over a long distance, but, near to, I believe it would seriously inconvenience you.'

How he did it she had no idea. One moment the muzzle of the pistol was virtually pressed to his waistcoat and he was staring at her in apparent shock, the next the pistol was flying across the room and she was picked up and thrown on to the bed, Jack Ryder's long body pinning her into the yielding mattress.

He stared down into her furious face, his own showing nothing more extreme than irritation. He was, damn him, hardly breathing any harder than he had before. '*Madame,* you may walk out of here and come with me to England willingly, or you may leave this room unconscious and make the journey under restraint. It is your choice.'

Chapter Two

As a way of restraining her it was remarkably effective, Eva admitted to herself as she lay glaring up at the man pinning her to the bed. She could struggle—fruitlessly no doubt, given the size of him and the strength he had already demonstrated—but that would simply press her body into even closer contact with his. She had far too much dignity to do so and he obviously knew it. He would probably enjoy it, too.

She regarded the wicked glint in the grey eyes stolidly for a moment, then said, 'Would you kindly remove your person from my bed?' She could only admire the steadiness of her voice, especially as some part of her, a tiny, suppressed sensual part, was aching to arch against the hard masculinity that was dominating her. She fought down the urge; she had, after all, been fighting that particular instinct for two years.

Jack Ryder responded by raising himself on his elbows, the better to look down into her face. The movement caused even more disturbing pressure on her pelvis; Mr Ryder did not appear to be fighting his own inner sensuality very energetically. His eyes were hooded, watching her with speculation. 'In a moment, ma'am, when we have sorted this out. I am not sure what written proof of my identity and mission you would accept, given that, as you say, I could have stolen it. Will you accept your son's word?'

'Freddie? What do you mean?'

'When I was talking to him, telling him I was coming to fetch you, I asked him if there was a password I could give you in case you did not believe me. He thought for a moment, then said, "Ask Mama how Bruin and the Rat are. It's all right for me to say it, because we aren't at home."'

'Bruin? Oh, the little wretch! Mr Ryder—' She gave him a shove. It was like trying to shift one of the castle's wolf-hounds when they got on to the bed. 'Please get off—I believe you.' Too relieved to be indignant with him any longer, Eva sat up as Jack rolled off the bed to stand leaning against the bedpost, his eyebrows raised interrogatively. 'They are his nicknames for his uncles and I made him promise never to use them to anyone but me because they might be offended. At least, Antoine would be.'

'The Rat I presume?'

'Exactly. He has a long nose that twitches when he is agitated. I believe you, Mr Ryder—now, will you get me out of the castle?'

'That is my intention.'

'And help me raise resistance to Antoine?'

'No.'

'Why not?' Eva swung her feet off the bed and confronted him, all her indignation surging back. This official, this *postman* for the English government, had no right to dictate

to her. He was obviously a man of action, just what she
needed in these circumstances—he should do as he was told.
'It is your patriotic duty, sir.'

'Humbug.' Eva gasped. No one spoke to her like that. It was
so unexpected that she gaped at him. 'Leaving aside the fact
that I have no allegiance to this Duchy, it is not my duty to
get most of its male population massacred by French troops,
which is what will happen if Bonaparte wants this place and
you resist. If he doesn't, then you are risking a civil war for
nothing. My duty, as I have already explained to you, is to
remove you safely to England where you have the legal authority to look after your son until all this is over. It will also
remove one hostage from Antoine's grasp.'

'What, slink off and abandon the Duchy to Antoine and the
French just because I am a woman?' He obviously thought she
was some milk-and-water English miss. Despite him remembering—occasionally—to address her with due respect, he
had no idea of the role she had had to play these past two years
since Louis's death, nor the iron that had entered her soul as
she had done so.

'No, execute a strategic retreat because that is the
sensible thing to do,' he retorted. 'You do understand the
concept of sensible action as opposed to romantic gesture,
I presume?'

'How dare you speak to me like that? You insolent oaf—I
can perfectly well look after myself.'

'Indeed, ma'am? You have escaped two accidents and one
poisoning by the merest chance. If I was an assassin, you
would be dead by now. Your son needs you, and you need me.
Now, are you going to sit there on your—' his eyes flickered

to her body '—dignity, clutching an invisible coronet to your
bosom, or are you going to come with me?'

I should slap him, but he is too quick for me. How can *I
leave? This is my duty, my country now…but Freddie. This
Jack Ryder thinks I am an hysterical woman…*

'What about Philippe? He cannot be moved.'

'Then we leave him. He is the Regent, he accepted the risks
along with the office.' He spoke as though it was a matter of
leaving someone behind while they went on a picnic, not that
they might be abandoning a man to his death. Dear Philippe,
Freddie's favourite Old Bear… 'Can you help him if you
stay?' She shook her head dumbly. 'Then we go.'

'Now?' Her head was spinning. For so long it seemed she
had had to think for herself—now this man was calmly taking
over her decisions and her actions and the frightening thing
was, it felt like a relief to let him do so. Eva straightened her
spine and tried to think this through, ignoring the hard grey
eyes fixed on her.

'Yes, now. Unless you can think of any reason why leaving
in broad daylight might be safer. Can you change into something completely neutral—a walking or carriage dress with a
cloak or a pelisse? Something an ordinary lady would wear,
if you own such a thing.' His gaze swept down over the rich
figured silk of her crimson evening gown to the tips of her exquisite slippers, assessing it, and probably, she thought irritably, pricing it, too.

'I will need to pack,' she began. How was he going to get
them out of there?

'A valise only. Essentials—one change of outer garments
at the most. A discreet gown, nothing showy.'

'But it will take us days to get back to England, I need more clothes than that.' Court routine, even on a quiet day, demanded a minimum of four changes from rising to retiring.

'We can buy more as we go. Have you any luggage here?'

'Of course not. I will have to ring for my maid to help me change, and how am I going to explain why I need a valise at this time of night?'

'Tell her you want to pack up some clothes for the poor— No, better, you know of a deserving young woman in the town who has the opportunity for a post as a governess and you want make her a gift of a valise and have decided to give her one of your old ones. Then tell her you want to change into your nightgown because you have a headache and do not want to be disturbed again tonight.'

'And how, pray, am I going to get into a walking dress by myself?' She knew the answer as soon as the words left her lips and spoke before he could. 'I presume you are going to tell me that King's Messengers have training as ladies' maids?'

'No, but I am capable of tying laces with my eyes closed,' he confided.

'I am quite sure you are, Mr Ryder,' Eva said grimly. And untying them, too, no doubt. He would have a certain appeal for some women who liked the quietly dominant type, she could see that. It was fortunate that she was inured to male appeal. She tugged the bell pull and watched with a certain malicious interest to see where Mr Ryder was going to hide himself. It was a positive disappointment to see him drop to the floor and slide under the bed without any apparent discomfort.

She was beginning to wish she could catch him out in some way—he appeared to have an answer to everything. In fact, the only sign of humanity she had witnessed so far was the occasional glint in his eyes which, in anyone else, she would put down to mischief.

'Your Serene Highness?' It was Hortense, her dresser, slipping into the room with her usual soft-footed discretion.

'Fetch me my valises, Hortense, if you please.'

'Now, ma'am? All of them? You want to pack?'

'Yes, all. And now, and of course I do not want to pack, Hortense. I am thinking of ordering a new suite of hand baggage from Paris and I want to see what I have.' There was no reason why she should not have used Mr Ryder's ingenious excuse— it was sheer stubbornness on her part and she knew it.

She was not given to issuing capricious orders and made a point of being considerate to the castle staff, so such a quixotic demand at that hour of the evening was unusual. But Hortense was too well trained to register surprise. 'Yes, ma'am, right away.'

It took almost twenty minutes, but eventually the dresser was back with four menservants carrying fifteen bags between them. 'Thank you, Hortense. I had no idea I had so many. Put them over there, please.' She waited until the men had gone, then added, 'Help me undress, please. I am a little fatigued and I will not need you after that.'

'Yes, ma'am.'

It felt decidedly risqué to be undressing with a man under the bed, even if he could see nothing. Eva slipped her arms into a wrapper and tied the sash firmly. 'Good night, Hortense.'

As soon as the door shut behind the woman, she ordered, 'Stay there,' and began rummaging through her clothes presses for a suitable walking dress. She was answered by a faint sneeze as she threw her wrapper and nightgown aside and began to pull on her underthings again. A simple pair of stays which she could lace from the front solved one problem, but what to wear on top?

Finally she struggled into the plainest gown she had, which by almost dislocating her shoulder she could button up behind by herself, and found a stout pair of walking shoes to match. There was a large, but rather worn, valise in the pile and she added a good selection of undergarments before announcing, 'You may come out now.'

Jack Ryder slid out from beneath the bed and got to his feet as she was gathering up toothbrush and toiletries. 'That bag? No, far too large.' As Eva gasped, he delved into the valise, extracted the pile of frills, fine lawn and filmy silk and deposited it on the bed.

'*Mr Ryder!* That is my underwear!'

'How very dashing of you to mention it, I was endeavouring not to. French, I observe,' he added outrageously. 'That bag there will do, but you will need to halve that pile of frippery. Here.' He flipped through the pile, sorting it into two, and handed half to her.

Eva contented herself with one glare, dumped it into the small bag, then began to find the other items, trying to think which were the essentials to take. 'What about money?'

'I have enough. The journey to the frontier should only take us just over a week.'

'But Napoleon controls France!'

'He is in Paris, massing his troops. It would not do to show we are foreigners, but we should have no trouble passing as French travellers—it worked well enough on my journey down. Your French is perfect, mine good enough to pass as regional.'

Eva shrugged; he had got to Maubourg, true enough, now she just had to trust he could get them both back to England. 'How do we get out of the castle?' Travelling virtually the length of France seemed simple in comparison to walking out of her own castle with a strange man and a valise.

'Have you a cloak with a hood?' Eva nodded and went to take it from the press. Ryder folded it, placed it in another of the valises, then stripped off his own coat and added that to it. 'I need a sash.' He stood there, waiting for her to catch up with him; of course, in shirtsleeves with his dark waistcoat and breeches, he could be taken at a distance for one of the menservants, except that they all wore a red sash around their waists. But what did that achieve? She could hardly disguise herself the same way.

And if he could see from his hiding place under the bed the way that the footmen were dressed, what else had he been able to see?

Eva forced that worry away and rummaged in the press until she found a long scarf of almost the right colour. 'Let me.' She was so focused on being brisk and matter of fact that her arms were round his waist before she thought what she was doing. Jack stood very still for her, his arms lifted. Eva felt the colour rising in her cheeks; it was impossible to do this without touching him.

'The way it is knotted is distinctive,' she said briskly. 'There, that should do.' She stepped back, hoping her blushes would be taken for general agitation. The heat of his body had been disturbing for some reason. She forced herself to think clearly—it had to be the shock of the whole situation, otherwise what could account for the way she was reacting to this man? 'Now what?'

'Do you know which way to go to reach the lower courtyard without passing many guards?' Ryder was securing the pistol out of sight in the swathing sash, his movements crisp.

'Yes, of course, but we cannot avoid them all, there are two at the end of the corridor, for a start—my bodyguard.' She watched him, puzzled. 'I doubt I can disguise myself to deceive them, nor any of the others, for that matter.'

'You don't even try. Just walk with me, scolding me for something or another, then take the route for the lower courtyard using the least frequented areas.' He swung the small valise up on to his shoulder, casting his face into shadow, and lifted the other one in his other hand. With only the cloak and coat in it, it hung in his grasp, obviously light and apparently empty.

'I understand.' Eva found her face relaxing into a smile. It felt strangely stiff and she realised how long it was since she had found anything genuinely to smile about. 'Come on.' She pressed open the door and led the way out into the corridor. A short distance ahead, where the passage to her private suite joined the main gallery, guards stood on either side, pikes at the slant. At the sound of her voice, they snapped to attention, their weapons crashing upright.

'I cannot imagine how it can take one man so long to mend a simple strap,' she complained, remembering at the last minute to speak the Maubourg *patois*. 'And how you can say you do not understand which valise I want to replace it with, defeats me! I suppose it will be faster to come and look at them myself. How long have you been employed here? I must speak to the major-domo about his selection of staff.'

They passed between the guards, Eva, nagging away, keeping herself between Jack's unprotected side and the right-hand man. There was no response from the guards as she marched along, her heels clacking on the stone floor, her voice raised peevishly. 'This way, man, I do not have all evening!'

Jack strode along in Eva's wake, suppressing a grin at her tone. Although, if she was this bossy in real life, it was going to be a tense trip back. It was hard to understand how such a feminine-seeming creature could be so hard. He had seen genuine tears when she had feared for her son's life, but beside that she seemed cold, arrogant and wilful. As he had been led to believe.

He kept his head down as they passed a knot of female servants, all too busy bobbing curtsies to look at him, and followed the willowy figure of the Grand Duchess.

She wound her way down spiral stairs, along narrow passages and through what were obviously the working areas of the castle with surprising confidence. Perhaps, despite her autocratic manner, she took a practical hand in the supervision of the household. Jack found himself admiring the way she moved, the swing of her hips in the plain gown, then made himself concentrate on trying to maintain his sense of direction and to keep count of floors.

Eva opened a heavily studded door, then stopped. Puzzled, Jack glanced at her and saw she had gone pale. There seemed nothing to account for it, no voices, nothing but the start of a dark spiral staircase. It seemed she braced herself, her fingers white on the ring handle, then she stepped forwards.

After that hesitation she led the way unerringly down the precipitous flight to the solid oak door at the bottom. She pushed it and they stepped out into a brightly lit hubbub of steam, cooking smells and bustling women. In the centre of the room a massive, florid-complexioned individual brandished a ladle and harangued his subordinates. 'Which criminal idiot put cream in this?' he was demanding. 'Do you not know what her Serene Highness likes? Do you wish to poison her?' He glanced across the room, caught a glimpse of the newcomers through the steam and gasped. *'Madame!'*

'Just carry on.' The Grand Duchess waved a hand imperiously and the workers turned back to their tasks, leaving the maestro goggling amidst his cooking pots. 'Through here,' she murmured and Jack found himself outside in the wood yard. A lad staggered past carrying a basket of logs, then the door into the kitchens swung shut and they were alone in the dark.

He put down the lighter valise and took out her cloak and his coat. 'Here, pull up the hood and hide your face as much as possible.' He kicked the empty bag into the shadows, took her arm and began to walk steadily towards where he guessed, if his internal compass had not failed him, the lower courtyard would be. The townsfolk had unrestricted access there; in a few moments they would be simply two passers-by.

It proved easier than he had hoped, although the Grand Duchess was stiff at his side. She was obviously unused to being manhandled by subordinates. There were guards, but only on the main entrance to the inner courtyard, and no one took any notice of one couple amongst so many townsfolk.

'I've a carriage waiting down by the East Bridge,' he said as he steered her out of the gates and past a group laughing as they headed for a tavern, then dodged a stallholder who had finally given up for the night and was packing his wares into a handcart. 'This is busier than I expected.' At least the woman was less trouble than he had feared she might be from the way she had been described. She had a cool head, even if she had a sharp tongue.

It was hard not to give in to the temptation to run—the slope of the street towards the river encouraged haste—but that would only draw attention to them. Below, Jack could just make out the glint of water and ahead was the creaking inn sign he had used earlier as a landmark. 'Down here.'

It was a steep lane, almost an alley, with steps down the centre and cobbles at the sides, and it led directly to the riverside. Beside him Eva was walking briskly along, clutching her cloak at the throat and showing no sign of fear. Now they were well embarked on their escape she was still calm. Jack offered up thanks for being spared an hysterical female and allowed himself to think they were going to make it.

Then, only yards down the alleyway, Eva slid away from him with a little gasp of alarm, her feet skidding on the greasy stones. He dropped the valise and used both hands to reach for her, but she tripped on the steps and was down with a loud noise of rending cloth.

'Ouch! Oh, that is *hard*.' She sat up, batting irritably at the tangling folds of the cloak. In the gloom he could make out the white oval of her face, and the moth-shapes of her moving hands, but that was all.

'Are you hurt?' Jack dropped to one knee and reached out to support her.

'Bruised, I expect, nothing serious.' Eva began to get up, then clutched for her cloak. 'Oh, the wretched thing! The fastening at the throat has broken.' Jack helped her to her feet and steadied her. She moved well, he noted automatically. She was fit, slender, active. That was a relief—he had feared finding a pampered, plump princess on his hands. The cloak slipped away, invisible in the shadows at their feet.

'Just stand there a moment, I'll find the cloak and bag,' Jack began, then froze at the sound of loud voices. The flare of torch-light lit up the mouth of the alley with dramatic suddenness as booted feet hit the cobbles. He spun back against the nearest shuttered shop front, pulling Eva to him. The narrow lane filled with torchlight. 'Make this look good,' was all he had time to say before he bent his head and fastened his lips over hers.

'Mmmf!' she protested against his mouth, trying to jerk her head back. Jack applied one palm firmly to the back of her head, held her ruthlessly around the waist with the other hand and focused on giving a demonstration of blind rutting lust in action. It was not easy when the lady in question was trying to bite your tongue with vicious intent.

'Hey! What have we here?' The voice was loud, cultivated and arrogant. 'Can we all join in, friend?'

Jack raised his head, catching a glimpse of furious, rebellious brown eyes in the second before he pressed Eva's face into his shoulder, muffling her snarl of fury in the cloth. 'Sorry, but this lady's all mine.' There were half a dozen of them, officers in the pale blue-and-silver Maubourg uniform that he had learned to recognise as he had scouted the castle and its defences. They had been drinking, but only enough, it seemed, to make them boisterous and over-friendly.

He kept his accent pure Northern French, gambling on them finding that more intimidating than provocative—which was more than could be said for the Grand Duchess's efforts to free herself from his grip. He had his hands full of scented hair and sweet curves and she was pressed intimately against him. He tightened his hold, which had the unfortunate result of pressing her harder against the part of his anatomy that was entering into the deception with enthusiasm, and growled, 'Patience, sweetheart, wait until these gentlemen have gone at least.' Her reaction was to attempt to plant a knee in his groin. 'Friends, give us some privacy, the lady's husband will be looking for her—have some fellow feeling.'

That provoked the predictable lewd reaction, guffaws of laughter and cries of encouragement. They turned away, beginning to descend again to the river, when one, the most senior by the glimpses Jack had of his epaulettes, stopped.

'Why, the lady has dropped her cloak. Allow me.' He stooped, gathered it up and stepped close to lay it over Eva's shoulders, holding up the torch, all the better to see exactly what he was doing, and, Jack guessed grimly, to catch a glimpse of the lady in the case.

Chapter Three

*C*olonel *de Presteigne!* At the sound of his voice Eva stopped her efforts to free herself from Jack's outrageous embrace and clung to him instead, pressing her face into the angle of his neck. This was not a group of young subalterns who could be relied upon not to recognise their Grand Duchess in a plainly clad figure glimpsed in a dark alleyway. This was a senior officer who knew her all too well.

Against her lips she could feel the pulse in Jack's neck, strong and steady, and tried to stay as calm. 'Here, allow me, *ma chère.*' The weight of her cloak settled heavy on her shoulders and the colonel's fingers trailed, lingering, across the nape of her neck. He had done exactly the same thing two nights before as he had restored her gauze shawl at a reception, counting on her not knowing whether it was deliberate or accidental. Now she could recognise that it was quite deliberate, no doubt a favourite ploy of his he could not resist trying on any female, whether noble or bourgeoise.

'*Merci.*' Jack's hand came up, ostensibly to smooth the

cloak around her shoulders, in effect bringing the edge of his palm sharply against the colonel's groping fingers. '*Bon nuit,*' he added pleasantly. Under the words the threat of violence hung like a lifted rapier.

Eva could feel the atmosphere crackle between the two men and knew instinctively that Jack had let his gallantry override his common sense. It was foolhardy, yet she felt a *frisson* of pleasure run through her that he had reacted that way. To be protected as a woman and not as a grand duchess was so novel she felt quite flustered. Or was that simply the effect of his outrageous kisses?

She felt Jack's arm tighten and could tell from the way the muscles flexed that he was preparing to push her out of harm's way if the other man reacted. There was a second where everyone seemed to have stopped breathing, then de Presteigne laughed. '*Bon nuit. Bon chance, mon ami.*' The officers clattered off down the hill, leaving them in darkness and silence. Eva felt herself slump against Jack in relief as she felt both her poise and her balance desert her. She dragged down a deep breath and tried to stiffen her shaking knees, even as her arms clung to him.

Before she could free herself, Jack lifted both hands, cupped her face and kissed her again with a fierceness that spoke of relief, tension released and, quite simply, sexual demand. His mouth was hot, hard and experienced and Eva surrendered to it, swaying into his embrace again with a sensation of letting go. Physical pleasure, direct and straightforward, was such a liberation that she felt her mind go blank and let herself slide into the moment, ignoring the squalid little alley, the greasy cobbles underfoot, the danger of pursuit.

Her mouth opened to the thrust of his tongue, its message echoed by the hardness of the male body she was clinging to. Behind her closed lids stars spun against blackness. Need flooded her body like the kick of a glass of spirits at the male taste of him, the scent of his skin.

'Hell.' He lifted his head, still holding her tight against him, and reality and reaction hit her simultaneously.

Hell? They were very nearly making love on the cobbles and all he could say was *Hell?* She must have been mad—what would have followed if that moment of insanity had happened in her bedchamber? How dare he presume to touch her? How could she have allowed it?

'You…' she began furiously.

'I forgot myself, indeed.' The rueful admission was tinged with a satirical note, reminding her of her own part in what had just occurred. In the darkness she could not read his face; it was perhaps as well he could not see hers. 'Relief and tension do strange things to us. Shall we go on?'

It was, certainly, the most dignified course to say nothing at all about the incident. Discussing it would lead nowhere but into more embarrassment—as it was, thinking about it made her skin hot all over. 'Certainly, Mr Ryder,' she said haughtily. 'Have you the valise?' Eva clutched the broken cloak clasp at her throat, feeling her pulse race against her knuckles.

'Here.' He stooped, a dark shape in the shadows, then took her arm. Knowing another fall risked injury, she made herself accept his touch, and tried to focus on something other than the newly re-awakened demands of her body.

'Who is looking after the coach?' She had not thought to ask, but this was the real world outside the castle, the world where coaches did not appear with drivers, grooms and out-riders ten minutes after one had the whim to drive out. In this world people stole horses if you left them unattended. It was a world she had been insulated from for almost ten years, one she was going to have to learn to understand and survive in very rapidly.

'My groom, Henry.' Jack's pace increased as the hill levelled out and they reached the quayside. Light spilled out from taverns and bawdy houses all along its length; the destination, no doubt, of the colonel and his companions.

'What if someone speaks to him?' Eva pulled up her hood and watched her feet as they stepped over mooring ropes stretched taut across the quay.

'He spent two years in a French prison, so his grasp of the language is adequate, if colourful.' Jack sounded amused and alert, not at all like a man who had been indulging in a torrid kiss with a virtual stranger not minutes before. She only wished she had his *sangfroid*. Perhaps he had not found her very exciting. Now, that was a dampening thought. 'Here we are.'

The carriage was drawn up opposite the entrance to what Eva was quite certain was a brothel, as though waiting for its owner to return from his pleasures. A group of men were standing outside, talking over-loudly, and a bruiser with fists like hams stood watching them in the doorway. From the brightly lit windows came the sound of music and laughter.

The driver must have been on the lookout, for Eva saw a figure in a greatcoat sit up straight from its huddled position on the high box seat. 'There you are. *Quel surprise.*' He bent down as they came alongside and addressed Jack in accented French and with a familiarity that amazed her. 'Thought I'd be picking your broken bones off the rocks come morning. Quite resigned to it I was. This the lady, then?'

'No, just one I picked at random,' Jack said sarcastically, opening the carriage door and helping Eva inside. 'Of course it's the lady. Did you have a scout round this afternoon like I told you to?'

'Yes, guv'nor.' The man had dropped into English. 'And a very nice little burgh it is, too, not up to Paris, of course, or even Marseilles, but a man could have a bit of fun here, given the time.'

'Well, we haven't got any time, and speak French, damn you,' Jack retorted. 'Did you see the perfume factory?'

'I did. Ruddy great place and smelling like a Covent Garden flower stall. Why? Were you wanting to buy any presents?'

'No, I want to break in to it. Take us there now, and go steady, I don't want to attract attention.' Jack swung into the carriage, closed the door and lay back against the squabs opposite her. He breathed out a heartfelt sigh and Eva glimpsed the flash of white teeth. 'Phew. That all went better than I had expected.'

There did not seem to be much to say to that, at least, not anything that didn't risk an allusion to that episode in the alleyway. 'Do you really intend that we break in to the factory?'

'I am going to, you are not.'

'Mr Ryder, do I need to remind you who I am? I say where I go and do not go. Besides, I have the key.' The lights from the various establishments flickered into the carriage, illuminating Jack's face in flickering bursts. She caught a look of surprise before he had his expression under control again.

'Here? You have the key here? Why on earth would you bring it?'

It was tempting to pretend that she knew he would need it, but honesty got the better of her. 'It is in the pocket of this cloak; I forgot I had put it there last time I visited. It was when I discovered about the chemists Antoine is employing—I had gone down one evening to look in the old recipe books, because I had found a perfume receipt up at the castle that sounded promising and I wanted to see whether we had it at the factory already.

'I used to visit all the time, but since Philippe became ill I had stopped going. I don't think Antoine knows I have a key to the offices. What are we looking for?'

'*I* am looking for formulae, drawings, equipment— anything that might give me an inkling of what they are up to.'

'*We* will need to start in the offices, then,' Eva said, loftily ignoring his carefully selected pronouns. 'Then we can move to the laboratories if we find nothing there. The actual work- shops are unlikely, I think—after all, the production of perfume is continuing as normal, or I would have heard about it.'

'It will be easier if you draw me a sketch.' Jack rummaged in one of the door pockets and came out with some paper and a pencil.

'I told you, Mr Ryder, I am coming with you.' Eva pressed them back into his hands. Even in the gloom of the carriage with the occasional flashes of light, she could see from his ex- pression that he had no intention of agreeing. 'I have a perfect right to be there,' she said, with sudden inspiration. 'I can walk in with whomever I like—who is to refuse me? And the care- taker will not think to wonder what I am doing, he is so used to seeing me. It will reduce the risk, and hasten things, if you do not have to break in.'

'That is true,' Jack conceded. He must have sensed her surprise at his capitulation. 'I am not in the habit of turning down perfectly good arguments just because someone else makes them.'

'I thought you objected because I am a woman. Or because of my position.'

'Neither. What you do in your position is your choice. I have a history of disagreements with dukes, but not grand duchesses, and in my experience women have an equal tendency to good and bad sense as men.'

'Oh.' He had taken her aback and it took a moment to recover. Whatever their station, the men in her life made it quite clear—deferentially of course—that she must be treated with respect for her position and with patronising indulgence for her opinions. Even dear Philippe was prone to treat her as though she had hardly a thought in her head beyond gowns, good works and her son. A grand duchess was expected to be a dutiful doll.

She was beginning to relax a little too much with this man, beginning to like him. In her position it was dangerous to do any such thing just because someone did not treat you like a brainless puppet—and kissed like a fallen angel. 'Do you treat the dukes with as great a familiarity as you treat me? I have a title which you should use—'

'Your Serene Highness, if I address you as such, then not only will every sentence become intolerably prolonged, but we risk exciting interest at every point along our journey.'

'*Ma'am* would do excellently,' she retorted, finding all her irritation with him flooding back.

'What is your full name? Ma'am,' he added belatedly just as she drew in a hissing breath of displeasure.

'Evaline Claire Elizabetta Mélanie Nicole la Jabotte de Maubourg.'

Jack whistled. 'I can see why you are referred to as the Grand Duchess Eva. I think we are here.'

Eva looked out at the high wall and the double gates with a little wicket set in them. 'Yes, this is it.' She found the key and handed it to him. 'I shall tell the watchman that you are a French visitor from Grasse, interested in seeing how we make perfume here. And do try to remember to address me properly,' she added as Jack handed her down from the carriage.

'Yes, your Serene Highness.' The click of his heels was a provocation she decided to ignore.

Old Georges, the watchman, came out with his lantern before they were halfway across the courtyard. He was pulling on his coat one handed, his wrinkled face a mask of concern at being caught out. 'Your Serene Highness, ma'am! I wasn't expecting you, ma'am—is anything wrong?'

'No, nothing at all, Georges. This gentleman is from Grasse where they also make fine perfumes, as you know. He has no time to visit tomorrow, so I am showing him the factory tonight.'

'Shall I light you round, ma'am?'

'No, that is quite all right, just give *monsieur* your lantern. We will let you know when we leave.'

She opened the door into the offices, nodding a dismissal to the old man. Jack followed her in and closed the door. 'That was almost too easy,' he observed.

'What do you mean?' Eva opened the heavy day book and began to scan it. 'There is always just Georges on duty at night. Now, this is the outer office; I doubt if we'll find anything in here and the day book seems innocuous.'

'If you were operating a secret laboratory, would you leave just one old man on duty? He did not seem at all alarmed by our presence, so he cannot be in on the plot.' Jack scanned the room, opened one or two drawers, then moved into the next room. 'Therefore it must be well hidden.'

'I see what you mean.' Eva picked up her skirts and followed. 'The laboratories are through here; I have the master key.'

One after another the doors swung open until she reached the last one. 'We do not use this one any more. Oh, look— the lock has been changed.' Suddenly the familiar surroundings of the factory, which she had often walked through at night without a qualm, seemed alien and full of menace. She found she had moved closer to Jack and bit her lip in vexation at the betraying sign of fear. 'This key will not work on it.' She held it out as though to explain her instinctive movement towards him.

'I'll have to pick it, then.' Jack fished in his boot top and produced a bent piece of thin metal, then hunkered down and began to work on the lock. Eva picked up the lantern and came to hold it close. 'No, I do not need the light, thank you. I do this by feel and by sound.'

She watched, fascinated by his utter concentration. Again, the image of a swordsman, balanced and focused, came to her as she studied, not his hands, but his profile. His eyes were closed, his face relaxed as though listening to music, hearing and analysing what he heard at the same time.

Dark lashes fanned over tanned cheekbones. She saw a small crescent scar at the corner of his eye and observed the darkening growth of evening stubble begin to shadow his jawline. He was a very masculine figure, she thought, aware of the ease with which he balanced, the way his breeches moulded tightly over well-muscled thighs, the warmth of his body as she stood close.

I am too used to courtiers, too used to velvets and satins and posturing politicians and officials. Even the officers wear uniforms that speak more of the ballroom than the battlefield. This man looks dangerous, feels dangerous. And the biggest danger was, Eva realised, dragging her gaze away from his body to concentrate on the movement of the picklock, that she found him exciting to be with. Infuriating, insolent, casual and peremptory—and exciting.

It was something she had been wary of, these two years of widowhood, letting herself get close to another man, allowing the chill of her lonely bed to drive her into some rash liaison. You overheard too many people sniggering behind their hands as they recounted the tale of yet another widow of high rank taking a lover. It was risky, demeaning and ruinous to the reputation, for the secret always seemed to get out and, of course, it was inevitably the woman who was the butt of the jokes and the object of censure.

This feeling of arousal, this sense of hazard, was simply due to the shock of Jack Ryder's eruption into her life and the stress of her worries for the past weeks. Everything was heightened, from her fear, her anxiety, to her sensual instincts. That was all it was, all it could ever be.

'Got it.' The lock clicked and the door swung open. Inside was a room laid out as a drawing office, with two desks on one side, a wide, high table in the middle and two drawing slopes with stools on the other side. Along the back of the room was a range of chests fitted with wide drawers.

'Not a scrap of paper.' Jack pulled open the desk drawers. 'Empty except for pens and ink and rulers.'

Together they went to stand in front of the chests. Eva reached out a hand and touched the dark wood, noticing how heavily the piece was made. 'Look at the locks. I have never seen anything like that before.'

'Neither have I, and I will tell you now, I cannot pick these.' Jack straightened up from a minute inspection of the locks, each made of steel, with double keyholes and strange rods and bars on its surface.

'We will just have to smash the chests, then,' Eva said robustly. 'There are fire axes in all the rooms. Look, here.' She lifted the axe from the corner where it stood next to a pail of water and swung it experimentally. It was heavy.

'If I do that, then there is no hiding the fact that we have been here.' Jack leaned back against the chest, folded his arms and regarded her steadily.

'Of course.' That much was obvious.

'When Prince Antoine discovers your disappearance from the castle he may give chase, he may not. It is unlikely to be a matter of such desperate urgency to him that he will throw great resources into the pursuit. But if he links your disappearance with a raid on his secret laboratory, he is going to tear the countryside apart to find you.'

'But we must find the proof of what is going on.' Eva knew she was frowning in puzzlement. Was he really asking her if she would put her personal safety before her duty?

'We have enough to confirm that Prince Antoine is experimenting with explosives. My orders are to get you back safely, not to engage in espionage.'

'Are you telling me that you will walk away from this?' Eva demanded.

'No, I am asking you whether you want to. It is your life. It is your son waiting in England.'

Eva found the axe was still dangling from her hand. She propped it against the nearest chest while she tried to sort through her thoughts. Jack was offering her the choice, as he would to another man. He was not trying to hide the dangers from her. He wasn't happy about it, but she was here inside the factory with him because he was prepared to listen to her ideas.

'If there is a risk that some weapon that might aid him falls into Napoleon's hands, then I would never forgive myself,' she said, meeting the cool grey eyes. 'I married a ruler of a country, albeit a small one. This goes with the territory.' And she knew that if her life was at risk, then so was Jack's—at greater risk, in truth, because she was coming to realise that if Antoine wanted her, he would have to go through Jack to get to her.

His lips curved in a smile that held admiration and a certain wry acceptance that she had just raised the odds stacked against them and that the counters she was pushing on to the gaming table represented both their lives. He held out his hand for the axe. 'Right, let's get started.'

Eva picked up the rough wooden handle, set her teeth and tightened her fingers. 'No, let me.' She raised it, her arms aching at the weight, and smashed it into the first lock. Wood splintered and the jolt as the blade hit metal ran up her arm. 'That is for Fréderic. How dare Antoine try to take what is my son's? I wish he was here at this moment!'

Chapter Four

Jack reached across and prised Eva's fingers from around the axe handle. 'Allow me. I fully appreciate your wish to decapitate your brother-in-law, but I think I may be faster at turning these into firewood.'

She nodded abruptly, letting him take the axe and stepping back, her eyes fixed on the chests with angry intensity. *God, that's a woman with backbone!* he told himself as he set to work to hack the locks out of their setting. She should be the Regent, she deserved to be. The way he was addressing her, the approach he had taken to their relationship, was simply because he could not afford for her rank to stand in the way of the mission. It was not through any lack of respect, whatever she might believe.

What the Whitehall officials who had sent him on this mission would say to him embroiling her in breaking and entering and spying, he shuddered to think.

The final lock in the first chest yielded in a mass of splinters and Jack began on the next. Beside him he was aware of

Eva pulling open drawers, taking out piles of papers and laying them in order on the big table.

The physical effort of swinging the axe, hacking into the solid wood, made the sore muscles around his ribs where the rope had cut earlier ache savagely. He had not realised the strain his body had been under while he was doing it—the mentally numbing effect of the drop beneath him as he had lowered himself over the battlements was probably enough to account for that.

Jack made himself concentrate on breaking into the chests as fast as possible. There was too much distraction already in this mission to be thinking about bruised ribs. The revelation about the Regent's health, the positive identification of Prince Antoine as the source of the treachery, the discovery of this factory and its secrets, were all outside his briefing and must be factored into his plans. And the impact that Eva was having on him was entirely unexpected and was going to need more than a change in tactics to neutralise.

He was not surprised to find himself admiring her for her coolness and courage, but he had not expected to find himself lusting after her. And that was what it was, there was no excuse for blinking at it. And it wasn't just beauty that was having this effect. Jack delivered a final blow to the last chest and began to wrench out the drawers. There was something else—a passion behind those steady brown eyes, an energy and anger concealed under cool grace and dignity. And her body in his arms, the sweet fury of her mouth under his when he had kissed her…

He stepped back as Eva came to lift out the sheets of drawings from the drawers he had just opened. She moved as though in a state reception, but her hair was coming down and her face was flushed from hurrying backwards and forwards in the stuffy room. Her cloak was in a crumpled heap on the floor and she had pushed back the sleeves of her gown to expose strong, slender forearms and fine-boned wrists.

The drawings were already arranged on the table, he saw, as she darted about, brow furrowed in concentration, sorting the latest collection. Jack put down the axe and leaned back against the splintered chest to watch her. He should never have kissed her, of course, although as a ruse in the crisis they had found themselves it, it had worked very well.

The frankness of her kiss when she had stopped fighting him, when the officers had gone, should not have surprised him, either. She had been a married woman, she knew what she was about. From the briefing he had received, if she had taken a lover she had been very discreet about it—he may have been receiving the benefit of several years of chaste frustration.

They had both been under pressure, in danger, and that embrace had been a response as natural as two soldiers going out and getting drunk after a battle—a life-affirming release. It seemed she had dismissed it now, and so should he. Which was easier said than done.

'Mr Ryder. Have you gone to sleep?' The tart enquiry was sufficient to dampen any wandering fantasies of unpinning the rest of her coiled conker-brown hair and letting it flow over her shoulders.

'No, ma'am, merely keeping out of your way until you had finished.' The meek response had her narrowing her eyes at him, but he kept his face straight and she turned back to the table with nothing more than thinned lips to show her displeasure. Grand Duchess Eva had a knack of ignoring unpleasantness and skimming straight over it—presumably a useful skill in court life. 'How have you sorted the papers?'

'These are drawings of different mechanisms, but I think they all go together.' She frowned and Jack found his hand lifting to smooth away the little crease between her brows. He jammed his fists in his pockets and came to stand next to her. 'I have stacked each one with the most recent drawing uppermost; they are all dated.' Eva pointed to a pile of black-bound notebooks. 'Those are all figures and calculations. Formulae. They make no sense to me.'

'To me, neither.' Jack flicked through the topmost one and turned his attention to the drawings. 'These are rockets.'

'Fireworks?' Eva leaned over close to his side to see and Jack drew in a sharp breath between his teeth. Her body was warm and fragrant and conjured immediate memories of how she had felt in his arms.

'No, artillery weapons.' Jack shifted round away from her as though to show what he was talking about. 'They were invented by Congreve and the British have been using them at sea and on land since about 1805. Napoleon offered a reward for anyone who could invent one for the French army—but they haven't got them yet. They aren't very accurate, though.' He leant over to study the other drawings. 'See, these are frames and carriages for firing the things—I wonder if they have worked out a way to aim them better?'

'And the notebooks might be formulae for the explosive powder?'

'Yes, that could be it. We need to get these back.' A look

which could only be described as smug passed fleetingly over Eva's face. 'Ma'am, if you are about to say "I told you so"—'

Her eyes opened wide in hauteur. 'I would say nothing so vulgar, Mr Ryder. Just how do you suggest we get them all out past Georges?'

'We don't. Not all of them.' Jack picked up a pair of shears and began to cut down the top drawing from each pile, removing every scrap of waste margin. 'We take the most recent of each of these, the most recent notebook, and we destroy the rest.'

'The fireplace.' Eva nodded and began to scoop up the remaining drawings, jamming them into the cold fireplace in the corner of the room. She picked up the notebooks and started to tear the pages out. 'They'll burn better loose.'

The half-dozen reduced drawings folded into a neat packet with the notebook. Jack jammed them into the breast of his coat and lit a spill from their lantern. The paper flashed into flame, blackening and falling apart in moments. Jack beat out the ashes with the poker and straightened up, observing, 'How to make a prince angry in one easy lesson.'

'Antoine will be beside himself,' Eva agreed, picking up her cloak and shaking the dust out of it with a *moue* of distaste. Jack took it and put it around her shoulders. 'Thank you, Mr Ryder. We had better be off, had we not?'

'Indeed.' Jack scanned the floor until he found what he was looking for: a shard of broken metal smaller than his little fingernail. 'I'll lock the door behind us.' It was a matter of moments to flick the lock shut with the pick, then he eased the fragment of metal into the keyhole and tried it again. The fine pick jammed and grated against the foreign body. 'There, they won't be able to get the door open, but at first they will simply think the lock is faulty. It might buy us a little time.'

Eva led the way back out into the yard, keeping up a steady flow of polite chitchat that could only have come from years of practice at mind-numbingly tedious parties and diplomatic events. The caretaker came out and stood waiting for them. 'Ah, there you are, Georges. We are off now; I am sorry to have disturbed you. Is your daughter well? Excellent.'

Jack paused to hand the lantern to the old caretaker and followed his gaze as the Grand Duchess made her way across the cobbled yard with all the dignity and grace of a woman stepping on to the ballroom floor. Her hair was coming down at the back, her face was flushed and there was dust around the hem of her skirt. Her dirty, crumpled cloak looked as though it had been used as a bed by a pair of hounds. It gave him an idea.

'Thank you.' Jack pressed a coin into the gnarled hand and lowered his voice. 'Her Serene Highness can count upon you to be discreet, I am certain.' The man stared at him, comprehension dawning on his face, then he nodded vigorously.

'God bless her, *monsieur,* she deserves someone to care about her.'

Jack let one eyelid droop into a slow wink and sauntered out of the yard in Eva's wake, the bulge of the documents flattened under his arm.

Eva allowed herself to be assisted back into the carriage and sank back against the squabs. 'That wretched little rat! If Philippe recovers, he is going to make himself ill all over again when he finds out about Antoine. To ally us with Bonaparte is treachery enough, but to create weapons to put into his hands, that is beyond forgiveness or understanding.'

Now they were out of the factory, the full magnitude of what they had found was beginning to dawn on her. Inside it had all seemed an adventure. She had found it exciting, even though she had been frightened. She had enjoyed the give and take with Jack, both of words and, as she had swung that axe, of physical effort. He brought something alive in her, something that had been repressed for a very long time. It was enjoyable, and it must be resisted.

'How long will that lock hold them, Mr Ryder?'

'Quite a while. They will have to get a locksmith and although they will be impatient, I do not think they will realise it has been sabotaged. A locksmith will realise at once that it has been jammed, of course, then they will break the door down, I should imagine.' He sounded as though he was frowning in thought. 'From the weight, it may have been reinforced—they'll be cursing their own precautions by the time they get inside.'

'And then they will ask Georges who was there and he will tell them, he has no reason not to. I should have spoken to him.' Eva shook her head, angered at her own lack of foresight. 'Although what I could have said to explain such a request without exciting curiosity, I do not know.'

'I think he will be circumspect.' There was something in Jack Ryder's voice that made her suspicious. Perhaps if it had not been almost dark, she would have missed it, but relying only on her hearing seemed to make her more sensitive to his mood.

'Why?' she demanded, suddenly suspicious. 'What did you say to him?'

'Nothing at all of any significance. I tipped him, said I was certain he would be discreet…'

'And why should he think that was needed?' A stray lock of hair tickled the dip of her collarbone. Eva put up a hand and discovered that half of it was down. As she touched her face, she felt how warm and damp her skin was. Her cloak, she recalled now, was crumpled and dusty from being on the floor.

'I walk in to a deserted building after dark with a man and I emerge an hour later, dishevelled and flushed and crumpled and he asks the caretaker for discretion,' she said flatly, working it out as she went. 'Georges thinks…you *encouraged* him to think…that we were making love in there!' The magnitude of it swept over her, leaving her hot faced and sick inside with humiliation. 'How could you?'

'It will be effective. And he appeared most sympathetic. I imagine your people would not grudge you a little harmless diversion.'

'Harmless? Diversion? Is that how you categorise adultery and dissipation? Is it?' She kept her voice down with an effort. A grand duchess does not shout. Ever. 'Think of my position!'

'It could not be adultery,' the infuriating man pointed out. 'Neither of us is married.'

'Oh! You render me speechless.'

'Patently not, ma'am.'

Now he was being literal with her! He deserved to be thrown into the castle dungeons. If only she had access to them now—they would be full of rats and spiders and he could hang there in chains next to Antoine, she thought vengefully. They deserved each other. Then the memory of what else lay under the castle sent a shudder running through her. No, best not to think of that, not here, not now, in the darkness.

'Mr Ryder. Let me be plain. If I were to so far forget myself—and what is due to my position—as to take a lover, I would not chose an insolent, ill-bred adventurer and spy.'

'You made me a spy,' he countered.

That was true. Eva caught herself on the verge of an apology. This was outrageous—how was Ryder managing to put her in the wrong when he was quite obviously the one at fault? 'Just because I did not remonstrate as I should when you took those outrageous liberties with me in the alleyway, there is no reason to assume you can blacken my name—'

'Liberties, ma'am?' His voice, with its faintly mocking edge, cut into her diatribe like a knife into butter. 'Forgive me, but when those officers had gone I do believe that you returned my kisses with as much enthusiasm as I gave them. Either that, or you are an exceptionally talented actress.'

'I was in shock,' Eva protested, guiltily aware he was perfectly correct.

'Of course you were,' he agreed smoothly. 'I perfectly understand. And, please forgive me, but that incident had nothing whatsoever to do with my exchange with Georges just now. I am afraid he leapt to a conclusion and it seemed to fit our purposes all too well.' There was a pause, which Eva filled by gritting her teeth together and concentrating on breathing slowly and calmly through her nose. 'Would you like me to go back and explain he has jumped to an incorrect conclusion, your Serene Highness?'

'No!' Deep breathing was not as calming as it was supposed to be. 'It is too late now. The damage is done. Where are we?' She looked out of the window and saw the glint of the river below. 'Driving back into Maubourg? But why?'

'Because it is the last place they would expect you to be by now if you have been missed. This coach is going to drive slowly, and very visibly, through the middle of the town. Henry is going to ask the way for the Toulon road at least three times, at each point making certain that the rather gaudy red door panels are well illuminated. We will then drive into a dark alleyway, remove the door panels to reveal a tasteful—and fictitious—crest, and equally sedately, make our way out of the Northern gate with me driving. By the time daylight comes Henry will be driving again, the door panels will be plain and to all intents this will be a third carriage, one which has not been seen in Maubourg.'

'And if they have not missed me yet?' The precautions and layers of planning took her aback. If she had thought at all about what would happen after they had left the factory Eva had simply envisioned driving as fast as possible towards the coast. 'No,' she answered her own question. 'I see. They will question the guards and time my escape by us leaving my bed-chamber, so they will be checking up on the coaches leaving tonight. Mr Ryder—do you do this sort of thing a great deal?'

'Abduct royalty? No, this is the first time.' He must have felt the intensity of her glare in the gloom, for he continued before she could explode. 'Missions into Europe during the war, yes, some. Mainly I carry out intelligence work for the government, and occasionally for private individuals.'

'What sort of thing? Following errant wives?'

'Checking that suitors are what they seem, occasional bodyguard work. Recently I assisted a gentleman who had misplaced his wife ten years ago.'

'Goodness. How very careless of him. And you earn your living from this?' He spoke like a gentleman, with the hard edge and decisiveness of a military man. Her jibe about lack of breeding had been far from the mark. He wore no jewellery and she could make no judgement from his clothes, other than they seemed suitable for climbing down walls.

'I have an adequate private income. I do this because I enjoy it.'

'You do?' How very odd, to enjoy fear and danger. Then Eva realised that she was enjoying it, too, in a perverse sort of way. She was scared, worried sick about Fréderic, embarrassed by much of what had happened today, but she was also alive. The blood was pumping in her veins, her mind was racing, she had been pitchforked from a life of predictability and privileged powerlessness into one of complete uncertainty—and she felt wonderful.

Only the day before she had gazed at her own reflection in the mirror and struggled to accept the fact that all that lay ahead of her was a decline into graceful middle age.

In a few months she would be twenty-seven. For nine years she had been a dutiful wife, then a dutiful Dowager Duchess. She had done nothing rash, nothing impulsive, nothing exciting. As Freddie grew up, then married, she would step further and further back into respectable semi-retirement. It was her duty. She might as well be dead.

'Ma'am?'

'Yes, Mr Ryder?'

'You sighed. Are you all right?'

'I am contemplating the thought that it is dangerous to wish for things. I had been finding my life a trifle dull and wanting in diversion recently. Then Napoleon returns, Philippe is struck down, someone tries to murder Freddie and me and you leap through my bedchamber window and take me burgling. I appear to be about to enter an adventurous phase in my life.'

'I can promise you that.' The coach stopped again, for what must be the third time. Eva listened to Henry's rough French accent and the response from the watchman standing under the streetlight. She drew back further into the shadows.

'Why are we not taking the Toulon road?' she asked as they started forward once more.

'Because, although it is faster, it is also riskier. Support for Bonaparte is strong to the south, and it is the obvious route for us to take. Then how do we find a boat to take us to England from a French port? I am going north, up into Burgundy, and then north-east towards Brussels, which is where the king has fled. Wellington has had his headquarters there since early April. We will go from there to Ostend.'

The coach turned sharply, lurching over a rougher surface, and pulled up. 'Excuse me, we will be on our way in a moment. Henry will sit with you for a few miles.'

After some scraping and banging at the sides of the vehicle, the coachman climbed in, doffing his hat. 'Begging your pardon, ma'am.'

'That is quite all right.' This at least was easy. One's entire life appeared to be made up on some days of holding conversations with tongue-tied citizens. 'Have you been a coachman long, Henry?'

'I'm a groom, ma'am. Least, that's what I am official-like. Most of the time I'm whatever the guv'nor wants me to be, depending on what we're about.'

Hmm, not so tongue-tied, which could be useful. 'So sometimes you have to be a gentleman's groom, when Mr Ryder is at home in London?'

'Aye, ma'am. When the guv'nor's being himself like, which isn't often.'

'That must be difficult for his family,' Eva persisted, fishing as carefully as she could. 'For his wife, for example.' Though he had said he was not married… 'Or his parents.'

'Would be, indeed, ma'am, if he'd a wife. As for his respected father, top-lofty old devil he was, if you'll pardon me saying so; nothing the guv'nor did was ever right for him, so I don't reckon he'd give a toss, even if he was alive. Which he ain't.'

That had not got her very far. He was not married and a *top-lofty* father confirmed his origins were respectable. It was an odd choice of words, *being himself*—it implied two very different lives. And London was *home*. Just who was Jack Ryder?

'We're out the Eastern gate,' Henry observed. 'Another hour and we'll be snug at the inn, ma'am. I'll wager you'll be glad to be settled for the night.'

'You know where we are staying tonight, then?'

'Why, yes, ma'am. The guv'nor doesn't leave things to chance. All booked, right and tight on the way down, and the landlord expecting us late, so no suspicions there. It's a nice little place used by gentlemen on hunting expeditions in the foothills, but it's quiet now.'

Eva sank back against the squabs and fell silent. Henry was certainly not in need of setting at his ease in her presence, so, strange as it felt, she did not have to make conversation. It was curiously peaceful to realise that she had no duties, none at all, other than to survive this adventure and reach England.

* * *

'Ma'am!' She jerked upright, startled to find they had stopped moving and there were lights outside. 'You'd dropped off, ma'am,' Henry added helpfully.

'Yes, thank you,' Eva said repressively. Goodness knows what sort of appearance she must present with her gown crumpled, her cloak filthy and her hair all over the place. She pushed it back and pulled her hood up to shadow her face as best she could. People saw what they expected to see, and this innkeeper would not be expecting a weary traveller to be his grand duchess. She must just be careful to do nothing to attract his attention.

The door opened, Jack helped her down and the landlord came bustling out to greet them, cheerfully prepared for their arrival at this late hour.

'Welcome, sir, welcome, madam! Come along inside, if you please.' Eva let the familiar local patois wash over her as the horses were sent off to the stables, their luggage carried in and Henry vanished in the direction of the taproom. 'The room is just as you ordered, sir. The bed has been aired and I am sure your wife will be comfortable.'

The man led the way up the stairs. Eva stopped dead at the bottom, the last traces of sleep banished. 'Room? Wife? Which room are *you* in?'

'Ours.' Jack took her arm and began to climb. Without actual violence she had no option but to follow him. 'Thank you.' He took the branch of candles from the landlord's hand and pushed her gently through the open door at the head of the stairs. 'This looks excellent. Some hot water, if you will.'

Eva stood in the middle of the room and looked around.

One dresser, two chairs, a rug before a cold grate, a clothes press, a screen and a bed. One bed. 'And just *where* are you sleeping?' she enquired icily. Beneath her bodice her heart was thudding like a military tattoo.

'With you. In that bed. Why? Where else do you expect me to sleep?'

Chapter Five

'I expect you to sleep in your own bed, in your own room.' Her mouth had gone dry, her stomach was full of butterflies.

'I am your bodyguard. I need to be close to you.' He was touching the flame to the other candles in the room, his hand steady as he did so. Eva felt her irrational panic building. What was she afraid of? That he would ravish her? Ridiculous. Somehow common sense did not stop the unsettling physical reactions.

'Then sleep on the floor.' She pointed to the far corner, hidden behind a screen.

'Why should I be so uncomfortable?' Jack enquired. 'The role of the modern bodyguard does not include sleeping at your threshold like a faithful troubadour. I have had a long hard day. That looks like a very large, very comfortable bed. I'll put the bolster down the middle of it if that would make you feel any better.'

The click as he turned the key in the lock brought the

panic bubbling closer to the surface. 'It is scandalous,' she stated. 'I am—'

'My wife,' Jack said, turning from the door to face her across the expanse of snowy-white quilt. There was not a trace of amusement on his face. 'For the rest of this journey you act, think, live as my wife.'

'No!'

'Eva, what are you afraid of? Do you think I am going to insist on my conjugal rights? That would be carrying the deception a little too far. This is for your safety.' It was not a small room, but his masculine presence seemed to fill it. Part of her mind registered that he had called her by her first name; part of it dismissed that as an irrelevance. The forefront of her consciousness was full of the reality that she was going to have to spend this night, and goodness knows how many nights after it, in bed with this man.

'Of course I do not think that.' She was fighting *not* to think of it! 'And I am not afraid of you.' She tilted her chin haughtily and tried to stare him down.

No, she was not afraid of him, she was afraid of what he was reminding her she missed, afraid that every hour spent with him would tear away a little more of the screen she had erected round her needs and desires. Afraid that she might turn to him in the night for strength and comfort and… It was easy to resist temptation when it was not a fingertip away, easy to ignore yearnings when there was no way of satisfying them.

'You are tired. We both are. They will bring hot water up soon and you can wash and go to bed.' As he spoke there was a tap at the door. Eva watched, startled, as Jack slid a knife from his boot and went to open the door. By the time the little maid had come in with the pitcher of water, the knife was out of sight. He turned the key in the lock again once she was gone and gestured towards the washstand and screen. 'Go on.' He lifted her valise and placed it behind the painted wooden panels.

'Thank you.' Eva forced the words out of stiff lips and stepped past him into the fragile privacy. She was going to have to use her cloak as a dressing gown. Her hands shook as she delved into the valise, but she lifted out the scanty contents, shook out the one spare gown he had allowed her and sorted through the rest. *Oh, no!*

'Mr Ryder.' It was the tone she used to point out some grave dereliction of court protocol and it normally produced a reaction of instant, anxious, attention on the part of the person so addressed.

'Yes?' His voice sounded muffled, but unconcerned. Eva had a momentary vision of his shirt being pulled off over his head and turned her back on the join in the screen panels resolutely. For a moment she had wanted to peep, like some giggling maidservant spying on the grooms.

'When you took those things out of my valise at the castle, you apparently removed my nightgown. What, exactly, do you expect me to sleep in?' If she hadn't been so angry, she would have considered her words more carefully. As it was, there was a long silence from the other side of the screen. *He is laughing at me, the beast,* she decided grimly, just as a white linen garment was tossed on top of the screen.

'Have one of my shirts.'

'You have plenty, I assume?'

'Of course, I knew how long I was packing for.' *He is laughing.* Eva fumed as she stripped off and washed hastily, then dragged the shirt over her head. It came midway down her thighs, the cuffs dangling well below her fingertips. She pulled it down as much as possible, rolled up the cuffs and unpinned her hair. At least he had left her hairbrush in the case.

The long, regular strokes had the soothing power of routine. She did the requisite one hundred and hesitated, half-tempted to do another set. Then another. She braided it hastily. 'Where are you, Mr Ryder?'

'In bed.'

'Then close your eyes.'

'Very well. They are closed. Will you snuff out the candles?'

A cautious look around the edge of the screen revealed that Jack was indeed in bed, his eyes closed as promised. There was no doubting that he was awake somehow; he seemed to radiate alertness. The covers were pulled up to his chin, not giving her any hint as to what he might—or might not—be wearing and the odd lump down the centre of the bed showed that he had inserted the bolster as a gesture to modesty.

Eva emerged, resisted the undignified urge to scuttle from candle to candle and then dive into bed, and instead went round carefully snuffing each until the bed itself was just a white glimmer in the room. She slid under the sheet, pulling it up tight to her throat.

'Good night, Eva.'

No more *ma'am*, not until they reached safety. It was a curiously liberating thought. 'Good night,' she responded coldly. *Jack.* Liberating, or dangerous? Protocol was a straitjacket, but it was also an armour. Behind it one could maintain a perfect reserve, perfect privacy for the emotions. This adventure was going to throw her into an intimacy of thoughts and fears with this man that was at least as perilous as any physical closeness.

She should have been exhausted, ready to drop into sleep the moment her lids closed. The bed was comfortable, clean, and there was the reassuring touch of the bolster down her spine to remind her that she did not need to fear turning and touching Jack in the night. Of course she trusted him, and really, it was no different to him sleeping on the floor on the far side of the room, she told herself stoutly.

So why could she not sleep? Eva closed her eyes and tried to relax, starting with her toes and working up. She tried counting sheep, reciting recipes, recalling Italian irregular verbs. Hopeless.

Was he asleep? She held her breath to listen to his, steady and even. There was an interruption as he shifted slightly, a soft sigh, then the even rhythm resumed. Jack Ryder was obviously one of those infuriating people who could sleep anywhere, under any circumstances. She just hoped he would wake up as quickly if danger threatened.

Eva turned her thoughts resolutely to her son, her lips curving into a smile as she did so. How soon before she could see him? He would have grown so much. What new clothes would he need? Would he look more like his father now as he grew up, or less? Would he still throw himself into her arms to be kissed, or was he too grown up for that now? Without realising it, she relaxed and drifted off to sleep.

Jack opened his eyes on to darkness and lay still, trying to work out what had woken him. Eva's breathing was soft and regular, she was lying curled up with her back turned and had managed to push the bolster a good three-quarters of the way across the bed towards him. A woman used to sleeping alone.

Distantly a dog was barking, the bored yap of a lonely animal, not the aggression of a threatened one. The yard below was silent. He dredged into his mind and came up with the sound of a closing door outside. It must be about three o'clock—who was abroad at this time? He had chosen this inn, a hunters' favourite off the main road, for its isolation.

He eased out of the bed, pulling on his breeches before taking four silent strides to the window. He unlatched the shutter, pushed it back and stood looking down until his eyes adjusted to what dim light there was. Minutes passed, then he saw a familiar figure come out of the shadow of the stable opposite and walk across the yard. In the centre the man stopped and looked up, directly into his eyes, although he could not have seen Jack.

He eased the window wide and leaned out. 'What's the matter?' He pitched the whisper to reach Henry and no further.

'Nothing,' the groom hissed. 'I was restless.'

Jack raised a hand in acknowledgement and silently closed the window again. Henry was lying, of course, he had probably been prowling about every half-hour or so throughout the night. He never seemed to need much sleep—the result, he claimed, of becoming accustomed to very little when he was a prisoner of war.

The man drifted out of sight as soundlessly as he had appeared. Jack turned to go back to bed and found himself face to face with a white spectre. 'What the hell!'

It was Eva, of course. How she had got out of bed and across the room without him hearing her was a worry—was he losing his sharpness of hearing, the instinct that warned him of danger? But, of course, Eva was not a danger. Not, at least, in the sense that she was likely to knife him in the back.

'It is me,' she whispered. 'What's wrong? Is it Antoine's men?'

'No, nothing's wrong. I was simply checking. Henry is on guard below,' he said reassuringly. 'Go back to bed.'

'Very well.' Eva started to turn, stumbled, put out her hand for balance and hit it sharply against his naked ribs. The gasp of pain as her nails grazed across his bruises was out before he could choke it back. 'What's the matter?'

'Nothing. You scratched me slightly and made me jump, that's all.' She stood, looking up at him as though she could read his face in the near darkness. Her own was a pure oval of white, only the shadow of her eyes discernible.

'I do not believe you,' she said after a moment, and spun round towards the bedside table, the movement sending a faint rumour of warm skin and gardenia wafting, achingly, to his nostrils. 'Stay there.' There was a scrape and a flame flared up. She touched it to the candle and carried it over to where he stood. '*Mon Dieu!* Your ribs, your chest! Turn around.'

'It is nothing, just bruises from the rope.' Jack tried to urge her back to the bed, but she stood her ground. Eva should have looked ludicrous in his oversized shirt, her slim legs and slender feet emerging from beneath the hem, but she looked tousled and delectable and the fact she was wearing something of his was oddly arousing. No, *extremely* arousing.

'What rope? And turn around, I am not going to hurt you, you foolish man.' She seemed to have no conception that he might not obey her.

The implication that he was frightened had him turning before he could catch himself. Then he froze as a cool palm touched lightly on the diagonal welt across his back. 'You didn't think I climbed down the castle wall to your window like a lizard, did you?' It was suddenly difficult to control his breathing.

'Rational speculation about how you appeared in my room was the last thing on my mind,' Eva said drily. 'You could have flown there on a broomstick for all I knew.' She made a soft sound of distress as she moved the candle to see the full extent of the damage. Jack stood watching their shadows slide across the bedchamber wall and fought the urge to turn and take her in his arms. Her feminine concern, the gentleness of her touch, almost banished the constant awareness of who she was. But the Grand Duchess was all too aware of it; Jack reminded himself grimly of the fact, and turned round.

It did not help that the suddenness of his movement gave her no time to move her hand and they ended up almost chest to chest, her right arm wrapped around his naked ribcage, her left hand holding the candlestick out to the side in an effort not to scorch either of them. Oddly, the intimacy did not appear to be concerning her.

Eva tutted again, moving away to put the candle down safely. 'I don't suppose you have anything useful like medical supplies along with all those clean shirts, have you?' He was breathing like a virgin on her wedding night now and Eva was perfectly composed. *For God's sake, man, get a grip.*

'Of course.' Offering up a quick prayer of thanks that he had stopped to put on his breeches, Jack lifted one of his valises on to the bed and opened it. 'There. Not that I need anything.'

'I will be the judge of that.' Eva began to lift things out of the case. 'What on earth are these?'

'Probes for removing bullets.'

'Urgh.' She opened her fingers fastidiously and dropped the instrument on to the bed. 'I hope Henry knows what to do with them, or that you stay well out of the line of fire, because I am certainly not using them. Here, witch hazel, that is just the thing. And some lint.' She shook the bottle and pulled out the stopper, releasing the strange astringently aromatic smell into the room. 'Sit on the corner of the bed, please.'

The liquid was cold on his sleep-warm skin and Jack could feel the goose bumps forming as she dabbed her way up his back and across his shoulder along the lines left by the rope. He found himself wondering with a sense of detachment if she was going to deal with his chest with such aplomb. It seemed she would. For some reason a woman who baulked at sharing his bedchamber could cope quite easily with his half-naked body provided there was an injury to deal with.

Eva moved round, tipping the bottle on to the lint again to re-dampen it. She paused to survey the darkening bruise, then caught his eye. 'What is it?' *Damn the woman, can she read minds?* His ability to keep a straight, unreadable, face was one of his most valuable professional assets. So he had believed.

'I was wondering why you do not appear to find this embarrassing,' he answered frankly. 'We are both half-dressed and in a bedchamber, and earlier that appeared to be a major obstacle to a good night's sleep.'

She looked down her nose, suddenly every inch the Grand Duchess, despite her makeshift nightshirt and bare feet. 'You are injured; that is something that must be dealt with, whatever the situation. On the other hand, finding myself constrained to share a bed with a strange man was something I would hope to avoid if at all possible.'

'So modest behaviour depends on circumstance? Ouch!'

'Sorry.' She peered close to see why he had jumped, then carried on dabbing. Her breath fanned warmly over his collarbone, playing havoc with his pulse rate. 'Of course it depends. If I was in my bath and the place was burning down, I would not expect you to wait politely outside the door until I got dressed before breaking in to rescue me.'

Jack fought with himself, biting the inside of his cheek in an effort not to laugh, then he caught Eva's eye and watched while she imagined the scene she had just described. Her lips twitched, the corners of her eyes crinkled and she burst out laughing. He had never seen her laugh before; he hadn't known whether she had a sense of humour. The only smiles he had seen were polite social expressions, but this was another woman. One hand pressed to her lips, she hurried to put the bottle down safely, then collapsed on the bed in a paroxysm of giggles.

'Oh, Lord! I can just imagine our chamberlain doing just that! "I regret to inform your Serene Highness that the castle is on fire. Might I suggest you complete your coiffure at your earliest convenience, ma'am, as the flames are licking around my feet, ma'am…"'

She looks eighteen, a girl, so fresh, so natural, so sweet. The laughter drained out of Jack as he stared at her. Eva sat up at last, hiccupping faintly and mopping her eyes with the cuff of the shirt.

'I am sorry, it must be the strain.' She smiled at him hazily.

'I can't remember the last time I laughed out loud, or even found something silly enough to laugh about.'

Jack put out a hand towards her, not knowing what he wanted, only knowing he needed to touch her. Eva put her hand in his, her eyes questioning. He did not speak—there was nothing to say, nothing that he could articulate. For a moment she held his gaze, then awareness of who she was and where they were became clear from her expression and she looked away, chin up. Jack freed her hand and stood up.

'Back to bed, we will need to be up in a couple of hours. You require your sleep.'

She nodded haughtily, very much on her dignity and got up, skirting carefully around him to slide under the covers on her side. 'Good night.'

'Good night.' He stoppered the bottle of witch hazel, grateful for the way its heavy odour blanked out the feminine scent of her, and pulled the covers up firmly over his shoulders.

It was no part of his plans to be attracted to a woman, least of all a grand duchess. He had not thought himself so susceptible, nor so unprofessional. It was not as though he was short of feminine comfort for his physical needs—a succession of highly skilled barques of frailty made quite certain of that—for he had long since recognised that his chosen path was not one a wife could be expected to tolerate.

Not that the examples of marital life about him had made him eager to commit himself to such a relationship, so it was not such a deprivation. His recently widowed sister, Bel, had once confided that her husband was so dull she could hardly stay awake in his presence, his father had been a serial adulterer, and his friends, one after another, appeared to be sacrificing themselves on the altar of respectability by marrying simpering misses straight from the portals of Almack's.

Flirting with young ladies of good breeding was boring and risked raised expectations and broken hearts. Flighty matrons and dashing widows required more emotional commitment than he was prepared to invest—which left the professionals, with whom one could at least be assured there was no hypocrisy involved.

So why was this woman making him hard with desire? Why did he want to shelter her to an extent that went way beyond his brief to bring her back safely to England? She was hurt, anxious and vulnerable despite her efforts not to betray that and she had got under his skin in a totally unexpected way.

It was the novelty, obviously, Jack decided, stopping himself turning over restlessly for the third time. He was unlikely to find himself on such intimate terms with a member of a royal family again, that was all it was. Satisfied he had put that anxiety to rights, he closed his eyes, willed himself to sleep, and forbade himself to dream.

On the other side of the bolster Eva was wrestling with her emotions, her body's reactions and her sense of decorum and duty. She had woken, roused by instinct—for she was certain Jack had made no sound—and had lain for a moment looking at the silhouette of his head and torso against the pale frame of the window. His body was a beautiful shape, the classic male outline of inverted triangle over a narrow waist, enhanced by a musculature in the peak of fitness—hard, sculpted and wickedly exciting to a woman who had lived a life of celibate respectability for over twenty months.

Then the sleep had cleared from her mind and she forgot erotic considerations in anxiety about what he was looking at. That anxiety had carried her across the room to his side without self-consciousness, or any modest concern for how she was dressed, and no sooner had she recollected these things than she had been distracted again by the realisation that he was hurt.

Small boys with scraped knees were a matter of routine for a mother; grown men needing bandaging and nursing were part of a wife's duties, and somehow that had carried over into caring for her brother-in-law, and now Jack. She simply had not thought of him as anything but a body to be mended until he had looked into her eyes and held out his hand to her.

What was he asking? What did he want? After the skill of that kiss in the alleyway she had no doubt he could make a fine attempt at seducing her, if that was what he desired. She would find him hard to resist, she acknowledged that. Eva had long since abandoned self-deception as a method of dealing with her situation in life, and she was not going to risk everything by pretending she did not know temptation when she saw it. For years she had been able to turn away flirtation, thinly veiled offers and outright attempts at seduction without the slightest quickening of her pulse rate, not a moment's sleep lost. Now she felt as unsteady as a young girl in the throes of her first infatuation.

Was it simply friendship she had seen in Jack's gaze, in his outstretched hand? Or was it the first move of a skilled seducer? She could afford neither, for if friendship brought her closer to him she feared her own need would betray her, and if he was intent on seduction, then only a rigorously maintained distance and discipline would save her from herself.

Eva closed her eyes and made herself lie patiently waiting for sleep.

There was no virtue in remaining chaste while there was no temptation, she told herself severely. The morning would bring new resolution and greater strength, she had to believe that.

Chapter Six

The sound of booted feet on the floorboards brought Eva awake with a start of alarm. Sunlight was flooding through the window, morning had broken and she was still abed while pursuit could be at the door. She sat bolt upright. 'What time is it?' How could she have slept so soundly? 'How are your bruises?'

'Six, that is all. But time you got up, all the same. And my bruises are much better, thank you.' Jack straightened from fastening a valise and smiled at her, a casual smile that held none of last night's unspoken complications. He was fully dressed, clean shaven and alert. It felt very odd to have a man in her bedchamber while she was still in bed. 'There is warm water on the washstand. I'll wait downstairs unless you need any help with…er…' he waved one hand in an effort to find an acceptable word '…buttons or anything.'

'Thank you, no,' Eva replied, suppressing the information that she had carefully selected garments that did not require assistance with laces, buttons or any other fastening. Yesterday she would have probably blurted that out; today she was resolved to retain the utmost dignity compatible with sharing a room with a man to whom she was not married.

'Very well, I will order breakfast for twenty minutes' time.' He paused, one hand on the key. 'Lock the door behind me.'

She made it downstairs with five minutes to spare and was rewarded by a raised eyebrow as Jack stood and held a chair for her in the deserted parlour. 'I have a busy schedule that requires frequent changes of clothing,' she explained, answering the unspoken comment on her punctuality and accepting a proffered napkin with a nod of thanks. 'Where is Henry eating?'

'In the kitchen, I imagine.' Jack helped himself to a hearty slice of ham, two eggs and a length of sausage.

'I would prefer that he join us.' She poured coffee into the large cups and added a generous amount of milk, still frothy from the milking pail.

Jack accepted a cup, frowning. 'Why? He can hardly chaperon us in the bedchamber, so his presence at breakfast seems a touch superfluous.'

'Even so. I wish to retain the appearance of respectability so far as I am able.' How direct he was! She had hoped to raise the matter without mentioning chaperons or bedchambers, but, no, Jack made no concession to conventions, or to the mild hypocrisies that oiled the wheels of real life. Eva tried not to either blush, or look like a prude, and suspected she had ended up merely looking starched-up. Not such a bad thing.

'As you wish.' Jack got up, put his head round the door to catch a passing potboy with the message and resumed his seat. 'I am not sure Henry would add to any lady's credit, but I cannot provide you with a lady's maid.'

'No, I agree. It would not be fair to her, and she could slow us down in an emergency.' Eva buttered bread sedately, resisting the fragrant dish of ham and eggs until she had taken the sharpest edge off her appetite. Dinner last night had been unusually early and she had had nothing since, but she was not going to bolt her food. Years of eating in her room so she could be seen dining in public with the appetite of an elegant bird had left her awkward about tucking into a meal in company.

'Quite. A very practical assessment.' Jack was regarding her with a quizzical air. Eva stared haughtily back and carried on nibbling her bread and butter. 'Is anything wrong?'

He was always catching her off-balance, she thought resentfully. Half the time he was coolly expressionless, practical and seemed to expect her to just get on with things as he did himself. Then there would be a flash of sympathy, of understanding or concern, and his grey eyes came alive with a warmth that made her want to reach out and take his hand again.

'Whatever could there be wrong?' she said lightly, feeling her smile tighten. She added, with an edge of sarcasm, 'This is all quite in the normal run of my experience, after all.'

'Treating me like a awkward ambassador is not going to— Henry, good morning. *Madame* would like you to join us.'

'Strewth.' The groom stood turning his hat round in his hands. 'You sure about that, ma'am? I mean, I've been seeing to the horses this morning and all.'

'Entirely sure. Please sit in that chair there, Henry. Now, would you care for some coffee?'

Eva poured, served herself ham and eggs, made careful conversation with both men in a manner that effectively forbade the introduction of any personal matter whatsoever and finally rose from the table, satisfied that she had set the tone for the rest of the journey. 'Where are we travelling to today?' she asked over her shoulder as Jack pulled out her chair for her at the end of the meal.

He shook his head slightly and she caught her breath. She had been beginning to feel safe, lulled by the routine domesticity of breakfast. Of course, walls had ears, people could be bribed to pass on tittle-tattle about earlier guests. The cold knot in her stomach twisted itself together again, not helped by the squeeze he gave her elbow as she preceded him out of the room. She was not used to being touched. It was meant to be reassuring, she was sure, but it succeeded all too well in reminding her just how much she needed him.

Jack waited until the carriage had rattled out of the inn yard and Henry had turned west before speaking. 'Grenoble, Lyon, Dijon, then north to the border with the Kingdom of the Netherlands by whatever seems the safest route at the time,' he said without preamble as she folded her cloak on the seat.

'Through so many big towns? Is that wise?' The watchful grey eyes opposite narrowed and Eva caught a glimpse of displeasure. *He does not like my questioning his judgement,* she thought. *Too bad, I want to understand. I need to.*

'In my judgement it is,' Jack responded evenly. 'We need the speed of the good roads and travellers are less obvious in cities. However, if we run into trouble, then I have an alternative plan.' She nodded, both in comprehension and agreement. 'I am glad you approve.'

'It is not a question of approval,' Eva snapped, then caught at the fraying edge of her temper. Grace under pressure, that was what Louis had always insisted was the mark of rulers. Grace under pressure at all times. 'I wish to understand,' she added more temperately. 'I am not a parcel you have been charged with delivering to the post office. Nor does my position make me some sort of mindless figurehead as you seem to think. If I understand what we are doing, why we are going where we do, then I am less likely to make any mistakes to earn your further displeasure.'

'It is not my place to express displeasure at any action of yours.' Jack's retort was even enough to tip her emotions over into anger again. He was humouring her, that was what he was doing. He wanted it both ways—he wanted to call her by her first name, carry on this pretence of marriage and sharing a room, yet the moment she tried to take an active part in their flight he fell back on becoming the respectful courtier.

'No, it is *not* your place, Mr Ryder, but I thought we had agreed that for the duration of this *adventure* I was not a grand duchess, that you would call me by my given name. I had assumed that meant you would also stop treating me as if I was not a real person. I hate it when I visit a village and they have painted the shutters especially. How do I know what lies behind them? Are they prosperous or are they poor? How much money was wasted on that paint? I want the truth, Mr Ryder, not platitudes, not your equivalent of painted shutters.'

Her angry words hung in the air between them. She saw the bunching of the muscles under the tight cloth of his breeches and wondered if he was about to jump up, pull the check cord and transfer to the box, leaving her in solitude to fume.

Then Jack leaned back into the corner of the seat and smiled. It was not a sign of humour, it was the kind of smile she produced when she was deeply displeased, but it would not be politic to say so, a curving of thinned lips. Had that hard mouth really been the one that had slid over her warm lips with such sensual expertise?

'Very well.' Eva jumped, dragging her eyes away from his lips. 'If you must have it without the bark on it. The amount of danger we are in all depends on whether Antoine wants you back, and, if he does, whether he has a preference for alive or dead.' Eva tried not to flinch at the brutal analysis. 'He might simply be satisfied with you disgraced, in which case we are doing his work for him—last night was enough to ruin you. Or, of course, an accident on the road has the advantage of simplicity.

'If he wants you ruined, he just has to leave us alone, spread the rumour that you have fled with your lover and make sure every newspaper in Europe picks up the tittle-tattle.'

'When I get back to England and I am seen to be received by the Prince Regent and the Queen—'

'The damage will be done by then, the dirt will be on your name. No smoke without fire, they will say.'

'I wonder, then, that you chose to share my room last night.' Cold shame was washing over her body—what would Freddie think? Small boys were cruel; someone would make certain he heard of his mother and the smutty tales about her. 'It was poor judgement on your part.' All this time worrying about her reputation and knowing that taking a lover was out of the question, and now this.

'I put safety above respectability. Better slandered than dead.' There was a flash of white teeth in a sudden grin, then the grim humour was gone. 'And besides, Prince Antoine has all the ammunition he needs without confirmation from an innkeeper about which beds were slept in. You were seen leaving with a man and some baggage.' He paused, watching her face. 'If I had pointed this out, back in the castle, would you still have come?'

'Yes, of course I would have come!' Of course she would have. 'What does my reputation matter against Freddie's safety or my duty? And what difference does it make to our choices whether Antoine wants me alive or dead?'

'If he wants you back in Maubourg so that people can see you, while he controls you as a puppet by threats to your son, then he will have to capture you and transport you home. That requires some logistical planning, more people. It may be easier to spot. If he wants an accident…well, then that is harder to see coming.'

'Yes, that is putting it without the bark on,' she agreed, trying not to let her voice shake. This was the man she had begun to think she understood and now realised she had been underestimating. Jack seemed so cold, so unmoved by the fear and danger behind his analysis. 'Are you ever afraid?' she demanded, the words leaving her lips as she thought them.

'Of many things,' he said evenly, surprising her. 'The knack is not to admit to it, not even to yourself.'

'I am scared of spiders,' she confessed. 'But I am not prepared to say what else.' Even referring to her recurring nightmare obliquely made it hideously real. Those dark passageways under the castle, the shifting lift of the torches making half-seen shapes move in corners. The rectangular shapes and the knowledge of what was in them… She pushed it away with an inner shudder. 'I understand what you mean; it does not do to conjure such things up. Instead, tell me what I should to do to help protect us all.'

'Do what I tell you, always, at once and without question.'

Eva blinked. She had been hoping he would give her a pistol, and show her how to use it, or demonstrate how to hit an assailant over the head, or some other active form of defence. 'That was very peremptory, Mr Ryder.'

'Are you going to argue about it? And call me Jack.'

'Yes, I am going to argue, *Jack,*' she said. 'What if I do not agree with what you are telling me to do?'

'We stand there and debate it while the opposition takes the advantage, or I hit you on the point of your very pretty chin and do whatever it is anyway.'

'My… What has my chin got to do with it?'

'It is the easiest part of your anatomy to hit in a crisis.' He appeared to have regained his good humour. 'Then Henry and I bundle up your unconscious body and make our escape with you slung unflatteringly over Henry's shoulder.' The smile reached his eyes, crinkling the corners in a way that was infuriatingly attractive.

'There is the death penalty in Maubourg for striking a member of the Grand Ducal family,' Eva stated. *And see how you like the thought of a coarse hemp noose around your neck, Mr Ryder!*

'What a good thing we will not be in Maubourg if such an eventuality transpires.' They sat in silence. Eva glared out of one window, Jack looked out of the other, his lips pursed in a soundless whistle.

Eventually the coach turned, lurched and began to ride more smoothly. Eva dragged her attention back to the landscape and away from a satisfying daydream of seeing Mr Ryder dragged off in chains to the scaffold. They had reached the post road to Grenoble.

'Are you going to sulk all the way to Brussels?' Jack enquired.

'I am not sulking. I have simply not got anything to say to you, you insolent man.'

'I see. I apologise for the remark about your chin.'

'What part of that remark, exactly? Threatening to hit it?'

'No, making an uncalled-for personal remark.'

'Has anyone told you how inf—' She broke off at the sound of a fist being banged on the carriage roof.

'Hell.' Jack sat upright. 'That means trouble. We are almost at the border—do you normally have it guarded? There was no check when we entered the Duchy.'

'No, never. Our army is minute and there are far too many passes and back roads to make it worthwhile putting on border guards. What do we do?' Jack would have a plan for this, he couldn't intend that they stop, surely? Eva braced herself, expecting the horses to be whipped up to ride through whatever obstruction lay in their path.

But Jack was on his feet, balancing against the swaying of the coach as Henry began to rein in. Eva stared as he groped under the edge of the seat he had been sitting on. There was a click and the whole top folded up leaving a rectangular space. Jack threw her valise into one end and gestured. 'In you get. There are air holes.'

'No!' It gaped, dark and stark as a sepulchre. Eva could feel the panic constricting her throat. *Don't talk about nightmares...it makes them come real...* The edges of her vision clouded as though grey cobwebs were growing there. The shadows in the corners shifted... the sound of stone grinding on stone...the scratch of bone...

'In!' Jack gestured impatiently, his attention on the scene

outside as the carriage came to a halt. There were voices raised to give curt orders. 'Now!'

Duty. It is my duty to survive. It is my duty to be strong. Eva scrambled in, and sat down. The air seemed to have darkened, she was light-headed. *Don't shut it, no! Don't!* The scream was soundless as Jack pushed her down until she was lying prone. He said something; but the roaring in her ears made it hard to hear. Then the lid closed on to darkness. Forcing herself to breathe, she raised both hands until the palms pressed against the wooden underside and pushed up. It was locked tight. *Trust him, he will let you out. Trust him. Trust…he will come.*

Jack sat down in the corner of the carriage, ran his hands through his hair, crossed one leg negligently over the other and drew a book out of his pocket. He raised his eyes to look over the top of it as the door was flung open. 'Yes?' It was a soldier in the silver-and-blue Maubourg uniform. Sent by Prince Antoine, no doubt.

'Your papers, *monsieur.*'

'But of course.' Jack put down the book, taking his time, and removed the documents from his breast pocket. His false identity as a Paris lawyer was substantiated by paperwork from a 'client' near Toulon who wished for advice on a family trust. He fanned out the documents without concealment, extracted the passport and handed it across.

The man took it and marched away towards the front of the vehicle without even glancing at it. Damnation. That probably meant an officer. Jack climbed down and walked forward to where a young lieutenant was scanning the papers, three soldiers at his back.

'You are on your way back to Paris, *monsieur?*'

'Yes. I have been on business near Toulon.' The young man's thumb was rubbing nervously over the wax seal. The lieutenant was inexperienced, unsure of himself and probably wondering what on earth he'd been sent out here to deal with.

'What other vehicles have you passed since yesterday?'

'I have no idea.' Jack stared at him blankly. It was a useful trick. People questioning you expected you to lie, to make up an answer, to be able to catch you out. An honest admission of ignorance took the wind out of their sails and made you seem more credible. 'I have been reading, sleeping. I take no notice of such things. *Henri,* what have you seen?'

Henry shrugged. 'All sorts, *monsieur,* all sorts. What is the lieutenant looking for?'

'A woman,' the young man began, then reddened at the grin on Henry's face and the sound of his own men choking back their laughter. He glared at his men. 'A fugitive. A woman in her mid-twenties, brown hair, tall. With a man. Probably in a travelling carriage.'

'No idea.' The groom was dismissive. 'Can't see inside anything closed from up here. Could have passed the Emperor himself and a carriage full of Eagles for all I know.'

'Very well. You may proceed.' The officer handed Jack the passport and stepped back.

Jack climbed into the carriage and sat down without a glance up at Henry. Inept and badly organised was the only way to describe that road block. It must have been the first response last night, to send troops out on the main roads. He did not fool himself that this would be the extent of Antoine's reaction to the disappearance of his sister-in-law.

The rapid tattoo on the roof told him that no one was following them. All clear, he could let Eva out. What a fuss she had made about getting in—no doubt she thought the box contained the dreaded spiders she had confessed to fearing.

Jack unlatched the seat, lifted the lid and caught his breath. For one appalled moment he thought she was dead. Her face was grey, her eyes closed, her hands, clasped at her breast, had blood on them. Then her eyes opened, unfocused on some unseen terror. 'No,' she whispered. 'No! Louis—don't let them in!'

Chapter Seven

'Eva.' A dark shape loomed over her. *He* had come, just as she knew, just as she feared. The figure reached down, took her shoulder and she gasped, a little sound of horror, and swooned.

'Eva, wake up.' Her nostrils were full of the smell of dust, of the tomb he had just lifted her from. She was held on a lap, yet the male body she rested on was warm, alive, pulsing with strength, not cold, dead…

He shifted her on his knees so he could hold her more easily. 'It's all right, we are quite safe, there is no one else here.' *Jack?* She could not trust herself to respond. A hand stroked her cheek, found the sticky traces of half-dried tear tracks. Flesh-and-blood fingertips against her skin, not the touch of dry bone. She came to herself with a sharply drawn breath. 'Eva, you are safe,' he said urgently.

'Oh. Oh, *Jack.*' She burrowed her face into his shirtfront.

'Are you all right now?' He managed to get a finger under her chin and nudged it up so he could look into her face. 'You frightened me. What was all that about?'

'I am sorry.' She tried to sit up, but he pulled her back. 'It is just that that was…is…my worst nightmare. A real nightmare. I keep having it.' *I am awake, I am safe. Jack kept me safe. He did not come.*

'Tell me,' he prompted.

She had never spoken of it to anyone. Could she do so now? Admit such fear and weakness? 'When I first came to the castle Louis, my husband, took me down to the family vault under the chapel. At first it was exciting, fascinating, like a Gothic romance—the twisting stairs, the flickering torches. I didn't realise where we were going.'

The smell of the air—that was what had hit her first. Cold, dry, infinitely stale. Old. Louis had held, not a lantern, but a torch, the flames painting shapes over the pillars and arches, making shadows solid. 'Then he opened the door into the vault—it seems to go on for ever, right under the castle, with arches and a succession of rooms.'

She had been a little excited, she remembered now. These must be the dungeons. It was all rather unreal, like a Gothic novel. Until she had realised where they were.

'We were in the burial vaults. All there is down there are these niches in the walls, like great shelves, each one with a coffin on it.' Jack must have felt her shudder at the memory and tightened his hold.

'The newer ones were covered in dusty velvet, there were even withered wreaths.' How did the flowers and leaves hold their shape? she had wondered, still not quite taking in what she was seeing. They had moved on, further and deeper into the maze of passageways. 'The older ones were shrouded in cobwebs. Some of them were cracked.' There had been a hideous compulsion to move closer, to put her eye to those cracks and look into the sarcophagus as though into a room.

'Then Louis started to show them to me, as though he were introducing living relatives; it was horrible, but he seemed to think it quite normal, and I tried not to show what I was thinking.' Already, by then, she was learning that she must not show emotion, that she must show respect for Maubourg history and tradition, that weakness was unforgivable. Somehow she applied those lessons and did not run, screaming, for the stairs. Or perhaps she had known she would never find them again.

Then they had moved on. She had felt something brush against her arm and had looked down. 'There was one—an old wooden casket where the planks had cracked and a hand had come out.' She had tried never to think about it while she was awake, but whenever the nightmare came, this was the image that began it. 'A skeleton hand, reaching out for me as we walked past. It touched me.'

Her voice broke. Jack made a sound as if to tell her to stop, that it was too distressing, but she was hurrying now. It must all be said. 'And then he came to two empty shelves and said "And these are ours". I didn't understand at first, and then I realised he meant they were for our coffins.'

One day she would lie there, enclosed in a great stone box, sealed up away from the light and air for ever. There would not even be the natural, life-renewing embrace of the soil to take her back.

'I don't know how I got out without making a scene. That night I dreamt I had died and woken up in my coffin. I knew I was down there, and *they* were all out there, waiting, and that any moment Louis would lift the lid and he would be dead, too, and— I am sorry, such foolishness.'

Eva sat up, smoothing her hair back from her face with a determined calm. *Discipline, remember who you are.* There was pity and respect in Jack's grey eyes as he looked at her. She could not let it affect her. 'Ever since then, I have been afraid of very tight, dark, spaces.'

'I'm not surprised, that is the most ghoulish thing I have ever heard. Did your husband not realise what an effect it was having on you?'

'Louis was a firm believer in self-control and putting on a good face,' Eva said with a rueful smile. 'I soon learned what was expected of me.'

'Did you love your husband?'

'No, of course not, love was not part of the expectation,' she said readily. She had just confessed her deepest fear—to tell the tale of her marriage was easy in comparison. 'I was dazzled, seduced and over-awed. I was seventeen years old, remember! Just imagine—a grand duke.'

'A catch, indeed,' Jack agreed. There was something in his voice that made her suddenly very aware of where she was and that Jack's body was responding to holding her so closely

'I… Mr Ryder, Jack, please let me go.' She struggled off his lap, suddenly gauche and awkward, knowing the colour flaming in her cheeks. 'Thank you. I appreciate your…concern.'

She settled in the far corner, fussing with her skirts and pushing at her hair in a feminine flurry of activity. 'You say you have the dream quite often?' Jack said slowly.

'Yes.' She nodded, keeping her head bent, apparently intent on a mark on her sleeve.

'Very well. You must remember, the next time, that when the lid begins to move, it is me opening it. I will have come to rescue you. There will be nothing unpleasant for you to see, and I will take you safely up those winding stairs, up into the daylight. Do you understand, Eva? Remind yourself of that before you go to sleep.'

'You? But why should you rescue me in my dream?' No one has ever rescued me before.' He had her full attention now. She fixed her eyes on his face as she worried over his meaning.

'You did not have me as a bodyguard before,' Jack said simply. 'All you need to do is believe in me, and I will be there. Even in your dreams. Do you?'

'Believe in you? Yes, Jack. I believe you. Even in my dreams.'

It was a fairy tale. Eva looked down at her clasped hands so that Jack would not see that her eyes were suddenly swimming with tears. Such foolish weakness! She was a rational, educated woman; of course he could not stride into her nightmare like a knight, errant to slay the ghosts and monsters. And yet, she believed him. Believed *in* him.

Only the year before she had found an enchanting book of fairy stories by some German brothers and had been engrossed. What was the name of the one about the sleeping princes? Ah, yes, 'Briar Rose.'

And it was a dangerous fairy tale, for she wanted more than protection from her knight errant—she wanted his lovemaking, she wanted him to wake her from her long sleep.

Jack wanted her, too, she knew, if only at the most basic level of male response to the female. He could not hide his body's response from a woman nestling in his lap. And that frightened her, for she realised that she had responded to it, been aroused by it, before her mind had recognised what was happening to them. She should have been alert to that danger, she had thought she was. Had she not resolved to maintain everything on a strictly impersonal level, as recently as this morning? That attack of panic had upset all her carefully constructed aloofness like a pile of child's building blocks.

'What are you thinking about?' He was matter of fact again. It almost felt as though he was checking on her mental state in the same way as he would check on the condition of a horse, or test the temper of a blade he might rely upon.

'Fairy stories,' she said promptly, looking up, her eyes clear. Telling the truth was always easiest, and this seemed a safe and innocuous subject. Her early training came back—find a neutral topic of conversation that will set the other person at their ease. 'I found a wonderful book of them last year.'

'The Brothers Grimm? Yes, I enjoyed those.' He grinned at her expression. 'You are surprised I read such things?'

'Perhaps you have nephews and nieces?' she suggested.

'No, none. And I do not think it is a book for children, do you? Far too much sex, far too much fear and violence.'

Flustered by how closely this was impinging on her fantasies, Eva said hastily, 'Yes, of course, you are quite correct. It is not a book I would give to Freddie.'

'I doubt he sits still long enough to read anything except his schoolbooks,' Jack said.

'Oh, of course. I forgot, you actually spoke to him.' How could she have forgotten that? She had been fighting her fears about Freddie, fretting over how he was, and here was someone with news of him that was only weeks old. 'Tell me how he looked.'

'As well as any lively nine-year-old who has just had a severe stomach upset,' Jack said. 'A touch green round the gills, but so far recovered that he was able to enjoy describing exactly, and in minute and revolting detail, how his mushrooms had reappeared and what they had looked like.'

'I am sorry.' Eva chuckled. 'Little wretch.'

'He's a boy. I was one once— I am not so old that I cannot remember the fascination of gory details.'

'How tall is he?' Eva asked wistfully. 'Hoffmeister writes me pedantic reports on a regular basis. "HSH has attained some competence with his Latin translation, HSH has been outfitted with new footwear, HSH smuggled a kitten into his room. It has been removed." But it doesn't help me *see* Freddie.'

Jack stood up, braced himself against the lurching of the carriage with one hand on the luggage rack and held the other hand palm down against his body. 'This high. Sturdy as a little pony now—but any moment he is going to start to grow and I think he will be tall. His hair is thick, like yours, and needs cutting. His eyes are hazel, his face he is still growing into. But I saw he was your son when I first set eyes on you.'

He sat down again and Eva felt the tension and fear of the past hour ebb away into relief and thoughts of Freddie. 'Oh, thank you so much, I can just picture him now! He was such a baby when Louis insisted he went to England. The first thing I am going to do when I am settled there is to have his portrait painted.'

'With his mother, of course?'

'No,' she said slowly, thinking it out. 'Alone. His first official portrait. I will have engravings done from it and flood Maubourg with them. It is time people remembered who their Grand Duke is.'

'Ah.' Jack was watching her, sizing her up again in a way that made her raise her chin. 'The Grand Duchess is back.'

'She never goes away,' Eva said coolly. 'It would be as well to remember that, Mr Ryder.'

His half-bow from the waist was, if one wanted to take offence, mocking. Eva chose to keep the peace and acknowledged it with a gracious inclination of her head. Then she let her shoulder rest against the corner squabs and closed her eyes. One could never take refuge in sleep in public as a grand duchess, but she was coming to see it was a useful haven in everyday life.

'Grenoble.' Jack spoke close to her ear and Eva came fully awake as the sound of the carriage wheels changed and they hit the cobbles.

'What time is it?' She sat up and tried to stretch her neck from its cramped position.

'Nearly eight. We made faster time than I feared we would.'

'And where are we staying?' Water glinted below as they passed over a bridge. The Drac or the Isère, she could not orientate herself.

'Another eminently respectable bourgeois inn. And this time we have a private parlour adjoining our bedchamber, Madame Ridère.'

'So that's who I am, is it? I suppose it is easy to remember—Ryder or Ridère. And this was all booked in advance for tonight?' He nodded. Eva could make out his expression with some clarity, for the streets were well lit. 'You were very confident that we would get here, were you not?' Jack smiled, looked as though he would reply, then closed his lips. She added sharply, 'I suppose you were about to say that you are very confident because you are very good.'

'It is my job.' Infuriatingly he did not rise to her jibe. Eva was stiff, hungry and tense, for all kinds of reasons. A brisk exchange of views with Jack Ryder was just the tonic she needed. It seemed she was not going to get one. 'We are here.'

'Bonsoir, bonsoir, Monsieur Ridère. Madame! Entrez, s'il vous plaît.' The innkeeper emerged, Eva forced herself to think in French again, and the ritual of disembarking, being shown their room, ordering supper, unwound.

'That bed is smaller,' she observed as they sat down in the parlour to await their food. 'In fact, it is very small.'

'Indeed.' Jack was folding a rather crumpled news sheet into order in front of the fireplace. 'No room for the bolster, then, which is a good thing—you nearly pushed both it and me out last night.'

'I am *not* sleeping with you in a bed that size. There is a settle in here.' She pointed to the elaborately carved example of Alpine woodwork on the far side of the room.

'That is a good foot shorter than I am, as narrow as a window ledge and as hard as a board. And it appears to be covered in very knobbly artistic representations of chamois. I am not forgoing a comfortable bed.' She bristled. Jack snapped the newspaper open and regarded her over the top of it. 'Do I appear to you to be crazed with lust?'

'I… You… *What* did you say?'

At this critical juncture the waiter appeared with a casserole dish, followed by various other persons bearing plates, bread, jugs and cutlery. Eva folded her lips tightly and went to take her seat at the table.

Jack put down his newspaper and joined her. *'Du pain, ma chère?'*

'Don't you *my dear* me,' she hissed, only to subside as the waiter returned with a capon and a dish of greens. *'Merci, c'est tout,'* she said firmly.

'Non, non, un moment, la fromage.' Jack wielded the bread knife and passed her a slice.

'Coward! You cannot hide behind the servants for ever.' She forced a smile as the waiter brought the cheese. The door closed. 'How dare you?'

'I thought the *my dear* added verisimilitude. Some wine?'

'Yes, please.' A stiff drink was what she really needed. Brandy at the very least. 'That was not what I was referring to and you know it. How dare you refer to lust in my hearing?'

'I apologise for my choice of words.' Jack passed her a glass of white wine and took a thoughtful sip from his. 'Amorous propensities? Uncontrollable desire? Satyr-like tendencies? Ardent longings? Any of those any better?'

All or any of them involving Jack would be sinfully wonderful, as would throwing the cheese board at him. Eva gritted her teeth and persisted. 'It would be highly improper for us to share that bed. It is far too small.'

'And you expect what, exactly, to occur as a result?' Jack began to carve the legs off the capon. Something about his very precise knife work suggested repressed emotion at odds with his dispassionate tone.

'We might touch. Inadvertently.' Eva took a deep swallow of wine, nearly choked and took another. A capon leg was laid on her plate. 'Thank you.' Even when discussing lust one could maintain the courtesies, she thought hazily, reaching for the decanter and refilling her glass. 'Some greens?' She lifted the serving spoons competently.

'Please.' Jack passed her the butter and took the lid off the casserole with a flourish. *'Pommes Dauphinoise?'*

'Allow me…' *To upend it over your head.* Eva wielded a serving spoon with practised elegance.

'Thank you. Has it occurred to you that we have been touching—inadvertently or otherwise—all day?'

'Of course. It was unavoidable. Butter?'

'Thank you, no. And?'

'And nothing. Touching in bed is quite another matter.'

'That, my dear, is indubitably true.'

Eva almost choked on a further incautious mouthful of wine and stared at Jack across the steaming dishes. 'I do not need you to tell me that. I am a mur…married ludy. *Lady.*'

'Widowed lady,' he corrected gently. 'More wine.'

'Yes.' She was obviously tired, despite that nap in the carriage. Otherwise why was her tongue tangling itself? 'Please.'

'So.' Jack chewed thoughtfully. 'How to avoid this undesirable inadvertent touching? Whilst allowing me a decent night's sleep.' He reached across the table and lifted the second bottle of wine and the corkscrew. 'What forethought on my part to order two bottles.'

'It is a tolerable vintage,' Eva allowed, fanning herself with her napkin. It really was warm in here. 'As to the bed, thatsh—I mean, that's your problem, Mr Ryder. You arranged it.'

'What if I sleep on top of the bedclothes and you under them? More capon?'

'Thank you.' She was obviously hungry or why was her head spinning so? 'Wearing what?'

'Me or you?'

'You, of course.' Her glass was empty again. It really was a most excellent vintage.

'A nightshirt.' He lifted his wineglass, then glared at her over it as she snorted. It wasn't a very elegant reaction, Eva acknowledged vaguely. Grand duchesses never snort, but really!

'What, exactly, is there in that to provoke a snort?' Jack demanded.

'Men look ridiculous in nightshirts. Hairy legs sticking out of the bottom.' *Did I just say that?* She blinked at the wineglass. It appeared to be half-full now. How many had she drunk?

'Well, in my case you won't be looking, so if you can just steer your imagination away from the aesthetic horror of it, we will be all right.'

He isn't pleased I commented on his hairy legs. I suppose he has got hairy legs, all men do, don't they? He has a hairy chest. Not very hairy, though, just nicely hairy. Some remnant of restraint, surfacing through the effects of four glasses of wine on a nearly empty stomach stopped her complimenting Jack on the niceness of his chest. A creeping feeling of unease that perhaps this conversation was not all it should be began to steal over her.

'I think I am going to go to bed. Into bed. Under the covers.'

Jack stood up. 'Can I be of any assistance? The door is over there.'

'I know that,' she said with dignity, gathering her skirts around her and paying particular regard to her deportment. 'Good night, Mr Ryder.'

The effect of this exit was somewhat marred by a very audible hiccup.

Chapter Eight

Eva woke, far too hot and with a thunderous headache. She hadn't recalled the bedclothes being quite this thick—but then her memories of the previous evening were somewhat uncertain. She had drunk far too much, that was indisputable. She had discussed lust and beds and nightshirts with Jack in a most outrageous manner. Eva screwed her eyes tighter shut and prayed that she hadn't actually *said* anything about hairy legs. Had she? Or worse, chests. *Please, God.*

She shifted restlessly under the weight of the blankets and found that it was not layers of woollens weighing her down, but one long masculine arm thrown over her ribcage that was pinning her to the bed. At the risk of a cricked neck, she turned her head and found herself almost nose to nose with Jack.

'Good morning. Do you have a headache?'

'What are you doing!' It was a shriek that almost split her head as she uttered it. Eva closed her eyes again with a groan. Warm breath feathered her face.

'I must have turned over in the night. No inadvertent touching, though,' he pointed out with intolerable self-righteousness.

'Will you please remove your arm?'

The weight shifted. Eva opened her eyes cautiously and found that his arm might have moved, but Jack had not. They were still close enough for her to have counted his eyelashes, should she have had the inclination to do so. They were unfairly long, very dark and framed his eyes dramatically. She was also in an excellent position to note that his eyes might be grey, but there were black flecks in them. The pupils were somewhat dilated and his regard intense. She found herself unable to stop staring back, directly into them.

'One of us has got to blink,' Jack observed, 'or we may mesmerise each other and never get up.'

It seemed to Eva that someone had certainly been exerting powers of animal magnetism upon her, although she thought she had read somewhere that the effect required immersion of the subject in magnetised water. Or was it just her headache making her feel like this?

'Yes, and it will have to be you because I am completely pinned down with you lying on these covers,' she pointed out crisply. Thank goodness she still seemed able to speak with clarity and authority; she had been half-afraid she would open her mouth and mumble inanities.

'Very well.' Jack rolled away and stood up, stretching as he walked to throw open the shutters. He was dressed in a crumpled shirt and breeches, his feet bare on the boards.

'You said you were going to wear a nightshirt.' Eva sat up in bed, pushing her hair back off her face with both hands. She hadn't even plaited it last night.

'And you expressed horror at the suggestion. I believe an aversion to hairy legs came into it.' Jack turned back from the window and stood regarding her, hands on hips, a smile tugging at the corner of his mouth.

'I didn't say that, did I? Oh, Lord.' Eva buried her face in her hands. If she didn't look, then he wasn't really there, she didn't have to face the hideous embarrassment of knowing she'd been completely tipsy—no, *drunk*—and totally indiscreet. What must he think of her? She knew what she thought of herself.

'Eva.' The bed dipped beside her and a hand settled on her shoulder, large, warm, comforting.

'Stop it. Don't touch me,' she snapped. It lifted again. 'I'm sorry, I am finding this very difficult.' Silence. 'I'm not used to this intimacy with someone. I'm not used to someone being so close, so involved with what I'm doing, what I am thinking.'

She dropped her hands and looked at him, desperate to communicate how she felt. 'I do not know how to *be* with you, because this relationship we have is outside anything I've known before.' Jack's face, intent, listening, gave her no clue as to his feelings—except that he did not appear to be inclined to laugh at her.

'We are forced into this closeness and it is as if I am adrift without any chart to guide me. You are not a servant, you are not one of the family, you are not a professional man I have hired, like a doctor or a lawyer. What *are* you?'

She did not expect an answer, far less the one he gave her. 'A friend.'

'A friend?' Why did that word hurt so much? It was as though he had shone a light on the great empty loneliness at the heart of her life and forced her to confront it. 'I do not have any friends.'

'You have now.' Jack picked up her right hand as it lay lax on the counterpane. 'Eva, you have shared a dark secret fear with me, you have told me how you feel about your son, how you felt about your husband. You have got tipsy with me and you have confided your prejudices about nightshirts. We are jointly engaged on a dangerous adventure. Today we will go shopping together. These are all things you do with friends.'

Her hand seemed small, lost within his big brown one, the long fingers cupping it protectively, not gripping, just cradling it. Eva found herself studying his nails. Clean, neatly clipped with a black line of bruising along the base of three of them, a rough patch on the index fingernail as though it had been abraded against a rough stone. That damage had been done as he had climbed down the castle wall to her room. Absently she rubbed the ball of her thumb over it, welcoming the distraction of the rasping sensation.

'Do you make friends of all your clients?' She did her best to sound like the Grand Duchess and not Eva de Maubourg, not disorientated, half-afraid, confused.

'You are not a client, his Majesty's Government is my client. But, yes, I do make friends with some. Not all. Some I do not like, many are in too much trouble to want to do anything but see the back of me when it is all sorted out. When we are in England I will introduce you to Max Dysart, the Earl of Penrith, and his wife; you will like them, I think.

'But why have you no friends? Girls from your come-out in England? The Regent, the ladies of the court...'

'Philippe is twenty-five years my senior, he is like an uncle.

Antoine, I have never trusted. The ladies of the court, as you put it—no. Louis did not encourage me to make friends here, or to retain them from before, and that became established. I do not think there are any kindred spirits amongst them in any case.' She assayed a confident smile, knowing it was a poor effort. 'Certainly there is no one I could get drunk with, or have an adventure with, or risk telling a weakness to.'

'Then I am the first.'

I am the first. The words Louis had used as he had undressed her on their wedding night, his green eyes heavy with desire. It had been very important to him that she was a virgin. Now, no longer an innocent, she knew it had titillated the jaded palate of a man she was to learn was one of the most energetic, and promiscuous, lovers in Europe. Theirs had not been a love match, but she could not complain that Louis had ever left her physically unsatisfied. Just emotionally empty, and yearning for affection. She had learned to be a good grand duchess, and to do without love.

'What is it?' Jack's hand closed shut around hers. 'Another nightmare?'

'No. Just a memory. Thank you, I would like to be your friend.' She looked up, relaxing, expecting to see something uncomplicated in his expression. He was smiling, but in his eyes there was something else, something she knew he was trying to mask. Heat, intensity, need. She recognised them because she felt them, too. The ordinary words she had intended to say caught in her throat. Somehow she not could pretend to herself that she did not see, or that she did not feel.

But I want… No, I cannot say it. I cannot say I want you, because if I do the world changes for ever.

Jack lifted her hand and pressed a kiss on her fingertips that were all that could be seen within his grasp. 'You were right, ma'am, from now on we need a considerably bigger bed and then I can sleep under the covers and safely wear a nightshirt.'

'Oh!' Eva was startled into a gasp of amusement. 'How can you make a joke about it?'

'Because laughter chases away fear and it also puts many things in perspective. Are you hungry? Because I am starving and I don't know where they are with the hot water.' Jack tugged at the bell pull and retreated behind the screen.

'I am ravenous.' And suddenly she was. And strangely happy as though a weight had been lifted. Perhaps it was simply the cathartic effect of telling Jack how she felt. Except, of course, the fact that that she desired him. *He feels the same way.* The memory of the heat in his gaze as it had rested on her made her feel warm and fluttery inside and ridiculously girlish. Even though they had not acknowledged what that exchange of glances meant, the fact that an attractive, intelligent man found her desirable was the most wonderful boost to her confidence. *Perhaps I'm not so old and past it after all.*

There was a knock on the door and she hopped out of bed to open it, remembering at the last minute to ask who it was before she unlocked the door. Feeling wonderful was no excuse for laying them open to attack.

The chambermaid staggered in with two steaming ewers, set them both down beside the screen and went out, sped on her way by Eva's insistence on a large breakfast as soon as possible.

'Are we really going shopping?' She climbed back into bed and sat up, her arms round her knees, listening to the sounds of splashing. She had never listened to a man's morning rituals. Louis had always retreated to his own suite after visiting hers. He had never, after their wedding night, slept with her until morning.

'Of course. You need a travelling wardrobe.' There was a pause and a sound she guessed was a razor being stropped. 'They won't be the sort of shops you are used to,' he warned.

'I do not care.' Eva flopped back against the pillows. 'I don't get to see many shops, everything comes to me. It is so boring—I love window shopping and looking for bargains.' The noises from behind the screen were muffled. 'Do you hate shopping, or are you shaving?'

'Shaving.' He sounded as though he had a mouthful of foam. She waited a few minutes, then, more clearly, 'I have very little experience of shopping with women.'

'Oh. No—what is the phrase—no barques of frailty you wish to indulge?'

'What do you know of your weaker sisters, your Serene Highness?'

'Nothing at all, except that my husband kept a great many of them, if you add them all up over the years.'

Silence. Had she shocked him? 'I am about to emerge, ma'am, if you would be so good as to close your eyes or otherwise avert your gaze.' Eva obediently closed her eyes and pressed her hands across them, as well, for good measure. Something was bubbling inside her, some ridiculously youthful feeling. There was the pad of bare feet on the boards. 'Did you mind the other women?' Jack asked from somewhere on the other side of the room. 'My back is turned, if you want to get dressed.'

'Mind? Not really. I was ridiculously shocked at first, but

then, I was ridiculously young to have married a man like that.' She slid out of bed and risked a glance in Jack's direction. He was standing in front of the open window, his back to her, pulling on his shirt. The sunlight shone through, throwing the silhouette of his body against the fine fabric as he stretched his arms above his head. Eva bit back a sigh, dropped her eyes, found she was staring at the admirable tautness of his buttocks and the elegant line of his legs in the tight breeches and hastened to get behind the screen before her imagination got the better of her. *Friends,* she reminded herself fiercely. *My friend—don't spoil it.*

'You surprise me.' She followed Jack's movements about the room by ear as she washed. 'I would have expected that to have upset you greatly.'

'He never pretended to love me,' Eva explained, shaking out the remnants of her clean linen and making mental shopping lists while she talked. 'And I was too young to have formed a real attachment. It was my pride that was hurt more than anything, once I had got over my shock. Then, by the time I realised that he was not the sort of man to devote himself to one woman, I had Freddie and I was beginning to carry out my duties. It wasn't so bad, and there were some benefits to being married to one of the most accomplished lovers in Europe.'

In the crashing silence that followed this remark, Eva thought she could have heard a pin drop. The handful of underwear fell back into the trunk from her lax grip. How tactless was it possible to be? She had just intimated to a man who had kissed her—with such skill and feeling that her knees still felt weak when she thought of it—that she would have been mentally comparing his technique with the legendary erotic skills of her late husband.

Worse. This was a man who she was quite certain wanted her. Eva grimaced, wondering what she could possibly say to make things better. Nothing, probably, unless she wanted to dig the hole even deeper. To say anything acknowledged the attraction between them.

'Do you have grounds for comparison?' Jack asked coolly into the aching silence.

'Only Louis's own assessment,' she replied, then came to a decision. She could not leave this. 'Personally I have had no basis for comparison—only one kiss. On the basis of that Louis need not have been so confident.'

'Nothing? In all that time?' Jack sounded as though he was just the other side of the screen. She should step out, have this exchange face to face, but somehow Eva guessed it would be more truthful like this. 'No one?'

'No one,' she affirmed. 'No one while he was alive, no one since.'

From that, she supposed, he could conclude she was a love-starved widow, ready to turn to any personable man once she was away from the close scrutiny of the Grand Ducal court, or that she was cold and had not felt the lack of love and of loving.

'The man was a fool,' Jack said abruptly. It wasn't until she heard the snick of the latch that she realised he had walked out and left her. Eva stood for a moment, filtering the few words through her mind, listening to the emotion behind the curt statement. Her friend was angry on her behalf. Her eyes filled; no one had ever understood what it must have been like being married to Louis, and yet a man she had just tactlessly insulted grasped it immediately with warmth and empathy.

'Thank you, Jack,' she whispered to the empty room.

* * *

Shopping with a woman was a new experience. At the age of twenty-nine one did not have many of those, and certainly few that were so entertaining. If his sister, Bel, had asked him to accompany her through the fashionable lounges and shops of London, he would have pretended an attack of mumps sooner than oblige her, but Eva's delight at being let loose in the bourgeois shops of Grenoble was infectious.

In her travel-worn gown and cloak she darted from shop window to shop window, ruthlessly dragging Jack with her. 'I must have a hat,' she declared. 'I feel positively indecent without one. Which do you think? The amber straw with the ruffle or the chip straw with the satin ribbons?'

'Have both,' he suggested, ignoring the inner warning that a carriage stuffed with hatboxes was not the efficient vehicle for clandestine travel he had designed it to be.

'Really? May I?' He was still looking into the window as she glanced up at him. Something about the reflected image of himself standing there with this lovely woman on his arm, her head tilted to look up at him with delight in her eyes, hit him over the solar plexus like a blow from a fist. They looked right together, and the sight gave him an entirely unfamiliar sensation of possessiveness. Jack tried to analyse it, but Eva was still talking.

'Only I haven't bought a gown yet, and I ought to buy that first and match the hat.'

'Really? Is that how it is done?'

'I think so—when I have new ensembles made they all come together with a selection of hats and shoes and so forth. I'm not used to shopping like this.' Her nose wrinkled in doubt and Jack grinned. That was an expression far from the grand duchess he was used to.

'Come on, let's break the rules.' He pushed open the door and held it for her as the little bell tinkled, summoning the milliner. 'And you will need something in case we have to ride.'

'If we do, that will be an emergency? Yes?' Eva stopped inside the door and lowered her voice.

'Yes. We'll be picking up saddle horses a bit further north as a precaution.'

'Then I need breeches.' Jack felt his brows shoot up. 'I will explain later, but I can ride astride.' Eva turned to the shop-keeper, who was bobbing a curtsy. 'There are two hats in your window I would like to try, if you please.'

Ride astride? How in Hades had she learned that? It was certainly useful—if they had to take to horseback then it would be because they had to abandon the carriage and move both fast and unobserved. His mind strayed to wondering how one bought riding breeches for a woman off the peg in Grenoble. Eva was tall and slender, but definitely rounded in a way that no man or youth was.

'*Jacques.*' He pulled himself away from a frankly improper contemplation of the curves hinted at by the fall of her gown and found himself confronted by a nightmare he had heard other men gibbering about. He was expected to make a judgement between two articles of clothing worn by a woman. 'Which do you think?'

Eva was wearing the chip straw, the bow tied at an angle under her jaw. The deep green of the satin ribbon did things to the colour of her eyes he could not explain, but which made him want to cover a bed with velvet in exactly that shade and lay her upon it. Naked.

'Delightful. It definitely suits you.' He remembered to talk in French just in time.

'Or this?' She replaced it with the amber straw. The brim framed her face, the colour brought out golden tones in her hair. The daydream changed to a bed strewn with amber silks. 'Delightful. Have them both.'

'Yes, but then I saw this.' She was biting her lower lip in thought. Jack closed his eyes for a moment's relief and opened them to see a pert confection he had no name for. The only word for it was *sassy* and it made his dignified grand duchess look like a seventeen-year-old, ripe for a spree.

'Wonderful. Buy them all.'

'*Jacques,* you aren't taking this seriously. You must prefer one of them, or don't you really like any?' It was exactly what friends had moaned about. Women asked you for an opinion and then were upset whatever you said.

'I think they all look marvellous on you,' he said, trying to inject sincerity into his voice. 'But I think that whatever the hat, you would look good, so it is very difficult to express a preference.'

'*Ah, monsieur.*' The milliner obviously thought this was a suitable answer. Eva cast him a roguish glance that made something deep inside respond. He knew his pulse rate was up and drew in a deep breath to steady it.

'Thank you. I think I will have the chip straw and…that one.' She pointed to the sassy little hat.

'Not all three?' Jack queried as the gratified shopkeeper hastened to pack the hats in their boxes.

'We have only just started shopping.' Jack found himself grinning back in answer to Eva's smile.

It was madness. Here he was, Jack Ryder, King's Messenger, a man who chose danger as a way of life, looking forward to hours spent exploring dress shops, haberdashers and shoemakers. If Henry found out, he would never live it down.

Chapter Nine

Two hours later, laden with parcels, Jack called a halt and dragged Eva into a confectioner's. 'Enough! Can there be a single shop of interest to ladies in this town we have not explored?'

'Not one.' Eva smiled happily at him over the rim of a cup of chocolate. 'Tell me what you bought for my riding clothes.'

'Breeches, shirt, waistcoat, coat and boots. You can use one of my neckcloths.'

'But how did you know my size?' She blushed adorably, he mused, wondering how else he could provoke that reaction without overstepping the bounds of friendship he had set himself.

'I can measure your height against myself, likewise your feet.' He let his booted foot nudge against hers under the shelter of the tablecloth and lowered his voice. 'As for the rest, well, I have held you in my arms.'

'Oh.' The rose-pink colour reached her temples this time. Jack tried not to imagine how soft the skin would be there, how it would feel to nuzzle along to the delicate curve of her ear and explore the crisp moulding before nibbling his way down… 'You have a good memory.'

Confessing that he had been recalling those few minutes in vivid detail ever since they had occurred was out of the question. 'I doubt the breeches will be a good fit.' Eva looked a question. 'Any youth quite your, er…shape would be an unusual young man. They are certain to be too large in the waist.'

'Never mind. Better than too tight.' Eva put one elbow on the table and rested her chin on her palm while she nibbled at a macaroon biscuit. 'Thank you for today.'

'What, the clothes and fripperies? His Majesty's Government coffers are paying for those.' The range of items she had enjoyed browsing through had been a revelation to a man used to buying jewellery as a present for his mistress of the moment, or handing over cash for them to make their own purchases.

'No. For the holiday. For letting me take my time and relax and for pretending you enjoyed it, too.'

'I did enjoy it.' She finished her biscuit and cupped her chin in both hands, regarding him sceptically. 'It was a new experience for me. Shopping.'

'Don't men shop? Surely you do?'

'Yes, but we don't flit so much.' He ignored her *moue* of indignation at his choice of verb. 'I go to my tailor, my shirtmaker, my bootmaker, a perfumier for toiletries and so forth. But I know what I want before I set out, they are all within a very small compass of London streets, and I do it only when I need to.'

'Then what did you enjoy about today?'

Jack poured them both more hot chocolate and tried to explain. 'I enjoyed your company, I enjoyed your good taste. It was an interesting glimpse into a feminine world—and I enjoyed seeing you enjoy yourself.' And he had enjoyed just watching her, fantasising about making love to her, setting himself up for a night of disturbed sleep and physical discomfort thinking about her.

'Thank you.' The sceptical look was gone. 'I am so glad we are friends.' She put out her hand impulsively and lay it on his for a fleeting moment, then jerked it back, obviously embarrassed at doing such a thing in public. 'Jack, are we in danger here?'

'Here and now? I doubt it, unless whoever is chasing us has decided they need light refreshment. I somehow do not think this is what your brother-in-law would be expecting us to do just now. But if you mean in Grenoble, yes, certainly.' There was no point in lying to her; besides anything else, neither of them could afford to be complacent.

'It will be most dangerous from here to Dijon because there are so few alternative routes if we wish to avoid high mountains or areas that have come out strongly for Napoleon. After that, there are several possible routes.'

'And Antoine may have found out about the factory by now, and know we know about the rockets.' Jack nodded, watching her thinking. Now her guard was down with him, he found Eva's brown eyes extraordinarily expressive. 'Should we have stopped for so long? Shouldn't we travel all night? But you will tell me you know best and not to worry, I expect.' She bit her lip. 'I am not holding you up, am I? I could have managed without more clothes. Or was that an excuse to give me a rest?'

'You call that a rest? No, it was part of my plan. We could not have got more than one bag out safely, but it would draw attention to us if you are shabbily dressed.' He gestured to the waiter for their bill. 'I plan to leave early tomorrow, before sunrise. Always providing we can pack all this stuff away.'

'We can put it under the seats if there is too much for the luggage racks,' Eva suggested, gathering up the myriad of smaller packages. He was well aware that her demure expression was to hide her amusement at seeing him burdened by two hatboxes—well stuffed with lighter objects around the hats—three parcels and the unwieldy package containing the riding boots.

'No, we can't. One is full of equipment, and we may need the other one again.'

'For me.' She said it flatly and he could have kicked himself for reminding her. 'It is all right Jack. I know you will let me out.' Then she threaded her free hand through his elbow and nudged him lightly in the ribs. 'And if you are found, apparently all alone with a carriage full of female apparel, what exactly is going to be your explanation?'

'A demanding wife who expects a lot of presents,' Jack retorted promptly and was rewarded by her rich chuckle. 'Oh, and by the way, I have explained to our host that my fussy spouse finds the bed too narrow and has thrown me out, so I expect to find a truckle bed in our room when we return.'

'Did you receive much masculine sympathy?' Eva asked.

'Of course. He now regards me as intolerably henpecked, but apparently he surmised that from first seeing us.'

'Whatever made him think such a thing?' Eva demanded indignantly.

'I have no idea.' Jack sighed. 'I had thought I was bearing up so well.' This time it was not so much a nudge as a jab.

'Beast.'

* * *

'Have you any family?' Eva curled up in the corner of the carriage, her shoes reprehensibly kicked off and her feet tucked up under the skirts of her new forest-green walking dress. Jack lounged in the corner diagonally opposite, his hands thrust deep into his coat pockets, his eyes moving between her face and the road as it unwound behind them. She thought she had never seen a man who seemed more at home in his own body. He was totally relaxed now, and yet she would wager a large sum that, if there was a crisis, he would be alert, balanced, ready for instant action. It was, she acknowledged ruefully to herself, very appealing.

'A half-brother, older than I am, and a full sister who is younger. My mother is widowed and lives out of town.'

'Not very many relatives, then?' she commiserated. It would be wonderful to have brothers and sisters and it was a deep regret that she had not been able to give Freddie any siblings.

'You asked about family.' Jack rolled his eyes. 'Relatives I have by the dozen.'

'Truly? Do you get on well with all of them? You are lucky, I wish I had lots. Any, in fact.' She sighed, smiling in case he thought she was being self-pitying.

'One aunt, three uncles and nine cousins. Plus the Scandalous Aunt we do not talk about—she may have any number of offspring, for all we know.'

'What did she do that was so shocking?' Eva asked, agog. It was so refreshing to be able to indulge in some vulgar gossip—Jack would tell her if she overstepped the mark, but his expression when he mentioned his aunt did not seem at all forbidding.

'No one will tell us *children*. Even my mama, who is considered scandalously freethinking by the others, plies her fan vigorously and blushes when questioned. All she will say is that Poor Dear Margery was wild to a fault and fell into sin. The only clue is that whatever sin she succumbed to was highly lucrative, for Mama also confided that no amount of money can wash a soul clean from moral turpitude.'

'Have you never been tempted to find out? If anyone can, I should think it is you.'

'I might at that.' Jack smiled lazily. 'I have to admit, the last time Aunt Margery was mentioned by my Wicked Cousin Theophilus, I felt a certain stirring of irritation at being designated a child at the age of twenty-eight.'

'*Theophilus?* I don't believe anyone called Theophilus could possibly be wicked.'

'He was more or less destined for either extreme virtue or vice, poor Theo. His father is a bishop and his mother the most sanctimonious creature imaginable.'

Theo sounded rather amusing. Eva wondered if there was any chance of meeting Jack's numerous relatives. 'So, you are twenty-eight?' Younger than he looked, Eva decided. She had guessed at thirty and tried to work out why. The steady, serious, watchful eyes possibly. Or the air of total competence and responsibility.

'Twenty-nine, I have just had a birthday.'

'Congratulations! And did your brother and sister and all your cousins come to your party?'

'I spent it on the road on my way south to Maubourg.' He must have seen her frown of regret, for he added, 'Birthday parties are not my sort of thing. I suppose I am not used to them. My father considered such things too frivolous for children.'

'Then you do not know what you are missing,' Eva said robustly, thinking, *Poor little boy. Not so little now, but everyone should have the memory of a happy childhood to grow up with.* Hers was always there at the back of her mind, a candle flame to warm her soul by in hard times. A man who forbade a child a birthday party was unlikely to have been a loving father in other ways.

'I give wonderful parties for all ages and you must come to Freddie's in December.' She tried to imagine Jack playing the silly party games she invented and failed. There was nothing wrong with his sense of humour, and he certainly did not stand on his dignity, but there was something lonely and distant about him in repose. She wondered if there was something else, other than a father who, she recalled, Henry had referred to as top-lofty, and felt an ache inside for him. Not that he would thank her for pitying him, for there was an armour of pride and quiet self-confidence behind his easy competence.

'I am not used to children's parties, but I would be honoured by an invitation.' Jack managed a bow that was positively courtly, despite his casual posture.

'No nieces or nephews, then?' Children would like him, she decided. He wouldn't condescend to them. Freddie must have liked him, otherwise he would never have trusted him with the secret nicknames for his uncles.

'My sister, Bel, was widowed before they had any children.'

'Your brother?' Eva prompted, curious that his eyes, which had been open and amused as they spoke, flicked back to the view from the window. His profile was unreadable. There was some secret here.

'I think it highly unlikely that Charles will ever have children,' he said, his voice so neutral that her suspicions were confirmed. In the face of that blankness, she could hardly continue to probe.

A silence fell, not cool exactly, but not comfortable, either. Perhaps the poor man was an invalid and it pained Jack to speak of it. Eva shifted to stare out of the window on her side and brooded on what else Jack had told her.

A large extended family then. A bishop for an uncle and general outrage at a sinful aunt spoke of respectability, even minor aristocracy, maybe. But then, aristocrats did not spend their time as private investigators, or King's Messengers, come to that. A puzzle, her new friend. *Friend.* That was the word she had to keep repeating in her mind. Friend. Not lover, however much she wished he was. If she thought about it, it would show in her face, Jack Ryder was no fool and he knew women, she had no doubt of that.

'Where are we staying in Lyons?' she asked, more to test his mood than for any particular anxiety to know.

'On the Presqu'île, in the business district. A modest, respectable inn patronised by silk merchants and other business men. They do an excellent dinner.'

'We can't go out, then?' The previous day's expedition had been such fun and Lyon was famous for its silks. Eva knew that more shopping was out of the question—not on borrowed money, at any rate—and the carriage was already stuffed with parcels, but she would dearly have loved to do some browsing. Despite everything the sense of being on holiday, of being let off the lead of respectability and duty, was heady.

'No. This is where it gets dangerous. Lyon came out strongly for Napoleon. Besides that, Antoine will know what we have seen, guessed at what we will have stolen. And now he has had enough time to organise the pursuit. If you are up to it, I intend that we ride to Dijon from Lyon and leave Henry to drive.'

'But that will put him in danger,' Eva protested. It no longer felt right to be curled up so casually. She sat up straight and slipped her shoes back on, as though to be ready for action.

'There will be nothing to betray him. A humble coachman carrying presents from his mistress's sister back to her in Paris. We will be taking the back roads and the plans will be with us.' He flicked her a sideways glance. 'Are you up to it?'

'Yes.' Eva nodded firmly. She had ridden all day on occasion when Louis had held one of his week-long hunting parties, although not recently. She would manage; the thought of being a burden to Jack, of slowing him down, was not to be contemplated. Everything was going so well, all according to his smooth planning, she had to do her part.

But even the most careful plans come adrift. Eva stood beside Jack in the entrance of the Belle Alliance inn and watched his face as the *patron* explained all about the fire in the kitchen. The stench of wet ash and charred timber filled the air; it had hit them as they entered, but the man assured them the bedchambers were unaffected and it was only the kitchens that were not functioning.

'There are many good places to eat along the *quais, monsieur,*' the *patron* hastened to explain. 'On either the Rhône bank or the Saône bank. You take any of the *tra-boules*—those are the passageways—'

'I know what they are,' Jack interrupted him. 'Very well, we will go out now, while there is still some light. I do not wish my wife to be abroad in a strange town after dark. *Henri*.' He jerked his head towards the small pile of luggage. 'You'll see these taken up to our room?'

The groom nodded. 'I'll eat over there.' That was a small, and rather greasy-looking, eating shop immediately opposite the entrance to the Belle Alliance. 'I like to keep an eye on who comes and goes.' It was only because she was looking for it that Eva caught the unspoken message between the two men. Warning, reassurance. Did Jack suspect the fire was deliberate?

She asked him directly as they made their way through one of the famous Lyonnais *traboules* that cut down to the rivers, wending their way through private courts and gardens as they went. Eva wanted to look around her at the vibrant glimpses of everyday life that they passed, the women gossiping, the looms visible through windows, merchants slapping hands on a deal, but Jack kept his hand under her elbow and walked briskly.

'No, I don't suspect that; Antoine could not possibly have found where we were going to stay and organised such a thing. But his men may start checking the lodgings and I would prefer to be inside looking out if that happens.'

'I see. Jack?'

'Yes?' He looked down at her and his eyes crinkled into a smile that seemed not so much one of reassurance but simply of pleasure to find her there on his arm.

'Are you armed?'

'To the teeth,' he assured her, the smile belying his solemn tone.

'Don't be flippant.' The tone of crisp reproof was still there when she needed it, she found. 'I cannot see any weapons.'

'I should hope not.' She narrowed her eyes at him in exasperation and he relented. 'Knives in my boots and in a chest harness. Pistols in my pockets. Hence,' he added as she glanced sideways at him, 'the dreadful cut of my coats.'

There was nothing wrong with his coats at all. This one fitted admirably over broad shoulders and snug at his waist. It was, if what he was telling her was true, exceptionally well tailored, and probably very expensive, for all its lack of fashionable flourish.

'Stop fishing for compliments,' she chided. 'You know perfectly well that coat is very smart. Why wouldn't you let me wear my cloak and hood?'

'Because that was what you were last seen in. If those officers who interrupted us in the lane have worked out who you were by now, they ought to be able to describe your clothing. 'That hat…' he flipped the brim irreverently '…is not the sort of thing a grand duchess wears. When you skim a crowd, searching, your eye stops when it sees something familiar. It is like hunting—you look for the shadowy outline of deer and ignore foxes. They search for a great lady and might miss a lovely young girl in her pert new hat.'

'Young!' Eva tried not to think about the rest of that description, but she couldn't repress a blush.

'Now who is fishing?'

'I am not, but really, Jack, I am twenty-six years old—'

'So ancient! Quite on your last prayers, obviously. I almost fell off your damnable window ledge with the shock I had when I first saw you. They did not tell me, you see, that you were both young *and* beautiful.'

'Are you flirting with me, Monsieur Ridère?' she enquired suspiciously as he steered her through the door of a re-spectable seeming eating house.

'Of course, Madame Ridère. A friend may, may he not? This place looks acceptable.' Eva forgot the compliments and the teasing as she watched him assessing the *bistrôt,* trying to work out what he was looking for.

'A back door, plenty of people, a table over there with a good view of who is coming in?' she suggested.

'Yes. Precisely, you are learning to get the eye. Let's hope the food is good, too.'

It was. And so was the atmosphere. Eva had never been anywhere like this. She found her elbows were on the table, that she was singing along with the group near the door who had struck up an impromptu sing-song while they waited for their order, and the simple casserole of chicken and herbs, washed down with a robust red wine, seemed perfect.

'I am enjoying this,' she confessed, as the waitress set down a platter of cheese.

'So am I.' Jack caught the hand she was gesturing with and held it. 'I enjoy seeing you relax.'

'This is so different for me,' Eva admitted. 'No one is staring. I don't have to pretend.'

'Don't you?' Jack murmured, almost as though he were asking a rhetorical question. Eva tugged her hand free, finding his warm grasp rather more disturbing than was safe and Jack let go at once, taking her by surprise. Her arm flicked back, caught the little vase of flowers set on the table and knocked it off.

'Oh, bother!' Eva jumped to her feet to retrieve it just as

the door opened and a group of men walked in. She straightened up, the flowers in her hand and found herself staring, across the width of the *bistrôt,* straight into the eyes of a tall blond man with sharp blue eyes and a sensual mouth set over a strong chin.

Good-looking, arrogant, unmistakable. It was Colonel de Presteigne.

Chapter Ten

The colonel had seen her, recognised her. There was no way to avoid him. The way the hunter's smile of sheer triumph slid across his face sickened her. Eva clenched her hand around the slender vase, as she counted the men standing at his back. Three of them, all ordinary soldiers out of uniform by the look of them—there were no impressionable young officers to appeal to here.

Behind her she felt Jack slide out from behind the table, then stand, almost as if to hide behind her. But Jack was not a man to hide behind a woman—he had a plan, she knew it. He moved smoothly, so she was not surprised that the men kept their attention on her. His hand closed round her left wrist. 'When I tug, throw that vase and run with me.' The words were a breath in her ear and she nodded fractionally in response as he released her.

'*Bonsoir, madame.*' De Presteigne, feigning deference. 'Dining in style with your gallant lover, I see.' His lip curled in a sneer at the sight of Jack apparently hiding behind the shelter of her skirts. How had she ever thought the colonel charming?

Eva sensed Jack shifting his balance, her whole body attuned to him as though they touched. Out of the corner of her eye she watched the waitress come out of the kitchen door with a steaming tureen and walk across to a table. Their escape route was clear. She shifted her balance slightly.

'Better a humble *bistrôt* than a formal dining room in the company of traitors,' she retorted, seeing the smile congeal into dark anger on his face.

'You call supporters of the Emperor traitors?' he demanded, raising his voice. People shifted in their chairs to stare, the amiable faces of the diners changing to suspicion. Lyon, she remembered, supported Bonaparte.

'You betray your Grand Duke,' she flashed back as the colonel took a stride towards her. She felt Jack's hard tug on her wrist and she threw the vase full in de Presteigne's face. Water and flowers went everywhere as the man roared in shock and clawed at his eyes.

Eva saw no more, she was running with Jack, through the door, into the kitchens towards the back door. Kitchen staff scattered. They passed a rack of knives, she snatched one, a small vegetable peeler, then they were outside in a cobbled alley, rank with the smells of food waste. A cat bolted away, hissing with fright as Jack made for the mouth of the alley. Behind them the door crashed back. Eva risked a glance over her shoulder.

'Two of them, not de Presteigne,' she gasped.

'Here's the rest.' Jack skidded out on to the street just ahead of the colonel and the other soldier, turned, reached inside his coat and threw something. With a grunt the man toppled and fell and de Presteigne went down with him, tripped beyond hope of balance.

'Run!' Jack pushed her. 'The waterfront's that way.' They took to their heels, splashing through foul puddles, leaping piles of garbage, dodging the few passers-by. The pounding feet behind them were relentless. Eva heard de Presteigne's voice cursing the men for not catching them as they erupted into a little square.

Jack made for the far exit, then recoiled. 'Dead end.' It was enough to bring their pursuers up with them. Jack pulled a pistol from his pocket and held it steady, his back almost to the wall, his left arm outstretched, urging Eva behind him.

It was as she had known instinctively: he would stand and protect her at the risk of his own life—and the odds were too great. She edged behind him, then further, out into the open, towards the alley to her right. Keeping the little knife concealed in her skirts, she waved the reticule that was somehow, against all probability, still swinging from her wrist. 'Is this what you want, Colonel? The plans? The notebooks? Don't you wonder what we took, what we know? Who we told?'

'Eva!' Jack lunged for her, but she had done what she had meant to do, split their attackers. De Presteigne shouted, 'Ducrois, with me! Foix, break his neck', and dived towards her. She spun round and ran, light-footed, impelled by the desperate urge to leave Jack with manageable odds. There was the bark of a pistol—his or Foix's? Then she was out on to the quayside. Which river? It hardly mattered, either would have boats, surely?

The edge of the quay was slippery beneath her feet. Wary of

mooring ropes, she began to edge along it, half her attention on the swirling water, half on the colonel and the soldier who had come to a halt when they saw her and were now, with the caution of hunting cats with a bird in their sights, padding forward.

'Stand still, you silly bitch,' de Presteigne said irritably. 'Where the hell do you think you are going to?'

'*You* are the one going to hell,' Eva retorted. 'That is the place for traitors and turncoats.' She risked another glance down. It seemed a long way to the river's dark surface and there were no rowing boats in sight yet. *Where is Jack?* There was a shout echoing from the little square, the soldier half-turned and stopped at his officer's curse.

'Never mind them. Get her.'

Eva held her knife that had been concealed by the reticule in front of her. 'Try,' she invited.

The man rushed at her, grinning at her defiance. She slashed at him, he ducked away, slid on the slippery surface and pitched into the river with a yell of fear and a loud splash. 'Colonel?' she invited politely. The light from the lanterns hung along the fronts of the warehouses glittered off the little knife.

The tall man reached into his coat and produced a pistol. 'No. You come here, or I'll shoot you. And then, if your lover isn't dead yet, I'll shoot him.'

Slowly, trying to control the trembling in her arm, Eva held the reticule out over the river by her fingertips. It hung with convincing heaviness, thanks to the novel that she had tucked inside it that morning. 'Then you'll never get these.'

He shrugged. 'So? They'll be at the bottom of the river.' He stepped forward. 'Come on, don't be such a little fool. Back to Prince Antoine.' Eva's head spun as she tried to decide what to do. *Drop the reticule, then he won't look anywhere else... Jack...*

As she thought it he came out of the alleyway. Even at that distance she could see his bared teeth, the killing fury in every line of his body as he came, his pistol hand rising to level on the colonel. De Presteigne snatched at her as her attention wavered, caught her by the arm and held her, his own pistol swinging round towards her breast. 'Stop right there or I'll kill— Aagh!'

Eva fastened her teeth on his hand and he released her, scrabbling for balance. For a moment she was free, poised on the edge of the quay, then the momentum of her movement took her and she felt herself falling towards the river. There was the crack of a pistol, a shout immediately above her, then she hit the water and stopped thinking of anything but survival.

Despite the warmth of the summer night the cold almost knocked the breath out of her. Some corner of her brain registered that the river was fed by snowmelt as she kicked off her shoes and clawed at her bonnet strings and the fastenings of her pelisse.

I can swim, I can swim well, she told herself, fighting to calm the panicking part of her that was wanting to thrash and scream. It was a long time, but as a child she had swum naked in the river that ran through the grounds of their château. As a young woman she had swum in the private lake in the castle grounds. *I haven't forgotten, thank God...*

With her heavier outer clothing gone she was managing to stay afloat, but the current was sweeping her downstream at terrifying speed. In the darkness things loomed out of the water, swept by her before she could register them as either dangerous or a potential lifeline. A wave slapped her in the face and she gagged on foul water.

It was useless to try to swim against this current, she had to stay afloat, go with it and trust to a rope or a bridge pillar to cling to. Eva struggled to orientate herself. This must be the Rhône, rushing down to its confluence with the Saône. A vision of swirling cross-currents and whirlpools where the two rivers met almost frightened her into stopping breathing, then something struck her shoulder.

Instinctively, she reached for it, and found herself grasping a large branch, the leaves still on some of the twigs. It supported her weight just enough for her to draw in a sobbing breath and raise her head to look around. She was in midstream, the banks seeming to flicker past at nightmare speed as she pitched and rolled with the current. Ahead the right bank seemed to vanish; the confluence was almost on her.

It did not seem possible she could survive this. Even with the support of the branch her limbs were losing sensation with the cold and the effort, her head was spinning and her throat raw. Eva tried to pray—for Freddie, for Jack, for herself—and clung on.

De Presteigne went down with a shout of pain as the ball lodged in his shoulder, his own shot whistling somewhere over Jack's head. Jack did not stop to check whether the man was alive or dead as he began to run downstream, his eyes straining to search the surface of the water. Lights sparkled and flashed off the choppy surface, dazzling and confusing in some patches, leaving the river in darkness in others.

He sought mental balance, knowing that to give in to fear

and panic would kill Eva as surely as walking away. If she could not swim, or catch some sort of float, she was dead already. He pushed that knowledge back and scanned the surface again. *There!* A tangle of foliage and, in the centre, a dark head, the flash of pale cloth, a raised arm. She was well ahead of him, there was no way he could reach the point where the two rivers joined before her.

People scattered in front of him as he ran, then a rider emerged from a side street, slack reined, relaxed, perhaps on his way home to his supper. Jack drew his remaining knife, reached up and dragged him from the saddle, his bared teeth and the menacing blade between them enough to have the man backing away, hands thrown up in surrender.

The animal reared, alarmed at the violent movements, the strange weight on its back, then it responded to heel and voice and they were away at a canter. With the added height he could see better, realised he had to get off the Presqu'île and on to the far bank, and dragged the horse's head round to make for the foot of the last bridge just ahead. It all wasted time, lost him distance and Eva was fast vanishing into the maelstrom of waters.

Jack blanked the thought that he was losing her from his mind, tightened his grip and kicked.

Ignoring traffic and obstacles and shouted abuse, he galloped downstream towards the place where he could recall the newly joined rivers' turbulence wearing itself out in a tangle of sandbanks and islands before resuming its long smooth passage towards the sea. If he was going to snatch her out, that was the place. If she made it so far, if he could get there first, if he was strong enough to reach her.

The stolen horse baulked and shied as he forced it through the shallows to the first sandbank. He flung the reins over the branch of a spindly willow and tore off his boots. His coat followed as he ran over the sand and shingle, vaulted a pile of driftwood and plunged into the first channel.

Even here the current was strong. He clawed his way out the far side and ran to the edge of the main stream, his eyes straining upstream for a sight of Eva. The light was surprisingly good; a glow still hung in the sky from the sunset, lights from boats and cottages laid ribbons of visibility across the water.

He did not have long to wait. The leafy branch was still afloat, the glimmer of white cloth still tangled within it as it swirled down towards him. But the figure that lay in its cradle was unmoving. Jack entered the water in a long, shallow dive and struck out to intercept it, refusing to feel the cold water biting into muscles, the enervating pull of the current, the clutch of fear at his heart.

The river was so strong it was trying to drag her out of her branch, so savage she could swear it had hands. Eva clung on, her fingers numb. She should just give in and die, this hurt so much and was so hopeless. Yet she could not— would not—surrender.

'Eva,' the river gasped in her ear. 'Eva, let go.'

'No!'

'Yes! Look at me!'

Jack's voice? Jack? With an effort that seemed to take her last ounce of strength, Eva turned her face from the rough bark it had been pressed to and saw him.

'You came for me?'

'Always.' It sounded like a vow. 'Always.' The world went black.

'Eva!' Someone was shouting at her, slapping her face, her hands.

'Stop it,' she protested feebly, then rolled on her side, retching violently as what seemed like most of the river came up.

'Good girl, that's right.' Someone was praising her for being sick? Eva let herself be lifted and found she was bundled into some strange, bulky garment far too big for her. 'Come on, up you come.' Jack. Jack was lifting her. She forced herself to full consciousness, her body unwilling to make the effort, her will screaming that she could not just leave him to cope. He must be cold, exhausted, perhaps wounded.

For a moment she indulged herself in weakness and lay against his chest. Cold, wet cloth clung to his chilled skin, his body heat fighting to warm them both. He was plodding through shingle and underbrush, she could hear. Hard going, he was stumbling slightly, but his grip did not waver.

'Put me down.' She cleared her throat and said it again, more clearly. She couldn't bear to burden him, like a sack of stones on an exhausted pack animal that somehow kept going despite everything.

'When we get to the horse.' With her ear against Jack's chest she could hear the effort to control his voice, the way he steadied it like a singer so she wouldn't hear the fatigue.

'No. Now.' She put every ounce of authority she possessed into the command.

To her amazement he gave a snort of amusement and

trudged on. 'Remember what I said?' he asked. 'Do what I tell you, always, at once and without question.'

'This doesn't count.'

'Why not?' Jack stopped, she felt him brace himself, then plough on up the steep edge of the bank on to shingle.

'Because you are being a stubborn idiot! Put me down this minute before you fall down!'

'Yes, your Serene Highness.' Eva found herself set on her feet.

'There. You see? That's better.' Her legs buckled and she swayed against him, surrendering to the support of his arm around her waist. 'Oh, bl…*bother.*' They stood there, locked together and dripping. Jack must have wrapped her in his coat, she realised, trying to get her arms, and the flaps of the coat, around him. Her face was pressed into his chest and his heartbeat was slowing even as she stood there. *Very fit,* the logical part of her mind, the part she always thought of as the *Grand Duchess* observed, while the other, entirely feminine, entirely private, part just revelled in his strength and courage and wanted him. *You do chose your moments, Eva,* she thought ruefully.

'Were you wounded?'

'No. I don't think so.'

'Don't think so?' Eva arched back against Jack's arm to see his face, which was almost impossible now.

'I'm sure so,' he amended. There was a flash of white; she thought he was smiling. 'I had other things to think about. Come on, the horse I stole is just over here; if we stand still much longer we'll freeze.'

'Which would save us from being hanged for horse stealing,' Eva observed, as they picked their way back to the horse standing patiently by the willow tree. Jack boosted her up into the saddle and swung up behind her, settling her so she sat across his thighs.

'Hold tight.' The horse scrambled down into the shallow channel, then up the other side and on to the road. 'Henry can "find" it wandering tomorrow and hand it over to the authorities,' Jack added. 'I want to get you back and into a hot bath.'

'You, too.' She felt his chin pressing down on the crown of her head and let herself drift. She thought she felt him chuckle and blushed at the improper thought of them both in the same steaming bath.

'Are you asleep?' He didn't wait for her answer. 'Don't. Wake up and talk to me, it is dangerous to drift off when you are this cold.'

'Talk? What about?' Eva felt like grumbling. It was very difficult to think of conversation when you were numb from head to toe, dripping wet and perched on a horse. She wanted to sleep, to dream about making love with her fantasy of Jack, not be bossed about by the real, wet, battered hero who wanted to be her bodyguard and her friend and would let himself be nothing more. But there was something she had to say to the real man.

'Thank you. Have I said that? Thank you, Jack. You saved my life. I cannot believe that anyone else could have done what you did.' *And if you say it is just your job, you will break my heart.*

His arms tightened, then she felt his chin move and realised he had lay his cheek against her hair for a fleeting moment. 'I thought I was going to lose you,' he said at last. 'And that didn't seem like an option I could accept.' There was a pause. Eva filled it trying to work out whether he meant that personally or professionally, and failed. Jack was just too good at keeping his emotions out of his voice. And yet, she could not forget the echo of his voice as she had slipped into unconsciousness in the river. *Always.*

Chapter Eleven

'Bloody hell, guv'nor!' The outburst of swearing was Henry's voice, Eva realised vaguely. They had stopped. She looked round, her head feeling like lead on her aching neck, and saw they were in front of the inn.

'Stubble it,' Jack growled, then, 'Help *madame* down, will you?'

'Gawd help us, you're soaked, both of you.' The groom caught Eva with as much respectfulness as was possible and set her gingerly on her feet. 'And frozen.'

'Get this animal out of sight. I've stolen it—you'll need to *find* it in the morning and return it to the authorities.'

Henry took this news with a calm that said volumes about his expectations of life with Jack, Eva thought, amused despite her weariness. It seemed impossible that she should ever stop shivering, and as Jack took her arm to steer her into the inn she felt the betraying vibration under his skin, as well.

'Upstairs, try not to be seen. If de Presteigne is in any fit state, he will start enquiries round the inns for soaking wet guests. At least we've stopped dripping.'

They went upstairs with all the caution of a pair of illicit lovers and regained their chamber with such relief that Eva found herself clutching the bed post with tears in her eyes. Jack leant back against the closed door as though he could no longer rely on his legs to hold him up. South facing and high up, the room still held the warmth of the day, but that mild air could not touch the bone-deep chill that racked her.

'Get undressed.' Jack straightened and pushed her towards the dressing screen, tugging the bell pull as he passed it. Eva began to fumble with buttons and hooks, set in swollen, sodden fabric. There was a tap at the door. 'Hot water, lots of it. And a hip bath. There's more of that if you make haste.' She heard the clink of coin and the retreating scuffle of feet.

'Here.' A large towel landed on top of the screen.

'I can't undo the fastenings,' Eva said, cursing under her breath as a softened fingernail tore. 'Oh, *damn.*' It was all too much, she just wanted to be back in Maubourg. She wanted a flock of ladies' maids and footmen, she wanted her dresser and to be warm and dry, to curl up, sleep, forget.

'Here, let me.' She gasped in shock as Jack came round the screen. He was stripped, clad only in a large linen towel slung round his narrow hips. 'You can open your eyes,' he said after a moment in a tone that hung somewhere between amusement and irritation. 'I would suggest that dying of cold and exhaustion but unsullied by a glimpse of my naked flesh is observing the proprieties too far.'

'Yes. Yes, of course.' Eva tried to sound brisk and matter of fact as she opened her eyes, trying to unfocus them at the

same time. It was ridiculous to be prudish under the circumstances. Jack was her bodyguard and her friend. She had been
a married woman—it was not as though she had never seen a
naked man before. And, in any case, neither of them was in a
fit state to do anything imprudent.

Jack began to work on the row of buttons that fastened the
bodice of the dress, swore under his breath, and undid it by
the simple expedient of tearing it open with both hands.
Buttons pinged off in all directions. 'Jack!'

'It is ruined anyway,' he pointed out reasonably, pulling the
bodice apart and dragging it down her arms.

'I..er… I can manage now.'

He ignored her, lifting the water-sodden skirts over her
head and dumping the garment in a heap on the floor, then
standing, hands on hips, regarding her as she shivered in stays,
petticoat and chemise.

'Did you tie these with a bow or am I going to have to
cut the strings?' He advanced on the neat row of lacing that
secured the corset. Eva squeaked. 'A bow. Excellent
woman.' The stays landed on top of the gown just as the
maid knocked on the door. Eva retreated, leaving Jack to
deal with the procession of inn servants with tub and
steaming ewers.

She peeked through the gap in the screen, her lips curving
in amusement at the sight of the maids reduced to blushing
giggles by Jack's well-displayed physique. They could not be
blamed, she told herself, conscious that she was admiring the
view just as much as they were. The bruises had begun to turn
yellow across his back and chest. She ignored them as she
studied the cleanly defined musculature, the narrow hips and

the well-shaped calves. Hairy, but just right, she decided, as a violent shiver shook her, reminding her just how serious their situation was. *Stop it!* she chided herself. *Ogling like one of the maids, indeed!*

The door shut and Eva hastily bent to untie her garters and roll down her stockings. Jack reappeared around the edge of the screen. 'Come on, hurry up, your teeth are chattering.'

'Go away, then! Because if you think I am taking another thing off while you are— Jack! Put me down.' He bent, swept her up and deposited her, petticoats and all, into the deep tub the girls had brought up. 'Oooh. That's *wonderful.*' Warmth seeped through her, making her skin tingle and her frozen toes ache. But the momentary discomfort was worth it. She even began to believe that the bone-deep chill would disappear in time. 'What a huge tub.' It was big enough for her to tuck in her feet, provided she kept her knees bent up, sticking above the surface.

Jack began to scoop water up in his cupped hands and pour it over her knees and her shoulders. He paused, his hands and arms deep in the hot water for a moment, letting the warmth seep into him.

'I'll be quick, you need to get in,' Eva said hastily.

'No, you aren't warm through yet, and your hair needs washing.' Jack picked up one of the ewers. 'Close your eyes.' He poured the water through her tangled hair, then found the scented soap and began to work up a lather and rub it in. 'Sit still, don't wriggle or you will get soap in your eyes.' He seemed quite at home doing it. Eva wondered vaguely if he bathed his mistress. *Mistresses, more like,* she reflected, moving her head languidly to the pressure of his hands. She could not believe that this man would find much attraction in celibacy.

'You're purring.' His chuckle was close to her ear. 'Keep your eyes closed, I'm going to rinse it.' The warm torrent drowned her protest that of course she was doing no such thing, then she found her head swathed in a towel and realised he was rubbing it dry. It was so easy to let go and allow him to do it. Eva's eyes stayed closed, even when the towel was lifted away and she heard Jack moving across the room. He came back almost at once, lifted some of the damp weight of her hair and began to comb it.

'Jack, don't bother with that, you'll get chilled, I must get out.' Eva opened her eyes and found he was very close, his fingers working carefully through the tangles.

'No, I'm warm, here in the steam, I promise. Relax while I comb this.' The grey eyes that could be so hard and cold were gentle as he watched her, the lines of his face relaxed out of their habitual vigilance as she had never seen them before, even in laughter.

Her eyes drifted shut again. The memory of being cold, of being afraid, seeped away under the strokes of his hands. 'Lean forward.' She found herself resting against his chest, her forehead on his shoulder as he reached round her, plaiting her hair into a thick tail. Then he coiled it on her head, fastening it with a pin he must have found with her comb.

The heavy weight of it made it difficult to lift her head up off his shoulder, or so she told herself. Against the skin of her forehead she could feel the hard line of his collarbone, smell the scent of him through the soap-scented steam. River water, chilled flesh, man. Jack. Her lips moved, touching lightly on the flat plane of his chest and he shifted, his hands slipping down from her hair to hold her against his body as he knelt there beside the tub.

'You are cold,' she murmured against his skin.

'Warm me, then.'

Awkward, her wet petticoats tangled round her legs, Eva shifted in the tub until she was kneeling up, breast to breast with Jack. Her hands slid, palms flat, up his back, holding him close to her, pressing herself to the length of his torso so her heat soaked into him. Her nipples peaked, hard under the soaked petticoat, rubbing against the subtle friction of wet linen as she buried her face in the angle of his neck, feeling the thud of his pulse close to her ear.

Jack's breath was hot on the side of her face, feathering her ear so that she caught her own breath, the almost-forgotten heavy heat of arousal settling low in her belly. She expected him to touch her ear, perhaps run the tip of his tongue around the curl of its moulding; instead his hands moved down to cup her buttocks.

The sensation of the two palms, cooler than her own hot flesh, the gentle grasp of the long, clever fingers, had her pressing closer so that when, without warning, Jack stood up, she was lifted with him in one smooth motion. He shifted, taking her off balance so that she clutched at him, then he was standing in the hot water with her.

They were so close that she could feel the hem of the towel he wore around his waist pressing against her knees, the roughness of wet hair where one of his legs pressed between hers. The sodden fabric she was wearing might as well not have been there as her body melted into his, the touch of hard nipples against her breast, the unmistakable heat and pressure of his arousal against her stomach.

Eva lifted her face from the shelter of his neck, his hair spiky with wet as it brushed her cheek. 'Go,' he said huskily.

'What?' she whispered. His eyes were closed, the lashes as wet on his cheeks as though he had wept, but the skin below was dry.

'Go. Get into bed.' Still blind, his mouth curved into a smile that had her longing to touch her lips to the corner of his. 'I think you have warmed me as much as a friend might be expected to.'

Jack stood motionless, following Eva's retreat behind the screen by sound. When he heard the flap of a towel from the direction of the screen he opened his eyes, poured in the remaining ewers of hot water and, discarding the towel, took her place in the tub.

The heat took him into its embrace like a lover and he leaned back against the high back of the tub, his knees hooked over the other side and his feet dangling. It was possible, he thought hazily, that he would just lie there all night, luxuriating.

If only he did not have to think. To plan. To try to get some sort of perspective on what had happened just now. The warmth was doing absolutely nothing to subdue the evidence of just how much the sensation of holding Eva in his arms had aroused him.

What had gone wrong? Cold, battered, exhausted, all he had intended was to get her tucked up in bed, warm and safe. If he had been asked, he would have laughed at the thought that he could have summoned either the strength or the inclination to think about sex. It seemed he did not know his own body as well as he thought.

There was a discreet cough and he closed his eyes as Eva's footsteps padded past, wondering if she was looking at him, wondering, for the first time, what she thought of the man she saw.

Arrogant devil, he chided himself, as he fished blindly over the edge of the tub for the soap. What she saw was an adventurer, a man she could rely on for violence, low cunning and an insolent disregard of her status and position. She saw a man who promised to be her friend and who had damn nearly taken her there and then, dripping wet, on the floor beside this tub.

But he hadn't. Why not? Jack began to scrub the smell of the river water and mud off his skin, grimacing as he realised he'd picked up Eva's soap and not his own. He would reek fragrantly of gardenias as a result, but he felt too relaxed to get out and find something else. He hadn't even kissed her, hadn't bent his head to sweep his tongue over those taut nipples he had felt fretting against his own chest, hadn't let his hands take the sweet weight of her breasts in their palms.

Because I want to make love to her, not just have sex with her. And make love when she is fully awake and aware of what she is doing, he thought grimly, *not clinging to me because she is exhausted, frightened and I have saved her life—just.*

And what the hell am I thinking? Jack demanded of himself savagely as he slid down so his head went under the water. He emerged, streaming, and scrubbed his hands through his hair with intentional force.

That was a grand duchess in that bed, not some game pullet, not even a sprightly matron who was interested in showing her gratitude for a well-executed commission in ways that went beyond paying his bill. That happened now and again. He never sought it, sometimes took steps to evade it and sometimes found it a mutually satisfying, if short-lived, encounter.

This was different. The Grand Duchess Evaline was different. There was an innocence about her that was at odds with her marriage to one of the most hardened roués in Europe, a softness under that imperious manner that she could adopt at the blink of her long-lashed eyes. The memory of those lashes against his skin sent a stab of lust lancing into his already aching groin.

It was going to be a long night. He might want to make love to her, she might, in her vulnerability and disorientation, turn to him, but Jack knew full well that he could not let it happen. She was chaste, he could tell that almost at a glance, and she would have had countless opportunities discreetly to be otherwise. The fact that she had not meant that this was something that was important to her, to what she was as a woman, and he could not destroy that.

He opened his eyes, saw nothing but a mound under the white covers to show where Eva was, and began to scrub at the soles of his feet which seemed irrevocably black. Had she spurned de Presteigne at some point? His instinct told him that she had. The man would take that as an insult, would nurse it in his breast as a slight to be repaid. It made him even more dangerous—if he still lived.

Jack climbed out of the tub, registering dispassionately the muscles that ached, the ones that felt least responsive. Weaknesses he could not afford, gaps in his training to be worked on. Tomorrow he wanted to ride, if Eva was up to it.

Two of their pursuers were dead, he had made sure of that. But there remained de Presteigne—wounded certainly, and if alive no doubt as furious as a scalded cat—and the soldier who had fallen in the river who might have been able to swim.

Pursuit was either still on their heels, or as far away as Prince Antoine, waiting impatiently in the brooding castle of Maubourg for news of the hunt. Ahead was safety. He rested one foot on the edge of the tub as he scrubbed the leg dry and reconsidered that thought. Safety unless Antoine had had the sense to send agents on ahead of de Presteigne in the hope that the colonel would act as the ferret down the rabbit hole and drive them headlong into his hands.

Without ever having met Eva's brother-in-law, Jack felt a deep dislike of the man, a traitor both to his own family and his country and the attempted murderer of his nephew and the boy's mother. But that did not make him a fool, and to misjudge him could be fatal.

Dry and warm at last, he padded over to the bedside and looked down at Eva. The thick plait had come loose from his inexpert attempt at pinning it up and lay on the covers, making her look heart-wrenchingly young. He thought about just falling into bed, then spent several minutes extricating the long bolster without waking her, and setting it down the middle of the bed. He might be resolved now to fight her sensual spell, but he would not have wagered so much as a groat on his body paying any heed to that if he touched her as he slept.

The soft mattress took him like a cloud as he finally slid between the sheets and sleep swept over him even before he could pull the covers up to his shoulders.

* * *

The tattoo of knocking on the bedchamber door had Jack out of bed with his pistol in his hand before he was even conscious of moving. The sun was streaming in through the window, the old clock in the corner registering eight. He took a steadying breath and called, *'Oui?'*

'C'est Henri, monsieur.' It must be, no one could imitate the groom's atrocious accent.

Jack turned the key in the lock and let the man in. 'Thought I'd better check, seeing the time's getting on.' He glanced round the room and added reprovingly, 'You know, guv'nor, you shouldn't be walking about like that, stark naked with your wedding tackle on show. There's a lady to consider, and not just any lady. She's a grand duchess, when all's said and done.'

He looked defiant as Jack glared at him, but the retort came, not from him, but icy—if somewhat muffled—from the bed. 'The Grand Duchess in question is right here, Henry, and the reason I am stuck under these very hot covers is to spare myself the sight you so graphically describe. If you *gentlemen* would be kind enough to remove yourselves, dressed or undressed, I would like to get up now.'

Jack dragged on his breeches and shirt, scooped up the rest of his things and strode out of the room. 'We will be in the private parlour, *ma'am*. Please be so good as to lock the door behind us.'

The lock clicked before they were three steps along the landing. Jack dropped his shoes, swore mildly, and kicked them ahead of himself into the parlour. 'You don't half whiff, guv'nor. Like a flaming lily,' Henry observed.

'Gardenias,' Jack corrected, dragging off his clothes again

so he could put on his drawers and stockings. 'Better than smelling like the banks of the Rhône, believe me.'

'Can believe that.' The groom hitched one hip on the window ledge and regarded Jack critically as he dressed. 'You hurt any? You look banged about.'

'Nothing that won't heal soon enough.' He felt as though he had been stretched on the rack, then beaten with broom handles, but admitting to that would only lead to Henry offering one of his brutal massages.

'Good enough.' The groom looked uncomfortable. 'Look, guv'nor, you really shouldn't be getting involved with her Highness like this.'

'Like what?' Jack demanded.

'No, don't you go pokering up on me, guv'nor, you look like your late unlamented father when you do that, and it's enough to give a man the colic, with all due respect…'

'The chance of some due respect would be welcome, but I suppose you are going to have your say,' Jack retorted grimly. To an outsider the liberties he allowed the groom would have been inexplicable, but Jack was prepared to listen to a man whose loyalty and courage had been proven over and over again, even if his tendency to embarrassing frankness was legendary.

'I am that. She's a real lady, that one, and royalty, almost. You shouldn't be—'

'I'm not.'

'Yes, that's all very well for you to say, but when you come hopping out of her bed in a state of Abram, who's going to believe that?'

'You are, if I tell you so, you suspicious old devil. There's a bolster down the middle of the bed every night—stop laughing, will you!'

'Are you two going to indulge in whatever crude conversation is amusing you for much longer?' a frosty, disapproving voice enquired from the doorway. 'Because I want my breakfast.'

Jack saw Henry's jaw drop and turned slowly. The figure standing on the threshold was clad in breeches, boots, a snug-fitting waistcoat and white shirt. Her hair was bundled into a net at her nape and a neckcloth dangled from her hand. 'Can one of you show me how to tie this?' Eva enquired calmly, her eyes defying them to comment on her attire. 'I must say, I had no idea how difficult it is to get into men's clothes.'

The unfortunate turn of phrase was too much for Henry, who collapsed in hoots of laughter. Eva went scarlet. 'You should meet Mr Brummell,' Jack said, attempting to save her blushes by pretending not to notice the *double entendre.* He kept his face straight with an effort that hurt and aimed a kick at the groom's ankle. 'He would assure you it takes two hours at the very least.'

Chapter Twelve

Embarrassment and her own sense of the ridiculous fought inside Eva and humour won. Her lips curled in a reluctant smile. 'I am not used to using my English every day,' she admitted. 'Thank you, Jack, it was, as you kindly assumed, the difficulties of dressing as a man I was referring to. You,' she said with calm reproof to Henry, who was still spluttering gently, 'have a dirty mind.'

'Me! Now, that's unfair, ma'am, I was only this minute lecturing the guv'nor on proper behaviour.'

'Hmm.' She handed the cravat to Jack. 'Please?'

'Fold it like this, then wrap it round once, and again and then… The devil—I can't explain. Sit down, please.' Eva sat obediently while Jack went to stand behind her and took the ends of the cravat in each hand. The warmth of his body was pleasant, although she could almost feel the tension in him as he tried to avoid pressing close to her. 'Then under here, spread it out, tuck it in… Let me see.' He came round to the front and regarded her, hands on hips. 'Not bad.'

'Thank you,' Eva responded demurely. Jack was different this morning, she concluded sadly. He was pleasant, apparently cheerful, yet there was a reserve underlying his words and his eyes were impossible to read when she managed to catch them directly—which was not easy.

Last night, of course, that was what was concerning him. They had almost—what? Made love? But he had made no move to caress her, to seduce her, only to hold her. The fact that she had found the entire experience utterly arousing would, she suspected, surprise him. He seemed not to have any vanity about the effect he must surely have on any woman who had the slightest interest in the opposite sex.

She let herself be concealed behind a screen while the maids laid the table and brought breakfast in, hardly listening to Jack's explanation that she must not be seen in men's clothes by the inn staff in case they were questioned later. It must be, she concluded, that he saw the problem as his own desire for her—and she had too much experience of the instinctive masculine response to any halfway attractive woman to be greatly flattered by that—and did not have any concept of how much she was coming to want him.

Eva could feel the bedrock of her preconceptions, of the limits she had set on her life, her rules of conduct, begin to shift subtly. It was disturbing, like sensing that the ground you were on might slip, yet not being able to see any fissures yet. Was it just that she was too weak to resist temptation? Or that something had changed?

'Safe to come out now,' Jack called, and she emerged, frowning, to take her seat.

'What is it?' Jack put out a hand as though to smooth the line she could feel between her own brows, then turned the gesture by pulling out her chair. 'Are you very tired after yesterday?'

'I am well, a little stiff, but that is all. It is nothing. No, perhaps not nothing after all. Something I need to think over and perhaps talk to you about later.' When she had some idea if she was just overwrought and adrift, or whether she really did need to think again about her life and how she lived it. 'Where are the horses?'

'At a livery stables on the Lyon road. We will travel that far with Henry, and then you and I will leave him to the post road and we will take to the minor roads that parallel it.' Jack cut a healthy slice off a beefsteak and bit into it with the appetite of a man who had exercised hard.

Eva toyed with the preserves spoon. 'And we meet at the inn tonight?'

'No. We travel separately, with rendezvous points we have already agreed. It will be easier then to spot danger, see if we are followed.'

Henry finished chewing his mouthful of ham. 'I called on our agent here first thing this morning. Word is that Bonaparte's moving troops towards the frontier. Thought you said they aren't expected until July, guv'nor.'

'Well, Wellington certainly wasn't expecting the French until then,' Jack said, frowning at his coffee cup. 'That timing was what persuaded us to plan for this route, otherwise I would have organised some convenient English smugglers at Calais.'

Eva supposed she should be anxious about this news, but somehow she couldn't manage it. She trusted Jack to get her back, and after last night she was half-convinced he could work miracles. In any case, she felt too strange to worry.

He put down his fork and eyed the slice of bread and butter she was nibbling. 'Eat! That is not enough to keep a sparrow alive. Eggs, ham, black pudding.' Jack pushed the platter towards her. 'Goodness knows when we will get our next square meal.'

Obediently Eva helped herself, piling the food on her plate until Jack nodded approval. Jack was the expert—if he said eat, she would eat, even though she had little appetite. Possibly it was the water she had swallowed last night, or perhaps it was the unsettling, hot, ache inside her that had started last night and now would not leave her. When she looked at him it got worse.

Desire. *I should be ashamed.* But where, exactly, was the shame? she pondered, dutifully chewing her ham like a small child told to eat up. She set her own standards, it was herself she was letting down if she fell short of them, and it was her own conscience she must consult.

But there were two people in this equation. Eva looked down and saw her plate was empty. Suddenly finding her appetite restored, she reached for the bread and butter and spread a slice with honey. There were Jack's standards to consider, as well, his conscience. She gave herself a little shake. They would ride, it would clear her mind. Then they would talk. Frankly.

The horses Jack had hired were fine animals, strong, sound and looked fit enough to carry them to the frontier, provided they kept to a steady pace. Eva stayed with the carriage until they were some distance from the stables, then Jack, leading her saddle horse and a laden pack animal, caught up with them and she was able to shed her cloak and mount.

'Oh, you lovely thing.' She ran her hand down the arching, satiny neck of the bay gelding, settling herself in the saddle while Jack checked the girth and adjusted the length of the stirrup leathers for her. 'It seems so long since I was able to ride anything so big and powerful. Since Louis died I have been expected to ride side-saddle at ceremonies, or on gentle hacks around the vicinity of the castle on a nice, quiet mare.'

'You can mange him, then?' Jack swung up on the black horse, a good sixteen hands, with a wicked glint in its eye. 'I hoped perhaps you could, because of the distances we need to cover, but I did have one in reserve.' He grinned suddenly. 'A gentle, solid little mare.'

'An armchair ride?' Eva enquired indignantly. 'Certainly not.' She did feel an inner qualm that perhaps she was so out of practice that she might not manage, or that she would slow him down. Jack's high expectations of her reinforced her determination to live up to them, gave her courage, even while part of her wondered sceptically if this was just good management of the forces under his command. She decided to test him. 'Why do you think now that I can ride this horse?'

'Because you've got guts, determination and a certain natural athleticism,' he said matter of factly, neck-reining one handed to turn his horse towards the track that led away from the post road. Eva stared at his retreating back. 'Come on.' Jack twisted in the saddle. 'Don't you believe me? When have I ever flattered you or been less than honest with you?'

'Never.' Eva dig her heels into the horse's flanks and cantered up alongside him. 'I don't think so. Thank you.'

'Thank me later, when your muscles are remembering that they have not worked like this in months—'

'Years,' she said ruefully.

'Years, then. You will be convinced your posterior is one big blister and your shoulders will ache like the devil and then it will all be my fault.'

'I'll just have to look forward to a good deep hot bath,' Eva said without thinking, then went red to her ear tips at the recollection of last night's bath.

But Jack was already forging ahead, up the slope. 'I wouldn't count on it,' she thought he said. But that could not be right—any inn would be able to provide a tub.

The pace Jack set was steady but fast, wending their way between the small ponds, thickets and fields on the east side of the wide river. They would canter, then drop to a walk to spell the horses, then canter again. From time to time he would check a compass, glance at the sun or stop to study the black notebook he kept in his pocket. He took half an hour at noon to eat from the packages of food that were stowed in their saddlebags, then watered the horses and walked, leading them for half an hour before mounting again.

They spoke little, although Eva was aware of Jack's eyes on her from time to time. Something strange was happening to her as the lush countryside unrolled beneath their horses' hooves, as the wildfowl rose in honking panic from the pools or the cattle raised their heads and watched them pass with great liquid brown eyes.

The wind was in her hair, the air was sweet in her lungs and it was as though she was stripping off some heavy, uncomfortable robe, freeing her limbs so she could run and laugh. Reality narrowed down to the landscape around them, the feel of the horse beneath her, her awareness of the man by her side.

Slowly, very slowly, the realisation came to her that she was herself again, not the girl who had left England, a wide-eyed bride, not the Grand Duchess with the weight of a tiny country on her shoulders, but herself, the Eva who had always been inside. For years she had looked out through her own eyes as though viewing the world from behind a mask, and in time she had become to believe that that was who she was.

I was beginning to think I was middle-aged, she thought in amazement as she followed Jack's lead and popped the gelding over a low post and rail and whooped in delight at the sensation of flying. *I was a mother, a widow, a Duchess. They are all important, but they are not me, not all of me. I'm me* and *Freddie's mother. Me! Eva, having an adventure. Last night I nearly died and now I feel more alive than I ever have in my life.*

Jack reined in and pointed upwards and she squinted into the blue sky at the pair of kites wheeling above them. Free. She was free. What did she want? What was important for her, inside? Inside, where she was a woman…

Despite her euphoria she was beginning to flag, to think longingly of the inn ahead. As the sun dropped low over the hills of the Beaujolais to the west, Jack reined in. 'This will do, I don't want to press on past Châlon tonight.'

'What? Where?' Eva stood in her stirrups and looked around. There was no sign of so much as a farmhouse, let alone the snug inn she was imagining. 'Are we going back down to the post road?'

Jack, she saw suspiciously, had the air that seemed to be shared by every male with a guilty secret from small boy to King's Messenger. He was trying to look innocent—and failing.

'Well?' she demanded.

'We are camping out,' he admitted, cornered.

'Out here? What about my bath?' Now they had stopped she was painfully aware of her sore bottom and the fact that she was going to have to unbend her legs and stand.

'I did warn you. Look, there's a nice grove of trees and a stream.'

Nice grove, indeed! Eva considered grumbling. Complaining loudly even. She wanted a hot bath, she wanted a good dinner and she wanted a soft bed. She wanted her major-domo, her footmen, her Swiss chef and her maids. She wanted clean, soft linen. She sat on the tired gelding, absently rubbing her hand along his neck and watched Jack, who had swung down off his horse and was exploring the glade.

It *was* rather nice, now that she came to look at it. The trees whispered softly in the warm evening breeze, there was fine grass and the stream ran busily over glinting pebbles. And there was the man in the middle of it, stretching mightily, his hat tossed on the ground. As she watched he stripped off his coat and threw that down, too, then turned and smiled at her. And Eva smiled back, her aching muscles, her grumbles, her empty stomach forgotten. He was why she felt so free, so *new*. And she was going to have to decide what to do about that.

'It is lovely,' she called, and sensed, rather than saw, the way he relaxed. Had he expected her to be difficult? 'I don't think I can get down by myself, you will have to help me.'

It was part calculation on her part, a feminine wile to get his hands on her, and partly the absolute truth. Jack strolled across and held up his hands. 'Throw your leg over the pommel and slide,' he suggested.

'I don't think I can throw a shoe, let alone an entire limb,' she joked, slipping her foot out of the stirrup and creakily lifting the leg over. The horse, impatient to get at the water and soft grass, shifted and she slid, with more speed than elegance, into Jack's waiting embrace.

He caught her around her waist and held her for a second, feet dangling, then he let her slide down, sandwiched between his body and the horse. She was aware of every inch of his body, and of hers. As her feet touched the ground she realised she was holding her breath and raised her eyes to search his face.

It was expressionless, those searching eyes shuttered and uncommunicative. Jack opened his hands and stepped away. 'I'll gather firewood. Can you water the horses?'

'Yes, of course.' So, the door was still firmly closed. If she wanted him, she was going to have to be very explicit, not rely on hints or flirtation. Eva unsaddled the riding horses, removed their bridles and led them to the stream, then tied them on long leading reins to a sturdy branch. The pack horse stood patiently while she fiddled with straps and buckles, but soon he too was free of his burden and cropping the grass with the others.

'I did not expect you to do that.' Jack was back with an armful of wood. He crouched in the middle of the glade where travellers had obviously lit fires before and began to methodically stack the wood, sliding twigs and dried grass in at the base.

'Why not? I am perfectly capable of it.' Eva searched in the unloaded packs and found food, then bedrolls, which she shook out by the fireside. 'Can we eat all of this tonight? I am starving.'

'So long as we have something left for breakfast.' Jack finished lighting the fire and stood, studying his surroundings, shading his eyes against the setting sun as he watched the track and the fields that lay between them and the river. He looked back at the fire, apparently satisfied with the almost invisible trickle of smoke from the dry wood.

Eva busied herself setting out the meal, then went to scoop water from the stream. 'Shall we make coffee?'

'Why not?' Jack folded himself down on to one of the bedrolls with enviable ease for a man who had been in the saddle all day. 'Do you know how?'

'Er…no.' Eva passed the packet of coffee across and began to slice and butter bread. Somehow, in the last few minutes she had made up her mind what she was going to say to Jack, how she wanted to resolve the conflicts inside her.

'That was good,' Jack said at length, pushing away his empty plate and flopping down on his back. 'Are you warm enough?'

'Yes, thank you. It is going to be a very warm night.' *Now, while I have the courage…* 'Jack, I did not thank you. For last night.'

'For what? Fishing you out of the river? Yes, you did. When we were on the horse.' He was flat out on his back, one knee raised, the other foot balanced casually on it.

'No. I know I thanked you for that. I meant for later, in our room.' Eva took a deep breath and plunged. 'You could have seduced me with no effort at all and I think you know that very well.' The foot that had been describing lazy circles stopped. She had his full attention now. 'I was exhausted, vulnerable and I had been very frightened and I want to thank you for not taking advantage of that. In the morning I would have felt regret, whatever the night had been like.'

'I know.' Jack's voice was neutral, but she knew him well enough by now to hear the tension in it.

'I am not exhausted, vulnerable or frightened now,' Eva said deliberately. And waited.

His reaction seemed to take for ever. He put both feet on the ground, then levered himself up on his elbows and finally sat up, looking at her. The sunset painted gold and rose across his face. 'What are you saying, Eva?'

'That I feel myself now. More myself than I have for nine years and I can see clearly what I need and what is important to me. I have been chaste since my husband—'

'I know. I could tell almost by looking at you. Eva, you do not have to—'

'Let me finish.' She smiled at him, smiled at the serious expression in the grey eyes.

'Here, I am not the Grand Duchess. I am not a widow, I am not a mother. I am just Eva. And I am alone in a beautiful place with a man I desire and I trust and I like.' Jack moved abruptly, as though he was going to stand, and Eva held out a hand to still him. 'I am just a woman, asking a man if he would like to make love to me. If you say *no,* if I am wrong about what I see in your eyes, what I feel when you are close to me, then I apologise. If you lie to me, I will know and that will hurt far more than you explaining that you do not want to do this.'

'Not want? I have wanted you since I first set eyes on you.' The breath, so painfully held, left her lungs in a soundless sigh of relief. Jack pushed himself up so he knelt on one knee, the movement bringing him close enough to take her hand. 'I desire you so much it hurts, but I fear hurting you far more than I fear that pain. Eva, have you thought about this?'

'Idiot man,' she said roughly, tears forming behind her eyes. 'I have thought of very little else since I turned and saw you in my bedchamber, brought there by magic.'

'I don't believe that,' Jack said. *Oh, thank God, he is smiling...*

'Well, I admit I think a lot about Freddie, and Philippe and the Duchy and how we are going to get back safely and whether I have a blister on my behind. But in all the gaps between I think of you and how I want to be in your arms and feel your mouth on me.'

'Do you want to sleep on it?' He was still regarding her with questioning eyes.

'No,' she declared roundly. 'I want to sleep *with* you.'

Chapter Thirteen

Jack searched the wide brown eyes looking so candidly into his. She meant what she said, and he could believe that she had been thinking about it, seriously, all day. Something like this, for Eva, was not to be taken lightly. And for him, after an adult life treating such encounters as either a matter of amicable business, or simply a fleeting moment of mutual pleasure, the responsibility of what she was offering felt as heavy as the duty laid upon him to keep her life safe. She, for some bone-deep reason he could not understand, and was afraid to analyse, was different from all the women before.

'Well, that was definite enough.' He smiled at her decisive declaration, fascinated by the play of colour under her creamy skin. She was shocking herself, he could tell, seeing the soft pink ebb and flow in her cheeks. But she was enjoying that sensation at the same time. 'Eva, we are out of our real worlds here, for as long as this journey lasts. What happens when we get back to England?'

'I do not know,' she said frankly. 'I do not care.' She shook her head. 'No, I do know—it must stop then, I cannot risk the scandal. But we may never get there, for all your skill and courage. I do not want to add losing this to the list of my regrets.'

'Come, then.' Jack stood up with a sensation that he had cast the dice, laid his bet and that his life would change for ever with the fall of those fickle white cubes. Which was madness. She was right; this liaison, whatever it was, could last only as long as it took to feel the swell of the English Channel under their boat's keel. How could that change his life?

He held out his hand to Eva and she took it, with a certain formality, and got to her feet. 'Let me put these together.' He shook out the two bedrolls to their widest, laying one upon the other and raked the fire, adding a thick log. He did not want her becoming chilled; he sensed she was nervous enough, despite the strength of her declaration.

When he turned, she was balanced on one foot, tugging at her boot. 'I'll do that,' he promised, 'and you can help me with mine. Let's start at the top.' The neckcloth he had tied for her that morning was still firmly in its knot. Jack untied it, un- wrapped it from around her neck and folded it carefully in his hands before raising it to his face and inhaling. He held her startled gaze as he filled his senses with the fragrance of her skin.

'But I didn't wear any scent this morning,' she murmured.

'I know.' Jack put the neckcloth into his pocket. 'I can smell gardenia perfume any time I want. I cannot bottle the scent of you.'

Eva reached up and began to untie his neckcloth, her face serious as she fiddled with the knot. He ached for her to hurry, desperate to ignore clothes and simply pull her to the ground and take her here, now, while he still felt he had any control left. But this was Eva, and for her this night was not something to be taken lightly, and for him his whole focus and pleasure must be her delight.

She had managed the knot and was untangling the neckcloth, pulling it free and bunching it in her hands, burying her nose in it in imitation of his gesture. 'Man, warm cloth, bay soap—Jack.' She folded it and put it in her own pocket. 'For nights when I may need courage to sleep,' she said simply, starting on his waistcoat buttons, her lower lip caught between her teeth in an agony of concentration. Jack imagined her applying the same intensity to touching his body and shifted, uncomfortably aware of the constriction of well-fitting breeches.

To hasten matters he threaded his arms through hers and began work on her waistcoat. The effect as their release allowed her bosom to swell free was far more interesting than the equivalent result in his case, he was certain.

'This feels very odd,' he observed, his fingers grazing against fine suiting cloth. 'No ribbons or bows, it's like undressing myself.'

'Indeed? Her eyebrows went up in mock-outrage, then, as though teasing was too dangerous a step into intimacy, she slid her hands up hurriedly and pushed his coat from his shoulders, then his waistcoat. The warm air was delicious through the fine linen of his shirt. Jack felt his eyelids grow heavy as he contemplated the effect of that breeze on bare skin. His, hers.

Jack copied her actions, pushing off her coat and waistcoat, and studied the result. The breeches, which he had chosen with some care, moulded her rounded hips and thighs, but were inevitably too big in the waist. She had cinched it in hard with a leather belt and her hands were hovering, uncertain, over the buckle.

Jack reached out, brushing her fingers away and undid it. He had to stand closer to do so, no longer able to see the whole of her, but close enough now to observe how her pupils had dilated, and trace the flickering pulse under the fine skin at her throat. His own pulse was thundering in his ears as though he had run full tilt up a flight of stairs as he drew the length of plaited leather slowly through the belt loops. It dropped away, a warm snake in his hands.

With a snap of his wrist he flipped it around her again, this time lower, around her buttocks, catching the free end in his left hand and using it to pull her in against him. With both hands holding the leather he could not hold her, but she leaned in of her own accord, her face tipped up for his kiss.

He took a deep breath, drawing in not just the familiar scent of her but the sweet musk of arousal that seemed to perfume her skin, just on the edge of his ability to sense it. Could she detect that on his skin yet? Soon, very soon, he knew their urgent bodies would be sending that thrilling signal unmistakably; now it was as tentative and shy as Eva felt against him.

But this wasn't a virgin trembling so close that the tips of her breast brushed in agonising unpredictability against his chest. This was a woman who had been married, even if she had been alone for a long time.

There were some benefits to being married to one of the most accomplished lovers in Europe.

Hell and damnation. He had tried so hard not to remember those words, not to dwell on them, to tell himself that, just as he never thought of one of his former lovers when with a new one, she would not remember Louis when she was in his arms. That was all very well when the thought of making love to her was just a fantasy to keep him painfully awake at night, or to distract himself with while he should have been thinking of practical matters. Now he was about to put that theory to the test and he knew, perfectly well, that while he could dismiss any number of lightly undertaken affairs, Eva's memories of lovemaking were going to be clear, specific and important to her.

Well, Jack, he told himself ruefully, *you had better do your very best.* And he lowered his head, took her soft mouth with his and found that rational thought fled before the sensual shock of her yielding.

At last! She had dreamed of his mouth on hers again ever since that fierce, intense kiss in the alleyway, dreamed how it would be, wondered if it would be as overwhelming the second time. He was so gentle, yet so certain, in the way he kissed her. He did not even use his hands to hold her; he did not need to. His mouth angled over her lips, seeking, tasting, the flicker of his tongue teasing at the seam until she opened to him with a little gasp of surrender.

Eva found her hands were locked around his neck, her interlinked fingers brushed by the thick black hair at his nape where the strong tendons braced against the pull of her urgency. He explored her mouth slowly, as though seeking to understand something, tasting perhaps, as she tasted him, coffee, the freshness of the celery he had crunched and a taste that just had to be him. Jack.

Louis hardly had ever kissed her like this, taking his time, caressing. It almost seemed that for Jack this was enough, an end in itself, not a hasty part of a rush to consummation. Perhaps she could be more active... Eva let her tongue tangle with Jack's then, greatly daring, thrust it into his mouth, almost gasping at the intensity of the experience. Something slithered across her bottom; he had dropped the belt, catching her in his arms and straining her against him in a blatant gesture that pressed her intimately against the hard ridge in his breeches.

Eva burrowed closer, twining herself wantonly against him, rubbing like a cat urgent for stroking, the hot ache low down where their bodies throbbed together, crying out for him to assuage it.

Jack left her mouth and began to lick and nuzzle at her neck, bending her back over his strong arm so that she arched like a bow in the hands of an archer while he followed the curve of her throat to where her breasts, unconfined by corset or waistcoat, swelled in the vee of her shirt.

'You are so beautiful.' His voice was husky, the words murmured against the aching curves as he lowered her on to her back on the blankets. He followed her down with a control that spoke of his strength and his care of her and lay against her flank, propped up on one elbow as he slowly opened the buttons to reveal her. 'It is like pushing back the petals of a rose to find the fragrant, golden centre.'

As the sides of the shirt fell open, he made no move to caress her, only lay there, watching her, his warm hand lax on her ribs. As she breathed in and out she was conscious of the roughness of a rider's calluses on his palm, the slight friction of his nails as his curved fingers touched her.

The intensity of his gaze shook her confidence. What was he looking at? What was he seeing? Surely she could never match up to his mistresses who thought of nothing else but how to make their lithe young bodies and smooth faces attractive to men. Her certainty wavered.

'What is it, sweet? He sensed her mood instantly, his hand coming up to cup her cheek. 'Are you cold?'

'No.' She shook her head, her lashes falling to hide the embarrassment she knew must show in her eyes. 'Jack, I'm not a girl any more…'

'No,' he agreed instantly, his voice a sensual growl. 'I can see that.'

'I'm nearer thirty than twenty, I've had a child…' He cut off her stumbling words by pressing his hand over her lips as he sat up. The other hand caressed over the fullness of her breasts, stroking and cupping the weight of them, his thumb flicking from one nipple to another until she bowed up, moaning against his palm.

'You are a woman, Eva,' he said huskily. 'A beautiful, sensual woman. I am a man and what I want—what I *need*—is a woman. Not a girl, and not a woman pretending to be one, either. A real woman. You.'

She heard him, believed him, but she could not reply, for he was kissing her breasts now, suckling her pebble-hard nipples until she thought she was going to climax from that alone. Her fingers dug into his shirt; she felt the fine cloth tear and, reckless, ripped it more so that she could feel the skin of his back, hot satin, under her fingertips.

Jack's hands were at the waist of her breeches, fighting with the fastenings, dragging them down over her hips, taking her drawers with them. He reached her boots, swore and spun round on his knees to drag them off, then sat down, pulling his own off with equal force. By the time he turned back to her she had kicked the tangle of cloth away. The heat of his gaze on her naked body stilled her and she crouched there, her eyes wide on his face as she absorbed the look in his eyes. Desire, heat—and something so fragile, so tender, it took her breath. This hard man, this adventurer felt like that about her. *Her.*

'Jack,' she whispered. 'Jack, love me.'

'Yes.' He sounded as though his teeth were gritted in pain. 'Eva—'

Her hands were on the fall of his breeches, slipping under the cloth to caress hot flesh as she found the buttons and pulled, breeches and underthings with them, freeing him in all his awesome state of arousal. 'Oh. *Oh.*' She should be fearful—how long was it since her body had known a man? Would it be like losing her virginity all over again? She did not care; all she knew was that she wanted this magnificent man inside her, joined with her.

Coherent thought, even about her wants and needs, fled as Jack came down over her, his knee pushing hers apart, his long, clever fingers slipping between them to caress her intimately. 'Oh, so sweet, such honey.' He teased and explored, inciting her and opening her ready for him.

As he thrust, one long stroke of mastery and possession, Eva wrapped her legs around his waist and pulled him close, so close against her that she could feel their pubic bones together. He filled her, completed her and she pulled his head down to her lips as he began to thrust. Both of them were desperate for this, neither had any desire to temper the pace of their passion.

She felt his ardour building, meeting her, driving her and she knew only that she screamed as he took her over into dizzying oblivion and that the sound mingled with his shout as he left her body. And then the little grove fell silent.

The moon was riding high when they finally fell apart, lying side by side, fingers entwined, bathing in the silver light.

So this is what it can be, Eva thought in wonder. *This intense, this tender, this fierce.* It was as though she had found the counterpoint to herself, she marvelled. They had hardly spoken—single words, gasps of pleasure, murmurs of delight—yet he had known how to drive her in to ecstasy, time and again, and some sure instinct had steered her hands, her mouth to bring him there, too.

'Jack.'

'Mmm?'

'Just *Jack.*'

He chuckled and sat up, propped on one rigid arm, running his free hand down over her. 'Cold?' Without waiting for an answer, he stood and began to make up the fire. Eva found her shirt and pulled it on, leaving it loose. With the warm night air and the glow of the fire it was all she needed. *Warm inside,* she thought, wrapping her arms round her knees and sitting watching Jack.

In the moonlight, lit by the fire, he seemed like primeval man—naked, unselfconscious, beautifully made. The light slid over matte skin, highlighted muscle, threw intriguing shadows. She wished passionately that she could draw, could capture him, just as he was now.

He came and lay down again on his back with the relaxed,

unselfconscious grace of a big cat. Eva lay, too, propped on her elbows at right angles to him. She rested her chin in one cupped hand and began to run the other over Jack's torso.

'What are you about?' he asked lazily, his mouth twisting as she inadvertently tickled him.

'Exploring.' She let her fingertips trail down the line of hair below his navel, then drifted them lower to thread into the dark tangle of curls.

'There is nothing there but standard male equipment having a rest.' Jack sounded amused as she caressed him. 'And if you are hoping to provoke me into further activity, I give you fair warning, it will take a little while.'

'No, I'm not,' Eva assured him, meeting his eyes with a smile of fulfilled satisfaction. 'It is just that I've never been able to do this before, you see. As I said, I'm exploring.'

'What?' Jack levered himself up on his elbows, looking down the length of his torso to where she was cupping his testicles, gently weighing them in her palm.

'This. Louis would always leave my bed as soon as we had finished making love. I have never been able to examine a naked man like this, so closely. Your body is fascinating,' she explained seriously, then leaned forward and blew lightly as an experiment, intrigued by the way the skin contracted. 'This is all very sensitive, isn't it?'

'Very,' Jack said emphatically as she teased him with the back of one pointed nail. 'Why would your husband always retreat like that?'

'I don't know.' Eva pondered it, realising it had never struck her as odd before. But then, she had no basis for comparison. 'I think perhaps he would see it as a sign of weakness to be naked and vulnerable, and not at his most potent. Louis would always want to be rampant—like the lion on the Maubourg coat of arms. But I think it is more a sign of strength to be able to trust, like this.' On impulse she leaned even further and dropped a kiss onto the half-hidden flesh.

'Come here.' Jack sat up, pulling her almost roughly into his embrace, then lay back with her against him. Under her cheek the sound of his heartbeat was reassuring, his skin was warm, slightly rough from his chest hair. 'It must be trust for two people to do what we have just done, together. We made love *together.* That is new for me, that feeling of partnership.'

'I know,' she said sleepily burrowing into his shoulder. 'I felt it, too: counterpoint.'

'Music, yes,' she heard him agree as she drifted off, feeling him draw the blanket over her, cocooning her safe against his body.

Eva woke to warmth and to the drift of hands over her breasts and stomach. Sleepily, eyes closed against the daylight, she snuggled back into the hard body she was curled against.

'Good morning,' Jack whispered in her ear, and slid into her with one slow thrust. She gasped, shifting to accommodate this new position, then relaxing as he continued to move gently within her, his hands the perfect complement as they caressed with a total lack of urgency, focused only on pleasuring her.

It was bliss, but she could not touch him, could not kiss him. Except one way. Eva tightened her muscles around him, playing with the effect it had both on her and, from the gasp as she did it, on Jack.

It was blissful, languorous, sensual beyond belief. Eva had

no idea how long they lay curved together, only that when it came she lost herself entirely in the peak of sensation he brought her to, shuddering with delight in his arms.

She must have dozed again, for when she opened her eyes she was alone in the nest of blankets, water was heating on the fire and Jack was standing knee deep in the stream, washing. Eva got up and took herself off into the bushes, treading cautiously in bare feet. When she got back Jack was just rinsing off by the simple expedient of lying flat in the water. He emerged, shaking himself like a wet dog, and saw her.

'It's cold. Come in,' he invited.

Was she ever going to get used to looking at him? Get used to the way he looked and the effect it had on her? It wasn't simply the lines of his face, or that he was beautifully made and superbly fit. It was the fact that he did not appear conscious of those things that was so attractive. And that a man so self-contained, so disciplined, should let down his guard so totally with her still filled her with awe.

'Only if you get out first. Or we'll get…distracted again.' Eva kept the shirt firmly wrapped round her body.

'All right.' He splashed to the bank and climbed out, pausing beside her. 'I could become very easily…distracted.'

What if we never go back? What if we stayed here for ever? Eva tossed her shirt to one side and stepped off the bank. The cold water was enough to recall her to the real world—danger, duty and a small boy who needed his mother.

Chapter Fourteen

They rode on again all that day, up through the rich and gentle landscape of the Côte d'Or, halting at noon for their rendezvous with Henry in an inn in the little wine-growing village of Auxey Duresse, just south of Beaune.

Jack watched Eva as they rode. She was easy in the saddle now, apparently unaffected either by her ordeal in the river or their lovemaking. The memory of her supple body answering his, following where he led—sometimes, as her confidence grew, leading him—had him hard, the thought that tonight she would be even less inhibited, even more unreserved, had him aching with longing to hold her again.

From time to time, apparently prompted by some thought, she would turn in the saddle, her eyes warm and happy as she smiled at him. No one had ever looked at him like that, he realised, impossibly flattered when she reached out her hand and touched him fleetingly on the knee, as though it gave her pleasure just to know he was there.

Henry was at the inn already when they arrived. He had

made himself thoroughly at home as usual, Jack noticed, sitting on a bench under a spreading tree, a tankard on the table in front of him and a serving girl with a twinkle in her eye flirting as she talked to him.

'Here they are now. You be off inside, *mam'selle,* and bring out the luncheon, just like I ordered it.'

'Found an admirer?' Jack asked in French, swinging down from his gelding and keeping half an eye on Eva. It wouldn't do to draw attention to her sex by making too much of a fuss, but she dismounted easily, handed him the reins and went to sit beside Henry at the shadowy end of the bench.

'Huh.' Henry sniffed at the teasing, but smiled at Eva. *'Bonjour, madame.'*

'Are you all right? No adventures along the road?' she asked anxiously as Jack walked the horses round to the stable yard.

She looked serious when he returned, but the girl setting a laden tray on the table and laying out tankards and plates kept him silent until they were alone. 'Quietly, and in French,' he warned. 'Trouble Henry?'

'I think I've set eyes upon *màdame'*s brother-in-law.'

'Antoine?' Eva went pale and Jack put his hand over hers. She sent him a flickering smile of reassurance and freed herself. Embarrassed at the show of affection in front of the groom, Jack guessed.

'If he's a sharp-nosed streak of misery?' Henry asked. 'Brown hair, Maubourg uniform with enough silver braid for a general?'

'That's Antoine,' Eva nodded. 'But in uniform?'

'With a mounted troop behind his carriage, all pale blue and silver.'

'That is our uniform, but this is France. We're a neutral country, he cannot bring troops across the frontier like that, for goodness' sake!'

'You can if Maubourg is now allied to the Emperor,' Jack pointed out, then snatched his hand off the table as Eva slammed her knife, point down, into the wood. Henry jumped. Both men regarded her furious face with guarded interest; Jack had not seen her lose her temper since that first glimpse through the castle window.

'The bastard!' She glared as Jack tried to shush her. 'Oh, very well, I know, becoming angry does no good. But he has no right to take us to war with half Europe, the maniac—only Philippe can do that. How many men had he?'

'About fifty,' Henry estimated. 'Hard to see, they made so much dust.'

'Excuse me.' Eva slid off the bench. 'I cannot eat while I am this furious. I will be back in a minute.'

They watched her while she strode off towards the little river that vanished beneath the mill.

'They had outriders checking every vehicle going north,' Henry added, tearing a lump of bread off and spreading it liberally with pâté. 'Cantered up alongside, peered in, then off. Here, guv'nor, try this.' He pushed the pâté towards Jack, who took it and began spreading his own piece of bread, his attention half on Eva, who was standing, hands thrust into her breeches pockets, staring at the water.

'You didn't take any notice of what I said back at the inn, did you? Knew you wouldn't,' Henry said gloomily. 'You shouldn't have done it, you know, guv'nor, for all that she's a nice lady, and lonely with it.' He ignored Jack's glare. 'Look at her, she's all of a glow. Lovely to see, that is, but what about when you get to England?'

'Damn your impudence.' Jack grabbed the tankard and half-drained it. 'Of course she's glowing—she's furious.'

'No, before then. I could see when you arrived. She was all sort of soft and…glowing. And have you had a look in a mirror yourself lately?'

'If you tell me I'm all soft and glowing, I'll darken your daylights for you,' Jack warned ominously.

'You look happier than I've seen you look since I've known you, and that's since you were a lad,' Henry said frankly. 'I just hope you can stay that way. You don't want it all ending in tears.'

'Damn it, man, we're in the middle of a mission, this is no time for your romantic tarradiddles.'

But the impudent old devil's words struck home. So that was what it was he was feeling: happiness. An odd sensation he seemed to recall from a long time ago. Different from satisfaction, gratification, relaxation, contentment. Something deeper. Something that threatened to make him weak. Damn it, he was sitting here, eating pâté and listening to his groom, however trusted, however much of a friend, lecture him on how to behave with the woman he—

Jack's thoughts juddered to a halt. No. He was not going there, he was not going to think about Eva beyond the pleasure of making love to her between now and their return to England. He was not going to analyse this strange, warm, profound sensation and he was certainly not going to speculate on how he would feel when he handed her over in London.

'Jack?' She was there by his side, a rueful smile on her lips.

'I've sworn at a poor innocent moorhen, kicked pebbles at an inoffensive water lily and I feel better now.'

'Good.' He moved so she could sit down on the bench again. 'Eat up, this is good food.'

'No doubt tested on your way south.' She was tucking in with a healthy appetite, he was glad to see. The elegant toying with her food had vanished; this was a healthy young woman getting a lot of exercise in the fresh air. He caught himself grinning, recalling exactly what sort of exercise might have contributed to the appetite, and got his face straight before Henry noticed.

'Yes,' he acknowledged, 'And the wine is good, too. Henry will be collecting a number of cases before he leaves.'

'Wine?' Eva stared at him, then burst out laughing. 'You English! Such sangfroid. Here we are in the middle of Continental upheaval, the return of Napoleon, you are on a dangerous mission and you stop to taste wine? I had forgotten the English aristocrats' way of behaving as though nothing is a crisis, everything is a bit of a bore.'

'It makes us look like ordinary travellers, *madame*,' Henry supplied, then, with his regrettable tendency to over-explain, added earnestly, 'No aristocrats here.'

Her gaze slid sideways to Jack's face. There was speculation behind the amused brown eyes. 'Indeed?'

'Saving your presence, *madame*.'

'Hmm. So Jack, do we travel with the wine or are we taking to the back roads again?'

'We ride.' He had been intending to resume travelling by coach, but Henry's encounter made him wary. Prince Antoine could be taking those troops to Paris as a very visible pledge of his allegiance to the Emperor, or he could be intending to throw a cordon across the roads further north. Or both. 'Henry, we'll meet at the rendezvous near the frontier. If we aren't there by the seventeenth, or if you run into trouble, push on to Brussels. Have you supplies for us?'

'Aye, enough for a week if you get your fresh stuff in the villages. That'll get you there so long as you don't have to go making any big detours. There's bacon, some hard cheese, sausage, coffee and sugar. I reckoned you'd want to stay on the back roads when I told you about Monsieur Antoine and his little army. What'll you do if it rains?'

'Find some small inn off the beaten track.' The idea of making love to Eva on a goose-feather bed was powerfully attractive. Not that the prospect of another night under the stars was any less so. He caught her eye and saw she was having the same thoughts. She blushed and hastily reached for the cheese. Henry rolled his eyes.

Eva sat watching the carriage roll away down the dusty road towards Beaune. 'He knows about us, doesn't he? Did you tell him?' Jack was checking the pack horse's girth and she was amused to see the flush on his cheekbones at her question.

'Of course not. It is not something I would ever speak of— to anyone. But he has known me a long time, the insolent old devil. He says I look happy and that you are glowing.'

'Oh.' Eva was so taken by this unexpectedly romantic side to Henry that she had to urge her mount to a trot to catch up with Jack. 'I think that's lovely. But I expect you bit his head off.'

'I did. You don't need to worry that he would ever gossip.' Eva shook her head—no, she wouldn't imagine Henry ever doing anything that was against his master's interests. 'I'm not at all sure I like being so transparent, even if it is him.'

'You have a good gambler's face, I would guess.' Any excuse to gaze at Jack as they rode along was welcome—she had the urge just to sit and stare at him all day.

'I have. At least, I had thought I could bluff anyone. It seems I am wrong. You are a bad influence on me, Eva.'

'I am?' Eva's amusement fizzled out, leaving a hollow feeling inside. Jack had enviable focus and concentration—was she undermining that, distracting him? Even weakening him? Was that what Henry was anxious about? She had put his disapproval down to moral objections to a liaison, now she wondered.

Mortified, she rode in silence, picking up pace when Jack spurred on, wrapped in examining her conscience. Jack was a professional. He might have been attracted to her, but he had been keeping that attraction well in check. She had stormed straight through that armour.

He could always have said 'no', she told herself defensively. Or perhaps she was not doing any damage and was being over-sensitive. *Just because I have fallen in love, it doesn't mean that he...*

Eva swallowed hard. *Just because I have fallen in love. Oh, my God, I have done just that.* She thought she simply wanted comfort—physical comfort and the emotional relief of being close to someone who seemed to care about her. But she loved him. And it was impossible. She was a Grand Duchess, he was a King's Messenger at his most respectable, an adventurer at worst, even if he was the younger son of a good family, which she guessed he must be.

I can't ever tell him. She stared at Jack's broad shoulders, relaxed almost into a slouch as he rode at an easy hand canter. He even managed to be elegant when he was slouching. But it was not his physical beauty that made her feel like this, even if that had been a powerful attraction to begin with. She loved the man under that hard, cool, competent exterior. And she must not let him guess.

She had said that this could only be while they were out of England and he had agreed. Now she knew she must persuade him otherwise, without betraying her innermost feelings for him. She could not lose him so soon, it was too cruel.

'Eva?' He reined in and circled back to come alongside her. Eva realised with a start that she had come to a halt and was sitting gazing blankly into space. Hurting. 'Are you all right?'

'Yes. Yes, of course, I am sorry I was just thinking... about England.'

Jack reached over and touched her cheek fleetingly. 'You miss Freddie, I know. I'll try and get you back as soon as is safe. Come on, let's get past Beaune before we stop again.'

Guilt washed through Eva as she followed the black gelding along the vineyard terrace path. Freddie. His reaction to this had never crossed her mind. He must never know his mother had taken a lover, and she could not hope to keep it a secret in England under the close scrutiny of court and society. If Henry could see it, then others could, too. She had told Jack she would have no regrets if they were to become lovers, and she must never let him guess how she felt, how she had broken her implied word not to become involved.

Some people are never able to consummate their love, she told herself fiercely. *I have been fortunate, I have him for this little span of time. It must be enough. It must.*

* * *

Four days later they were across the border, the River Sambre just behind them after the bridge at Thuin. The days had been hot, the nights dry and they had not had to take refuge in an inn yet. Somehow Eva managed to push her knowledge of her love for Jack away to the back of her mind, not to think about it, only to feel—and in that way hide her feeling from him.

Or she tried. 'What is it, sweet?' he would ask, capturing her face between his big hands and staring deep into her eyes. 'Tell me what is hurting you.'

'Nothing,' she said every time. 'Just worries.' And she would stand on tiptoe and kiss him until he forgot whatever betraying expression had crossed her face. Until the next time.

By the fourteenth they had begun to hear cannon fire. At first it was so distant and irregular that she thought it was thunder out of a clear blue sky, but Jack shook his head. 'There's fighting up ahead, border skirmishes as they all sort themselves out, I expect. Now we begin to take great care.'

Dodging small groups of French troops became routine. Jack seemed to know the uniforms, jotting notes whenever they sighted them. Sometimes they were seen themselves, but Jack would let the horses walk, wandering along, doing nothing to raise suspicions that they were anything but innocent local riders. No one challenged them.

Making love by starlight in owl-haunted woods, or in meadows so soft and sweet you could almost taste the goodness of them, became completely natural. They had never made love inside, on a bed, and somehow that did not seem a loss to her, so it was a surprise when Jack sat studying the sky in the late afternoon.

'It is going to rain,' he said, taking the notebook out of his pocket and studying one of his meticulous maps.

'Is it?' Eva looked round, puzzled. 'I am no weather expert, but it looks just the same as yesterday afternoon to me.'

'No. It will rain.' Jack gathered up the reins and turned his horse's head down the fork in the track through the woods. Ahead, across fields, a church spire punctuated the low hills. 'Or there will be a heavy dew in the morning. Or a thunderstorm.'

'Or a plague of locusts?' Eva enquired, beginning to see where this was going. 'You are looking for an excuse to find an inn. Why not say so? Do you think I am going to accuse you of becoming soft because you want to bathe in a tub instead of a cold stream?'

'I think you might be alarmed if you guess the things I would like to do when I get you alone in the Poisson d'Or's best bedchamber with its big goose-feather bed.' Jack grinned, managing to look nearer twenty than thirty.

'Indeed?' Eva attempted a severe expression. She appeared to have forgotten how. 'What a very depraved imagination you have, Mr Ryder.'

'I am shocked you can know of such things,' he teased back. 'Tell me, what would *you* like to do in that big feather bed?'

'Ooh…' Eva pouted provocatively. 'I would like to take all my clothes off—very, very slowly. Then I'd brush out my hair, bathe in a deep hot tub with scented soap, climb out, dripping wet…' Jack's eyes were glazing in a very satisfactory manner. 'Dry myself, then climb into bed. And—go to sleep.'

Laughing at his expression, she urged her horse on, cantering down the track. It curved, perhaps fifty feet above the main road that cut across the country between them and the village. Some instinct made her glance to her left. Dust was rising above the scrub and spindly trees that covered the slope. Eva reined in, holding up her hand to halt Jack, who was rapidly catching her up. They moved into the shelter of a coppice and waited.

'Soldiers,' Jack breathed as the sound of tramping feet reached them, drowning out the song of skylarks over the wheat field. 'French soldiers heading towards Charleroi. A lot of them—this is different from what we have seen so far. I thought our luck would not last much longer.'

'Are we in danger from them?' Eva shaded her eyes and tried to make out uniforms, but her knowledge was not good enough.

'No, probably not. There is nothing about a pair of apparently unarmed riders to cause them any concern, provided we merely cross their path and do not appear to be shadowing them.'

He sat watching the slowly vanishing column of infantry through narrowed eyes. 'Wellington is assembling an Anglo-German army around Brussels, but our agents along the way so far have not known what the weight of troops were on either side, and they were very vague about where Bonaparte is heading. That is Fontaine l'Eveque ahead. I'm going to strike north-east tomorrow and aim for Nivelles.'

'You haven't been talking to me about all this,' Eva accused. 'I should have worked it out for myself—my brain must be turning to porridge. I suppose I have just been so focused on our own adventure I haven't been thinking about the wide world. Of course Bonaparte isn't just going to sit there in Paris, sending out a few scouting parties, and the Allies certainly aren't going to let him.'

'No.' Jack was scrutinising the plain. 'You know, that

cannon fire is a fair way off to the north and east, but it is almost continuous now. I think there is a battle going on.'

'And by making for Brussels we are riding right into the middle of it.'

'Maybe. If we do not take care.'

'Jack,' Eva asked with a calm she was far from feeling, 'have you been keeping quiet about this so as not to worry me?'

'Yes,' he admitted ruefully, surprising her by his frankness. 'My orders were to bring you back overland to Brussels; it seemed faster and safer than risking the sea route. It probably still is the right thing to be doing; we just need to avoid wandering into Napoleon's HQ or the no man's land between the two front lines by mistake.'

He dug his heels in and sent the black gelding and the packhorse trotting down to cross the main road. 'After today we ride hard and fast for Brussels and skirt round any trouble we see. I'll dump the pack and we can rotate between the three horses— it will keep them fresher. We'll do it in the day that way.'

'Have we been going too slowly up to now?' Eva asked, suddenly feeling guilty again. 'Have I been holding you up?'

'No, and, no you haven't.' Jack reined back to a walk. 'We were right to take to the horses—Henry's encounter with Antoine proved that. And I could see no merit in flogging the horses at such a speed that we would have had to be changing them as we went. It draws attention to us, and it was no part of my instructions to deliver you bruised and exhausted. We can make it to Brussels tomorrow, even if we arrive after dark.'

'So tonight is our last night on the road.' The last one alone with Jack. Things would be different in Brussels, she would become the Grand Duchess again then. Even if Jack was still her escort, that was all he could be. Did he realise? Had he thought about that? Probably not—he had a job to do and personal considerations would always come second. 'What is the date?' she asked, wanting to fix this night in her memory for ever.

'June 16th,' Jack said. 'Look, there is the Poisson d'Or.'

'What about my clothes?' she asked, suddenly recalling the way she looked. 'It hasn't been a problem because I have not been close to anyone yet, but I cannot hope to fool people close up.'

Jack seemed unconcerned. 'I will speak quite frankly to the landlord, and anyone else who stares, and say that I do not like my wife riding about the countryside with all these troops about. Of course, if we did not have to hurry to the bedside of your ailing grandmother in Celles it wouldn't arise, but you insisted, so here we are.'

Eva nodded—that was a good tactic, to confront the issue, not to try to keep her sex a secret and arouse suspicion. Jack rubbed his chin, rasping the stubble as though in anticipation of a shave in ample hot water. 'We will have a good dinner to celebrate our last night on French soil. Shall I order champagne so we can drink to the confusion of our enemies?'

'Of course,' Eva flattered herself that the smile she managed was perfectly natural. *To the confusion of our enemies and to the last night in Jack's arms.*

Chapter Fifteen

'To victory,' Jack said quietly in French, touching the rim of his glass to Eva's.

'To victory,' she echoed. There was no private parlour at the Poisson d'Or, but there was a low-beamed room with tables set around. The noise level from the other diners was high enough for them to talk quietly without fear of being overheard, but they kept to French so there would be no unfamiliar rhythms of speech to draw attention to them.

Outside, the rumble of the distant guns continued. Inside everyone pretended not to notice it. Yet there was a febrile excitement in the air, an unease, a whisper of rumour. Did these people really want their emperor back? Eva wondered.

Where were the Maubourg troops? Following where Antoine led them into the midst of a battle or reluctantly marching north and not yet in danger? Were they convinced of the rightness of joining the Imperial cause, or was it simple obedience that kept them with him? If she had been in the carriage when they had stopped it, could she have won them round, convinced them to go back to the Duchy, their families and safety? Eva gave herself a mental shake; thinking *what if* and *maybe* was futile, but when they reached Brussels she would do what she could to ensure the men were found and treated well.

Up ahead was bloody battle, men dying and being wounded and there was nothing they could do. Wellington would win, of course he would, she assured herself. Anything else was unthinkable.

'To victory, and to us,' she added to the toast, touching the painful subject like someone with toothache who cannot resist worrying at the sore tooth. 'It has been good, Jack, these last few days, has it not?'

'It has.' He watched her over the rim of his glass as he took a mouthful of wine before setting it down. 'And it is not over yet.' There was a familiar heat in his gaze, a heat that made her feel hot inside, roused the fluttering pulse of arousal so that she shifted on her chair. The anticipation of a night spent in that big soft bed made her mouth dry and she was uncomfortably aware of her nipples peaking against the restriction of her waistcoat.

'One more night,' she agreed, lightly. One more night and day while he was still hers and hers alone. One more set of memories to live on.

'And then Brussels, and the journey back to England.' Jack stopped speaking as the maid brought bread and a pitcher of water. He dropped his broad hand over hers and squeezed reassuringly. 'Fréderic will be beside himself to see you again.'

'If he remembers me,' Eva said. It seemed to be her evening for probing all her worries.

'He does!' Jack lifted her hand in his and kissed her fingers, earning himself a sentimental smile from a plump *bourgeoise* sitting opposite with her family. 'He told me so—not in so many words, but with what he said, what he mentioned of Maubourg and you. He has no doubts—lads of that age don't. He knows he will see you again, he knows you are there waiting for him, and he feels quite safe. It is you who has suffered, knowing that you have missed those years of him growing, knowing you have had to trust him to the safekeeping of others.'

'Thank you.' Eva blinked back tears, dropping her cheek momentarily to rest against his raised hand. He smiled at her, then she saw his eyes focus beyond her, the laughter lines creasing attractively. 'And who are you flirting with, might I ask?'

'Behind us. A most respectable dame who obviously thinks we make a pretty couple.'

'We do.' Eva dimpled a smile. 'Look, see the mirror to your right, you can see us in it.' Jack glanced across. She was right—on the wall was an ancient mirror, probably something that had found its way from one of the great houses of the district during the Terror, for it was too fine for this workaday place

The old glass was soft and kind, framing them as a portrait of lovers, hands clasped, heads close. Eva, so feminine despite her severe man's clothing, with her dark plait lying heavy on her shoulder. Him, just a man… Jack stared. That *was* him, it couldn't be anyone else, but somehow the reflection looked different. Younger, more—he fought for the word—more complete. Which was nonsense. It had to be the flattering effect of the mirror. But Henry had said he had changed, and he felt different.

He stared deep into his own eyes, deep into the eyes of a man in love. *Hell!* Jack shut his eyes on the betraying image, turned his head sharply and released Eva's hand. No, that was not going to happen, he could not let it, it was impossible and there was nothing there for him but misery.

But the trouble was, he knew it was too late. That warm centre of contentment, that feeling of completeness that threaded through the desire he felt for Eva, that stab of black misery that hit the pit of his stomach when he thought of leaving her—he had never felt those things before.

The bustle of the inn dining room faded around him as he sat there. He had fallen in love, the one thing he had sworn he would never do. And he had fallen in love with the most inappropriate, most unobtainable woman he could have chosen, short of one of the royal princesses. He felt his lips part without conscious volition and tried to control his instinct to say the words, here, now, at once.

'Jack? What is it?' Eva was staring at him, her lovely mouth curving into a smile that was half-amusement, half-concern. He must be gawping at her like the village idiot, that fatal declaration trembling on his lips.

'Nothing.' *Everything. My heart. My world. My soul.* 'Nothing at all important, just a thought that struck me. This chicken is good, is it not?'

'It is pork.' The smile became a teasing grin as he clenched his hands around knife and fork to stop himself reaching across the table and pulling her to him. 'Does champagne always have this effect on you?'

No, you do. 'No. It is not the champagne, it is pure, unadulterated desire.' He made himself match her bantering tone and found himself smiling as the ready colour stained her cheeks. She was so deliciously modest and reserved, yet when they touched she was utterly abandoned in her lovemaking. It was like her whole character. Outwardly she could be aloof, autocratic, reserved; inwardly she was warm, vulnerable, loving. 'We will take another bottle upstairs—I have wicked thoughts about what we can do with the contents.'

The brown eyes watching him opened wide with speculation that was both shocked and titillated. Jack called up reserves of self-control he had never had to apply to his own feelings before and made himself focus only on the here and now. This meal, this tension between them and the sound of cannon fire which was becoming fainter and less frequent as the darkness drew in, became the whole of the world. Jack felt the urgency draining out of him, to be replaced by a sense of anticipation that was thrumming through his body with almost orgasmic intensity.

He was going to make love to Eva tonight, and when he did it would be astonishing, even better than all the times before, and yet that was not all he wanted any more. He wanted—no, he *needed*—to watch her, see her in minute detail. He needed to learn the way she wrinkled her nose at a flavour she did not like, how she smiled when she thanked the maid for some small attention, how the colour of her eyes changed in the candlelight, how the tiny mole at the corner of her left eye moved when she frowned at him in mock-anger at a teasing word.

He packed away the pictures of her at every moment, the sound of her voice when she chuckled, the throaty laugh of real, uninhibited amusement, the sudden, serious, expression that kept transforming her face and which he could not persuade her to explain. All of these impressions he saved, learned, as he would a map of enemy territory or a complex brief from a client, storing them away for the time when they would be all he had of her. All he could ever have.

Eva pushed away her plate with a little sigh of repletion. He poured the last drops of the champagne into their glasses and gestured to the maid for another bottle. 'Shall we go up?'

Their chamber had been cleared of bath tub and shaving water. The puffy white eiderdown on the big wooden bed had been turned down invitingly and candles burned on the dresser and beside the bed. On the washstand a bunch of June roses made a blotch of warm colour in the pale room.

'Eva.' Jack reached for her.

'No.' She held up a hand, halting him. 'No, tonight I want to make love to you.'

'What have we been doing up to now?' he asked, conscious of the straining ache of arousal that had been building all evening towards this moment.

'You have been making love to me, we have been making love together,' she explained. 'Tonight I would like to…to lead.'

Had he the strength, the willpower, to let her set the pace? Jack swallowed, realising he wanted this, badly, and that his imagination was already threatening to tip him over the edge. Unable to speak, he nodded.

'Good.' She was blushing, but determined. 'Undress for me.'

He could not unlock his eyes from hers. By touch Jack pulled off his neckcloth, unbuttoned his waistcoat, shed it with his coat, careless of where they fell. He had hardly any recall of how his shirt got off, or his shoes, but he found himself standing there in bare feet, clad only in the light trousers he had changed into when they arrived.

'Everything,' she said huskily, releasing his eyes as her own gaze slid down his torso.

He was so hard his fingers fumbled momentarily on the fall of his trousers, then he was pushing them down, feeling the relief as his erection was freed from the constriction, hearing her gasp as she saw him. 'You have me excited almost beyond bearing,' he confessed.

'Do not apologise,' Eva murmured, apparently transfixed. Her intent regard made him swell harder, larger, as if that were possible. 'Lie on the bed. On your back, please.'

Intrigued, Jack did as she ordered. This was a new experience. What was she going to do now?

What she did was to proceed to torture him by slowly removing each article of her own clothing with deliberate intent to send him insane. She took off her coat and waistcoat with prim care, hanging them carefully on a chair while he admired the tight fit of her breeches over her buttocks and the slender length of her thighs.

She eased off her boots, sliding each down her leg in turn in a way that made him fantasise about sliding in and out of her body. Her neckcloth came next. She stood by the bed untying it, shaking her head reprovingly as he reached for her and only moving again when he lay back. Then she used it to trail down his body, the featherlight touch of the muslin wafting the subtle scent of her heat to him as it teased his nipples into hard knots, then slithered over his groin.

'Have some mercy!' He grabbed for it, only for her to

whisk it away, leaving him aching. Jack fought the urge to take himself in hand to gain some relief from this torment.

Eva began to unfasten her shirt, then turned her back on him as she slowly slid it over her shoulders, giving him the view of her slim, white back, and the merest hint of the curve of her breast as she moved. Jack locked his hands into fists in the sheet as the leather belt fell to the floor and she eased the breeches down over her hips, taking her linen underwear with them.

She was a Venus standing there, white and smooth and exquisite. But it was not a marble statue that looked over its shoulder at him but a warm, soft, curving female. How had she learned to be this provocative, this alluring? He sensed this had not been the way she had behaved with her husband. Eva was doing this for him and because of him. Unable to bear the throbbing need any longer, he curled his fingers round the hard flesh that was tormenting him.

'No,' she whispered, coming close, reaching down and unclasping his hand. 'No, I forbid it.' Her heavy plait fell forward, swinging down lie a soft pendulum above his groin, the very tip touching his swollen erection. He was going to disgrace himself, lose all control in a moment. Jack gritted his teeth as Eva loosened the ribbon and slowly, still letting the hair brush him like tiny lashes of fire, unplaited it until it swung, a silken curtain between them.

He was hanging on to his self-control by his fingertips, Eva realised, watching Jack's set jaw muscles, the clenched fists, the magnificent, straining evidence of his desire for her. Enough teasing—she hardly thought she could bear any more herself.

The bed was yielding as she climbed on to it, knelt up and

straddled Jack's body, keeping herself raised above him as she bent her head and let her hair fall in a cloud over his chest. His hands came up to cup her breasts, taking their weight as she hung over him. Her nipples, already sensitive, stiffened into aching nubs as his fingers found them. She put her hands on his shoulders and leaned further, giving herself up to his caresses, using her hair to caress in return.

Between her thighs she could feel his hips lifting, straining to rise enough to take her. Aching for him, she lowered herself to meet him, gasping as the hard flesh touched her, wriggling to take him into her, sighing with the exquisite sense of fullness as their bodies interlocked, sinking down until she could go no more and he was fully lodged in the core of her.

She had never done this before, but the feeling of power and control was intoxicating as she began to ride him, rising and falling, slowly drawing upwards, then, as he bucked beneath her, moving rapidly so that his head fell back and he grasped her hips with fingers like iron.

Her body was aflame, she could feel her control slipping, knew her rhythm was becoming ragged even as Jack took control, reared up and turned her over so he was on top. She knew he was close, knew he was holding on to take her with him and bowed up to meet him, feeling the swirling ecstasy possess her as he freed himself, cried out, hung rigid above her for a moment, then fell down to crush her into his embrace.

'What had you meant to with the champagne?' Eva murmured later, against Jack's shoulder. The candles were low, he had drawn the covers up over their entwined bodies and they had dozed lightly, occasionally stirring to murmur against each other's skin or trail the lazy kisses of lovers who had exhausted themselves, but not their desire to touch.

'Mmm? I wondered what it would taste like if I licked it off your body.' Jack lifted himself on one elbow to look down at her from under hooded lids. He looked tousled, sleepily replete, yet that fire was still there, banked down perhaps, but enough to warm her deep inside.

'Really?' Eva pondered this. 'That sounds nice.'

'That's what I thought. But it is a pity to waste it when we are both too tired to really concentrate on wine tasting. We'll take it with us.'

'To Brussels? But can we… I mean, where will we be staying?'

'I am sure that, wherever it is, your bodyguard will find it necessary to spend the night in your dressing room.'

'Armed to the teeth?' Happiness bubbled up inside her like the champagne they had drunk earlier. This was not to be the last night after all.

'Well, certainly fully armed,' Jack said with a certain male smugness, settling down again and pulling her into his arms. 'And ready to give you his undivided and close personal attention.'

'There was a battle at Ligny yesterday, that was what we could hear,' Jack told her as Eva came out to the stables. The inn had been in hubbub that morning, the staff distracted and the breakfast service haphazard. They had eaten up and stayed quiet, trying to overhear what was going on, but making sense of it was impossible. Jack had left Eva to settle their account while he went out to saddle up, hoping to get a more coherent account from the stable hands.

'Ligny.' Eva frowned, trying to place it. Jack opened a much folded map from his pocketbook.

'Here,' he pointed. 'And at Quatre Bras to the north-west of it.'

'Who won?' Jack was maintaining his usual neutral expression, but Eva could tell it was not good news.

'Napoleon, by all accounts. Wellington has pulled back towards Brussels. Quatre Bras is a key crossroads,' he added, folding the map away.

They mounted up and rode north in sombre mood until they were out of sight of the village. Then Jack halted and stripped the packs off the led horse, dumping out everything except weapons, water and some of the food. 'Will this fit in your saddle bag?' He flipped open the flap to push in a small loaf of bread. 'The champagne? Eva, what's that doing in there? We are supposed to be travelling light!'

'For tonight,' she insisted. 'You promised.'

'For tonight,' he agreed.

With the led horse free of its burden they made better speed, riding at a canter, constantly scanning the land ahead as they rode through the fields and along the dusty tracks. They saw nothing, for the local peasants seemed to have kept close at home for fear of what might be out there in the aftermath of the battle, but there was sporadic gunfire from their right.

Jack kept away from the main roads, crossing the rivers by little pack mule bridges, or splashing across fords. 'We're not far south of Nivelles,' he told her as they pulled up to a walk to rest the horses.

The edge of a wood curved ahead of them and they hugged it close, grateful for the shade. The sun was scorching now, the sky a queer brazen colour forewarning of thunderstorms to come. They rounded the curve and there, right in front of them, were the first troops they had seen all day.

A dozen men slumped on the ground or hunkered down around the pile of their packs. Weary horses stood, heads down, barely able to flick their tails to keep the flies away. The men were filthy, bandaged, and their uniforms were torn, disfiguring the familiar light blue cloth and the silver trimmings.

'Jack! They are the Maubourg troops!' Eva was riding forward even as she spoke, ignoring Jack's sharp order to come back. There were so few of them, perhaps half of the troop Henry had seen, but they were here, her men, and these, at least, were alive.

At the sound of the hooves they raised their heads, hands reached for weapons and a man strode out from behind the screen of horses, a pistol in his hand.

The long muzzle lifted, the tiny black eye unwavering on her breast as she pulled the horse to a slithering standstill. 'Antoine!'

Chapter Sixteen

'Fleeing the Duchy with your lover, my dear sister-in-law?' Antoine enquired. The pistol did not move. Behind her she could hear Jack's horse, stamping in impatience as he reined it in. The rest of the men got to their feet, staring.

'I am the Grand Duchess Eva de Maubourg,' she said, ignoring Antoine and raising her voice to reach the troopers. 'Prince Antoine has no right to lead you to war, no right to break our neutrality.'

'This woman is a whore, a traitor who has fled with her lover,' Antoine countered, drawing their attention back to him. 'Seize their horses, bring them here to me.'

Some of the men started forward. 'No! Remember who I am! I am the mother of your Grand Duke and I am on my way to him now.' But their faces showed nothing but exhaustion and dull shock. Would they even recognise this woman in man's clothing from the images that they would have seen of her, or the glimpses caught from a distance at parades?

What was Jack doing? Nothing, probably; seeing the aim

that Antoine was taking, there was little he could do without risking her being shot. Then she heard him, his voice pitched just for her ears, in English. 'Faint. Now, to the left.'

With a little gasp she slumped sideways, keeping a grip of the pommel just sufficient to break her fall. As she hit the ground, her horse between her body and the men, she saw the led horse gallop riderless through the gap, sending the troopers scattering. There was a sharp report—the pistol—she thought hazily, and then Jack was there, the big black gelding a wall between Antoine and herself.

Had he a pistol? Eva ducked down, peering under the belly of the two horses. Antoine was scrabbling in a holster for a loaded weapon, his horse backing away, frightened by the firing; three hefty troopers were hurling themselves towards Jack.

Eva swung back on to her horse, groping in the saddlebags in the hope that Jack had stashed a weapon there, but all her frantic hand met was the neck of the champagne bottle. She dragged it out, hefted it in her hand and kicked the animal into an explosive canter. They rounded the knot of troopers Jack was holding at bay with a long knife and bore down on Antoine. His second pistol was in his hand now, aimed at Jack. Eva dragged on the reins and swung the bottle. As her horse crashed into the prince's, the champagne cracked over his head and he slumped, unconscious, beneath her hooves.

'Jack!' She pulled up the bay on his haunches as the big black horse erupted towards her through the group of troopers.

'Ride!' His hand came down on the bay's rump and both animals flew along the track at a gallop. 'Keep down!' Eva flattened herself over the withers, expecting the crack of musket fire behind at any moment, but nothing came. Jack kept up the pace, zigzagging through the trees until they reached the far edge of the wood. Even there, he only slowed to a canter, twisting in the saddle to check behind them for pursuit.

'Jack,' Eva called across to him. 'I must go back—those are my troops, my men, I cannot leave them.'

'You can and you will.' The face he turned towards her was implacable. 'Philippe may be dead. If that is so, who will rule Maubourg for Fréderic? You. I cannot risk Antoine being in a fit state to rally them, and I cannot risk your life for the sake of a handful of men who made the wrong choice.'

'No,' she protested, but even as she said it, she knew he was right. It was her duty. The very fact that Antoine had dared bring the men north to the Emperor made her fear that Philippe was indeed dead, that the moral influence of his position, even in sickness, had gone, leaving his brother free to do his worst. If anything happened to her, then who would be there for Freddie, alone in a foreign country, however benevolent?

'Are you hurt?' Jack slowed the pace.

'No. Just shaken.'

'We'll ride on, then, but steadily—we have only the two horses now, we cannot keep this pace up.'

It was then that her bay put his foot in the rabbit hole. Eva was flat on her back on the grass before she knew what had happened, the breath knocked out of her. She sat up, whooping painfully, to find Jack kneeling beside her. 'I'll try that question again.' He smiled reassuringly. 'Are you hurt?'

'No.' She shook her head as he helped her to her feet. The bay gelding was standing, head down, his offside fore dangling.

'Hell and damnation.' Jack strode across to his mount, pulled the long-muzzled pistol from the holster and began to reload. 'Don't look.'

'This really is not our day,' Eva said shakily as she wrapped her arms round Jack's waist and tried to get a comfortable seat behind him as the black horse walked stolidly north under its double burden. The track was uneven, which made keeping her balance even harder.

'You could say that.' She could hear the rueful smile in his voice. 'I could try buying a horse, although I doubt we'll find one. This is going to be a long day.'

They had ridden, then walked, then ridden again, for perhaps three miles, before Jack was confident they had bypassed Nivelles to the west. 'Another seven miles or so to Mont St Jean, then, surely, we will be close enough to Brussels to risk the main road.'

The journey seemed to take for ever on the tired horse. Gradually Eva felt herself flagging, leaning against Jack's straight back, her cheek pressed between his shoulder blades. It should have been uncomfortable and flashes of memory of Antoine's face, the muzzle of his pistol, the sound as she had hit him, kept jolting her with fear, but the solid warmth gradually filled her with a sense of safety and she slipped into sleep.

'Eva, wake up.' It was Jack, twisting in the saddle. 'It's started to rain—we need to get under cover.'

Sleepily she shook herself awake and looked round, surprised to find how dark it had become. The sky was black and heavy drops of rain were hitting the dusty track. 'Where are we?'

Jack threw his leg over the pommel and slid down, holding up his arms for her. Eva almost fell into them. 'Nearly at

Mont St Jean, just over that rise, but I don't want to go blundering into a village in the middle of a rainstorm when I can't see what's going on. It could be full of French troops. There's a barn over there.'

Barn was a somewhat optimistic description—leaky hovel was closer to it—but Eva was not about to start complaining, not when the rain started hitting the thatch like lead shot. Jack brought the gelding in and unsaddled it, tethering the animal near a pile of hay. It lipped at it suspiciously, but when he lugged in a bucket of water from the well outside it drank deeply.

'Eva, come and lie down and get some sleep.' She stumbled obediently to where Jack had laid his coat on some straw, then stopped, the memory flashes coming back to almost blind her.

'Have I killed him?' she blurted out, suddenly realising what was causing that cold lump in her stomach.

'I don't know,' Jack said with the honesty he had always shown her. She certainly would never feel patronised with him, she thought with a glimmer of rueful humour. He put down the saddle bag he was sorting through and came to take her in his arms. She leaned in to him with a sigh that seemed to come up from her boots: *Jack will make it all right.* But he couldn't, not if she had killed her own brother-in-law. 'He was trying to kill us, Eva. Whatever has happened to him, it was self-defence. If you had not ridden into him, one of us would probably be dead. You saved my life, as well as your own.'

'He's Freddie's uncle,' she whispered. 'What do I tell him?'

'That his uncle was misguided, that he took some troops to join the Emperor and that he was killed on the battlefield. If Antoine survives, he'll be on the losing side and in no position to make accusations about two people he tried to kill.'

Jack was rubbing his hand gently up and down her back; it filled her with peace and a sense of his strength.

Comforted, she tipped her head back to look up into his face and caught her breath at the unguarded expression of tenderness she caught there. Then it was gone and he was back to normal: calm, practical, austere. But the wicked glint she had learned to look for was missing from the grey eyes and in its place was something akin to sadness.

'Jack?'

'We're both tired.' His lids came down, hiding his expression from her. 'We'll sleep while this rain lasts; it is so heavy that no one is going to be moving troops around in it.'

'All right.' Eva nodded. She was too tired and bemused to try to read what had changed in Jack. He was here, with her, and for the moment that was all that mattered.

Jack woke cold, and lay still with his eyes closed, trying to work out what had roused him. It was safer, he had found from experience, to check out his surroundings before revealing that he was awake. There was a slanting scar over his ribs to remind him of that on a daily basis.

His internal clock told him it was early, not long after dawn perhaps. His ears could detect nothing amiss. The rain had stopped, birds were singing, the horse was mouthing hay. Against his chest he could hear the soft, regular breathing of the woman who slept in his arms. His mouth curved in an involuntary smile. Nothing alarming there to have awakened him. He inhaled deeply. Eva: gardenias and warm, sleepy female. Horse. Damp thatch and dusty hay. The comfortingly domestic smell of bacon.

Bacon? The very faintest hint of frying ham was threading its way through the chill, damp air. Jack shook Eva gently. 'Wake up, sweet.'

'What is it?' She sat up, pushing back the stray hair that had escaped her plait in the night. Her eyes were wide and soft with sleep and his heart lurched painfully. *My love.*

'Someone is frying bacon.'

'Oh, good. Breakfast.' She rubbed her eyes, then, suddenly completely awake, stared at him. *'What?'*

'Stay here.' He got to his feet, checking the knife was still in his boot top and picking up the pistol that had lain by the makeshift pillow all night.

Outside the day was sodden and chill. The ground was soaked, the heavy clay turned to mud by the torrential downpours of the night before. Jack scanned the field in front of him, but it was empty, the wisps of misty steam already rising as the faint early sun, struggling through the grey clouds, struck the moisture.

He slid round the corner of the barn and made his way up the slope. Beyond the hedge that formed the northern boundary the land rose for perhaps fifty yards, then dropped away. What lay beyond was invisible, but smoke rose in a myriad of thin trickles. Camp fires. The breeze shifted, bringing with it the smell of cooking again and, faintly, the sound of many voices and of barked orders. Troops.

'What is it? The French?' Eva, was at his elbow.

'I don't know, I can't see. And I told you to stay put.'

'I needed to find a bush, so I had to come out,' she said with dignity. 'Are we going to find out who it is, then?'

Ordering her to remain behind was probably futile. How he

had ever imagined he could compel any obedience from this woman he had no idea. 'Watch my back from here.' Jack put the pistol into her hand. 'Don't use that unless it is absolutely necessary or we will have two armies down on our heads.'

'I can do that better if I follow you,' she said stubbornly, taking the pistol.

'You will be safer here. Will you do as I tell you? Please!' He felt his voice rising and lowered it hurriedly.

'I know it is your job to keep me in cotton wool, but, Jack, don't you see—'

Something snapped. He yanked her into his arms without conscious thought, heedless of the pistol that ended up pressed against his ribs. 'I *see* that I almost lost you in that damn river,' he snarled, heedless of her white-faced shock. 'I see that I almost lost you yesterday. Can't *you* see, you pig-headed, in-dependent, bloody-minded woman, that I—' Some sense returned, from somewhere, God knew where. 'Can you not see,' he finished more moderately, 'that you are more than a *job* to me? And if I get you killed or captured, I will punish myself for it for the rest of my life?'

Those soft, red lips parted in a little gasp, but the colour was coming back into her face. Jack tightened his grip on her upper arms and lifted her bodily against him, his mouth taking hers in an uncompromising kiss. His tongue plunged into the warm sweet moistness: mastery, ownership, desperation. Then he set her down roughly on her feet again. 'Now, damn well stay here.'

'Yes, Jack.' Her shocked whisper just reached him as he ducked through a gap in the hedge and, crouching, made his way up the slope. Training and discipline kept him focused on what he was doing and not on who he had left behind, or what he had almost told her. Heedless of the mud, he dropped to the ground and squirmed forward on elbows and knees until he could see down the slope in front of him.

Dark blue uniforms covered the ground below and to the right of the continuation of the road they had left the night before. In the bottom of the valley he could see a crossroads and beyond it a small farm-like château with red coats around it. Beyond that, on the crest that he knew hid the hamlet of Mont St Jean, he could see more red coats.

So, the French were between them and the Allied army and the road to Brussels. Jack slid further forward. There was artillery below and to his left, the guns trained out over the Allied flank, but most of the troops were to the right. It was a scene of an anthill from this distance: hundreds of tiny figures, some grouped around campfires, some with horses, others moving guns or clustering around officers.

The light was good, despite the cloud. Why then, he wondered, had the fighting not begun? He realised why not as he watched a horse team struggling to move a gun limber stuck in the mud. Bonaparte needed to manoeuvre his artillery and he couldn't do it in these conditions. How long would it take for the ground to drain?

Long enough, if they started now, for them to get to the Allied lines before the firing began. Jack studied the slope to the left, then eased back from the edge and ran back down to the barn.

Eva had found a spot where she could watch both the field and the road. 'I've seen no one,' she reported. He saw her take in his mud-soaked clothes, but she did not comment, nor did she make any reference to how they had just parted. He should apologise, he knew, but not now.

'The French are drawn up below us, all along this scarp. The Allies are on the opposite ridge, and they are also holding a farm, half a mile below in the valley. If we can get down there, we can make our way up through the lines to the Brussels road.'

'Right.' He saw her throat move convulsively as she swallowed, but Eva showed no fear, only determination. 'What do we do?'

Fifteen minutes later they were trotting steadily to the west, away from the French, the Allied flank still visible on the ridge to their right. Eva clung on grimly, determined not to complain at the jolting.

'Ah!' At Jack's sigh of satisfaction she leaned round the side of him and saw what he had been looking for. Ahead was a small farm and a track led down from it into the valley. 'See—' Jack pointed '—we can cross the road down there and take the track into that farm in the valley with the Allied troops around it.'

'More of a small château,' Eva said, squinting in an effort to make out detail. 'I can see why the Allies want to hold it, it gives a good command of the valley floor.'

Jack turned the gelding's head downhill and, screened by a thick hedge, they made their way to the valley bottom. 'Get down, Eva.' He helped her slide down, then, to her surprise, stayed where he was, reaching down for her. 'Come on, up in front of me.'

Puzzled, she let herself be pulled up, swung a leg over the

horse's neck and found herself settled on Jack's lap. Then, as he urged the gelding forwards again, pulling her back tight against himself, she realised what he was doing. If there was a sniper with them in his sights, it was now Jack's broad back that would take the bullet.

'Have you got anything white we can wave as we approach?' Jack wrapped his arms round her waist and sorted the reins out.

'Only my shirt,' she retorted tartly, 'And if you imagine I am going to go cantering up to companies of soldiers half-naked, you have another think coming, Mr Ryder.' They were cantering, and she was still fuming before she realised what they were doing and then it was too late to be scared. 'You wretch,' she shouted, above the sound of the hooves. 'You are trying to distract me.'

'True.' He sounded smug. 'It worked, too.'

'Can we gallop now, please?' she demanded, trying to keep the shake out of her voice.

'No, I want to give the troops ahead a chance to see who we are.'

'Jack, I do not want you to get shot.' *Of all the daft things to say,* she chided herself. *As if he can help it if some sniper is sighting down his rifle barrel even now. He doesn't need me wittering nervously at him.*

'Neither do I.' Now he sounded amused, almost as though he was enjoying himself. Men were very strange creatures and being married to one, giving birth to one and having another as a lover did nothing to make them any more comprehensible. 'Look, the piquet have seen us.'

They were closing with the white, buttressed walls of what

looked like a large barn forming the western boundary of the château. Jack did not slacken their pace as they closed with the line of soldiers who were training their weapons on them.

'Wave!'

Eva waved, then shouted, 'English! English!' as the black gelding finally skidded to a halt in front of the troops.

'Who the devil are you?' The Guards officer who strode forward stared up at them. 'Good God! Raven—'

'Jack Ryder, Captain Evelyn. We met in London last year at Brook's, if you recall.'

'Ryder? Yes, of course, forgot. What are you doing here of all places?' The other man seemed ready to settle down to a thoroughgoing gossip. Eva stirred restlessly. She could almost feel the imaginary sniper's hot breath as he sighted at the middle of Jack's back.

'Can we go inside? I am escorting a lady and I doubt she wishes to sit under the eye of our friends up on the ridge much longer.'

'Yes, of course.' The captain recollected himself. 'There, through that gate. Swann, escort them. Oh, and Ryder, the Duke's here.'

'What did he call you?' Eva demanded, trying to twist round as they rode through the narrow gate and into the barn. 'Raven? Is that a nickname?'

'A mistake, he has a poor memory. Do you want to meet the Duke?'

'You know him, I suppose?' Eva gave up for the moment; now was not the time to try to probe Jack's reticence.

'We have spoken.' Jack sounded amused. 'At least, I should say, he has barked at me on occasion.'

Their escort led them out of the other side of the barn into a courtyard. It was indeed a château they had arrived at, but a small one, more of a glorified farm than anything. Through another gate and they saw a group of horsemen. The figure in the cocked hat and black cloak could only, if the nose was anything to go by, be the great man himself. He was surrounded by a group of officers, all in earnest talk. Jack rode across and four faces turned to view them.

Eva saw eyebrows rising as they took in the fact that she was a woman, then the Duke doffed his hat. 'Madam. From the fact that you are with this gentleman, I assume you are not sightseeing on the battlefield?'

'Ma'am,' Jack said, without a quiver in his voice, 'may I introduce his Grace the Duke of Wellington, Commander of Allied forces?' Eva bowed, as best she could given her position. 'Your Grace, I am escorting this lady to England. I regret that at the moment I am unable to effect a proper introduction.'

The Duke doffed his hat and the others followed suit. 'I presume that Rav…Ryder is taking you to Brussels?'

'Yes, your Grace. I must not distract you from the task in hand, forgive me.' Another *mistake* with Jack's name. What was going on?

'We will ride back together, ma'am, and find you a mount. Allow me to present General Baron von Muffling, Prussian liaison, and Major the Viscount Dereham.' He rose slightly in his stirrups and the other officers who had been standing further out moved forward attentively. 'Lieutenant Colonel McDonnell, gentlemen—you have your orders, this place is to be held to the last extremity, I have every confidence.'

Chapter Seventeen

The Duke and the Prussian general rode off ahead, through the orchard gate and into a sunken lane that led up towards the crest. The younger officer drew up alongside and grinned cheerfully across at them. 'You have chosen a hot day to visit us, ma'am.'

Eva smiled back, trying to make her mind work; it was beginning to feel decidedly bruised, as though it had been hit by little hammers for hours. *Pull yourself together, you can do this.* What was his name? Ah, yes, Dereham, and he was a viscount and a major. 'You must all be very wet and uncomfortable after last night, Major.'

Dereham shrugged. 'I can think of better ways to recuperate between battles, but I have no doubt we'll all have our minds taken off our wet feet before much longer.'

Eva liked him on sight—with his blond hair, blue eyes and devil-may-care expression he was the opposite of Jack's dark, serious, hawk-like looks. 'I hope you have managed to get a good breakfast this morning. The French are frying ham.'

'Stale bread and cheese, ma'am, washed down with rain-water. I'll tell the men about the ham, it'll make them even madder to get at the French.'

'I should imagine they would follow you anywhere, ham or not,' Eva said, meaning it. Under his cheerful exterior the major looked like a man who would inspire loyalty and trust.

'Stop flirting,' Jack murmured in her ear. 'I do not want to be fighting duels over you in the middle of Allied lines.'

'Nonsense,' she murmured back. 'Flirting, indeed!'

They breasted the crest as she spoke and the teasing words dried on her lips. In front of them were the massed ranks of Allied troops, muddy, damp, many of them bandaged or weary looking. She could see individual faces as they rode past, read the suppressed fear, the determination, the sheer professional spirit of the men and her heart contracted. How many of them would walk away from this place by evening?

Their eyes followed as she rode past; one or two raised a hand, or called a greeting to the major. Eva was just about to ask him what troops he commanded when there was a sharp crackle of gunfire from the valley below. Dereham swung his horse round and stared down the way they had come.

'They're attacking Hougoumont at last. The Duke put some backbone into the troops in the wood when we were down there, I just hope they stand firm now.' He spurred his horse on, 'Let's get you a mount, ma'am—the sooner you're away from here, the better.'

In the event, when Jack saw the raw-boned, hard-mouthed troop horses that were all that were available, he slid off the gelding and gave her the reins. 'He's tired, but I know he's reliable. I'm not having you carted halfway to the French lines on this brute.' He swung up on to a massive grey and hauled its head round away from the lines. 'Come on, you lump, I'm doing you a favour today, taking you off to Brussels and a nice quiet stable.'

'God's speed.' Dereham touched his hat to Eva and stretched out a hand to Jack. 'Perhaps we'll meet at a party in Brussels tomorrow night. I deserve one—I missed the Duchess's ball, after all.'

'Ball?' Eva queried as they left him and wove their way through the last of the lines and into the baggage train.

'Duchess of Richmond, I'd guess,' Jack said. 'Brussels was *en fête* when I came through. The whole mob of diplomats and their wives had arrived from the Congress—picnics, parties, you name it. A ball on the eve of battle would be no surprise.'

Behind them there was the boom of artillery as the guns began to fire. Eva looked back over her shoulder, knowing she was taking a last look at history being made.

'Come on.' Jack kicked the reluctant troop horse into a canter. 'I want you well away from those shells.'

'Your Serene Highness, welcome.' A bowing butler, curtsying housekeeper, an expanse of polished marble flooring and a sweep of staircase. She was back. Back in the real world of status and duty and loneliness.

Eva smiled, stiffened her spine, said the right things and searched Jack's face for any expression whatsoever. She found none. A respectful half-dozen steps to her left, hat in hand, he waited while their host went through his ceremonious greeting.

'Would your Serene Highness care to go to her suite?' She dragged her attention back to what Mr Hatterick—no, Mr

Catterick—was saying. A wealthy banker, he was apparently part of the network of contacts, agents and safe houses that Jack and his masters maintained across the continent.

Just at the moment Mr Catterick was struggling to keep up the pretence that the Grand Duchess standing in his hallway was not dressed as a man and thoroughly grubby and dishevelled into the bargain. His question translated, she knew full well, into *Please go and make yourself respectable so I know what I am dealing with.*

'Thank you, Mr Catterick.' Eva produced her most gracious smile, then felt it turn into an involuntary grin as Henry emerged from the baize door at the back of the hall. 'Henry, you are all right! I was worried about you!'

'Yes, I'm safe and sound, thank you, ma'am, and all the better for seeing you and the guv'nor here. Did you know there's a battle going on out there?'

'Thank you, Henry,' Jack said repressively, the first words he had spoken since introducing her to their host. 'We had noticed. Are her Serene Highness's bags in her room?'

'Aye.' The groom's bushy eyebrows rose at the tone, but he took the hint and effaced himself into a corner.

'I will go up now,' Eva announced. The housekeeper hastened to her side and gestured towards the stairs. 'Thank you, Mrs—?'

'Greaves, your Serene Highness.'

'Ma'am will do nicely, Mrs Greaves. Have you been in Brussels long?' Eva maintained a flow of gracious small talk aimed at putting the nervous woman at ease. It carried them up to the bedchamber and she felt her shoulders relax as the turn of the stair took her out of Jack's sight. She could feel the brand of his eyes on her back as clearly as if he had pressed his hand there.

The room, an over-decorated chamber that was doubtless the best in the house, was a bustle of maids unpacking baggage and pouring water into the tub she could glimpse behind an ornate screen. Eva almost sent them all away, then stopped herself. She was a Grand Duchess, she must behave like one and try to put the dream that had been the last few days behind her.

Sipping hot chocolate while lying in a tub of hot water while twittering maidservants flitted about with piles of towels, soap, a back brush and enquiries about gowns and stockings made such a contrast to how she had spent the morning that it would have been easy to convince herself that she had been in a fever and had only just awakened.

'There only seems to be one suitable day gown, ma'am,' Mrs Greaves said dubiously from the other side of the screen. 'Most of your luggage must be missing.'

That gown was one she had bought in Grenoble with Jack; it was not, Eva thought defensively, anything to be ashamed of, however simple in cut and construction. She remembered him in the milliner's, his expression desperate as he tried to find the right words to answer her queries—the only time she had ever seen him at a disadvantage. Her eyes swam with moisture for a moment and she pressed a towel to them, pretending soap had made them teary.

'Indeed?' she said languidly. 'Never mind, that one will do for now, although I regret I will not be able to dress for dinner. I trust Mr Catterick will not be offended.' Mr Catterick, she was sure, would not be offended if she chose to turn up for dinner in masquerade costume, he was so thrilled at her presence.

Clean, dressed and refreshed by a cold collation, Eva drifted downstairs, maintaining an outward calm she was far from feeling. The sound of gunfire was constant, the scene in the street when she had looked from the window was chaotic, the servants were barely concealing their agitation at the closeness of the French, and out there, in country she could picture vividly, the men she had seen this morning, the officers who had been so pleasant, were fighting for their lives in mud, blood and smoke and a hellish din.

Bonaparte had won, so they said, at Quatre Bras. Was he going to triumph again here at Mont St Jean?

And where was Jack? The butler, materialising just as her feet reached the marble of the hall floor, informed her that Mr Catterick and Mr…er…Ryder were in the study, making preparations for her onward journey to England. Could he assist her Serene Highness with anything?

Mr…er…Ryder, indeed! 'Yes, thank you. I wish to consult an English *Peerage* if there is one in the house.'

'Certainly, ma'am. If you would care to step into the library, ma'am, I would beg to suggest you will be comfortable in here while I fetch the volume down.'

Eva sat at a velvet-draped table and waited until the red leather volume was laid before her. 'Thank you. That will be all.'

Ryder. *Rycroft…Riddle…Ribblesthorpe.* She made herself stop thumbing rapidly and began to work through carefully. There. Lord Charles Ryder, Earl of Felbrigge, deceased. Married… Children… Lady Amelia Ryder married his Grace, Francis Edgerton Ravenhurst, the third Duke of Allington. 'Hmm. Dukes might be considered to be top-lofty,' she mused out loud, recalling Henry's vivid description of Jack's father. But surely…

She searched again, this time for Allington. The current duke was Charles, definitely too old to be Jack, and *his* mother was not Lady Amelia and had died years ago. Ah, there it was, married the second time to Lady Amelia, the previous duke had fathered two more children. Sebastian John Ryder Ravenhurst and Belinda Ravenhurst, now Lady Cambourn.

Jack, she seemed to recall from her days in England, was a familiar form of John. So, Jack was, in fact, Lord… Eva frowned in concentration as she worked out the proper form of address for the younger son of an English duke. Ah, yes, first names. Lord Sebastian, and his wife, rather strangely she had always thought, would be Lady Sebastian.

Only of course he did not have a wife. And he was, by all accounts, at odds with his family. No, that was not quite right. He had spoken with somewhat wry affection of his numerous relatives. It was his father he appeared to have had the strained relationship with. That, and his own position as an English aristocrat.

He was not living this adventurer's life for lack of money, nor, from the way Wellington had spoken to him, because of any disgrace. He just seemed to enjoy it.

Her lover, she mused, was a lord. A duke's son. A very respectable position for a lover, in fact. Only she did not care tuppence whether he was a lord or a labourer, she just loved him. And he was no longer her lover. He might come to her tonight, if it could be done without risk of scandal, but it would not be the same. Out there, anonymous fugitives, they had been free, simply Eva and Jack, with only

Henry's sniff of disapproval to remind them of what the real world would say.

Now, when she thought of him, looked at him, she had to guard her expression every second. When she was close to him she must be constantly vigilant in case she reached to touch him. When they were alone they were in peril every moment of being spied upon or overheard. In constant danger of having something that was heartfelt and honest and beautiful turned in to a squalid scandal for the gossip columns to hint and snigger at.

Eva closed the heavy volume and stood up, weighing it in her hands. Then she took it over to the bookcase it belonged in, pulling over the library steps so she could reach the shelf. It slid back easily into its rightful place, but she stayed where she was, seized with inertia.

They had been travelling to such purpose; now they had stopped, if only for a while, and it all seemed strange and purposeless. She had no control, she was simply the queen on the chessboard being moved about by invisible players. Should she even be here now—or should she be in Maubourg? What if Philippe had succumbed to his illness, or Antoine had made his way back? Or perhaps there was no one there in control. She wanted to be with Freddie so much it hurt, but the anxiety over what was the right thing to do nagged painfully.

'What are you dreaming about?' Jack was so close beside her that she jumped and almost overbalanced on the steps. He reached up his hands, and, heedless of all her mental warnings to herself, she let him lift her down, sliding down the length of his body, aware that he was finding that contact as instantly arousing as she was.

'Those trousers are too snug for this sort of thing,' she remarked, letting her eyes linger on the very visible evidence as she stepped away. 'I was thinking about chess,' she added.

'Indeed. And you are quite right, I had best stay in here studying something dull while you remove yourself.' He seemed serious under the flash of humour, turning to study the rows of books.

'No…actually I was thinking that perhaps I should go back to Maubourg, now. What if Philippe has died? Or Antoine has got back there? What if King Louis discovers our troops came across the frontier and invades? The French would love an excuse.'

Jack turned slowly on his heel and regarded her. 'Are you saying you want to turn round now and go all that way back, into God knows what and with Bonaparte still on the loose?'

'I think perhaps I should.' Eva found she was twisting her hands together in her skirt and made herself stop.

'And your son?'

She shook her head, helplessly. 'I know what I want, to be with him, but is it *right?* How can I tell what my duty is?'

'To hell with your duty,' Jack said explosively. 'I do not know, and I do not care, about the Grand Duchy of Maubourg, but I do know what *my* duty is—and that is to get you back to England and reunite you with a small boy who needs his mother.'

'Do you think that isn't what I want?' she demanded. 'Do you think I want to meddle in politics rather than be with Freddie?'

'I don't know—do you?'

'No! Oh, for goodness' sake, can't you see I love my son more than anything? But Maubourg is his inheritance.'

'If he loses his mother, that is irretrievable. If something happens to the Duchy, then the Allies will sort it out.'

'Possibly they will—some time, when all the big, important things have been done. Or they'll find a good use for it and we'll be helpless.' Eva found she had marched down the room in a swirl of skirts and swung round, infuriated by Jack's lack of understanding. 'Jack, I think I should go back. I'll write to Freddie, let him know I will join him as soon as I can.'

She paused, catching her breath on a sob as she thought of Freddie reading such a note, expecting Jack to answer with a solution that would make it all right, but he was silent, watching her. As she glared he folded his arms, casually, as though waiting for her tantrum to blow itself out.

'Do not stand there like that!' Goaded, Eva jabbed one long finger at him. 'Say you'll take me back'

'And do not do that,' Jack retorted, unmoving. 'I am not your footman to be hectored. I will not take you back, and if you try to arrange it yourself I will take you back to England by force.' For the first time she saw the full power of his anger turned on her. It was not in his voice, or his tone—both were calm and polite—but it was in his eyes, hard flint that were sparking fire.

'Oh!' Exasperated, frightened by what she read in those eyes, Eva acted without conscious intent. The flat of her hand swung for his right cheek, even as she realised what she was doing and that Jack had not even troubled to move to avoid the blow. His hand came up with almost insulting ease and caught her wrist and they stared at each other, so close that the angry rise and fall of her breasts almost touched his shirt front.

Then both her wrists were held tight, she was pulled against his chest, and, as he had in that field above Hougoumont, he punished her with a kiss. But then, as she had known full well at the time, it was a reaction to his fear for her safety, a plea to her to obey and stay safe. This, she realised with the part of her mind that was still capable of rational thought, was pure temper and her own rose to meet it.

Her fingers flexed into claws in his grip, her body arched against his, struggling to be free, yet wantonly provoking his reaction. Her lips opened under the assault of his and his tongue claimed her, thrusting arrogantly in a quite blatant demonstration of intent. Everything in her responded, love and fury and anxiety mingling into molten heat that pooled in her belly, driving her almost wild with desire.

Eva jerked both wrists down, surprising Jack just enough to free herself, then she had fastened her arms around his neck and was kissing him back with all the passion she was capable of, her body burning against his, her hips urging her tight into the hard, aroused masculinity she craved. She rocked, rubbing herself against him in blatant invitation until she was rewarded by the sound of his growl, low in his throat.

Somehow he had pushed her against the bookshelves; hard leather spines pressed into her shoulders and buttocks as his knee worked between her thighs, opening her as flagrantly as if she was wearing not a stitch. And still, neither could break the kiss, the furious, all-devouring, heated exchange that threatened to topple her into utter abandon.

What would have happened if there had not been the knock on the door Eva had no idea. Possibly they would have stripped each other naked and made angry, brazen, heated love on the library's rich Turkey carpet.

She wrenched herself away, her hands flying to her hair, her décolletage, her skirts. 'Get out,' she hissed. 'Just get out!' Without a second glance at Jack she ran across to the pair of globes which stood by the desk, turned her back on the door and called, 'Come in!'

'Ma'am, Mr Catterick wondered if you would care to join him for tea?' It was the butler. Eva looked back over her shoulder. Jack was apparently engrossed in a vast folio of maps on a stand that effectively hid whatever state of dishevelment he was in.

'Certainly. Please tell Mr Catterick I will join him in a few moments.'

'Ma'am. And Mr Ryder?'

'I am going out, I have arrangements to make,' Jack said curtly. 'I will be back for dinner.' He looked directly at Eva. 'Henry will remain here.' It was a warning not to try to leave.

'Certainly, sir.' The butler bowed himself out. Eva stepped across to the over-mantel mirror and surveyed her flushed face and wide eyes. At least the day was becoming uncomfortably hot, that at least might be taken as some excuse.

Grand Duchesses, she reminded herself desperately, do not plump down in the middle of the floor in the library and burst into tears of frustration, they get themselves under control and make small talk over the teacups. She gathered her skirts and swept out without so much as glance towards the atlases. She had foreseen this *affaire* ending in heartbreak—she had not expected it to fizzle out amidst bad temper and macaroons in a Brussels merchant's house.

Chapter Eighteen

Eva could not recall shedding a tear since the day Louis bore Freddie off to school in England, leaving her frantically weeping in the schoolroom, his slate clutched in her hands. Weeping was undisciplined, an unseemly weakness she had learned to do without.

Now, in her bed, the maids finally departed, a single candle on the nightstand, she leaned her head back on the pillows and let the tears trickle down her cheeks. From the street came the hubbub of laughter and shouts and cheering. The news had been coming in since about half past eight that the French were beaten. The early rumours became hard fact, as more and more messengers arrived. The Prussians were pressing hard from the east, the Foot Guards were advancing and then the French were in full retreat, the Old Guard alone standing firm to the last to allow the Emperor to escape the field.

Dinner had become a celebration of toasts, of speculation, of vast relief. She tried to tell herself Maubourg would be safe now, whatever fate had befallen her brothers-in-law. Someone was going to have to explain to King Louis XVIII why his neutral neighbour had invaded with a small troop of men, but at least the monarch had more pressing things on his mind just now.

And throughout the meal Jack had been distant, correct, formal. It was exactly how he should have been of course, and she thought her heart was breaking. Would he have been like this anyway, once they reached Brussels, or had her attack of nerves and indecision, her demands, alienated him?

She scrubbed at her cheeks, angry at herself for being so weak. There was so much to be happy about. Jack had at least taken the choice away from her, she must do what she wanted so passionately to do. In a few days she would see Freddie, hold her son in her arms. She could get news of the Duchy, hopefully of Philippe's recovery, Europe was saved from more years of war…and all she could think about was Jack's face, the feel of his mouth, hot and angry on hers, the knowledge that something magical had gone for ever.

The clocks began to strike, past one. The noise in the streets was dying down, or perhaps people were moving to the Grand Place to celebrate. Wearily Eva blew out the candle and closed her eyes. Tomorrow they would be travelling again; she had to get some sleep.

She opened her eyes on to pitch darkness, to chill, musty air, to a sense that the walls were closing in around her. Then she knew where she was: in the tomb, in the vaults. The terror coursed through her; she threw up her hands, desperately pushing against the unyielding stone. It did not move one inch.

Defeated, quivering with fear, she fell back, feeling the grave clothes shifting around her, her unbound hair slipping about her shoulders. Into the silence, broken only by her rasping breath, came the sound of the stone gritting above her. Louis. Louis had come for her. Somewhere, glinting in the black fog of panic, she glimpsed another thought and grasped it. Jack. Not Louis, Jack. He had said it would be him who would come, he had promised to rescue her. The stone lid slid further, she saw fingers gripping it as light flooded in.

'Jack!' He smiled down at her, reassurance, strength. 'You came.'

Without speaking, he reached in and lifted her against his chest and she buried her face in his shoulder so as not to see as he carried her back through the vaults, past the tombs, out to the stairs and the air and freedom. With a sigh Eva closed her eyes against the white linen of his shirt and let herself drift into peace.

When she opened her eyes again there was a candle burning on the night stand, her cheek was pressed to damp white linen and she was held against a warm, male body. 'Jack?' Disorientated, Eva twisted so she could look up at him. 'I was sleeping—dreaming. I had that nightmare, but you came into it, just as you promised. But that was a dream.' What was he doing here? He was angry with her, yet here he was, cradling her in his arms.

Jack looked down into the sleep-soft eyes and felt a wave of tenderness swamp every other confused emotion he had brought with him into her bedchamber. When he had curled up on the bed next to her he had kissed her cheek and tasted salt. He had made her cry.

He loved her, nothing could change that; he feared nothing

ever would. There was a puzzled furrow between her brows and he bent his head to kiss it away. 'Don't frown. I came to say sorry. You were asleep, so I stayed.'

'But…'

'Your reputation is quite safe. Everyone thinks we are being somewhat over-protective of you, given that the battle has been won, but Henry is asleep in an armchair on the landing and I, as you will have realised, am sitting in your dressing room with a shotgun.'

That made Eva laugh, as he hoped it would. 'That was not what I meant.' She wriggled out of his arms and sat up, half-turned so she could watch him. 'I should apologise, not you; I was foolish to waver now, when I had agreed to go to England, and I did not mean to try to make you go against your orders. To *hector* you.' Jack grimaced. Was that what he had said to her?

'You weren't. I was angry and I overreacted.' How to explain, when he hardly understood the violence of his reaction himself? This was probably all to do with falling in love, against all sense and reason. No wonder he did not understand himself any more. Eva was waiting; that damned furrow was back again, making him feel guilty for upsetting her. Hell, he *never* felt guilty!

'The thought of you in danger makes me afraid,' he admitted at last. 'I am not used to being afraid, it makes me irritable.'

She wrinkled her nose in what he could see was an effort not to laugh at him. 'Irritable? Is that what you call it?' Those frank brown eyes were looking so deep inside him he was afraid she could see his love for her written there. 'Are you truly never afraid? Isn't that rather dangerous?'

'Yes. I am. Of course I am, often. I meant afraid for someone else, afraid and not able to do anything about it.'

'Oh, I see.' Her face lit up. 'You mean, like I am afraid for Freddie? I try and be brave for myself, but even if it is irrational, I worry so about him. But…he is my son. I love him.' That little furrow of puzzlement was back as she looked at him, her head tipped slightly to one side

It was almost a question. Almost *the* question. He could answer it truthfully, and have her turn away, embarrassed by such an inappropriate declaration, or he could think damn fast, and learn not to get into intimate conversations about feelings in the small hours.

'I get like that about clients,' Jack said lightly. 'Very protective.'

'Oh.' The puzzlement had gone, replaced by a slight haughtiness. 'And you become the lover of many of them?'

'Only the women.' He tried to make a joke of it.

'*What?*' she demanded, bristling.

'One or two,' Jack admitted, knowing he was burning his boats. But this liaison, which was all it could ever be for her, had to end soon and it was best a line was drawn under it.

'I see. You mean, I am the latest in a long line?'

'Eva, I never pretended to be a virgin,' Jack began, feeling the conversation slipping wildly out of control. Then she buried her face in her hands and her shoulders began to quiver and it was as though he could feel the salt of her tears in his mouth all over again. 'Hell! Eva, sweet, don't cry. I didn't mean that. There isn't a long line, just a… Damn it, I'm not a saint.'

The quivering got worse, then she looked up, her eyes brimming with tears. Of laughter. 'Pretending to be a virgin?'

she gurgled. 'You know, Jack, I don't think you would have deceived me for a moment.' She rubbed the sleeve of her nightgown over her eyes. 'Don't worry, I am not such a hypocrite that I expected you to have been saving yourself for me. In fact,' she added, a decidedly wicked twinkle in her eyes, 'I'm glad you didn't.'

Jack reached for her. 'Get back under the covers and go to sleep. It is late and tomorrow we are going to Ostend. I want you on a ship before half the English army decides to head home.'

'Won't you stay?' Something of his feelings must have shown, for she added hastily, 'I mean just sleep.'

'While you drop off, then,' he said, resigning himself to the bittersweet pain of having her so close, perhaps for the last time.

'That's what I used to say to Freddie,' she murmured, wriggling down between the sheets, then turning on her side so she could wrap an arm across his chest.

'I'm not singing you a lullaby.'

'No?' She sounded almost asleep already.

'No.' Jack settled her more comfortably against his chest and lay back. He had never understood the need women seemed to have for cuddling, until now. You made love and then you slept, he had thought. But now, as always with Eva relaxed in his embrace, he felt a calm soaking into his bones, despite the lurking knowledge that he might never experience this again. This was love, damn it. Love.

'Is this the road to Eton?' Eva demanded, trying to read signposts as the post chaise bounded up the road from the coast.

'No. London.'

'But I don't want to go to London, I want to go to Eton to

see Freddie.' She twisted round on the plush upholstery to glare at Jack indignantly. 'You know I do.'

'And my instructions are to take you to London.' Eva opened her mouth to protest, but Jack shook his head before she could get the words out. 'We have a charming house for you in the heart of fashionable London. I am taking you there, then I will check with the Foreign Office and, if you still want to, we will go to Eton tomorrow, after you are rested.'

'But I don't want to rest! I've tossed about on that wretched boat for twenty-four hours—without getting seasick—and now I shall be stuck in this bounding carriage for hours. Compared to days in the saddle and sleeping under the stars, I am perfectly rested.'

And no lovemaking to make her feel languid and lazily inclined to do nothing but curl up in Jack's arms until one or other of them began those irresistible caresses that ended, inevitably, in ecstasy and exhaustion. She ached for him, but ever since they had set foot on the sloop he had waiting at Ostend, Jack had behaved with total circumspection.

It made her restless and impatient now, and, when she let herself brood, miserable for the future. The thought of seeing Freddie had been buoying her up; now that treat had been snatched away and she knew she was reacting like a child told to wait until tomorrow for her sweetmeats. Well, she was not going to stand for it…

'Don't even think about it.' The corner of Jack's mouth twitched, betraying his awareness of her rebellious thoughts.

'What?'

'Getting on your high horse and ordering me to take you to Eton, your Serene Highness.'

'Surely you are not frightened of a lot of Whitehall clerks, are you?' She opened her eyes wide and was rewarded by his grin at her tactics. Wheedling was not going to do it.

'I thought you understood the concept of duty,' Jack said mildly.

'I do. But would it matter so much if I were one day late arriving in London?'

'Yes.' Jack produced a travelling chess set. 'This will wile away the time.'

'No, thank you, I have no desire to play chess. Please? Take me to my son, Lord Sebastian.' That got his attention. Jack placed the box deliberately on the seat next to him and leaned back into the corner of the chaise.

'So that was what you were doing up a ladder in Mr Catterick's library.' Eva nodded. 'I do not use my title when I am working.'

'Why not?'

'Because it makes me more of a target, less invisible. I am two different people, Eva. You have not met Lord Sebastian Ravenhurst, and I doubt you will.'

'Why not?' she demanded again, kicking off her shoes impatiently and curling up on the seat facing him.

'Lord Sebastian is a rake and a gamester and does not mix in the sort of society that grand duchesses, even on unofficial visits, frequent.'

'Is that why you fell out with your father?' That would explain it, an estrangement between the duke and his wild-living son.

'Actually, no. My father rebuffed my efforts to be a dutiful younger son, learn about the estate, make myself useful in that way. He supplied me with money beyond the most extravagant demands I might make and sent me off to London to become, in his words, *a rakehell and a libertine.*'

'But why? I do not understand.' Jack's face was shuttered. Eva leaned across the space that separated them and put her hand on his knee. 'Tell me, I would like to understand.'

'I think because he was disappointed in Charles, my elder brother, and he did not want to admit it. I am very like my father, probably very like what he expected Charles to be. But Charles was—is—quiet, reclusive, gentle. My father maintained he was perfect in every way and dismissed me so he would not see the contrast proving him wrong at every turn.

'By the time I was ten—and my brother twenty—I was careering round the estate on horseback, ignoring falls and broken bones. I was pestering him to teach me to fence, to shoot. Charles was stuck in his study, reading poetry. By the time I was sixteen I was in trouble with all the local light-heeled girls, Charles had to be dragged to balls and virtually forced to converse with a woman. And so it went on. Eventually the contrast was too extreme, but my father's sense of duty to the family name, the importance of primogeniture, was too strong. He could not admit he loved me more, so he had to pretend the opposite. I had to go.'

'How awful,' Eva said compassionately. What a mess people got themselves into with their expectations and their pressures. Why could they not accept each other for what they were? 'Did you miss your family and your home very much?'

Jack shrugged. 'I was eighteen, the age when you want to get out and kick your heels up. He didn't show me the door, I still came home, saw Charles, my mother, Bel, my sister. But for a few days, every now and again. And my father got the constant comfort of people comparing his sober, quiet, dignified elder son with the wild younger one.'

'Then why aren't you drunk in some gaming hell now?' she asked tartly, to cover up the fact that she felt so sad about the young man he was describing. In nine years Freddie would be that age.

'Nothing was expected of me,' Jack went on, gazing out of the window as though he were looking back ten years at his younger self. 'Nothing except to spend money and to decorate society events. I did my best. I can spend money quite effectively, I scrub up quite well, I can do the pretty at parties— but I was bored. Then I found myself helping a friend whose former valet was blackmailing him over indiscreet love letters. One thing led to another and I found that I liked Jack Ryder far more than I did Lord Sebastian Ravenhurst.'

'Aren't they now the same person, just with two different names?' Eva asked. 'Hasn't Lord Sebastian grown up with Jack Ryder?'

'Perhaps.' He shifted back from the window to regard her from under level brows. 'It makes no difference to you and me. The Grand Duchess Eva de Maubourg does not have an *affaire* with a younger son any more than she does with a King's Messenger.'

'That was not why I wanted to know.' *Oh, yes, it was, you liar. It was curiosity, certainly, but something was telling you that this man was an aristocrat and that would make it all right.* 'It was curiosity, pure and simple. I dislike secrets and mysteries.' She said it lightly, willing him to believe her.

The way the shadow behind his eyes lifted both relieved

her and hurt her. He did not want their *affaire* to continue. Why not? She thought he would be as sad as she at its ending. But then, by his own admission, he was a rake. Loving and leaving must be as familiar as the chase and the seduction. Only he had neither chased nor seduced her, when he very well could have done.

'What do I call you, now we are back in England?' she asked. 'Mr Ryder, or Lord Sebastian?'

'I am Jack Ryder. As I said, you will not meet my *alter ego*.'

'You are not invited to the best parties?'

'Duke's sons are invited everywhere, even if fond mamas warn their sons against playing cards with them or their daughters against flirting. I do not chose to accept, it is as simple as that.' He looked out of the window again. 'And here is Greenwich. Another hour and you will be almost at your London house.'

Eva sighed. Even if she could persuade him, it was too late to set out to Eton now—there was the whole of London to traverse before she could be on the road to Windsor.

'Don't sigh—it is a very nice house.'

'How do you know?' Eva sat up straight and found her shoes. Time to start thinking and behaving like the representative of the Duchy in a foreign country, not an anxious mother or a sore-hearted lover.

'I chose it.'

'Really? You were very busy before you left.'

'I mean, I had bought it, for myself. I was finding my chambers in Albany a touch small these days. But I am in no hurry to move in. The staff are all highly trustworthy, employed by the Foreign Office for just such eventualities.'

'So you have never lived there?'

'No.'

That, at least, was a mercy. The thought of living in the midst of Jack's furnishings, the evidence of his taste, of his everyday life, was disturbing. Eva set herself to talk of trivia, of London gossip, and the last hour of the journey passed pleasantly enough. It was as though, she thought fancifully, they were skating serenely on a frozen sea, while beneath them, just visible through the ice, swam sharks.

'Here we are.' Jack opened the chaise door and jumped down, flipping out the steps for her before the postilions could dismount. She lay her hand on his proffered arm and walked up to the front door, gleaming dark green in the late afternoon sunshine. Jack lifted his hand to the heavy brass knocker, but the door swung open before he could let it fall.

'Your Serene Highness, welcome.' An imposing butler, with, she was startled to see, the face of a prize fighter, ushered them into the hall, then stood aside.

Facing her across the black-and-white chequers was a boy, sturdy, long-legged, with a mop of unruly dark hair. Hazel eyes met hers and for a moment she was frozen, unable to believe what she was seeing. Then Eva flew across the hall and fell to her knees, her arms tight around her son. 'Oh, Freddie, you're here!'

Chapter Nineteen

'Mama!' The pressure of his arms around her almost took her breath away. This was not the little boy she had last seen— he was so grown she could glimpse the young man he would become. And they would not be separated like that again, never, that she vowed. Disentangling herself with an effort, Eva sat back on her heels and stared happily at her son.

'You've grown,' she managed to say. 'How you have grown!'

'Well, the food's pretty grim,' he confided, startling her with his perfect English accent. 'But I stock up in the shops in the High—Uncle Bruin keeps me well supplied with the readies, you know.' He stared at her, his eyes solemn. 'You look just as I remember, Mama.'

'Good,' Eva said, fighting to keep the shake out of her voice. 'You have been very good at answering all my letters.'

'I missed you.' He was biting his lower lip, the desperate need to maintain his grown-up dignity fighting with the urge to hug his mother and never let her go. 'Are you going away again soon?'

'We are both going back to Maubourg together, just as soon as the situation in France is calm and we can travel safely.' She hesitated. 'You know Uncle Philippe has been ill?' He nodded. 'I don't know if he is better yet, or worse. And I am afraid that Uncle Antoine might have been…hurt in all the confusion with Bonaparte invading.'

Too much information. She was pouring it out, kneeling here on the hard floor, her hands tight around his upper arms, terrified of letting him go in case he proved to be a dream after all.

Awkwardly Eva made herself loosen her grip and tried to stand. Her legs felt shaky. Two hands reached for her and she placed her own, one in each. 'Thank you, Freddie, Ja…Mr Ryder.' For a long moment they stood there, linked. Like a family group, she thought wildly, releasing Jack's hand as though it were hot. Then Freddie let go, as well, and held out his hand to Jack.

'Mr Ryder. Welcome back. Thank you for looking after my mama.'

Jack shook hands solemnly. 'Your Serene Highness. It was a pleasure. I am glad to see you so well. You were a trifle green when we last met.'

'Mushrooms, Mama,' Freddie explained.

'I know. Mr Ryder kindly told me all the horrid details.'

Her son chuckled. 'I was very sick. Did you know this is Mr Ryder's house?'

'Yes. It is very kind of him to lend it to us.' She looked around. The pugilistic butler was still standing, statue-like, in the corner. A pair of equally large footmen were at attention at the foot of the stairs and a small covey of female domestics were gathered behind them. 'Have you been here long?'

'Long enough to know everyone; I arrived yesterday morning,' Freddie said importantly. 'This is Grimstone, our butler.' *It suits him,* Eva thought. 'And Wellings and O'Toole, the footmen. And Mrs Cutler is a spiffingly good cook. And Fettersham is your dresser.'

A tall woman dressed in impeccable black came forward and curtsied. 'Shall I show you to your room, your Serene Highness?'

'Ma'am will do nicely,' Eva said automatically. 'Yes, I will just take off my bonnet and mantle and I'll be right back down, Freddie. Then we'll have tea.' *And talk and talk and talk...* 'You will look after Mr Ryder, won't you?'

She almost tripped over the stairs because she keep looking back to make sure he was still there, her son. Just as the turn of the stairs took them out of sight, she saw Freddie slip a hand into Jack's and tug him towards what she assumed must be the salon. They looked so right together, the tall, lean man and the eager boy.

'Are you quite well, ma'am?' Her new dresser was regarding her anxiously. 'You went quite pale a moment ago.'

'Quite well, thank you, Fettersham. It was a wearing journey.'

In the event it took her longer to return downstairs than she had intended. Her gown proved sadly salt-stained, her hair was tangled, Fettersham found it hard to locate a full change of linen in her limited baggage and a mix-up in the scullery resulted in cold water being sent up, not hot.

Half an hour later, leaving a wrathful dresser descending upon the kitchen quarters to complain, Eva went downstairs to find Freddie sitting alone on one side of a tea table laden with cakes and biscuits, which he was eyeing greedily. He stood up punctiliously.

'I am ready for the tea now, thank you, Grimstone.' The butler bowed himself off. 'Where is Mr Ryder?' Eva sat down opposite her son.

'Gone. May I have a scone, Mama?' She nodded absently, shifting slightly to give the footmen room to deposit the teapot and cream jug on the table beside her.

'Gone where? Thank you, that will be all.' She did not want to discuss Jack in front of the domestic staff.

'I don't know, Mama. Oh, and he said would I please make his excuses to you, and…' Freddie frowned in concentration '…he said I must take care to get this right—he said to say goodbye, and that it was better that he went now, as his job was done and he did not want to make complications. And that you were to remember him if you ever have a bad dream.' A mammoth mouthful of scone vanished and Freddie chewed valiantly. 'Mama, do you think that means he isn't coming back at all? I didn't think anything of it at the time, but—'

'Don't talk with your mouth full,' Eva said automatically. 'Yes. I think that means Mr Ryder is not coming back.' He had walked away, without a word, without a kiss. There was just the memory of the pressure of his hand when the three of them had stood together in the hall and the knowledge that she would love him and miss him and want him for the rest of her days.

'That's a pity.' Freddie picked up a slice of cake, looked at it and put it down. When his eyes met Eva's, they glistened with a shimmer of tears. 'I like him. I'll miss him.'

'You hardly know him,' Eva said bracingly. What was upsetting Freddie so much?

'Yes, I do. He came to see me three times at Eton, and we had long talks. He wanted to know all about the castle and my uncles and you. I said I didn't remember very much, but he said I was intelligent, so if I put my mind to it, I would recall lots— and I did. It was really exciting. He said I was briefing him for his mission, and he would send me coded dispatches, and he did.'

'He did? How?' And why hadn't Jack told her so she could have sent messages, too?

'They went through his agents to the Foreign Office. And when the first one arrived, they sent Grimstone with it to stay with me. *They* said he was just a butler, but I think he's a body-guard, don't you, Mama? Because the first message from Mr Ryder said there was danger and I had to take great care and Grimstone started going everywhere with me. I got ragged a bit, but then the chaps shut up, because Grimstone showed everyone how to box.'

'How dare he worry you like that?' Eva banged down the teapot, disregarding the splash of hot liquid from the spout. 'And if I'd known he was writing to you, I would have sent a message.'

'Mr Ryder said the messages had to be short and you wouldn't like me to be worried, so you'd fuss. But Mr Ryder said I was old enough to understand and start taking care of myself. Are you *growling,* Mama?'

'Yes, I am!'

'But he was right, wasn't he? Things *were* dangerous. I don't expect Uncle Bruin's really just ill, I expect someone's tried to poison him, like they did me with those mushrooms.'

'Freddie!'

'It's Uncle Rat, isn't it? He's a Bonapartist.' Freddie's clear hazel eyes regarded her solemnly over yet another piece of cake.

'Yes. Freddie, I wasn't going to tell you all this, all at once. But I'm afraid Antoine has been very...foolish. He may be...hurt.'

'Mr Ryder said he was trying to develop rockets for the Emperor, and he was trying to kill both of us and he took Maubourg troops into France—so I expect I'm going to have to write to King Louis and say sorry, aren't I?—and he may have been killed, but we can't be certain.'

Eva picked up her cup with a hand that shook and took a gulp of tea. It did not help much. 'When did he tell you all this?'

'Just now, before he left. He said it's called a de-brief and he had to tell me because you probably wouldn't, because of mothers worrying. May I have a macaroon?'

'You'll make yourself sick,' Eva said distractedly.

'And he said you were a heroine, and found out about the rockets and helped him raid the factory, and fought off Uncle Rat's agents and probably saved his life.' The macaroon vanished and Freddie sank back with a happy sigh of repletion. 'And he said I wasn't to worry if you seemed a bit upset about things, because you had had a very difficult time, and finding I was all right would actually make you more upset, because that's the way shock and relief work.'

'Did he?' Eva took a macaroon and ate it rather desperately. Sugar was supposed to be good for shock, was it not?

'I like him a lot,' Freddie said again. 'And I think he likes me. And I thought perhaps, when I saw him looking at you, that he likes you, too. And now he has gone away.' He scuffed a toe in the Aubusson carpet. 'He's just the sort of person a chap would like for a friend, don't you think?'

'Yes. He would be a very good friend,' Eva agreed, filling up her son's teacup. Jack appeared to have handled breaking the news of all this to Freddie much better than she would have. She was angry with him, of course she was…but it was all part of the role he had assumed when he undertook to bring her back to England. *Do as I say, when I say it.* When Jack was with her, she knew he would look after her. Totally.

She would have resisted him telling Freddie about the danger, but her son was so much more grown up and perceptive than she had realised. He would have spotted the new bodyguard for what he was, and, in the absence of information, would have worried. Jack had involved him in the adventure, treated him like an intelligent young man so it became understandable and exciting. *What a wonderful father he would make for Freddie.*

'Mama! You are spilling your tea.'

'So I am.' Eva put down her cup, and dabbed at her skirt. A father for Freddie. *I am thinking of marrying him,* she realised. *And that's impossible, of course, Dowager Grand Duchesses do not marry King's Messengers. Only he's a duke's son…*

'What are you thinking about, Mama?'

'I am having a very silly daydream about something that cannot possibly happen,' Eva said briskly. 'Now, let's go and sit down, kick off our shoes, and we can talk until we are hoarse.'

It took three days before the invitations began to arrive. Three days during which Eva and Freddie did indeed talk themselves hoarse, she shopped exhaustively for a new wardrobe and they explored the house until it became like a second home and the staff familiar faces.

It was not just Grimstone who was a bodyguard, she soon realised. The pair of large footmen were never far from the door of any room she and her son were in. They stuck to her like burrs whenever she went outside the house, politely refusing to wait in the carriage whenever she entered a shop. Eventually she tackled the butler. 'We are here and safe, Grimstone. Surely there is no risk now? Prince A… The source of danger may not even be alive.'

'But his agents will be, ma'am,' the butler pointed out in his gravelly voice. 'This has just come for you from the guv'nor, ma'am.'

'Mr Ryder?' Eva snatched the letter off the silver salver before she could school herself into an appearance of indifference. She broke the seal and read the three lines it contained. The handwriting was black, sprawling, undisciplined, a complete contrast to Jack's methods of operation. Or was this Lord Sebastian writing? she wondered.

The absent troops returned home with the body of A. It has a bullet wound in the back. From very close range. P. improves daily. Show this to Grimstone and assume A.'s agents are still at large and may not yet know of his death. It was signed with a J., a slashing flourish across the bottom of the page.

Wordlessly Eva handed the letter to the butler, who read it through with pursed lips, then gave it back. 'Own men shot him by all accounts,' he commented. 'Didn't like being made traitors of, especially in view of what happened. P. will be the Regent, ma'am?'

'Yes, my brother-in-law, Prince Philippe.' Eva folded the paper and slipped it into her reticule. It was the only thing of Jack's she had. 'I will go and tell Master Freddie the good news.'

Master Freddie, as the entire staff called him, was in his favourite place, the kitchen, charming sweetmeats out of Cook. Eva tried to imagine him back in the castle. It was not hard—within the week he would have even the tyrant of the kitchens his devoted servant, the footmen would all be polishing armour for him to play with and he would no doubt be attempting to introduce cricket to the bemused inhabitants.

'Freddie, good news from Maubourg. Uncle Philippe is on the mend.'

'Can we go back soon, then?' He scrambled off the table, eyes wide, mouth ringed with raspberry jam.

'As soon as the Foreign Office tells me it is safe to travel. Shall we go and write to Uncle?'

She followed that letter up with one to the Foreign Office, asking about travel and received, not a response on that subject, but the first, and most imposing, of a flood of invitations. The Prince Regent, Freddie's godfather, begged the honour of her company at a reception in her honour at Carlton House in two days' time.

'Oh, Lord,' she lamented to Fettersham. 'I suppose that means feathers?'

'Yes, ma'am.' The dresser was agog with the thought of court dress. 'Hoops are no longer worn, though,' she added with a tinge of disappointment. 'The full-dress *ensemble* you ordered yesterday will be most appropriate.'

'Well, thank goodness for that. It is difficult enough walking about with those wretched feathers in one's coiffure without worrying about hoops flattening every small table in sight every time one moves!'

The gown arrived from the modiste on the morning of the reception along with the hastily purchased set of ostrich plumes. 'My goodness, waistlines are up,' Eva complained as Fettersham fastened the gown. 'There is very little room for my bosom in this!'

'I think that's the point, ma'am,' the dresser observed, tweaking the narrow shoulders so they sat securely. 'It's a very good thing you have such excellent shoulders, ma'am, otherwise I don't know how this style is expected to stay decent.'

They regarded the effect in the long mirror. The gown, in palest almond green, fell from under Eva's bosom to exactly the ankle bone. She was not convinced about the decency of showing so much ankle, either, although she was prepared to admit the fuller skirts were charming. The hem was banded with satin ribbon, of exactly the same shade, the texture making it show up subtly against the silk, and the whole lower half of the skirt was heavily embroidered in wreaths of flowers. The pattern was repeated on the puffed sleeves and the deep vee of the neckline was dressed in lace, which went some way to preserving the decencies.

'Very striking, ma'am,' Fettersham pronounced.

'Very dashing,' Eva amended. 'I do not recall it seeming so at the fitting!'

Long kid gloves with lace at the top to match the bodice, simple slippers, a gauze scarf at the elbows and the nodding weight of the feathers completed the ensemble. It was certainly striking enough for the occasion, Eva decided, wondering wistfully what Jack would make of it. She was managing very well, she congratulated herself. She thought of him only a dozen times an hour during the day. It was the nights that were so hard, when all she could do was toss and turn, aching for the sound of his voice, the caress of his hands, the heat of his mouth.

Fettersham produced the diamond eardrops, necklace and cuffs borrowed from Rundell and Bridges, the jewellers who had proved only too willing to oblige the Grand Duchess, in return for her tacit agreement to them making as much capital out of the fact as they wished.

'Mama?' It was Freddie, knocking at the door. 'May I see?'

'Wow!' he said as the dresser let him in. 'How do you dance in those feathers, Mama?'

'I do not have to,' she explained, stooping to kiss him. She was loving rediscovering her son, getting to know him again, not as the little boy she had left, but this new, much more independent and lively nine-year-old. 'Now, you will be good and go to bed when Hoffmeister tells you?'

'Yes, Mama.' She gave him high marks for refraining from rolling his eyes. The arrival of his private secretary-cum-tutor from the Eton lodgings had restarted the rivalry between the German and the butler. Freddie played one off against the other with what Eva tried to tell herself was precocious statesmanship, but she had to uphold Hoffmeister's authority when it came to bedtime and study periods.

Carlton House was just as she had seen in pictures, and even more stiflingly hot, crowded and elaborately ornate than she could ever have imagined. The Regent was gracious, over-familiar to the point of discomfort and determined she would enjoy herself. He insisted on escorting Eva around the crowded reception rooms, introducing her to one person after another until her head spun. She searched the rooms as they went, but there were no tall, elegant, dangerous men with grey eyes and a wicked smile.

'I am quite out of practice with this sort of thing,' she confessed to Lord Alveney. 'My brother-in-law Prince Philippe has been unwell for several months, so our court has been extremely quiet. Please, sir…' she turned and smiled prettily at the Regent '…I beg you not to neglect your other guests for me, I have so much enjoyed seeing these wonderful rooms in your company, but I can see I will be very unpopular if I monopolise you.'

The Regent beamed, blustered a little, then took himself off with a pat on her arm and a promise to show her the Conservatory later.

'Nicely done, ma'am,' Alveney said with a lazy smile. Eva was spared from replying to this sally by the arrival of a tall young woman who bumped into her and knocked her feathers all askew.

'Oh, my goodness!' I am so sorry! And you are the Grand Duchess and I haven't even been presented to you and I do this! Oh, dear! Oh, look, there is a retiring room, please, your Serene Highness, if we just go in there I am sure they can be pinned back…'

Eva sent Alveney an apologetic smile and allowed herself to be swept off into the retiring room, which was empty save for a maidservant with a sewing basket, smelling salts and a bottle of cordial. *Every eventuality covered.* Eva was thinking with amusement when the young woman snapped, 'Out, now,' to the maid. The key turned in the lock and the stranger was standing with her back to the door, eyeing Eva with angry grey eyes.

Antoine's agent? Here, in the Regent's own house? Eva edged towards the dressing table, hoping to find scissors or a long nail file. 'What do you want?' She spoke calmly, as though to someone mentally disturbed. The words she had spoken the last time she had been in this predicament—*So, you have not come to kill me?*—did not seem appropriate now. This young woman looked as if she intended to do just that, for all her lack of an obvious weapon, and asking the question seemed likely to inflame her further.

But even if her defiant words to Jack when he had appeared like magic in her room were not the ones to use now, she could not help but feel a strong sense of *déjà vu*. Why? Because she was cornered and in fear for her life? Or because…

Eva stared at the other woman. She was like a feminine, younger version of Jack. The tall, elegant figure, the dark hair, the clear, intelligent grey eyes with their flecks of black. She found her voice.

'What do you want?'

'I want to know what you are doing to my brother—and I want you to stop it. Now.'

Chapter Twenty

'Your brother? You are Jack's sister?'

'Sebastian.' The flurried and apologetic young woman was gone, replaced by a determined, poised and angry one.

'I know him as Jack.'

'Oh, it is the same thing! I don't care how you—'

'It is not the same thing,' Eva said firmly. 'And I am doing nothing to your brother, and have done nothing to justify your behaviour now.'

'You have broken his heart,' the other retorted.

'Nonsense! Why, that is complete nonsense. Your brother left my house without a word to me a week ago. There had been no disagreement, I had not dismissed him. Broken heart, indeed, what melodrama. If Jack Ryder has anything to say to me, he knows where I am.' *Broken heart? I know whose heart is broken—but I did not leave him.*

'You were lovers.' It was a flat statement. 'No, do not bother to deny it. He has said nothing about you, all I knew was that he had been in France, on a mission. Then when he came to see me, he had changed—something inside was hurt.'

Eva discovered that her head was beginning to ache, and so were her feet in their new slippers. 'Oh, sit down, please, for goodness' sake. What is your name?'

'Belinda. Lady Belinda Cambourn. I am a widow.' Eva nodded—Jack had mentioned Bel. 'I shouldn't be here, am still in mourning. But I love my brother very much, and I know him very well. And he is hurting. Deeply.'

'But—'

Bel waved a hand, silencing her. 'No one else would be able to tell, except possibly you.' She shot Eva a look of positive dislike. 'When he is on missions—when he is Jack—he is cool and calm and quiet, but there is still that wicked enjoyment of life behind those eyes of his. When he is Sebastian, he is the warmest, kindest brother you can imagine.' Bel directed another withering look at Eva. 'But now something has gone—the laughter has gone, the warmth inside has gone. He came to see me; he was very sweet, just as he always is. I asked him what was wrong and he laughed and said nothing, just a tiring mission in France.'

'There you are, then,' Eva said briskly.

'So I asked Henry,' Bel pushed on, as though she had not spoken. 'And he said that the guv'nor had got himself entangled with you. He said the pair of you were smelling like April and May and—' She saw Eva's blank expression. 'Like lovers, like people in love,' she supplied irritably. 'And he had warned Jack that no good would come of it.'

'If your brother does not choose to tell you about his personal life, I am certainly not going to.' Like April and

May…like people in love. She loved him. But Jack… Surely if he loved her he would never leave her like that?

'Don't you care about him? Henry says he saved your life.'

'Yes. He did.' Suddenly it was too much, she had to speak of him, about him, and this angry young woman with Jack's eyes at least cared enough about him to virtually kidnap her in the middle of a Carlton House reception.

'And, yes, we were lovers. And I have never had one before, in case you think I sleep with every good-looking man who comes my way,' she added militantly. 'And I had to ask him, because he was being so damnably gallant and gentlemanlike. We knew it could only last while we were in France—I cannot risk the scandal. We both knew that.'

Bel was watching her in wide-eyed silence now. At least she had stopped glaring. 'I fell in love with him. I didn't mean to, I really did not mean to. But I couldn't help it. I love him so much.'

'Then—?' Bel was thinking hard, her brow furrowed. 'Of course, you thought he was just a King's Messenger, a glorified bodyguard. No wonder you dismissed him when you got to England.'

'I knew he was more than that. And in Brussels I found him in the *Peerage*. But what difference does that make? I'd love him if he was a fishmonger's son. I told you—I did not dismiss him, he left me. He does not want me, or he would never have gone like that, without a word, just with a message to my son.'

Bel was biting her lip thoughtfully. 'Was it worth it?' she blurted out. 'Was having him as a lover worth all this heartache?'

'Yes! Yes,' Eva added more softly. 'But he never pretended it was anything more than an *affaire*.'

'He never *said* it was anything more, you mean,' Bel retorted. 'Did you tell him you love him?'

'No, of course not. Can you imagine telling a man you love him when you know he does not love you? How humiliating to see the pity in his face, the tact he will have to use to extricate himself.'

'Not if he loves you, too—how can you be sure he doesn't? I do not know about love, I was not in love with my husband and I have taken no lover. But I know my brother, and he is hurting. He is missing you.'

'Then why did he leave me like that?' Eva demanded. 'That hurt *me.*'

'I expect he thought a clean break was kindest for you. I imagine it must have been difficult to talk intimately in a houseful of servants and with your son there,' Bel said thoughtfully. 'Do you want to marry him?'

'Yes.' The word was out of her mouth before she could think. Yes, of course she did.

'And he can hardly ask the Dowager Grand Duchess, can he? I don't expect it is etiquette. You will have to tell him you love him and ask.'

'But…what if he says no?' Eva shut her eyes at the thought of it, every cell in her body cringing. She could almost hear that cool, deep voice, carefully and kindly masking his amusement at such a preposterous idea.

'What if he says yes?' Bel countered. 'You'll never know until you try, because, believe me, Sebastian is far too proud to plead with a woman who has been making it clear she wants no entanglements. And you have, haven't you?'

'Of course! I would never have got him to agree if he had

thought I was going to fall in love with him. What are you smiling about?' she added indignantly. Bel's mouth was curving into an unmistakable grin.

'The thought of my rake of a brother having to be asked if he wanted to make love to a beautiful woman,' she explained frankly.

'Is he a rake, then?' He had said as much, but somehow she had let herself think about gaming and clothes and racehorses, not mistresses and lightskirts.

'Shocking,' his loving sister confirmed. 'But somehow I doubt if he is seeking solace elsewhere this time.'

'Oh.'

'And, ma'am…'

'Eva. Please call me Eva.' Somehow this stranger had become someone she wanted for a friend.

'Eva. There is something Sebastian would never tell you, but if I am going to trust you with one of my brothers, I may as well trust you with both. Our half-brother—'

'The duke?'

'Yes. Charles. He is never going to marry. Possibly one day Sebastian will succeed him—he is ten years the younger, after all. But if you have a son together, the boy most certainly will.'

'The duke is unwell? Disabled in some way? Er…disturbed?'

'The duke does not find women attractive. Not sexually attractive. Do you understand me?'

'Oh. Yes.' One came across it, of course, although Louis had had to explain it to her. 'But is that not illegal?'

'Yes. You see how I trust you.'

'But in the case I knew of, the man married to get an heir.'

'Charles has lived, secluded on his Northumberland estate,

for eight years, very happily with his lover who, as far as the rest of the world is concerned, is his steward.'

'Ah.' Eva thought about it. 'That makes no difference to me, the thought of the title.'

'Good.' Bel beamed back. 'But it might to Sebastian, don't you think? Only he would never mention it, because he is so loyal to Charles.'

'So you think I should just find him and…propose?' It sounded the most frightening thing she had ever done. She could not imagine what it would feel like if he said *yes*.

'I think that I will inveigle him into escorting me to Lady Letheringsett's masked ball the day after tomorrow, and if you cannot find an excuse to carry him off and do the deed, then I wash my hands of the pair of you.'

'But I am not invited…' Bel with a plan was proving every bit as hard to resist as her brother.

'Then come and let me present her to you. She'll have arrived by now, I have no doubt. She'll invite you, never fear.'

'But if Jack finds out, he won't come.'

'Trust me.' Bel grinned. 'I will tell him at length how disappointed I am that the fascinating Grand Duchess Eva has declined! He will feel quite safe. Now, let's see if we can fix your feathers.'

'Don't you have to dress up?' Freddie enquired, obviously disappointed. He was perched on the edge of Eva's bed, watching while Fettersham dressed her hair to accommodate the half-mask she was to wear.

'No, just masks. It isn't a masquerade with fancy dress, but there will be a grand unmasking at midnight.'

The mask was pretty, she decided, holding it up so the dresser could thread the ribbons back into her coiffure to hold it securely. It was covered in tiny golden brown feathers, making her eyes seem a richer, deeper brown in its shadows.

Her gown was amber gauze over bronze silk, the neckline swooping low to expose the swell of her breasts and a generous décolletage. Eva was dressing for Jack tonight. Since that first night he had never seen her in anything but practical clothes. This was going to be a revelation.

'Jewellery, ma'am?' Fettersham proffered the selection the jewellers had sent. Diamonds, of course, or citrines or amber to match the dress. Eva hesitated, then chose diamonds set in gold with a diamond aigrette for her hair. She glowed, as she intended to, an offering to a man whose scruples must be overcome. She had seduced him once, on his own turf, now, on hers, the world of ballrooms and etiquette, she felt her confidence building. He would say *yes,* she had to believe it.

'Mr Ryder will like that gown,' Freddie said confidently. 'I think you look very pretty.'

'Why, thank you.' Eva stared at her son as his words penetrated. 'Why do you think Mr Ryder will be there to see it?'

Freddie sucked his cheeks in and managed to look like a cheeky angel. 'You are all fluttery, Mama.'

'Impudent child,' she scolded. 'Off to bed with you!'

Fluttery, indeed! The little wretch could read her like a book, even if he did not know the first thing about the relationships between men and women. *Just like his papa,* she thought. Louis had always been able to read her mind—except when he chose not to for his own ends, like that dreadful day in the vaults. She sincerely hoped her innocent son had not the slightest inkling of the sort of things that flitted through her mind when she thought of Jack.

'What a fabulous gown!' Lady Bel pounced on Eva as soon as she had entered the ballroom. 'And such a lovely mask—I wouldn't have known it was you if I hadn't been looking out very carefully. It is so nice to be out of mourning, although I shall be in such trouble if Mama finds out. I have four more weeks to go, really.' She swept Eva down one side of the crowded ballroom, ignoring the chattering throng, the men with their quizzing glasses scrutinising every masked lady, the towering floral displays and the glittering lights.

'Is this not a brilliant idea of mine?' Bel congratulated herself as they arrived in a slightly quieter semi-alcove. 'Because of the masks, no one is announced, so he will not have the slightest suspicion.'

'Where is he?' Eva craned to see. It appeared hopeless, then the crowd moved and there, leaning one shoulder against the pillar opposite, was a tall, dark-haired man in severe evening black, his mask a plain black slash across his face, his white linen the only relief from the starkness. She would have known him anywhere, and known, too, that, despite the relaxed half-smile on his lips, the casual attitude, he did not want to be here, that this evening was a penance undertaken to give his sister pleasure.

'I left him there and made him swear to wait for me,' Bel explained. 'There is a retiring room right behind that curtain, and the key is in the lock.'

'Do you know the location of every retiring room in London?' Eva asked, amused despite her tension. 'You make me suspect you have numerous outrageous flirtations.'

Bel coloured. 'I am boringly chaste—and unchased,' she said lightly. 'Go on, he is all yours. And good luck!'

Eva skirted round to approach Jack from behind. She paused, studying him. His hair had been cut since he got back; she could glimpse the whiter skin at his nape, and the memory of how that skin had felt under her fingers, against her mouth, took her breath.

There was so much noise with voices raised in conversation and the orchestra just trying its first few chords that she knew he could not have heard the soft tap of her slippers on the parquet floor, but as she reached the point where she could have stretched out and touched him, he pushed himself away from the wall and turned.

'You.' He kept his voice low, but it reached her none the less. His whole body was poised to move, the tension she had sensed on the quayside in Lyon was vibrating through him. He had hardly had to look at her and he knew her.

'Jack…' Eva held out her hand, but he did not take it. 'I need to talk with you.'

'This is Bel's doing, I take it?' His mouth was a hard line and Eva realised he was furiously angry.

'Your sister told me you would be here. Jack—' No, he wasn't Jack Ryder here. This, in the glamour of the ballroom, in his exquisite tailoring, his signet glowing dark on his hand, this was the other man, the one she had never met. 'Lord Sebastian. Please, there is a retiring room just here, I believe.'

'Very well.' Punctiliously he held the curtain back, opened the door for her and waited while she slipped inside.

'Will you turn the key? I do not wish to be interrupted.' She glanced around. A *chaise* against the wall, two chairs, a pretty little marble fireplace set across the corner, that was all.

'Jack…Sebastian. What do I call you?'

'Nothing,' he said harshly.

'You left without saying goodbye.' Eva meant it as a prelude; he took it as an accusation.

'It was better that way. I had hoped not to have this conversation.'

'What conversation? How do you know what I want to talk about?'

'I assumed you have changed your mind about wanting our *affaire* to end.' Jack's eyes were bleak, although his tone was neutral. 'I do not want it to end, either,' he added. 'But I know it is the wise thing. The only thing for two people circumstanced as we are.'

'No. That is not what I meant to say. I agree with you: an *affaire* is impossible here.' That, she was pleased to see, took him aback. 'But like you, I wish it were not.'

'Then why are we here?' Jack asked. The black mask made him seem different somehow, more aloof, more dangerous. 'In a locked room? Just one more time, perhaps?' Eva moved in a flutter of silk and gauze, needing to be closer, needing to see his eyes more clearly. She saw his control snap, suddenly without warning, like lightning from a clear sky. She was in his arms, crushed against his chest, his eyes were blazing into hers and his mouth came crushing down to silence her gasp of protest.

Damn it, did she think he was made of iron? She had taken him by surprise, with his guard down, and she came in silks and feathers and a cloud of subtle perfume that enhanced the scent of her and spoke of sin and sweetness and soft, soft skin. He was aching for her, had been aching with the bone-deep agony of something broken ever since that chaste night in Brussels.

He had expected it to get better; it got worse. He had thought it was purely lust and had tried to assuage it in the obvious manner. But he found his feet would not carry him over the threshold of the discreet house of pleasure that had enjoyed his custom so many times before.

If it were lust, then no other woman than this one, the one he could not have, could slake it. But it was not lust. He had admitted it to himself already—now he had to live with the reality of it. Love. He had found the strength to do the right thing and now she flung all that hard-won self-control back in his face, as though it did not matter, as though he would rather have slashed his own wrist open rather than walk away from that house without a farewell.

He had gone to the War Office and made them very happy with the rocket notes and then he made the effort to put Jack Ryder behind himself until this madness at least became a manageable agony. He had his hair ruthlessly barbered into the newest crop. He filled the white nights when he could not sleep with gaming, and won an embarrassing amount of money. He visited his tailor and ordered lavishly. Nothing helped, and, to add insult to injury, the highly fashionable, clinging knitted black silk of his evening knee breeches could not have been better designed to demonstrate the violently carnal effect Eva was having on him.

Then she had moved, bringing her warmth, her scent, to lash his senses, and he lost control.

Anger or lust or sheer desperation? Jack had no idea, and with Eva's body crushed against his, with her mouth warm and moist and soft under his, he stopped thinking. Her gown, already low over those milk-white breasts, slid away under the pressure of his hands and she spilled into his palms, the perfect weight so familiar, so arousing. He stooped and took one nipple in his mouth, nipping it, fretting it with his tongue mercilessly so that she cried out, gripping his hair, not in pain, but to urge him closer.

Closer? If she wanted closer, then she would have closer. There were buttons under his fingers, then they were free, the gown slipping down, over the curve of her hips, the perfect roundness of her buttocks. Under it she wore only the finest of petticoats, the simplest of corsets. They were no obstacle, it was moments and then she was naked except for her silk stockings and her mask, the effect wildly, indecently erotic. Behind the mask her eyes were wide and soft and fevered in its feathery shadows.

Almost roughly he pushed her down on to the *chaise* and began to tear off his own clothing. He was so hard for her, so aroused, the clinging silk almost refused to be removed. Impatient, he tugged and heard her gasp as she saw him. Had she forgotten his body so soon, or was this simply the result of the days of abstinence from her?

But Eva showed no fear, not of his anger, not of his size. She reached for him, drew him down to her, wrapped her long, slim, strong horsewoman's legs around him and pulled him hard to the core of her. She was wet for him, quivering, the scent of arousal fuelling his own state to the point where he thought he would lose all control before he even entered her.

There was no finesse, neither of them sought that, only possession, only oblivion. She cried out as he entered her without any preliminary caress, but the cry was feral, triumphant, demanding and he answered her by driving hard into the centre of her, again and again as she writhed and gasped and called his name, over and over until he felt her convulse around him and he somehow found the strength to wrench himself away before the tremors of her ecstasy sent him over into his.

Chapter Twenty-One

Eva came to herself to find Jack's weight still crushing down on her, the *chaise*'s hard bolster digging into the small of her back in the most uncomfortable fashion. They were hot, they were sweaty, she could hardly breathe and she had never felt physical pleasure like it. From outside the volume of noise from the music and the guests beat against the door; inside, the only sound was their panting breaths.

Slowly Jack raised his head so he could look down into her eyes. The black mask made him seem almost sinister, but the harsh lines of his mouth were softened, and the shadow of a smile lurked at the corner. With a sigh he dropped his forehead to rest against hers. She closed her eyes as his lashes brushed against her own lids and his breath stirred warm on her mouth.

'We are not very good at this abstinence thing, are we?' he enquired.

'No. It seems not. Jack…I cannot breathe very well.'

He levered himself up and sat at her feet, arms along the carved rail of the *chaise,* head thrown back. Naked except for the mask, he looked magnificent in the candlelight, his muscles long and smooth and powerful. She looked at the hand lying relaxed on the carved wood and felt the heat flood through her at the memory of what those elegant, clever, wicked fingers had been doing.

'Thank you.' She scrambled up until she was curled against the head of the *chaise,* just far enough away not to feel the heat of him, just far enough not to yield to the temptation to bend closer and run her tongue tip down his arm. 'Strange to say, I did not come here for this.'

'No? Eva, please, put something on. The effect of that mask and the silk stockings is quite outrageously arousing.'

Eva glanced down at herself, then at Jack, whose body was all too obviously stirring into life again at the sight of her. She dragged on her underthings. 'You'll have to tie my laces. I cannot get into this gown unless I am laced tight.'

He got up and came to do as she asked. Eva could hear the catch in his breathing as he gathered up the strings. She put her hands at her waist, drew in a breath and nodded. Jack pulled. 'More.' He pulled again. 'Enough. Tie them in a bow—although my dresser will know. Goodness knows what I am going to say to her.'

Jack stepped back as soon as the corset was done. 'And the buttons on my gown, as well. I am sorry, I cannot reach.' She stood as still as she could while he buttoned the amber silk. 'Thank you. Now, I will take care of my hair while you dress.' She found she could not look at him, she was nervous now.

The overmantel glass reflected back the entire room; Eva forced her eyes to focus only on her hair. This might be the last time she would ever see Jack naked, share the intimacy of getting dressed together. This might be the last time they ever kissed, caressed. The last time if she did not get this right.

'Well? What is it, Eva?' Jack stood at the foot of the *chaise,* his colour a little heightened, his neckcloth in a considerably simpler knot that he had arrived with, but apparently unruffled.

Eva sat down, certain her legs were not going to carry her, and gestured for him to sit likewise.

'I want to ask you something. And to tell you something,' she began. 'I need you so much it hurts to be without you.' It was out, far too abruptly, without any of the subtlety she had rehearsed. And the word she had sworn to herself she would use—love—would not pass her lips, not without some hint from him that he felt the same.

'Eva—'

'No, let me finish. I did not intend to feel like this. It is not just our lovemaking, although that is wonderful. When I asked you to be my lover, I was honest in my reasons, in what I told you. I said I was with a man I desired and trusted and liked. I thought I wanted physical pleasure, physical comfort, a strong man to hold me. That is all true. And then I found I cannot live without you.'

'Eva.' His head was down; he was regarding his clasped hands as though they held the answer. 'Eva, you honour me, and I—but that makes no difference to our problem. For you to take a lover, now you are back in the full glare of the public eye, is impossible if you wish to avoid scandal.'

'Jack, please look at me.' He looked up, met her eyes, his own still and watchful, and very dark. She sat quite still, her own hands, with a desperation to stop her from reaching for him, knotted in her lap. 'You do not understand. I am asking you to marry me.'

He was so silent that she thought he had not heard her. Then he stood up with the violent grace she had seen him use when he was fighting. From the other side of the little room, as far as he could get from her, he said, 'Are you insane?'

'No! I mean it.' His reaction shocked her. She had expected surprise, doubt, an argument. Not outright hostility.

'Have you forgotten who—what—you are?'

'I am the Dowager Grand Duchess. But I am not of the Blood Royal. My father was a French count, my mother the daughter of an English earl. You are the son of a duke. There is no disparity between our breeding.' She had thought that out very carefully. If Louis could marry her, then she could marry Jack.

'How very convenient that you discovered my bloodlines,' Jack said coldly. 'What would you have done if you had found I was plain Mr Ryder, simply an agent and an adventurer?'

'I have no idea,' Eva said flatly. 'I learned to need plain Mr Ryder, but I did not know just how much being separated from you was going to hurt until I got here. How do I know what I would have thought, what I would want to do, if you were not Lord Sebastian?'

'Not a convenient Maubourg title, then? That would have sorted out plain Mr Ryder. You might still want to come up with some sort of tinsel decoration, some sort of specially created title for me, or a senior rank in your army perhaps? Yes, that would do it. A handsome sash to wear on my new blue-and-silver uniform—or you could ask the Prince Regent to design something: he specialises in fantasy.'

'Stop it! You do not need a title, you have a perfectly good one of your own! If you want to take an interest in the army, then I am sure that would be very acceptable. What is the matter with you? Do you not want to marry me? Is there someone else after all?' He had never said those words, she realised, cold sweat beginning to trickle down her spine. She loved him, had hoped, when she asked him to marry her, that he would confess that he loved her, but had not felt able to say so. It seemed she had made a terrible misjudgement…

'No. There is no one else.' Jack took two strides, came up against the corner of the room and turned again, frustrated by the confining space. 'Don't you think, ma'am, that I might prefer to do the asking? Does it not occur to you that I have a life—two, actually—in this country? Marriages into Royal families happen for dynastic reasons, for heirs—there is one already; for international allegiance—I cannot bring that; for wealth—I am sure my resources are paltry in comparison to yours. What they are not intended for is so that the lady in question can enjoy the attentions of her lover without causing a scandal.'

'But that isn't why—I told you, I need you!' Eva got to her feet, her head spinning. This was not how it was supposed to go. She had told him how she felt, she made an offer that was the honourable one, fitting for both of them, and he threw it back in her face. Anger was beginning to stir under the misery.

'That is extremely flattering, ma'am. But as you know, I already have an occupation and being transplanted to virtually the Alps so I can service the sexual needs of a lady—however alluring and charming—does not fit in with my plans for my life.'

He did not even try to avoid it as she slapped him, hard across the cheek. Shaking her stinging fingers, Eva stared aghast at the scarlet mark of her hand branded across his livid face. She had hit so hard it would probably bruise.

'It is so much more than sex,' she whispered. 'So much more. I thought you felt the same. I was wrong. I am sorry, so sorry I spoke. I will go.'

'Eva.' Jack took her arms, holding fast as she tried to twist away. All she wanted now was to escape this humiliating heartbreak. 'Eva, What I feel for you went far beyond what happened just now in this room. You have been lonely, frightened, left to do your duty at whatever cost to yourself. I came along and gave you excitement and freedom and affection. It is not me you want now, and I cannot give you what you need. I am English, Eva, I live here, this is my home. I have purpose, identity, independence. I cannot give that up to find myself in a country not my own, where I have no role, where my life is bounded by the constraints of who I have married.'

'If you loved me, you would not say that,' she flung at him.

The silence between them seemed to fill the room. The music faded, the loud voices that had roared like the sound of the sea beyond the door became a whisper. 'If I loved you, my answer would be the same,' Jack said steadily. 'I cannot be caged into the life you offer me and, if you tried, I would finish by hurting you. I think you need to go back to Maubourg, Eva. Take Freddie, it is safe to travel now with the escort the Foreign Office will arrange for you. Go now, and forget me.'

Her hands were shaking so much that Eva could hardly unlock the door. She managed it at last, turning as she opened it for one last look at him. 'How can I forget?' she whispered.

'I love you.' It was safe to say it, he could not have heard her, the orchestra was just drawing a particularly noisy country dance to a triumphant conclusion amidst enthusiastic clapping. The dancers coming off the floor engulfed her, swept her away from the door as the Rhône had carried her, dizzy, weak, unable to fight her way to the edge of the room.

'Eva!' It was Bel, tugging her arm. That hurt; she remembered vaguely Jack gripping her just there, a hundred years ago. 'Come and sit down.' She steered Eva to a chair in an alcove. 'What happened?'

Eva could only shake her head, dumbly. Words seemed to have deserted her. 'You need a drink.' Bel looked around her. 'Why is there never a waiter when you need one? Theo! Yes, I know it is you, no one else in London is that tall with auburn hair, you numbskull. I need two glasses of champagne, at once. And a glass of brandy. Shoo!' She pushed the indignant young man off into the throng. 'My scapegrace cousin Theo,' she explained. 'Did he say no?'

Eva nodded.

'Why? Why on earth would he say no?'

'Because he does not love me, I suppose. Because I made a mull of it, because he does not want to end up as an adjunct to his wife in a foreign court.'

'You told him you love him? No?' Eva shook her head. A whisper he could not hear did not count. 'Why ever not?'

'Because I thought he realised that was why I was asking him, and then he told me he did not love me, so what was the point?'

'He told you?' Bel stared at her. 'In so many words? He actually said *I do not love you*?'

'He had told me he would not marry me and then he said

his answer would be the same whether or not he loved me. I think.' She shook her head, too stunned by the whole experience to trust her memory any more. The young man—Theo, was it?—came back with a waiter at his heels. Bel took a brandy glass, pressed it into Eva's hands and then scooped the two champagne flutes off the tray. 'Thank you, Theo.'

She waited until her cousin had retreated, then said, 'Drink it!' Eva tossed back the brandy, reckless now for something to take the edge off the pain, while Bel took a reviving drink of champagne, then removed the empty brandy glass and substituted the other flute for it. 'I will be drunk,' Eva protested.

'Good. I'd get tipsy and then go home if I were you, there isn't any purpose in waiting here for the unmasking, you'll only be miserable.' Bel sipped her drink, brooding. 'He may well think better of it in the morning,' she offered at length.

'I doubt it. I hit him.'

'Good.'

They brooded some more, the brandy and wine burning dully through Eva's veins. She recalled the last time she had been tipsy—a most infrequent happening in her well-regulated life. That had been with Jack in the inn and she had been utterly indiscreet. She felt more than indiscreet now, she felt desperate for action, to get away, not stay trapped here in this foreign country, miles from home.

'There's Lord Gowering,' Bel observed. 'See, in the red-sequined mask with one shoulder higher than the other. He directs all the agents in the Foreign Office, though you wouldn't think he was a spymaster to look at him. I have half a mind to go and tell him he should sack my brother for not taking care of you.'

The tall, stooping man was heading in their direction. 'Introduce me,' Eva said suddenly.

Bel shot her a startled glance, but got up and accosted the man. He bowed over Eva's hand. 'I had not expected to see you here, your Serene Highness. I understand we have to thank you for some very interesting armament designs. You are none the worse for your journey, I trust?'

'Perfectly recovered, I thank you, my lord. So much so that I wish to leave immediately for the Continent, with my son. I believe the butler and footmen at my present lodging are your men—I would like to borrow them for the journey.'

'But, of course, ma'am.' She gestured to the seat beside her and his lordship took it. 'There will be no difficulty with papers, naturally, but we had not expected you to wish to return so soon.'

'I am anxious about my brother-in-law, the Regent,' Eva explained, hearing her own voice fluently explaining how her son wanted to go home very badly, how she felt quite rested now—all as though there was some ventriloquist behind her speaking these words while she writhed in dumb misery. It must be the brandy. And years of training.

'Very well, ma'am, I will have papers for the staff sent to you first thing tomorrow. I wish you a safe and speedy return home, and we will hope to see you again in London when travelling conditions are a little less…exciting.'

He bowed himself off, leaving Bel staring at Eva. 'What am I going to tell Sebastian?'

'Nothing,' said Eva flatly. 'Nothing at all if you can help it. Bel, thank you for your support, your friendship. I would have loved to have you as my sister.'

'And I you. Oh, Eva, don't give up on him.' Bel took Eva's hand and squeezed it.

'I think for my own sanity, I must do so.' Eva stood up and shook out her skirts. 'Could you tell our hostess that I have a migraine and had to slip away?' She hesitated, Bel's hands in hers. 'Goodbye, Bel. Look after him for me.'

As she hurried away through the crowd, she caught Bel's wrathful parting words. 'Box his ears, more like.'

Jack stayed where he was after Eva had gone, waiting for his reddened cheek to subside enough to show himself again. The marks of her fingers would probably be there in bruises tomorrow; she had hit with intent to hurt him, and succeeded.

How he had had the strength to do the right thing and turn her down he had no idea. At least she had said nothing about loving him—he did not think he could have coped with that. She was lonely in that great castle, who could blame her? What they had shared had been a revelation for her, but they could not recreate those feelings, not in the humdrum world of court life.

It would be a disaster if they married and he loved her too much to risk it. Jack began to pace, the part of him that was trying to be fair, trying to understand, giving ground again to his pride and his temper. What had possessed her? He should have been the one doing the asking, not her. He should be the one with title and wealth and position to offer, not her. He could not be bought like a toy, and a husband was not something that was easy to throw away when you tired of him, either.

Leave England? Leave the estate that he had inherited from his maternal grandfather? Leave the rolling countryside, the broad river valleys, the green hills for a foreign country where he had no role except to please the first lady? He wanted sons who would be Englishmen, he realised, not exiles in another country where their half-brother had a status wildly different from their own.

Damn it! She should have guessed all that, she should never have asked him. He was an English gentleman, not some foreign gigolo—

'So you are skulking in here.' Hell and damnation, it was his interfering sister. Jack glared at Bel and she whipped off her mask and glared back. 'My goodness, that is going to mark,' she observed, apparently with some satisfaction, walking up to touch her fingertips to his cheek.

'Thank you, I do not need a second opinion on that,' he said tightly. 'I collect I have you to blame for this idiotic situation.'

'I suggested the ball and this room,' Bel said, sitting with some grace on the rumpled *chaise*. 'You are entirely to blame for the situation being idiotic.'

'You consider that I should have accepted her Serene Highness's flattering offer, do you?' He had never felt so out of charity with his sister.

'As you love her, I would have thought that was a logical thing to do.'

'Who told you I love her?' He saw the trap the moment he put his foot into it. Bel looked smug. 'I just did, didn't I?'

'I had guessed, that was why I wanted to help you both. Has it not occurred to you, numbskull, that she loves you, too? Or are both of you so determined this is all just about sex—' Bel went scarlet, but pushed on '—that you cannot see what is in front of your faces? Do you really think a woman like that is going to do something as difficult as asking a man to marry her if she did not love him?'

'She does?' Jack discovered his legs were feeling decidedly odd. The only place to sit was beside his sister, so he sat on the end of the *chaise* next to her and rubbed his hands over his face. 'Damn this thing.' He yanked off the mask and threw it on the floor. Bel just looked at him.

Eva loved him? He loved her, so it was not impossible, just something he had never dared to contemplate. She had wanted his lovemaking, his company, his friendship—was that not all she had wanted? Now his mind brought back the image of her face as she turned to him, her hand on the key of that door. What had she said, her lips moving, but no sound reaching him above the swell of the music?

He had learned to lip read as a useful espionage skill, but it needed a lot of concentration. This was Eva: she deserved that concentration. He closed his eyes, searched for the picture of her moving lips, his own moving as he tried out the words. *How can I forget? I love you.*

'Why did she not say so?' His sister, a woman, might be able to explain this mystery.

'Because she is shy, because she was afraid you would reject her, because she rather thought her idiot lover might have some inkling without having to be hit over the head with it,' his loving sister snapped.

'Oh.'

'So, what are you going to do about it?' Bel demanded after they had sat in silence for minutes.

Jack sat staring at the crumpled scrap of black fabric at his feet. 'Nothing.'

Chapter Twenty-Two

'What! Jack, you love her—now you know she loves you and you still say you will do *nothing?*"

'Bel, she is a Grand Duchess, for goodness' sake. I am a younger son.'

'Of a duke,' she retorted. 'Your breeding as a scion of one of England's oldest houses is as good as anyone's in this country. You know what you are, Sebastian John Ryder Ravenhurst? You are a snob.'

'A *what?*' Jack twisted round on the *chaise* to stare at her.

'A snob,' Bel repeated. 'An inverted snob. You refuse to justify your own position, to stand up for who and what you are because she has that title. One she married, not one she inherited, mind you. One of these days you could be a duke—your son certainly will be.'

'Bel!' She had truly shocked him now.

'You think I do not understand about our brother and his situation? If he is happy, I am certainly not going to judge him.

And you are an English gentleman; the Mauborgians should be grateful to have you as their Grand Duke's stepfather.'

'Mauborgeois,' Jack corrected absently.

'So, what are you going to do now?' Bel demanded again, ignoring his interjection.

'Nothing,' he repeated.

'Nothing.' His sister sprang up and regarded him, hands on hips. 'Nothing. Because your pride will not accept you having to stand one step behind your wife on state occasions. Because you will not compromise on how you live your life. Because people might talk. I could box your ears, Sebastian Raven-hurst, but a better woman got in first.'

The door slammed behind Bel. Jack stayed where he was, staring at the painted panels, trying to make some sense of his feelings. His head ached, his face ached, his heart…*ached* was an altogether inadequate word for how that felt. With a groan he flung himself back full length on the *chaise* cushions and found his nostrils full of the scent of Eva.

Pride, compromise, status, love. It was a word game, a riddle he had no idea how to read.

'How long may I stay in Maubourg?' Freddie demanded as the carriage rolled over London Bridge.

'Until the new term. This is not the end of school, young man, you know your papa wished you to be educated as an English gentleman.' Eva carried on settling all her things for the journey. Books into door pockets, her travelling chess set on the seat, some *petit point* in her sewing bag. Freddie's seat was cluttered with packs of cards, books, something he was whittling out of wood and a box of exercises Herr Hoffmeister insisted he took with him. They were doomed to stay there, Eva suspected—the tutor was taking a holiday, much to Freddie's well-suppressed glee.

'Why did Papa not let me come home for holidays?' Freddie persisted.

'I think because he wanted you to be thoroughly English,' Eva explained. 'Then when you were older you would have all the contacts you needed for diplomacy, and your English would be perfect.' Which it was. Now, they had slipped back into a mixture of French and the Maubourg dialect; she did not want her son arriving home sounding like a foreigner.

'I missed you.'

'I missed you, too.' She suppressed the nagging suspicion that Louis had wanted their son to grow up with less feminine influence, or even that, as Napoleon's influence grew, he had doubts about having married a half-French bride. Whatever it was, he had never chosen to explain himself to his wife, merely citing her tears as evidence that Fréderic was better off at school. 'Still, now you are so much older, I am sure Papa would have wanted you to spend your holidays in Maubourg.'

Freddie nodded thoughtfully. 'And I can study with Uncle Philippe so I will learn how to be a proper Grand Duke.'

'Yes, my love.' She smiled at him, tears of pride shimmering across her vision so that he became a blur. Last night, amidst the chaos of the preparations for their sudden departure, she had found no opportunity to shed the tears that filled her heart for Jack until she had reached her bed, and then, alone at last, she had wept for what might have been, but now never could be.

'Uncle Philippe is a very good Regent, isn't he?'

'Yes, dear.'

'But he doesn't know about things like sport and adventures and things like that, does he?'

'No, I don't think those interest him.' Her brother-in-law was the scholarly one of the family.

'I do wish you were going to marry Mr Ryder after all,' Freddie said.

'Freddie! Whatever makes you think—?'

'I thought you loved him. You were very sad when he went away and didn't say goodbye. And the way he looked at you. I may not know much about these things,' her nine-year-old son said with dignity as she gaped at him, 'but I can tell when two people like each other a lot. I don't understand why he didn't ask you to marry him.'

'Possibly because I am a Grand Duchess,' Eva said more sharply than she intended.

Freddie nodded. 'I did wonder about that. But then, he's a duke's son, isn't he? One of the chaps at Eton recognised him and told me. I know it's a long time since you've really been in England,' he explained earnestly, 'but it's a very important family; perfectly eligible. Do you think I ought to write and give him permission?'

'Freddie!'

'It is a difficult question of etiquette,' her son pondered, apparently oblivious to his mother's horrified expression. 'I shall have to ask Uncle Bruin. I mean, Mr Ryder is a lot older than me, after all.'

'Twenty years,' Eva said weakly.

'Old enough to be a proper father, and young enough to be fun,' the Grand Duke opined solemnly. 'Just right, really.'

'Freddie, promise me, really, truly, promise me you will not write to Mr Ryder,' Eva begged.

'Sure? Well, tell me if you change your mind, Mama.' Freddie found his pocket telescope and proceeded to risk motion sickness by trying to use it while the vehicle was moving.

Eva slumped back in the corner of the carriage. Bel thought he loved her. Her own son thought he loved her. She had hoped he loved her. But Jack had not said it. Were they all wrong—or was he deliberately not telling her?

Two days later Eva was still pondering. They were travelling at a reasonable speed, one of the footmen up on the box beside the driver with a shotgun, the other man, with Grimstone, riding on either side of the carriage. There had been no problems, no apparent danger—it seemed Antoine's plotting had died with him.

She looked out at the countryside, contrasting it with England and with Maubourg. She seemed never to have found a real home—their French château was a distant memory, she had been in England only a short while before Louis had married her, and Maubourg was hers by marriage, not by birth.

Jack struck her as a very English Englishman. She was not sure what that meant, but she had seen a change steal over him after they had landed, a sense that he was home, that he had taken a deep breath and relaxed. She had asked him to leave that without a single thought to how it would feel for him, without even asking what lands he held, how attached he was to them.

She had fallen in love with the man, without ever seeing

him in his true context. How could she hope to understand him? How could she know what she was asking him to give up for her?

Layer upon layer, Eva realised as the carriage rumbled over the cobbles in Lyon three days further on, she had failed to understand Jack. She should not have made that proposal; instead, she should have told him she loved him and waited for his response. She should not have demanded, she should have found some way of letting him know it was all right to propose—if he did love her. And she should never have started this without thinking through how she could compromise her way of life to fit with his.

She still could not imagine how that could be achieved. There was the Rhône, swirling past the road. The river that had almost taken her life, if it had not been for Jack. 'Not long now,' she said cheerfully to Freddie, and fell back into thought about compromise. But how? There was her son, her duty—and a country hundreds of miles from England.

The first sight of the castle struck Freddie dumb. Eyes wide, he stared, then, as the carriage rumbled over the bridge and began to climb the steep streets to the great gate, he darted from side to side, searching for familiar landmarks, places he could recognise.

There was a clatter of hooves and Grimstone spurred ahead, going to warn the castle of their arrival. And then they were there; guards were spilling out through the gate to line up on either side, townspeople coming running to see what was afoot.

The carriage drew up, the footman let down the step and reached to hand Eva down. 'No.' It was Freddie. With a dignity she did not realise her small son possessed, he said, 'Excuse me, Mama,' and climbed out first. Then he stood by the side of the door and held up his hand for her to take, making a little ceremony out of her appearance.

His expression as he looked at her was pure pride. Pride for himself, pride in her and a glowing pride at being home where he belonged.

Pride. Eva hung back as Philippe appeared in the gateway and walked steadily towards his nephew. Freddie started forward, almost at the run, then collected himself and walked up to his uncle.

'Your Serene Highness, welcome home.' The man bowed to the child and suddenly all the dignity was gone. Freddie threw his arms around his uncle's neck.

'Uncle Bruin! We're back!' He twisted round. 'Mama, see, Uncle Bruin is well again.'

'Yes, so he is.' Eva came forward, both hands held out to Philippe. 'Thank Heavens for it.' But in the back of her mind the word lingered. Pride. Pride and honour. So important to men, so easily forgotten by women who loved them.

'I am so sorry I left you,' she murmured to her brother-in-law as he took her arm to take her into dinner, hours later.

'It was the right thing. Your place was with Freddie, and by going you threw all Antoine's calculations into disarray.' The Regent patted her hand as he helped her to her seat next to him at the round table the family used when they dined informally alone. With Antoine gone, there was just the three of them now. Philippe's wife had died many years before, leaving him childless.

'You look well,' Philippe observed as the soup was served and the footmen retired to give them privacy. 'It may have been an odd holiday, but it has done you good to get away.'

'For the first time in over nine years,' Eva said. 'Yes, it was a…change. And the long days in the open air were invigorating.'

'I never understood why you did not go away before.' Philippe passed her the bread.

'Louis preferred that I did not travel,' she began.

'Louis has been dead almost two years,' his brother reminded her gently. 'You have been very obedient to all his wishes.'

Yes, she had, Eva realised. The rule that Freddie must stay in England, the rule that she did not travel. Yet Philippe was a more-than-competent Regent, it was hardly that she needed to be there all the time—only when Freddie was here in the holidays. And the rest of the time he was in England…

Compromise. Suddenly, in her mind's eye, she could see a compromise, a plan she could lay before Jack. He might still reject it—and her. But she had to go to him, put things right somehow, even if all that meant was that he felt he could write now and again to Freddie.

'Freddie. Philippe.' They broke off in the middle of an intense discussion about Napoleon's tactics at Waterloo that involved the salt cellars, a mustard pot and a bread roll, and turned to her politely. 'Would you both mind very much if I go back to England?'

'When?' Philippe looked startled, but her son's face was one big grin.

'Tomorrow. There is something I need to do.' She smiled back at Freddie. 'Someone I need to see.'

* * *

Eva was apologetic to her escort. She could take Maubourg men with her on the journey back, she offered. Grimstone and his two companions must be travel weary and saddle sore.

'No, ma'am.' The butler-turned-bodyguard was adamant. 'The guv'nor would expect us to stick with you, however long it takes. Where are we off to now, if I might ask, ma'am?'

'England,' Eva said firmly. 'Straight back to London.'

'Yes, ma'am.' The butler managed an estimable straight face. It sat oddly with his battered pugilistic features. 'Whatever you say, ma'am. Back to London it is, then.'

She did not leave until well on in the afternoon the next day. Partly it was because she wanted to enjoy the sight of Freddie rediscovering the castle, partly because she wanted to be completely sure that Philippe was well, but also because she was determined to retrace the route she and Jack had taken and to stay in the same inns. So, unless she was going to arrive ludicrously early at the first one, she needed to delay her departure. She was not certain what she would do when they reached the area where they had slept out under the stars, but she would deal with that when she came to it.

It was about six in the evening when the carriage, driven by a very bemused driver, deposited the Grand Duchess of Maubourg on the threshold of one of her more humble inns.

It was the same innkeeper who greeted them and he blinked a little at the sight of her again so soon, and with only servants at her back and no husband. But he did not recognise her true self this time, either, cheerfully ushering in *Madame,* lamenting that her esteemed husband was not travelling with her, and assuring her that the same bedchamber as last time was free. They had no other guests, he explained, directing her escort to a spacious attic room, although a hunting party was due in two days. What a fortunate occurrence that *Madame* could have the whole place to herself; he would light a fire in the parlour, for he was sure rain threatened and the temperature was dropping, did she not agree?

The promised rain came not as a shower but as a torrential downpour that made her think of the night before the battle. Then she had had only an open-sided hovel and straw to keep her dry and warm. And Jack's long body curled around her. But now she was in a snug parlour, surrounded by the carved woodwork and brightly painted earthenware the Maubourg peasants excelled at producing.

On the wide wooden mantel there was even the commemorative tankard that had been produced to celebrate her wedding to Louis. A good thing the image of her was so unlike. It was good of Louis though, she had always thought so. The handsome aloof profile stared blankly at the insipid representation of the new bride. So young, so innocent and so easily moulded to the dutiful wife her husband had demanded. Eva got up and turned the vessel around so the portraits faced the wall and the Maubourg crest was towards the room. That was better. She was another woman now.

There was a fire in the hearth to send red light chasing across the whitewashed walls and the curtains were drawn cosily across the casements. Distantly from the taproom she could hear the men talking. Here she was alone, but not lonely, thankful for the peace and the privacy to think about Jack. She had to get it right this time. Then upstairs was the bed they had shared, the memories of their first night together to relive when she finally felt sleepy. That first night—with a bolster down the middle of the bed!

Eva smiled. What would Jack think if he could see her now, nostalgically retracing their steps across France? Would he think her foolish, or would he understand?

The rain lashed down harder; it almost felt as though the sturdy little inn was a ship in rough seas, the waves battering at its sides. If it was like this tomorrow, she would not move on. It was madness to risk men and horses on roads that could become mountain torrents. Strangely it did not disturb her, the prospect of delay. She had made up her mind—she was travelling back to Jack almost fatalistically. He would be there when she arrived, she knew it.

There was a bustle outside, doors banged and the innkeeper shouted for the ostler. Some chance traveller caught in the storm, perhaps. Eva put down the book she had not been attempting to read and went to twitch aside the curtain. In the erratic light of the wind-tossed lanterns she saw that the ostler, huddled under the inadequate shelter of a sack, was leading a big horse towards the stable. Its coat was black, streaming with water, the saddle already soaked. She caught a glimpse of the skirts of a many-caped greatcoat as the rider vanished into the shelter of the porch.

A lone man, then. It seemed, unless he was content with the common taproom, that she must lose her privacy. Eva shrugged. She did not mind. One of the footmen could come in, too, to cover the proprieties.

'Such a surprise, *monsieur.*' The innkeeper was jovially greeting the newcomer. 'Come in, sir, come in! What a night to be sure, but you at least are certain of a warm welcome and your usual room. This way, sir, this way.'

A regular and favoured customer by the sound of it. But Eva was surprised that the innkeeper appeared about to usher him into the parlour, without a word to her.

'Here we are, sir.' The door swung open, making the candles gutter wildly. A tall figure, its bulk increased by the soaked greatcoat, filled the door. Water poured off the coat, pooled around the booted feet. The man's hat was in his gloved hands, but it could not have done much good, for his hair was plastered to his head.

The candles steadied as he took a step inside and Eva came to her feet. He looked weary, this traveller, there were shadows under the grey eyes and lines at the corners of his mouth that were new, she would swear, but as he saw her he went white, and under the blanched skin the bruised shape of four fingers stood out starkly.

'Jack. Oh, my God. Jack.' And then she was across the room, into his arms, her own around his neck, his soaking clothing leaching freezing wet into hers. And the heat of her love swept through her as he bent his head and his ice-cold lips met hers.

Chapter Twenty-Three

'*M*adame! *Madame?* Here, you, you can't go in there and…
Guv'nor!' Grimstone came pounding down the passageway
from the taproom, big fists clenched, then skidded to a halt,
his expression one of almost comical astonishment as Jack
turned, Eva in the crook of his arm.

'Thank you, Grimstone. *Madame* is quite safe with me.'

The bodyguard backed off, grinning. 'We're in the
taproom, guv'nor, if there's anything you need.'

'Divine intervention, probably,' Eva thought she heard
Jack mutter. 'You can get my boots off,' he added more
loudly, standing on one foot while the man tugged from the
back. The boot slid off with an unpleasant squelch and they
switched to the other.

'Landlord! A hot bath as soon as possible, if you please,'
Eva ordered, her hands already dragging off the heavy greatcoat. 'You are soaked, right through. You'll catch your
death, Jack.'

He shrugged off the greatcoat and coat together, bundled

them into Grimstone's arms and turned back to her. 'Don't fuss, sweet, I am tough enough to stand some rain.'

'You look like a half-drowned rat. Come to the fire.' She tugged, but he stood his ground, then stooping, swept her up in his arms and made for the stairs. 'Jack!' Eva registered the staring faces around them break into broad smiles and buried her face in Jack's shoulder. 'Jack,' she whispered, half in sheer embarrassment, half with the joy of being able to say his name.

'Forget the hot water,' he threw back over his shoulder as he climbed. 'I'll ring later.'

'Jack!' she was still protesting as he shouldered open the door and set her on her feet inside the bedchamber.

'Eva.' The door closed with a thud and the key clicked. 'Eva, what in Heaven's name are you doing here? Has there been an accident? Where's Freddie? You should have been in Maubourg by now.'

'He is, we were. I mean, we arrived yesterday. Freddie is with his uncle.'

'So why are you here?' Jack stood dripping, the water still trickling down from his hair and regarded her steadily. Oh, Lord, she had made such a mess of his face.

'I was coming back. To England.'

'But why are you here? If you left this morning, you should be well on your way by now.' He did not ask why she was returning, she noticed with sinking heart.

Jack would think her a foolish and romantic woman, but there was nothing for it but to explain. 'I wanted to stay in the inns we had used. And I could hardly turn up at ten in the morning at this one, could I? I have been here just two hours.'

He smiled then, his mouth curving into a tender line that made the tears start in her eyes. 'Why were you coming back? Had you forgotten your bonnet?'

'No.' She could not joke about it. And she had to say it now. 'I was coming to see you and say I was sorry. I handled it so badly.' She could not stand to be the focus of those intelligent grey eyes—they seemed to see right through her, into the muddle and fear inside. 'I thought about status and what I ought to do as Grand Duchess, not what I wanted to do as a woman. I hurt your pride, I made demands without thinking what you would need or want. I did not tell you the important thing.' The words stuck in her throat. Dare she say them? Once said, they could never be unsaid.

But he did not ask. Of course, he did not want her to say it. Eva felt her heart sink, all the warmth his presence had surrounded her with shrank away. Why, with her handprint on his face, would Jack want her explanations?

'Aren't you going to ask me why I am here?' The deep, amused voice did not sound like the angry man she had left at the masquerade.

'I assume you were driven here by the storm.'

'As it happens, I was heading for this place. Eva, has it not struck you as rather strange that I am here at all?'

'Oh.' She stared at him. 'Of course. I was thinking so much about you it never occurred to me. You should be in London!'

'I should be where you are,' he said gently, taking her hand and pulling her to him. 'I wanted to spend one night here before going on to the castle. One night to remember the first one, one night to get my speech in order.'

'Speech?' She was feeling stupid, numb, Somewhere a

voice was whispering that this was going to be all right, but she dare not heed it.

'The one where I fall to one knee and kiss your hand.' He knelt in front of her and lifted her hand to his lips with his cold, damp one. 'The one where I tell you I love you and ask you to marry me.' He waited patiently, his lips curving into a smile against her knuckles.

'But you said…' She stumbled to a halt, gazing down on the bent head, the otter-sleek wet hair, the vulnerable, exposed nape. 'You love me?'

'I love you. I should have told you then, in London. Instead I said a number of stupid, angry things. Eva, I let my pride get in the way of how I feel about you. I reacted without thinking about how we could make this work, and I know we can.'

'And I did not even think about how it *needed* to be made to work. I did not think about compromise, I just wanted you in my life. My old life, as though I could uproot you, demand that you fit into the court at Maubourg.'

'We need to invent a new life.'

'Oh, yes.' A new life, with Jack. Who loved her.

'There was an important thing you had to say to me,' he prompted.

'I have never said it to any man before.' Eva tugged at his hands until he rose and stood very close, looking down at her. Her heart was banging against her ribs. She had to explain that this was not an easy thing, a thing she had given before. She searched for the words. 'Louis did not expect me to love him, and although I respected him very much, I never felt anything more for him than that. But I want to say those words to you, and for you to know how important they are for me.'

'Which is why it is hard to say.' Jack nodded. 'I understand. If it were not important, it would be easy, that is how I felt. I have never said those words, either.'

'I love you.' Eva put one hand on his shoulder and lifted the other against the bruises on his cheek. His skin was stubbled and cold, but she felt as though she was warm right through from that one touch. 'I love you with all my heart, and I wish very much to marry you.' And then it was suddenly easy to say. 'I love you, I love you, I lo— Jack!' He swept her up in his arms again and carried her to the bed. She stared up at him from the soft white quilt. 'Jack, you must get warm, you are soaked through.'

'I intend to get warm, very soon.' He had discarded his neckcloth, his numb fingers were fumbling the buttons on his shirt; she knelt up on the bed to help. He tossed it aside and she found that her hand was pressed flat against the front of his breeches, against the only hot part of him. 'Just as soon as I get these off.' He moved her hands away and un-fastened the fall, pushing them off so he stood naked and magnificent and completely unashamed in front of her, showing her just how much he wanted her. 'There. Now you can warm me up.'

'Dry your hair first,' Eva said shakily, half-convinced she had fallen asleep in front of the parlour fire and was dreaming this.

'Undress.' Impatient, Jack reached for a towel and began to rub his hair, his eyes never leaving her.

There was no disobeying him, there never was. Eva slid off the bed and began to unbutton her gown, heeling off her slippers. She should undress slowly, she thought, tease him, but she was too impatient. Her fingers moved faster and faster, pulling at her petticoats, yanking at her corset strings, fumbling with her garters until she was naked.

Jack tossed the wet towel on to the tumbled heap of her clothes and turned to sit on the bed, pulling her towards him until she was standing between his legs.

'Now then, your Serene Highness, how do you propose going about this?'

'Like this.' Eva put her hands on his shoulders for balance and climbed up so she was kneeling on the edge of the bed, straddling the narrow hips, her thighs pressed tight against his flanks, the heat of her tantalising, just above the thrusting erection. She wriggled, seeking just the right angle, making him gasp and clutch her waist, then she slid down in one hard movement to take him, all of him, possessing and possessed.

Eye to eye they were still, her breasts pressed against him, his barely controlled, panting breath fretting their nipples together into an almost unbearable friction. Then she leaned her weight in, feeling the inner muscles gripping and holding the whole hot wonderful length of him as they fell in a tangle of limbs, back on to the bed.

Jack rolled her, his voice a growl, his mouth everywhere, tasting and licking and kissing as though to reclaim every inch of her. 'I love you,' he gasped in her ear, 'I love you.'

'I love you,' she answered, only to find his kiss swallowing the words as his mouth sealed over hers, drawing the breath and the soul out of her body. He drove into her, harder, deeper than she had thought possible, and began to move, driving her wild, her body arching under his, her legs curled round his hips, her heels locked, urging his taut buttocks down.

'I love you.' Which of them spoke? She did not know, only

that the world was turning into black velvet night, that she was spinning in space, that the pleasure flooding her body was his gift to her, just as she gave him all the love in her heart as he reared up, taut with ecstasy above her, gasped her name and collapsed into her embrace, their bodies still locked in delight.

Jack was conscious of determined hands dragging the covers up over his body, opened one eye and found he was burrowed comfortably into Eva's bosom. Bliss. He extended his tongue and touched one pink nipple and was rewarded by a squeak of outrage and a giggle. He shifted his position and began to give the stiffening peak serious attention.

'Jack—not again! My love, we ought to eat.' *My love.* He closed his eyes again and just luxuriated in the words.

'Must we?' he managed at length.

'Yes.' Eva wriggled upright, a deliciously arousing activity in itself. 'We have made love a positively indecent number of times and I am starving.'

'Mmm,' he agreed. Her change of position had brought his head into her lap; his tongue was quite prepared to explore down here, as well.

'Jack!' It was the imperious Grand Duchess voice. He rather thought he had not been dragged out of trouble by his ears since he was six, but he yielded, flopping over on to his back to smile up at her sleepily.

'Dinner,' he agreed. 'I'll ring.' His legs supported him as far as the bell pull, just. He yanked at it, then struggled into his shirt and breeches. 'Where? Here?'

'Yes.' Eva had slid out of bed and was groping amidst her clothes, complaining because the wet towel had made her stays damp. 'Oh, bother it.' She tossed her underthings aside, dragged on her gown, pushed her bare feet in to her slippers and went to braid her hair into a thick tail down her back.

There was a tap at the door. Jack put out his head and found Grimstone there, his expression so blank it was positively insolent. 'Food. Wine. Here. Quickly.'

'Guv'nor. It's one o'clock.' There was a pause. 'In the morning.' Another pause. 'I'll find something.'

Jack closed the door and leaned on it. 'Do you know what time it is?'

Eva's eyes were wide. 'I heard. Poor Grimstone.'

'I am sorry. Are you very tired?'

'No. Not at all.' His love twinkled at him wickedly. 'I had a very nice sleep after the last time.'

'Eva, we have to talk before we get to Maubourg. We have to have decided how this is going to work before we talk to Freddie and your brother-in-law.'

She got up and went to clear the small table that would take their food. With her hair in its simple plait and her rumpled skirts, she looked deliciously domestic. 'I had thought—and you must tell me if this is not all right—that we could be in England when Freddie is at school and then here when it is the holidays. But I do not know whether you have an estate in England.' She shook her head ruefully. 'I am so ashamed, I never even took the time to find out about your home.'

'That is a good compromise.' Jack found himself thinking about Knightsacre, how he had neglected it, how it needed a mistress to love it back into life. 'My estate is called Knightsacre. You would like it, Eva, it is in the West Country. Soft, green land, rolling hills, wide, clear rivers. You could learn to be the mistress of the house—it is three hundred years old, but with no towers and no dungeons. I have neglected it for years: it is waiting for you.'

'Oh, yes. I can imagine it, imagine you riding home from wide acres to the steps of an English mansion that we will make home again for us. But here—what will you do in Maubourg? Will you not be bored? That was what I was going to think about on the journey.'

The knock on the door halted her worries while Grimstone carried in his spoils from the kitchen and set them out. 'This all right, guv'nor?'

'Good, thank you. You go to bed now.'

'We're taking it in turns to sit up. Don't like to leave the place unguarded, not with *Madame* on the premises.' He inclined his head sharply to Eva and took himself out.

Jack pulled up a chair and waited for Eva to sort out the platters of bread, cheese and cold meats. 'You are worrying about me being bored—does that mean I have to work?' His mouth quirked. 'I was expecting to have a very smart cocked hat and to stand one pace behind you during ceremonials, looking handsome.' Her dismay at his teasing must have shown on her face. 'I am sorry, sweet. I thought I would be an additional tutor for Freddie—teach him to shoot and fence and improve his riding. And I wonder if there is something I can do to promote agriculture—growing flowers for perfume is all very well, but the arable crops look woeful.'

She reached across the table and touched his hand. 'You will be his father, not his tutor; he will love the attention. Thank you.' She took a sip of tea and frowned. 'Jack, will this stop your work for the government?'

'It will stop my private work. As for the government, I will have to see. I would not be able to do anything that could compromise the duchy.'

'Or dangerous.' He raised one eyebrow. 'Oh, all right, anyone would think it is fun! Well, nothing involving rescuing ladies, that I insist upon.'

'Very well.' He could promise that, at least.

'Jack,' she said again, still frowning in thought.

'Yes?' He watched her and tried to come to terms with being happy. It felt very odd.

'Before, when we have made love, you were very careful. Tonight you have not been.' She blushed rosily. 'I liked it even more. But does that mean you do not mind if we start a family?'

'I would like to, very much.'

'Oh, good.' Her smile made him feel he had given her the earth and the sea and the sky. It made him feel so powerful that he could do anything. 'A boy and a girl?'

'A boy and two girls,' he corrected. 'We need to keep the numbers even, and the girls will look like you, which will be delightful.'

'Very well. How wonderful if we had started our family tonight.'

'How soon can we get married?' He had not thought of that. A baby. There must be no scandal. And this was not something that could be achieved with a quick licence from the Bishop.

Eva frowned, a slice of bread halfway to her lips. She really did not look like a Grand Duchess. He tried to remember the imperiously angry creature he had found in her chamber the first night.

'Two weeks,' she pronounced. 'I will tell the Archbishop he must sort it out.'

Oh, yes! Imperious was back. 'Make it three,' he suggested. 'Then we can get the English guests here. I'll start a list.'

They carried the notebook and pencil back to bed, leaning shoulder to shoulder as they planned the wedding. 'Who gives you away?' Jack asked, and was answered by a soft murmur. Her head was on his shoulder, her eyes closed. He prised the paper from her hands and snuggled her back into the bed, then slipped out to douse the candles. As he got back she turned, curled her arm around his chest and snuggled close. Jack closed his eyes on the darkness and smiled. He had told her he would always come back for her, and he had. The miracle was, she had been there for him.

It had not occurred to Eva that anyone would recognise her. Their first visit, and then last night, had lulled her into a sense of security. But when they came downstairs the next morning they found in the entranceway Grimstone and both footmen, ostensibly discussing the state of Jack's boots with the landlord. There were also a plump woman, several maids and the ostler.

'*Madame,*' the landlord said seriously, breaking off the discussion and hurrying to the foot of the stairs. 'I must tell you, my wife has recognised you. I just wanted to say that all here are loyal supporters of the Grand Ducal house and we would sooner cut out our own tongues than gossip. You may be assured of our utmost discretion.'

She felt ready to sink, but Jack merely shook the startled innkeeper by the hand 'You are all invited to the wedding,' he said largely. 'Grimstone, see to it. Oh, yes, and a coat of arms for over the door. *By Appointment.*' He murmured in Eva's ear in English. 'I can do that, can't I?'

'Freddie can. You had better ask him.' She was going to collapse into giggles at any moment, which was probably better than strong hysterics, which seemed the alternative option. Jack was getting the hang of this very rapidly; she had forgotten that in his trade acting was a vital skill.

'I had better ask his permission to marry you, don't you think?' he added, handing her up into the coach.

'You would both be crippled with embarrassment,' Eva protested.

'Nonsense. I will be very solemn, call him by his title every other word. He'll love it. Then we can drink a toast in best Napoleon brandy.'

'Jack, he's nine!'

'I did say best brandy.' He grinned unrepentantly as she shook her head at him. 'Now brief me about everyone I am going to meet.'

'Well, as you've sent Grimstone on ahead, I should imagine the entire court will have turned out.' Eva made herself concentrate—staring like a moonling at her gorgeous lover and husband-to-be would have to wait. 'First of all there is Philippe…'

The entire court and the full Guard of Honour and all the staff appeared to have turned out. Jack helped her down amidst a trumpet fanfare and wild clapping from the onlookers.

'How do they know?' he hissed, nodding towards the townsfolk.

'They don't, but this is obviously an Occasion.'

'I am going to design myself a uniform,' Jack remarked as they solemnly paced across the flagstones to where Philippe was waiting, Freddie grinning hugely at his side. 'Something very severe and black with just a hint of silver braid.'

'There is no need, my love.' Eva waved graciously to the cheering crowd, her other hand very obviously resting on Jack's arm. She felt so proud she thought she was going to float. 'I have thought of a suitable office and title for you, and it doesn't come with a uniform.'

'None?'

'Not a stitch,' she said as they arrived at the foot of the steps. 'Master of the Bedchamber.'

Jack stopped and looked down at her, his eyes dark, and she wondered for a moment if the joke offended him. Then he tossed his hat at the crowd, took her firmly in his arms, and kissed their Grand Duchess full on the mouth. As the crowd roared its approval, he lifted his lips just enough to murmur, 'An office for life, I collect, my darling. I accept, with all my heart.'

THE OUTRAGEOUS LADY FELSHAM

LOUISE ALLEN

Author Note

My exploration of the lives and loves of THOSE SCANDAL-OUS RAVENHURST cousins began with the story of Jack Ryder and his Grand Duchess, Eva, in *The Dangerous Mr Ryder*.

At one point, Jack's sister Bel intervened in their romance—with almost disastrous results—so I thought it was time for Bel to have her own story. As the widow of a man known as the most boring member of the *ton*, Lady Belinda Felsham knows something has been missing from her life—specifically an exciting, handsome lover. And she knows, too, that she is far too well behaved ever to go out and find one.

But then Major Ashe Reynard, Viscount Dereham, arrives on her hearthrug at one in the morning, and Bel realises that she has found the man of her fantasies. Ashe is only too ready to oblige—for, after all, neither of them wants anything more than a commitment-free *affaire*. Or do they?

I had a great deal of fun, and some heartache, following Bel and Ashe through their tangled path to true love, hindered on the way by a polar bear, a bathing machine and a formidable aunt. I hope you enjoy the journey, too.

Coming next will be *The Shocking Lord Standon*—not that Gareth Morant, Earl of Standon, *wants* to be shocking. But sometimes a gentleman just has to make a sacrifice for the ladies in his life.

Chapter One

Late July 1815

I want a hero. The words stared blackly off the page into her tired eyes. 'So do I, Lord Byron, so do I.' Bel sighed, pushed her tumbled brown hair back off her face and resumed her reading of the first stanza of *Don Juan*. She and the poet did not want heroes for the same reason, of course. The poet was despairing of finding a suitable hero for his tale; Belinda, Lady Felsham, simply yearned for romance.

No, that was not true either. Bel marked her place with one fingertip and stared into space, brooding. If she could not be honest in her own head, where could she be? Her yearnings were not simple, they were not pure and they certainly were not about knights errant or romance.

Bel rolled over on to her back on the white fur rug and tossed the book aside, narrowly missing one of the candelabra which sat on the hearth and lit her reading. It was well past two in the morning and the candles were beginning to gutter; in a few minutes she would have to get up and tend to them or go to bed and try to sleep.

She stretched out a bare foot, ruffling the silken flounces around the hem of her nightgown, and with her toes stroked the ears of the polar bear whose head snarled towards the door of her bedchamber. 'That's not what I want, Horace,' she informed him. 'I do not yearn for moonlight and soft music and lingering glances. I want a gorgeous, exciting man who will be thrilling in bed. I want a lover. A really good one.'

Horace, unshockable, did not respond, but then he never had, not to any of the confidences that had been poured into his battered and yellowing ears over the years. At the age of nine she had fallen in love with him, wheedled him out of her godfather's study and moved him into her bedchamber. He had stayed with her ever since.

Her late husband—Henry, Viscount Felsham—had protested faintly at the presence of a vast and motheaten bearskin on his wife's chamber floor, but Bel, otherwise biddable and compliant with every stricture and re-quirement of her new husband, had stuck her heels in and Horace had stayed. Henry had always ostenta-tiously made a point of sighing heavily and walking around him whenever he made his twice-weekly visi-tation to her room. Perhaps he sensed that conversation with Horace was more exciting for his young wife than his bedroom attentions had proved.

Bel sat up, braced her arms behind her, and looked round the room with satisfaction. Her bedchamber was just right, even if she was occupying it alone without the lover of her dreams. In fact, she congratulated herself, somewhat smugly, the whole house was perfect.

It was a little gem in Half Moon Street, recently acquired as part of her campaign to emerge from eighteen months of mourning and enjoy herself.

It was still a very masculine house, reflecting the tastes of its last owner. But that was not a problem; it simply gave her another project to work on, and one that was possible to achieve, unlike the acquisition of a suitable lover, which was, as she very well knew, complete fantasy.

Bel was still becoming used to the blissful freedom and independence of widowhood. She would never have wished poor Henry dead, of course not. But if some benevolent genie had swooped down on a magic carpet and removed him to a place where he could lecture the inhabitants at tedious length on their drains, their livestock or the minutiae of tithe law, she would have rejoiced.

Henry had had a knack of being stolidly at her side whenever she wished to be alone and of stating his minutely detailed and worthy opinions upon every subject under the sun. And she had itched to have control of her own money.

But no genie had come for poor Henry, just a ridiculous, apparently trivial, illness carrying him off in what, people unoriginally remarked, was his prime. Her toes were becoming cold. Best to get into bed and hope the soft mattress would help lull her to sleep.

There was a sound from outside the room. Bel tipped her head to one side, listening. Odd. Her butler and his wife, her housekeeper, slept in the basement. The footmen were quartered in the mews and her dresser and the housemaid had rooms on the topmost floor. It came again, a muted thump as though someone had stumbled on the stairs. Swallowing hard, Bel reached out for the poker as her bedchamber door swung open, banging back against the wall.

Framed in the open doorway stood a large figure: long legged, broad shouldered, and dressed, she saw with a shock, in the full glory of military scarlet. The flickering candlelight sparked off a considerable amount of frogging and silver braid, leaving the figure's features in shadow. There was a glint from under his brows, the flash of white teeth. Her fingertips scrabbled nervelessly for the poker and it rolled away from her into the cold hearth.

'Now you are what I call a perfect coming-home gift,' a deep, slurred, very male voice said happily. It resonated in some strange way at the base of her spine as though she was feeling it, not hearing it. 'I don't remember you from before, sweetheart. Still, don't remember a lot about tonight. Thank God,' he added piously.

The man advanced a little further into the room, close enough for his booted toes to be almost touching Horace's snarling jaws. Bel scrabbled a little further back, but her nightgown tangled round her feet. Could she stand up? 'Who moved the bed?' he added indignantly.

He was drunk. It explained the slurred voice, it explained why he was unsteady on his feet and talking nonsense. It did not explain what he was doing in her bedroom.

'Go away,' Bel said clearly, despite her heart being somewhere in the region of her tonsils. Screaming was not going to help, no one would hear her and it might provoke him to sudden action.

'Don't be so unkind, sweet.' His smile was tinged with reproach at her rejection. 'It's not *that* late.' The landing clock struck three. 'See?' he observed, with a grandiloquent gesture that made him sway dangerously. 'The night is but young.' Despite the slurring, the voice was educated and confident. What she appeared to have in her bedchamber was a drunk English officer who could walk through locked doors—unless he was a ghost. But she could smell the brandy from where she was sprawled, and ghosts, surely, did not drink?

'Go away,' she repeated. Somehow standing up did not seem a good idea; she felt it might be like a rabbit starting to run right in front of a lurcher—certain to provoke a reaction. He appeared to be very good looking. Lit by the light of the two candelabra in the hearth his overlong blond hair, well-defined chin and mobile mouth were all the detail she could properly make out, but watching him she was conscious of something stirring deep inside, like the smallest flick of a cat's tail.

'No, don't want to do that. Not friendly, goin' away,' the man said decisively. 'We're goin' to be friendly. Got to get acquainted, ring for a bottle of wine, have a chat first.'

First? Before what, exactly? Suddenly getting up and risking provoking him seemed an attractive option after all. Bel glanced down, realising that not only was she wearing one of her newest and prettiest thin silk nightgowns, but that was all she was wearing. Her négligé—not that it was much more decent—was thrown over the foot of the bed. She inched back as the man took a step forward.

And put one booted foot squarely into Horace's gaping mouth. 'Wha' the hell?' The momentum of his stride took him forward, his trapped foot held him back.

In a welter of long limbs the intruder fell full length on the bearskin rug with Bel flattened neatly between yellowing fur and scarlet broadcloth. Her elbows gave way, her head came down with a thump on Horace's foolish stub of a tail.

'Ough!' He was big. Not fat, though—there was no comfortable belly to cushion the impact. She seemed to be trapped under six foot plus of solid male bone and muscle.

'*There* you are,' he said in a pleased voice, as though she had been hiding. His face was buried in her shoulder and the words rumbled against her skin as he began to nuzzle into it. His night beard rasped, sending shivers down her spine.

'Get off.' Bel wriggled her hands free and shoved up against his shoulders. It had rather less effect than if a wardrobe had fallen on her. At least a wardrobe would not have gone limp like this. There was absolutely nothing to lever on. 'Move, you great lummox!'

The only reply she got was a soft snore, just below her right ear. He had gone to sleep, or fallen into a drunken stupor more like, she decided grimly. This close the smell of brandy and wine was powerful.

Bel wriggled some more but he seemed to have settled over her like a heavily weighted blanket; there was nowhere to wriggle to. Under her there was Horace's fur, the thick felt backing, and, beneath that, the carpet. It all provided some padding, although rather less than her uninvited guest was enjoying. He appeared to be blissfully comfortable.

His knees dug in below her own. That was already becoming painful. With an effort she managed to move her legs apart so he was cradled between her thighs.

'There, that's better.' The answer was another snore, accompanied by a squirming movement of his hips as he readjusted himself to her change of position. At which point Bel realised rather clearly that this was not better. Not at all.

'Oh, my goodness,' she whispered in awe.

Bel had not been sure quite what to expect of marital relations from her mother's veiled hints during the *little talk* they had had just before her wedding day. She had expected it to be uncomfortable and embarrassing at first, and it was certainly all of that. But after the first three weeks of marriage, when the worst of the shyness wore off, she also realised that her marital duties, as well as being sticky and discomforting, were deadly boring. She tried to take an interest, for Henry would be highly affronted if she ever did nod off during his visits to her bed, but it was out of duty, not in the hope of any pleasure for herself.

It was not until the other young matrons with whom she began to mix forgot that she was a very new bride that she got her first inklings that she was missing out on something rather special. One day in particular stuck in her memory.

She had arrived early for Lady Gossington's soirée and found herself in the midst of a group of the very dashing ladies who always filled her with the conviction that she was naïve, gauche and ignorant. They settled round her like so many birds of paradise, fluttered their fans and prepared to subject every arrival to a minute scrutiny and a comprehensive dissection.

'My dears, look who's here,' Mrs Roper whispered. 'Lord Farringdon.'

'Now that,' one of her friends pronounced, 'is what

I call a handsome man.' Bel had studied his lordship. He certainly fitted that description: tall, slim with a clean profile, attractive dark hair and a ready smile.

'And so well endowed,' Lady Lacey purred. In answer, there was a soft ripple of laughter, which had an edge to it Bel did not understand. She felt she was being left out of a secret. 'So I am led to believe,' Lady Lacey added slyly.

Normally Bel would have kept silent, but this time she forced herself to join in; money, at least, was something she understood. 'Is he really?' His clothes were exquisite, but that was not necessarily any indication. 'I did not realise, I thought the Farringdon fortune was lost by his father.'

Their hilarity at this question reduced her to blushing silence. She had obviously said something very foolish. But how to ask for clarification? Lady Lacey took pity on her, leaned across and whispered in her ear. Wide-eyed, Bel discovered in exactly what way the gentleman was well endowed and just how much this characteristic was appreciated by ladies. It left her speechless.

Now she was able to judge precisely what her friends had been referring to. Her uninvited guest was pressed against her in such a way that his male attributes were in perfect conjunction with the point where her tangle of soft brown curls made a dark shadow behind the light silk of her bed gown. And he was drunk and unconscious or asleep and yet he was still...*oh, my heavens...* large. That appeared to be the only word for it. Her previous experience offered no comparison at all. Henry, it was becoming apparent, had *not* been well endowed.

Bel stopped all attempts to wriggle; the *frissons* the

movement produced inside her were just too disquiet-ing. The stirring of sensation she had experienced on first seeing the intruder were as nothing to the warm glow that spread through her from the point where they were so tightly pressed together. It felt as though her insides were turning liquid, but in the most unsettling, interesting way. Her breasts, squashed by his chest with its magnificently frogged dress-uniform jacket, were aching with something that was not solely the result of silver buttons being pressed into flesh. An involuntary moan escaped her lips.

Oh, my... Bel turned her head so she could scruti-nise as much as possible of the stranger. There was not a lot she could see except the top of a tousled blond head and a magnificent pair of shoulders that made her want to flex her fingers on them. This must be sexual attrac-tion! Or was it arousal? She was not very clear about the difference, or how one told. Whatever it was, it seemed alarmingly immodest of her to be feeling it for a man to whom she had not even been introduced. She wished Eva, her new sister-in-law, was in London to ask. But the newly weds were honeymooning in Italy.

Eva—erstwhile Dowager Grand Duchess of Maubourg and now most romantically married to Bel's brother Sebastian—very obviously knew all about sexual attraction. Not only had she been married to one of the most notoriously adept lovers in Europe, she was now passionately attached to Sebastian. Bel had hardly been able to turn a corner in the castle in Maubourg when she had attended the wedding two weeks before, without finding the two of them locked in an embrace, or simply touching fingers, caressing faces, standing close.

There was no one else Bel could trust enough to

discuss such things with; she was on her own with this new sensation. The man seemed nice enough, she brooded. She had observed that drink tended to emphasise any vicious tendencies in a man, so his apparently sunny and friendly nature could probably be relied upon. There was nothing to be done about it but to wait until he woke up and they could have a more civilised conversation. At a safe distance.

It was not easy attempting to sleep while squashed under the body of a large and attractive stranger and prey to one's first stirrings of intimate arousal. The candles began to go out, the room became dark and the only sounds were his heavy, regular breathing and the creaks of the house.

Now it was so dark Bel found her reactions were concentrated on touch and smell. Touch—even the warm caress of his breath against her throat—she tried to ignore, reflecting that if she became any more disturbed by that she would not know how to cope with it. She had heard—probably from one of Henry's pontifications upon the sins of society—that uncontrolled sexual feelings in a woman led to hysteria, and that was definitely to be avoided.

But her nostrils were becoming used to the smell of alcohol and behind it she was catching intriguing whispers of other scents. Soap—a subtle and expensive type—a hint of fresh sweat, which was surprisingly not at all offensive, and man. Henry had smelt just of Henry: rigorously clean and scrubbed at all times. He had used Malcolm's Purifying Tablet Soap, renowned for its health-preserving properties. This man was rather more complex, definitely more earthy and quite unmistakably male. And that, Bel realised, was another source of titilation.

Was this business of sexual attraction more complicated than she had assumed? Did scent and sight and
touch all play a part? And what about the mind? Love
songs and poetry, perhaps? Bel adjusted her head to the
most comfortable angle she could find and resolutely
closed her eyes.

She had not expected to sleep, but she must have
dozed, for when a warm, moist pressure around her ear
woke her, the room was already grey with the earliest
dawn light. Something was nuzzling her ear. Bel froze,
then remembered where she was and who it was. He
was mouthing gently at the sensitive whorls, his tongue
straying up and down them. It was bliss. Her eyelids
drooped again. And then he nipped gently at the lobe.

'Aah!' Bel had never felt so agitated. It should have
hurt; instead, she experienced a jolt of electrifying sensation in a most embarrassing place. Against the unyielding pressure of his chest her nipples hardened,
aching.

The lips left her skin instantly and the deep voice
murmured—with only a hint of a slur, 'Mmm…you're
awake. Good morning, sweet.' He settled himself more
comfortably between her legs with a thrilling tilt of his
pelvis and it was obvious that what she had felt before
was as nothing to what was happening now. He was
awake, he was amorously inclined and he thought she
would be receptive to his advances.

For a mad moment Bel thought of simply throwing
her arms around those broad shoulders and waiting to
see what would happen. She wanted a lover—here he
was. Then common sense and her upbringing came to
the rescue. It was one thing to choose as a lover a man

you knew and respected; it was quite another to lie with a complete stranger who appeared to have wandered in off the street, however deliciously tempting he was.

'Yes, I am awake.' She put her palms against his shoulders and shoved, even more annoyed with herself than with him. 'And thank goodness you are, at long last. Now, sir, please get up this instant.'

He did not stand, but at least he rolled off her, landing with a thump on his back. He turned his head and gazed at her with startlingly blue eyes fringed with thick golden lashes. Periwinkles, lapis, the sun on the sea. Bel gazed back, drowning, then pulled herself together and sat up.

'What, sir, are you doing in my house?'

'I was going to ask you the same thing, my sweet. I don't remember ordering you. Don't remember much, truth be told.' He sat up and rubbed both hands through his hair, rumpling it worse than before. 'God, have I got a hangover.'

'Kindly do not blaspheme.' Bel sat up. 'And I am not in your house, you are in mine. And stop calling me *sweet*. My name is—'

He stood up with a sudden lurch, grabbed for the bedpost, missed and looked around, swaying back on his heels. 'Who moved my bed? And what the dev… what on earth is *that*?' He pointed at Horace.

'A polar bear. You fell over him.' Bel got to her feet, her cramped muscles protesting. 'Who are you?'

'Reynard.' He ran a hand over his stubbled chin and grimaced.

'A fox?'

'No, not *reynard*.' His French accent was good, she noted. 'Reynard. Ashe Reynard. Major. Viscount Dereham. Didn't I tell you when I hired you?' He yawned mightily, displaying a healthy set of white teeth. 'I beg your pardon.'

'Dereham.' Of course. It made sense now. 'You sold this house. I live here now.' She had purchased it through his agent, who had told her that Viscount Dereham was on the continent with Wellington's army. That at least explained the way he had got in; she had not thought to change the locks.

'Ah. I sold it, then?' He swayed, sat down on the bed, and blinked at her. Then he looked down at the bearskin, the burnt-out candles, up at her nightgown. 'So you are not a Drury Lane vestal? Not a little ladybird I hired for the night. You are a lady. Oh, hell.' He drove both hands through the mane of golden hair as though to force some focus into his head. 'Have I just spent the night pinning you to the floor?'

Chapter Two

Bel glanced at the mantel clock. 'We have spent about two hours of the night on the rug.' He—Lord Dereham, for goodness' sake!—got up, hanging on firmly to the bedpost. His gaze appeared to be riveted on her body. She glanced down and realised all over again just what she was wearing and how the early light was streaming through it. She took two swift steps, caught up the négligé and pulled it on. Reynard rocked back on his heels as she brushed past. He looked as if he truly did have the most crashing hangover.

'My…'pologies…' His eyes were beginning to cross now.

'Come on.' She tugged his arm. Goodness, he was solid. 'Come and get some sleep in the spare bedroom.'

'Haven't got one. Remember that.'

'You did not, I do. I expect it was your study. Come along.' She closed both hands over his arm and tried to drag him like a reluctant child.

'In a minute.' Doggedly he turned round and walked off into her dressing room. Of course, he would know about the up-to-the-minute privy installed in a cupboard in the corner along with the innovative—and unreliable—shower bath. Bel left him to it and went across the landing to turn down the spare bed.

The little house had a basement with the kitchen, store rooms and the set of compact chambers occupied by Hedges and Mrs Hedges. Space on the ground floor was chiefly occupied by the dining room and a salon, with above them her bedchamber, dressing room and what had been a study, now transformed into her spare room by dint of adding a small canopied bed.

'You moved my desk,' Lord Dereham complained from the doorway.

'Never mind that now.' Bel took him by the sleeve again and towed him into the room. He was proving remarkably biddable for such a large man. 'Take off your jacket and your neckcloth.'

'A'right.' The slur was coming back. Those garments shed on to the floor, she gave him a push and he tumbled on to the bed. Which left his boots. Bel seized one and tugged, then the other, and set them at the foot. Reynard was already asleep as she dragged the covers over him, the blue eyes shuttered, the ludicrously long lashes fanning his cheeks.

'What *am* I doing?' Bel wondered aloud, bending to retrieve the jacket and neckcloth from the floor. But what was the alternative? She could hardly push him downstairs and he would probably fall if she made him walk. Rousing Hedges to throw him out seemed unfair to the butler, who would be up and working soon enough, and she could hardly leave him in her own bedroom. 'And I don't expect you will stir until luncheon time either, will you?' she asked the beautiful, unresponsive, profile.

His answer was a gentle snore. Bel hung his clothes over the chair back and took herself off back to bed, feeling that her eyes were beginning to cross quite as much as the major's had.

She was awoken, far too soon, by a female shriek. It seemed to come from the landing. Bel sat up, rubbing her eyes. Silence. Goodness, she was tired. And there was something she should remember; she was puzzling over it as her door burst open. Millie, the housemaid, eyes wide with shocked excitement, rushed in, followed by Philpott, her dresser, and bringing up the rear, Mrs Hedges, red in the face with the effort of running up the stairs.

'My lady,' Philpott pronounced in tones of throbbing horror, 'there is a man in the spare bed!'

A man in the spare bed? A man? Lord! Of course there was. Why had she not thought what her staff would find when they started the day's chores?

'Yes?' Bel enquired, more brightly than she felt. 'I know.'

All three women were staring at her bed, she realised. Staring at the smooth, untouched pillow next to her own, the tightly tucked-in bedding on that side, the perfectly unrumpled coverlet, the chaste order of the whole thing. She could almost see their thought processes, like the bubble above a character's head in a satirical cartoon. Despite the outrageous presence of a man next door, no one, quite obviously, had been in her ladyship's bed, other than her ladyship. She raised her eyebrows in haughty enquiry.

'If I had known your ladyship was expecting a guest—' Mrs Hedges crossed her arms defensively '—I would have aired the sheets.'

'I was not expecting him myself,' Bel said, adopting a brisk tone. 'It is Lord Dereham, from whom I bought the house. He was taken suddenly ill, most fortunately almost upon our doorstep, and, having a key, sought refuge in here.'

'But the front door is bolted, my lady. Hedges bolts it every night.'

'The back-door key, it must have been.' Bel wondered where she had suddenly acquired three such assiduous chaperons from. 'I assume his lordship was passing the mews when he became unwell.'

'Should I send for the doctor, my lady?' the house-keeper asked.

'Er…no. His lordship's indisposition is not medical, it is something that will wear off in the fullness of time.'

'He was drunk?' Philpott was aghast. 'It does not bear contemplating. What is the watch coming to, to allow such a rakehell to roam the streets in that condition? What outrage might he not have inflicted upon a helpless woman!'

'Lord Dereham was perfectly civil, and er…respect-ful.' If one did not count nuzzling her ear and giving her the prolonged benefit of the intimate proximity of his magnificent body. She stifled a wistful sigh at the thought of just how magnificent it had felt.

'What shall we do with him now, ma'am?' Mrs Hedges, ruffled, made it sound as if Bel had imported an exotic animal into the house.

'Leave him to sleep, I suppose.' Bel wriggled up against the pillows and tried to think. 'When he wakes up, then Hedges can fetch him coffee and hot water. My husband's toilet gear is in the small trunk in the dressing room, if you could find that, please, Millie; no doubt he will wish to have a shave. And then, depending on what time of day it is, it would be only hospitable to offer a meal.'

Her staff scattered, Mrs Hedges to bustle downstairs to update her husband on the situation, Millie to fetch her morning chocolate and Philpott to sweep around the room, tweaking everything into place. 'What shall I put out for you, my lady?' She retrieved the volume of poetry from the hearth, rattled the poker back into its stand and straightened Horace's head with the point of her toe. Bel watched out of the corner of her eye, suddenly incapable of looking Horace in the face.

'The new leaf-green morning dress, please, Philpott. I had intended walking to Hatchard's, but I suppose I had better not go out while his lordship is still here. The brown kid slippers will do for the moment.'

A new gown, her single strand of pearls and an elegant hairstyle would, she hoped, establish a sufficient distance between Lady Belinda Felsham and the scantily clad woman his lordship had crushed beneath him last night. Bel remembered the way his body had lain against hers, the way it had made her feel and the sudden heat in his eyes as they had rested fleetingly on her fragile nightgown.

The unsettling stirrings inside returned, making her feel flushed and uncertain. Was this the effect of desire, or of unsatisfied desire? Would she need to take a lover to stop these feelings disturbing her tranquillity, or, now they had been aroused, was she going to be prey to them for ever?

Bel leaned back on the embroidered linen of her pillows, turning her cheek against the coolness. But the little bumps of the white work embroidery pressed into her skin, reminding her forcibly of the pressure of the major's

buttons and frogging against her bosom. She waited until
Philpott went into the dressing room and risked a peep
under the neckline of the nightgown, expecting to find a
perfect pattern imprinted on her skin. Nothing, of
course—why then could she fancy she still felt it?

And how was she going to face Lord Dereham when
he awoke?

Ashe turned over on to his back and threw one arm
across his eyes as light from the uncurtained window
hit them. Even through closed lids the effect was
painful.

He lay there, waiting patiently as he had done every
morning for a month now, waiting for the noise of
battle, the shouts and screams, the boom of the cannon
and the crack of musket fire to leave his sleep-filled
brain. The battle was over. He was alive. The fact continued to take him by surprise every morning. How
much longer before he could accept he had not been
killed, had not been more than lightly wounded? How
much longer would it be before he could start to think
like a civilian again and find some purpose in the life
he still had, against all the odds?

Eyes remaining closed against the impact of a
massive headache, Ashe stretched his legs and came up
hard against a footboard. Odd. He did not appear to be
in his own bed. Vaguely, through the brandy fumes, his
brain produced the memory of a woman. A tall, dark-
haired woman with a glorious figure that had fitted
against his body as though she had been created to hold
him in her arms. A beautiful stranger. And a white bear.
A bear? Hell. How much had he drunk last night?

His nostrils flared, seeking her. Wherever the woman

in his memory—or had it been a dream?—had gone, she was not here now. The bed linen smelt fresh and crisp, there was no hint of perfume or that subtle, infinitely erotic, morning scent of warm, sleepy femininity.

Time to open his eyes. Ashe found he was squinting at a very familiar window. His study window, in his house. Only, the desk that always stood in front of it had gone, the bookcases had gone. The room had been transformed into a bedchamber. He threw back the covers and swung his legs out of bed, realising that he was still partly dressed. His boots were standing neatly at the foot of the bed, his dress-uniform jacket hung on the back of a chair. He had not the slightest recollection of taking either off.

The bell pull, thank God, was still where it should be. Ashe made his way across to it, swearing under his breath at the pain behind his eyes, and tugged it, then sat down on the edge of the bed to wait to see who would appear.

The part of his mind that was convinced he was at home expected his valet. The part that was crashingly hungover would not have been surprised to see the door opened by either a white bear or a lovely woman. He had not expected a completely strange, perfectly correct, upper servant in smart morning livery. The butler was bearing a silver salver with a glass upon it filled with a cloudy brown liquid.

'Good morning, my lord. I believe you may find this receipt efficacious for your headache. Would you care for coffee before I bring your shaving water?'

'You know who I am?'

'Major the Viscount Dereham, I understand, my lord.'

'And you are?' Ashe reached for the glass and downed the contents without giving himself time to think about it. Butlers like this one always knew the most repellent, and effective, cures. His stomach revolted wildly, stayed where it was by some miracle, and then stopped churning. He might yet live.

'Hedges, my lord.' The butler retrieved the glass. 'Coffee, my lord? Her ladyship has requested you join her at luncheon, should you feel well enough.'

Her ladyship? 'I am not married, Hedges.'

'As you say, my lord. I refer to Lady Felsham. I understand from her ladyship that you were indisposed last night and sought refuge here, finding it familiar, as it were.'

So he *was* in his own house, and he was not losing his mind. Only he had sold it—he could remember now he had been given a clue. He had written to his agent Grimball from Brussels three months ago. This comfortable little house had proved both too small, and too large, for his needs. He had the family town house—mausoleum though it was—for his mother and sisters on their unpredictable descents upon London, and after selling this house Grimball had taken chambers for him in the Albany for comfortable bachelor living.

But who the devil was Lady Felsham? Surely not the Venus in the translucent silk nightgown he could remember now his head was clearing? She must have been a dream. Women like that only existed in dreams.

The butler was waiting patiently for him to make a decision. 'Coffee would be a good idea, thank you, Hedges, then hot water. And my compliments to her ladyship and I would be delighted to join her for luncheon.'

He frowned at the butler. 'Where is Lord Felsham?' If he remembered correctly, Felsham was older than he—about thirty-five—staid to the point of inertia and widely avoided because of the paralysing dullness of his character and conversation. That did not bode well for an entertaining luncheon, but it was probably all his battered brain could cope with.

'His lordship, I regret to inform you, passed away almost two years ago as the result of a severe chill caught while inspecting the drains at Felsham Hall.' The butler cleared his throat discreetly. 'Her ladyship is only recently out of mourning. If you would care to remove your shirt, my lord, I will do what I can to restore it.'

Stripped to the waist, Ashe shaved himself with the painstaking care of a man who was all too aware that his finer reflexes had a way to go to recover themselves. At least he did not look too much of a wreck, he consoled himself, peering into the mirror after rinsing off the lather. Weeks out of doors drilling his troops had tanned his skin, tightened up his muscles, and one celebratory night of hard drinking did not show—at least not on the outside.

Internally was another matter. He was beginning to wonder what the devil he had consumed, if his memories of last night were so wild. The earlier part was no problem. He had called briefly at his new chambers, changed for the last time into his dress uniform and gone straight to Watier's, leaving Race, his valet, to unpack.

They had all been there, his brothers-in-arms who had survived Waterloo and were fit enough to have made it back to England. And as they had sworn they would the night before the battle, they settled down to a night of eating, drinking and remembering. Remembering the men who were not here to share the brandy and the champagne, remembering their own experiences in the hell that was being acclaimed as one of the greatest battles ever fought—and trying their hardest to forget that they now had to learn all over again to be English gentlemen and pick up the life they had abandoned for the army.

That much was clear. A damned good meal at Watier's, champagne for the toasts, then on through a round of drinking clubs and hells. Not playing at the tables, not more than flirting with the whores and demireps who flocked around them, attracted by the uniforms, but drinking and talking into the night. Doing and seeing the things they could do and see because they were alive.

Eventually, about half past two it must have been, he had turned homewards up Piccadilly towards the Albany. And there old habit must have taken control from his fuddled brain and steered his feet into the curve of Half Moon Street, through the mews and up to his own old back door. He could recall none of that, nor how he had got upstairs, nor what had happened next. Because whatever he might expect to find upstairs in the bedroom of the widow of the most boring man in England, a dark-haired Venus and a large white bear were not within the realms of possibility.

'Your shirt, my lord, and your boots.' Hedges materialised with the expressionless efficiency achieved only by the most highly trained English butler. 'And I have taken the liberty of borrowing one of the late master's neckcloths.'

'Thank you.' Ashe dressed in silence, got his hair into some sort of order, submitted to Hedges whisking the clothes brush over his jacket and followed the butler downstairs. In the blaze of silver lace and frogging he felt distinctly overdressed, but sartorial errors were apparently the least of his *faux pas*.

'Luncheon will be served in about twenty minutes, my lord.' Lady Felsham had not changed the function of the downstairs rooms around, he noted as Hedges opened a door, cleared his throat and announced, 'Major the Viscount Dereham, my lady.'

Taking a deep breath Ashe tugged down his cuffs and strode into the drawing room to confront the straitlaced widow whose home he had invaded.

The breath stayed choked in his lungs. He had expected a frowsty middle-aged woman in black. Standing in the middle of the room was his Venus of the night before, regarding him with steady grey eyes, the colour high on her cheekbones.

Only she was now decently dressed in an exquisite green gown that made her elegantly coiffed hair gleam like polished wood. Pearls glowed softly against her flushed skin and the memory of the scent of her almost drove his scattered wits to the four corners of the room.

'Lord Dereham.' Straight-backed, she dropped the very slightest formal curtsy. She could not be a day over twenty-six, surely?

'Lady Felsham.' He managed it without stammering like a callow boy, thank God, and bowed. There was a slight movement at the back of the room and he saw a plainly dressed woman of middle age in the shadows. A chaperon. Where the blazes had *she* been last night when he had needed her?

'Please, sit.' Her ladyship gestured at a chair and sank down on the chaise opposite. The woman at the back sat too. Not a chaperon, then, or she would have been introduced. Her dresser no doubt. 'I am glad you are able to stay for luncheon, Lord Dereham.'

'Thank you, ma'am. I am delighted.' *And I'm gaping at her like a nodcock. Pull yourself together, man!* 'I must apologise for invading your home last night. There is no hiding the fact that I had been celebrating rather too enthusiastically.' A faint smile curled the corner of her lips. The lower lip had the slightest, most provocative, pout. What would it be like to nip gently? He dragged his eyes away from it. 'I am somewhat confused about what then transpired. This is not helped by recollections of a white bear, which leads me to believe I was rather more in my altitudes than I had imagined.'

'Horace.' She might have been naming a relative. 'He is a polar bear skin on the floor in front of the fireplace.'

'Horace.' The damned bear was called Horace. What sort of woman gave her hearthrugs names, for heaven's sake? But at least he was not losing his mind. 'I think I must have tripped and measured my length on your Horace,' he added, the memories coming back now he knew the white bear was not a dream.

Ashe had thought her colour somewhat heightened when he entered the room. Now she flushed to her hairline. What the devil had he said? Lady Felsham could no longer meet his eyes. He closed them, searching the blurred pictures behind his lids. She had been lying on the fur. It was not Horace he had landed full length upon, it was her, and all those tantalising dreams of warm female curves, of the scent of her skin, of, Heaven help him, following the whorls of her ear with his tongue, were accurate memories.

Chapter Three

Ashe stared at his hostess and Lady Felsham gazed back, sitting there, outwardly composed, while inwardly she must be desperately wondering just what he could recall of all this—and whether he was going to gossip about it, or worse. In fact, the more he thought about it, the more anxious he realised she must be—he could ruin her reputation in one minute of indiscreet talk. It was not something he could hint about, and he had no idea to what extent she had confided in her dresser.

'Might I crave a private word, ma'am?' Her polite smile vanished and a shadowed look came into those frank grey eyes.

All she said was, 'Step outside for a few moments, please, Philpott, and close the door behind you.'

Ashe waited for the snick of the catch before speaking. 'I have placed you in a difficult position—'

'Not as difficult as the position in which I found myself at three o'clock this morning,' she interrupted him with some feeling. Ashe almost smiled; she could have been tearful or furious or even hysterical. As it was, her tart tone was refreshing.

'No. I imagine not. I am also aware that there is very little I can do to make things better other than to offer my profound apologies and to give you my word that I will not speak of this to anyone.' She nodded acceptance, her lips still unsmiling. The colour had ebbed from her cheeks somewhat, he was relieved to see; it seemed she trusted him. 'It must have been terrifying for you and I can only wonder at the fact that you did not have me thrown out on to the street the moment you were free to do so. To have given me a comfortable bed and the attention of your servants is charity I am far from deserving.'

'I doubt my nerves would have stood the results of screaming the house down and then being discovered pinned to the floor beneath an unknown gentleman,' she said gravely. 'Once you were on your somewhat unsteady feet I considered what to do and decided that my butler needed his sleep. In any case, the sight of your supine body on the front step would hardly have added to my consequence with the neighbours. I had plenty of time to assess you my lord, and I came to the conclusion that you were harmless enough.'

She was laughing at him now the anxiety was gone. The spark in those fine eyes was not mortification, nor indignation, but amusement. Ashe found an answering bubble of laughter rising and got it firmly under control. Lady Felsham might be prepared to see the funny side of this, but he still felt his own part to have been unforgivable.

'You are too generous, ma'am. I trust I did not injure you.'

'Not at all. Horace has thick fur and the carpet

beneath was also good padding. I have slept more comfortably, I must admit.' She smiled at last, a generous, warm smile that had him yearning to press his lips to it. 'But after almost two years in mourning, living in rural seclusion, a small adventure is not unwelcome.'

There was a discreet tap at the door. 'Come in!'

'Luncheon is served, my lady.'

'Have you an appetite, Lord Dereham?' Lady Felsham rose to her feet with a graceful sway that had him fighting to keep his eyes away from her hips. 'I can promise you that Mrs Hedges is an excellent cook.'

Mrs Hedges had indeed done them proud. Bel was thankful for the distraction the formalities of eating in company provided. Lord Dereham had greatly relieved her mind with his assurances of discretion and the impeccable way in which he was behaving, but even so, the sensations conjured up by even referring to the incident were physically most agitating. Bel shifted uncomfortably on her seat and tried not to fidget.

'Butter, Lord Dereham?' She helped herself to braised ham, then found herself staring at the big, capable hand with its long fingers and the healing scar across the knuckles as he replaced the butter dish on the table. It was the hand of a fighting man, a strong man, and she could not help but contrast it with Henry's white, soft and carefully manicured digits.

'You have not been back in England long?' She tried to imagine that she was presiding over a vicarage luncheon party and not to remember his mischievous twinkle as she had remarked that a *small adventure* was not unwelcome. 'Your agent led me to understand that you were with the army in Belgium.'

'I arrived the night before last from Ostend and reached London late yesterday afternoon.'

'Then no wonder you felt so…unwell yesterday. You must have been exhausted. The Channel crossing alone, I am sure, must be wearisome.'

'You are kind to find an excuse for me.' His smile really was very charming. Bel found herself smiling back. Seduced into smiling. He was dangerous. 'But I have none, in truth. I went out to join fellow officers and we talked and drank—with the result you saw.'

It was on the tip of her tongue to remark that they must have been celebrating when she sensed a shadow. It was not so much that his expression changed, as the light went out behind those remarkable blue eyes. He was sad, she realised with a flash of empathy. On instinct she turned and nodded dismissal to the footman who stood silently by the sideboard. If her visitor was experiencing mental discomfort, he did not need an audience for it.

'It must be so painful to remember all those men who could not be with you last night,' Bel said quietly. 'Is it sometimes hard to believe that you are alive and they are not?'

He had raised his glass to his lips as she spoke, but put it down at her words, untouched. Bel thought she caught the hint of a tremor in his hand, then he was in control again. 'You are the only person I have spoken to who was not there who understands.' He stared at the glass and at his own fingers wrapped around the stem. She waited, expecting him to say something further, but after a moment he lifted the glass again and drank. A sore spot, then, one to avoid. He was going to have a hard time of it though, once he went out into society

again. Everyone would want to lionise another returning Waterloo officer, talk about the battle, demand to
know about Wellington, ask about his experiences.

'We are both going to find our new lives difficult.
You have been in the army, I have been in seclusion,'
she observed. 'Unless you are going back into the army,
Lord Dereham?'

'No. I will go to Horse Guards today and resign my
commission. Quite frankly,' he added with a rueful grin,
'I am strongly tempted to bolt off to the country and rus-
ticate on my much-neglected estate rather than face
certain aspects of London life again.'

'Town is very quiet just now,' Bel reassured him.
'That is why I came up in early June—to replenish my
wardrobe and find my feet again without too many invitations. And then I found myself travelling to the
Grand Duchy of Maubourg, of all places, for my
brother's wedding.'

'Indeed? It sounds an adventure. That is an unusual
place for your brother to be wed, I must confess.'

'Not if you are marrying the Dowager Grand
Duchess of Maubourg.' Bel smiled reminiscently. 'It
was just like a fairy tale—or a Gothic novel, if one con-
siders the castle. Quite ridiculously romantic.'

'I am sorry, I should remember who your brother is,
forgive me.'

'My elder brother is the Duke of Allington. This was
my second brother, Lord Sebastian Ravenhurst.'

'Otherwise known as Jack Ryder! I knew there was
something familiar about you—you have the same
grey eyes.'

So, Lord Dereham knew Sebastian in his secret
persona as spy, investigator and King's Messenger. It

was probably a state secret, but she risked the question. 'Where did you meet him?'

'On the morning of the battle.' There was no need to specify which battle. Bel saw the realisation come over him. 'Then that very handsome woman in man's clothing was the Grand Duchess Eva? No wonder your brother looked ready to call me out when I tried a little mild flirtation with her!'

'Indeed, you were dicing with death, Lord Dereham,' Bel agreed, amused at the daring of a man who would flirt with any woman under Sebastian's protection. 'It is a most incredible story, for he snatched Eva out of Maubourg and back to England in the face of considerable danger.'

'You are a romantic, then?' He poured her more lemonade from the cut-glass jug at his elbow and watched her quizzically for her answer. Bel found herself drowning in that deep azure gaze, rather as she might surrender to the sea. He seemed to be luring her on to confess her innermost yearnings, her need to be loved, her wicked curiosity to experience physical delight. And just like the sea, he was dangerous and full of undercurrents. A completely unknown element. Of course she could reveal nothing. Nothing at all.

'A romantic? I...I hardly know,' Bel confessed, throwing caution overboard and wilfully ignoring the sensation that she might be heading for the reef without an anchor. 'I would not have said so a few weeks ago. I would have said I was in favour of a rational choice of marriage partners, of very conventional behaviour and, of course, of judicious attention to society's norms. And then, when Eva and Sebastian fell in love, I found I would have defied any convention in the world to

promote their happiness. I virtually gatecrashed a
Carlton House reception, in fact, then kidnapped poor
Eva to harangue her for breaking Sebastian's heart.'

'Passionate, romantic and daring, then.' He
sounded admiring.

Bel knew she was blushing and could only be
grateful that she had dismissed the footman earlier. 'In
the cause of other people's happiness, Lord Dereham,'
she said, attempting a repressive tone.

'Will you not call me Ashe?' He picked up an apple and
began to peel it, his attention apparently fixed on the task.

'Certainly not!' Bel softened the instinctive response
with an explanation. 'We have not even been introduced, ridiculous though that seems.'

'I am sure Horace did the honours last night,' Ashe
suggested. 'He strikes me as a bear of the old school.
A stickler for formality and the correct mode.'

'Even so.' Bel allowed herself the hint of a smile for
his whimsy, but she was not going to be lured into im-
propriety—her own thoughts were quite sufficiently
unseemly as it was. And she was not going to rise to his
teasing about her silly rug. Goodness knows what familiarity she might be tempted into if they became any
more intimate than they were already.

'Reynard, then?' He was not exactly wheedling, but
there was something devilishly coaxing about the expression in the blue eyes that were fixed on her face.

'I should not.' She hesitated, then, tempted, fell. After
all, it was only such a very minor infringement of propriety
and who was going to call her to account for it? Only
herself. 'No, why should I be missish! Reynard, then.'

'Thank you, Lady Belinda.' The peel curled in an un-
interrupted ribbon over his fingers as he slowly used the

knife. 'Now, tell me, why are you such an advocate of passion for other people, but not yourself?'

'You forget, I am a widow,' Bel said sharply. That was far too near the knuckle.

'I apologise for my insensitivity. Yours was a love match, I collect.' The red peel fell complete on to his plate and formed, to her distracted gaze, a perfect heart.

'Good heavens, no! I mean—' She glared at him. 'You have muddled me, Lord…Reynard. Mine was a marriage much like any other, not some…' She struggled to find the proper, dignified words.

'Not some irrational, unconventional, injudicious— do I have your list of *un*desirable attributes correctly?— storm of passion, romance and love, then?'

'Of course not. What a very unsettling state of affairs that would be, to be sure, to exist in such a turmoil of emotions.' *How wonderful, exciting, thrillingly delicious it sounds.* 'No lasting marriage could be built upon such irrational feelings.'

'But that is the state true lovers aspire to, is it not? Your brother and his new wife, from what you say, feel these things. It is not all so alarming.'

'And you would know?' she enquired, curious. Surely, if there was some blighted romance in his life, he would not speak so lightly; she might safely probe in return.

'The storms of passion? Yes, I have felt those on occasion. The more tender emotions, no, not yet.' He quartered the apple and set down his knife, watching her slantwise. 'Respectable matrons would warn you that I am a rake, Lady Belinda. We are immune to romance, although passion may be a familiar friend.'

'Are you attempting to alarm me, sir?' She had never knowingly met a rake before and she was not at all certain she had met one now; Reynard could very well be teasing her. Upon her come-out she had been strictly guarded by her mama, for the daughter of a duke was not to be left prey to the attentions of fortune hunters— or worse—for a moment. On her marriage there had been Henry to direct all her social intercourse and, as he would not dream of frequenting any place likely to attract the dissolute, or even the frivolous and fun-loving, such perilous men had not crossed her path.

'Not at all. If I was dangerous to you, that would be a foolish tactic for me to adopt.'

'Or perhaps a very cunning one?' she suggested, folding her hands demurely in her lap while he cut his apple into smaller segments and ate it, each piece severed by a decisive bite.

'Lady Belinda, I am too befuddled by last night's excesses and too bemused by your beauty to manage such clever scheming.'

'My beauty? Why, I do believe you are flirting with me, Reynard!' He *was*. How extraordinary to be flirted with again. She could hardly remember how it had felt and certainly not how to deal with it.

Lord Dereham wiped his fingers on his napkin and dropped it beside his plate. 'I was attempting to, I did warn you.' Before she could respond he was on his feet, standing to pull back her chair for her. 'That was a delicious meal, ma'am; you have heaped coals of fire on my unworthy head with your generous hospitality in the face of my out-rageous invasion in the early hours. And now I will remove myself off to Horse Guards and leave you in peace.'

'I hope your business goes well.' Bel held out her hand. There went her adventure, her glimpse into the world of excitement, scandal and loose living. And all it had left her were some very disconcerting sensations, which she could only hope would subside once a certain tall blond gentleman removed himself from her sight. Somehow she doubted it. Somehow she knew that Lord Byron's verse was going to be accompanied by some very vivid pictures from now on.

'Lady Belinda.' He shook her hand, his cool fingers not remaining for a fraction longer than was strictly proper. It was most disappointing, although doubtless the best thing, considering Hedges was hovering attentively in the background.

'Your hat and gloves, my lord. I found them upon the chest on the landing.'

The door closed behind Reynard and Bel found herself standing in the hallway, gazing rather blankly at the back of it. The sound of Hedges clearing his throat brought to herself with a start.

'I hope his lordship remembered to return his back-door key to you, my lady. I understand from Mrs Hedges that that was how he obtained entry last night.

'His key? Oh, yes. Of course,' Bel said brightly. 'Please ask James to be ready to accompany me to Hatchard's in fifteen minutes, Hedges, and send Philpott to my room directly.'

As she climbed the stairs, Bel realised that she had just lied to her butler without hesitation. Without, in fact, the slightest qualm. Of course Lord Dereham had not given her back the key. Had he forgotten it, as she had done up to the moment the butler asked about it, or was he deliberately keeping it? And was he really a dangerous rake, or was he just teasing her? Whatever it was that was fluttering inside her it was not fear, but it was a decidedly unsettling feeling.

* * *

Ashe walked briskly away from Lady Belinda's front door, reached Piccadilly, raised his hand to summon a hackney carriage and then, abruptly changing his mind, strode diagonally across the crowded road and into Green Park by the Reservoir Gate.

He needed, he found, space to think—which surprised him, for he had thought he had the next few days clearly planned out in his head. Horse Guards to resign his commission, then back to the Albany to settle in comfortably. There was the town house to check out for Mama, shopping to be done to fit himself out as a civilian gentleman once again, and letters to write. He had intended to stay in London for at least a fortnight before venturing west to Hertfordshire and Coppergate, his country estate.

He had been home on leave a mere six weeks ago, shortly before the battle. His family knew he was safe, where he was and that he had business which would keep him in London for a week or so. That would give him time to get accustomed to his new circumstances, allow him to mentally rehearse the stories he was prepared to tell his family about his experiences. If he told them the truth about the great battle, they would be appalled; he needed some distance from his recent past and space to create the comfortable fictions in order to shield them.

At Coppergate he would interview his estate manager, sort out his affairs and come back to town as soon as he decently could. Ashe loved his family, had missed them while he was away, but in the country he felt purposeless, empty and restless. Why, he had no idea. He enjoyed country sports, he was deeply attached to the estate and the strange old house at the heart of it. And there was certainly plenty he could be doing there, as his steward would tactfully hint.

And now, unexpectedly, he felt the same way here. It must be the hangover. He strolled around the perimeter of the Reservoir amidst the small groups of gossiping ladies with servants patient at their heels, the nursemaids and shrieking children and the occasional elderly gentleman, chin on chest, deep in scholarly thought as he walked off his luncheon.

The fresh air finished the work of Hedges's potion and a good lunch on his headache, but it did not cure his restlessness. Ashe struck off away from the water and headed for St James's Park, abandoning the idea of taking a hackney. He found he was avoiding thinking about last night, about Lady Belinda and about his reaction to her. He made himself do so.

It was a relief to realise that he had behaved with at least some restraint, although the feelings of a respectable lady on finding a drunken, amorous officer in her bedchamber defied his imagination, even if he had confined his assault on her person to falling full length upon her, licking her ear and then falling asleep for hours. He grimaced at himself. *Even!* He had treated Lady Belinda like a lightskirt and he was fortunate she was not even now summoning an outraged brother to demand satisfaction.

The dangerous Mr Ryder was safely out of the country, and the duke was where he always was, reclusive on his northern estates. Ashe wrestled with the conundrum of whether honourable behaviour required that he write to the duke, account for himself and make assurances about his behaviour, or rest upon the lady's remarkable forbearance. He decided, with relief, that he was under no such obligation to frankness. Nothing irretrievable had, after all, occurred.

Lady Belinda did seem to have forgiven him. Her straitlaced late husband could hardly have given her much cause to become used to gentlemen overindulging, so he supposed she must simply be a very understanding woman.

She had been embarrassed, though, he mused, kicking at daisies in the cropped grass as he walked. It was not as though she was one of those dashing widows who would greet the unexpected arrival of a man in their bedroom with opportunistic enthusiasm. Which was a good thing, he thought with a self-deprecating grin; he had been far too drunk to have performed to any lady's satisfaction, let alone his own.

Lady Belinda had been tolerant, sensible and pragmatic, he concluded, which was more than he deserved. The thought struck him like a punch in the gut that if she had chosen to be difficult she could, very easily, put him in a position where he would have had to marry her. And marriage was absolutely not in his plans. Not for another five years or so, by which time his mother's gentle nagging would become strident and she would cease merely hinting that Cousin Adrian would make a terrible viscount and order him to do something about the succession before his thirty-sixth birthday dawned.

He had almost succeeded in coaxing Lady Belinda into flirting, which had been agreeable. Ashe began to feel better. Flirting with pretty women was a cliché for the returning warrior, but it was certainly a good way to keep your mind off blood, death and destruction.

Ashe returned the sentry's salute and ran up the steps into Horse Guards. Perhaps civilian life in London, even out of Season, would not be so bad after all.

Chapter Four

Bel too, was contemplating her sojourn in London with rather more attention than she had previously given it. She had moved simply to assert to herself and her in-laws that she was an independent woman about to start a new life. Her lovely little house was a gem, she was enjoying the walks and the shopping and now she began to wonder if perhaps there was not some social life she could comfortably indulge in.

The fact that the extremely attractive Lord Dereham might form part of that social life was undeniably an incentive. Bel found she was gazing sightlessly at a row of the very latest sensation novels, plucked a volume off the shelf at random and went to sit in one of the velvet chairs Hatchard's thoughtfully provided for their browsing customers.

In place of her vague, innocent and completely uninformed dreams of a lover, of passion and excitement, her night-time visitor had presented her with a flesh-and-blood model of perfection. And some valuable, if highly disturbing, practical information about the male animal. Daydreaming about Ashe Reynard would doubtless be frustrating but…delicious. She flicked over the pages and read at random.

Alfonso, tell me I am yours, do not betray me to the dark evil of my uncle's plans! Amarantia pleaded, her eyes shimmering with unshed tears. Her lover strained her to his breast, his heart beating in tumultuous acknowledgement of her…

Bel gave a little shiver of anticipation and forced herself to consider the realities. She might see Reynard again. He might flirt with her. She might learn to flirt in return. That was, of course, as far as it could go. Actually taking a lover was a fantasy, for she would never dare to go any further than mild flirtation and he showed no sign of wanting to do so, in any case. Why should he? London was full of sprightly and sophisticated feminine company and Lord Dereham no doubt knew exactly where to find it.

No, it was just a game for her to play in the sleepless night hours. A fantasy. Lord Dereham was never again going to strain her to his breast, his heart beating hard against hers as it had last night. She sighed.

'Belinda!'

Bel gave a guilty start and dropped her book. The spine bent alarmingly. She would have to buy it now. 'Aunt Louisa!' Lady James Ravenhurst was fixing her with a disapproving stare over the top of the lorgnette she was holding up. 'And Cousin Elinor. How delightful to see you both.' She got to her feet, feeling like a gawky schoolgirl as Elinor retrieved the novel from the floor.

'The Venetian Tower,' she read from the spine. 'Is that a work of architecture, Cousin Belinda?'

'Er…no.' Bel almost snatched it back. 'Just a novel

I was wondering about buying.' Aunt Louisa seemed about to deliver a diatribe on the evils of novel reading. Bel hurried on, knowing she was prattling. 'I had no idea you were both in London.'

'As The Corsican Monster chose to escape from Elba at precisely the moment I had intended leaving on a study tour of French Romanesque cathedrals, my plans for the entire year have been thrown into disarray,' her aunt replied irritably. Her expression indicated that Bonaparte must add upsetting her travel arrangements to the list of his deliberate infamies. 'I had plans for a book on the subject.'

'Romanesque? Indeed?' What on earth did that mean? Surely nothing to do with the Romans? They did not build cathedrals. Or did they? Aunt Louisa was a fearsome bluestocking and her turn for scholarship had become an obsession after the death of Lord James ten years previously. 'How fascinating,' Bel added hastily and untruthfully. 'And you are in town to buy gowns?' After one glance at Cousin Elinor's drab grey excuse for a walking dress, that was the only possible explanation.

'Gowns? Certainly not.' Lady James trained her eyeglass on the surrounding shelves. 'I am here to buy books. Our expedition will have to be postponed until next year, so I will continue my researches here. Elinor, find where they have moved the architecture volumes to. I cannot comprehend why they keep moving sections around, so inconsiderate. You have the list?'

'Yes, Mama,' Elinor responded colourlessly. 'Britton's *Cathedral Antiquities of England* in five parts and Parkyns's *Monastic and Baronial Remains*. Two volumes.' She drifted off, clutching her notebook. Bel frowned after her. She could never quite fathom her cousin. Elinor, drab and always at the beck and call of her mother, was only two years younger than Bel. At twenty-four she was firmly on the shelf and certain to remain there, yet she neither seemed exactly resigned to this fate, nor distressed by it. She simply appeared detached. What was going on behind those meekly lowered eyes and obedient murmurs? Bel wondered.

'Belinda.'

'Yes, Aunt Louisa?' Bel reminded herself that she was a grown-up woman, a widow who was independent of her family, and she had no need to react to her formidable relative as she had when she was a shy girl at her come-out. It did not help much, especially when one had a guilty conscience.

'I hear you have purchased a London house of your own. What is wrong with Cambourn House, might I ask?'

What business it was of hers Bel could not say, but she schooled her expression to a pleasant smile. 'Why, Lord Felsham has it now.'

'I trust your late husband's cousin does not forbid you the use of it!' Lady James clutched her furled parasol aggressively.

'Certainly not, Aunt. I just do not choose to be beholden to him by asking to borrow it.' The new Lord Felsham was a pleasant enough nonentity, but his wife was a sharp-tongued shrew and the less Bel had to do with them, the happier she was.

'Then you have engaged a respectable companion, I trust?'

Bel moved further back towards the theology section, away from any interested ears browsing amidst the novels. 'I have a mature dresser and a most respectable married couple managing the house.' *And what would you have said if you could have seen me last night, I wonder?* The thought of the formidable Lady James beating a drunken Lord Dereham over the head with her parasol while he lay slumped on the scantily clad body of her niece almost provoked Bel into an unseemly fit of the giggles. She had the sudden wish that she could share the image with Reynard. He would laugh, those startling eyes creasing with amusement. His laugh, she just knew, would be deep and rich and wholehearted. 'I am very well looked after, Aunt, I assure you.'

Elinor drifted back, an elderly shop assistant with his arms full of octavo volumes at her heels. 'I have them all, Mama. I do like that gown, Cousin Belinda. Such a pretty colour.'

'Thank you. I must say, I am rather pleased with it myself; it is from Mrs Bell in Charlotte Street. Have you visited her?'

Lady James ran a disapproving eye over the leaf-green skirts and the deep brown pelisse with golden brown frogging. 'A most impractical colour, in my opinion. Well, get along, man, and have those wrapped, I do not have all day! Come, Elinor. And you, Niece— you find yourself some respectable chaperonage, and quickly. Such independence from so young a gel! I do not know what the world is coming to.'

'Good afternoon, Aunt,' Bel said to her retreating back, exchanging a fleeting smile with her cousin as she hurried in the wake of her mother. Lord! She did hope that Aunt Louisa retained her fixed distaste for social occasions and did not decide it was her duty to supervise her widowed niece's visits now that she was in London.

* * *

The afternoon post had brought another flurry of invitation cards. It seemed, Bel mused, as she spread them out on her desk, that she was not the only person remaining in London well into July this year. Perhaps the attraction of the officers returning from the Continent had something to do with it.

She took out her appointments book, turning the pages that had remained virtually pristine for the past eighteen months, and studied the invitations that had arrived in the past few days. Her return to town after the Maubourg wedding had been mentioned in the society pages of several journals and it seemed her acquaintances had not forgotten her now her mourning period was over.

Lady Lacey was holding an evening reception in two days' time. That would be a good place to start. No dancing to worry about, familiar faces, the chance to catch up on the gossip. Bel lifted her pen, drew her new-headed paper towards her and began to write.

'Belinda, my dear! Welcome back to London.' Lucinda Lacey enveloped Bel in a warm hug, a rustle of silken frills and a waft of *chypre* perfume. 'We have so missed you.'

'I have missed you too.' Lucinda had not written, not after the first formal note of condolence, but then Bel had not expected her to. Lady Lacey's world was one of personal contact, of whispered gossip and endless parties and diversions. She would not have forgotten Bel exactly, but she would never have the patience for regular correspondence with someone who could not provide titillating news in return.

'All your old acquaintances are here.' Lucinda wafted her fan in the general direction of the noise swelling from the reception rooms. 'We will talk later, there is so much to catch up upon.'

As her hostess turned her attention to the next arrivals, Bel took a steadying breath and walked into the party. At least her new jonquil-silk gown was acceptable, she congratulated herself, sending a quick, assessing, look around the room. The bodice was cut in a V front and back and the hem had a double row of white ruffles connected to the high waist by the thinnest gold ribbon. The length, just grazing her ankle bones, and the detail of the bodice and sleeves were exactly in the mode. It seemed strange to be wearing pale colours again after so many months.

She glanced down at the three deep yellow rosebuds she had tucked into the neckline. They had come from the bouquet of roses that had arrived the day after her encounter with Ashe Reynard, accompanied by a very proper note of thanks and apology. Bel had tucked the note into her appointments book, marking the day they had met. It was an absurdly romantic thing to do—just as absurd as her new habit of flicking back through the pages to look at it.

'Belinda!' The descent of three of her old acquaintances, fans fluttering, ribbons streaming, drove all thoughts of Lord Dereham from her mind. Therese Roper, Therese's cheerfully plump cousin Lady Bradford and Maria Wilson, a golden-haired widow with a sprightly air.

'Come and sit with us,' Therese commanded, issuing the familiar invitation to join the circle of bright-eyed ladies as they gossiped, criticised and admired the other guests. This was the forum that had convinced Bel that her husband's attentions in the bedroom fell far short of the bliss to be expected. She wondered what they would say if they knew their sheltered friend had been severely tempted by an intimate encounter with a handsome man on her bedchamber hearthrug and wished she could trust any of them enough to talk about it.

'Now that is a truly lovely gown,' Annabelle Bradford declared as they settled themselves on a group of chairs. 'I swear I am green with envy—divulge the modiste this instant!'

Obligingly Bel explained where she had purchased the gown, submitted to a close interrogation about the total lack of excitement in her rural retreat, agreed that Lady Franleigh's new crop was a disaster on a woman with a nose of such prominence and exclaimed with indignation at the revelation that Therese's husband had taken up with a new mistress only a month after promising to reform his habits and become a model of domestic rectitude.

'What will you do?' Bel was shocked and intrigued. Imagine Henry carrying on like that! It would have been unthinkable. Therese sounded far more annoyed than upset by the current state of affairs, but then she had had six years to become accustomed to Mr Roper's tomcat tendencies.

'I shall abandon my own resolution to be faithful, for a start.' Her friend lowered her voice to a conspiratorial tone. 'I have not yet decided who the lucky man is to be, for I am greatly tempted by two gentlemen, either of whom would be perfect. Let me tell you—oh, my—' She broke off, raising her gilt quizzing glass to her eye. 'My dears, just when I thought I had passed all the available gentlemen under review, yet another gorgeous creature arrives to distract me!'

'Where?' They turned like a small flock of birds, following the direction of Mrs Roper's interested gaze.

'Oh, my, indeed,' Mrs Wilson exclaimed. 'Now that is what I call a very handsome man. A positive Adonis. Where has he sprung from, I wonder?'

Elegant in corbeau-blue superfine, his legs appearing to go on for ever in tight black evening breeches and with the crisp white of immaculate linen reflecting light on his chiselled jaw, Lord Dereham strolled negligently into the room, deep in conversation with a man in scarlet regimentals. There was a collective sigh from the ladies, masking Bel's little gasp of alarm.

It was one thing daydreaming about meeting Ashe Reynard again, it was quite another to come across him in the company of three hawk-eyed ladies bent on either flirting with him, seducing him or observing who did.

'It is Dereham,' Lady Bradford decided after a minute scrutiny. 'I thought he was an attractive man last time I saw him, but a few years in the army have definitely added a certain something.'

Muscles like an athlete, an air of quiet authority that make goose bumps run up and down my spine and a gaze that seems to be scanning the far horizon, that is most definitely 'a certain something', Bel thought ruefully, wondering if she could find an excuse and slip out now, before he saw her.

Too late. The officer he was speaking to clapped him on the shoulder and strode off, leaving Reynard in the centre of the room. He turned slowly, scanning it, and Bel made a rapid decision.

'It is Lord Dereham's house in Half Moon Street that

I have purchased,' she confided, apparently intent upon the twisted cord of her reticule. 'He called the other day. A very pleasant man, I thought.'

'*Pleasant!* Is that the best you can find to say about him?' Therese stared at her. 'Is there something wrong with your eyesight, Belinda?'

Bel wrinkled her nose in disdain, searching for something to explain her faint praise. 'I find that blond hair rather obvious.' The others regarded her as though she had remarked that she was about to become a nun, then turned their collective gaze back on his lordship who was, Bel saw with a sinking heart, making his way over to her.

Sinking heart *and* racing pulse and fluttering insides would be more accurate, she realised, despairingly cataloguing her physical reaction to Reynard's approach even as she fought to attain some mental coherence.

'Lady Belinda, Lady Bradford, Mrs Roper, Mrs Wilson.' His bow was a masterpiece of graceful restraint. The ladies were bowing and simpering, returning the courtesy with a chorus of murmured greetings. He had scrupulously addressed them in order of precedence, Bel realised, getting her alarm that he had spoken her name first under control. There would be nothing there for the others to pounce and speculate upon.

Then his eyes fell on the rosebuds at her bosom and she saw a gleam come into them. What was it? Had he recognised the flowers he had sent? Perhaps he had just ordered his butler to see to a suitable bouquet and had no idea what had been delivered. His lips parted as though to speak.

'I must thank you again for calling the other day,' she said, cutting across Mrs Wilson who had begun to remark on how unexpectedly crowded London was.

Reynard's eyebrows started to lift and she hurried on. 'I was so grateful for someone to explain the idiosyncrasies of the plumbing on the first floor. Your agent seemed completely baffled.' Around her she could sense the amusement of her sophisticated acquaintances. *Poor little Belinda, she has this gorgeous man in the house and all he has come about is the plumbing!*

'It was my pleasure.' His eyebrows had returned to their normal level, but the gleam—the *wicked* gleam—was more intense as his voice slurred slightly over *pleasure*. Something wicked in her flickered into being in response and she could tell he had recognised it in her eyes. 'After all, the shower bath in the dressing room was put in at my insistence, but I fear the plumber had never come across such a thing before and it still works only intermittently.'

There was a flutter of interest. A shower bath was so novel, and the act of discussing bathing with a man so *risqué*, that the ladies fell to exclaiming and laughing. Reynard stooped to pick up the handkerchief that had fallen from her reticule and murmured, 'Clever.'

'You too,' Bel murmured back.

'A good team.' He pressed the scrap of lace-trimmed nonsense into her gloved hand, his fingers closing for a moment around hers, then his attention was back on the others. 'You were saying that London is very full of society, Mrs Wilson?'

'Quite amazingly so for July, do you not agree?' She batted her eyelashes at him. 'I think it is because all you wonderfully brave officers are coming back home and everyone wants to meet you.'

There it was again, that shutter descending, closing down the animation in Reynard's startling blue eyes.

'And all the *wonderfully brave* men as well,' Bel said abruptly, remembering something she had read in the newssheet only the other day about the wounded men still straggling back from Belgium. 'But they are not receiving so much positive attention, are they? After all, scars and missing limbs are not so glamorous shielded only by homespuns as they are beneath a scarlet dress coat.'

There was a collective gasp, but Reynard turned to her, a smile lurking behind his grave countenance. 'Indeed, that is very true, Lady Belinda. But doubtless society ladies are already rallying to form charitable organisations to help the men and their families, and urging their husbands to find them work.'

'One can only hope so,' she responded seriously.

'If you will excuse me, ladies? I am promised to Lord Telford for a hand of cards.' Reynard bowed again and left them to turn on Bel in a flurry of indignation.

'How could you drive him away like that? Honestly, Belinda, the most handsome man in the room comes to talk to us and you start prosing on about plumbing and amputations!' Annabelle Bradford scolded.

Bel schooled her face to meekness. 'I am sorry, I did not think.' Reynard did not want to speak about his experiences, and she was not going to let these feather-brained women torment him with them, not if she could help it. *A good team.* The words warmed her inside, adding to the strange hollow feeling that she was beginning to recognise as anticipation and the low, pulsing ache that she supposed was desire.

She turned her face resolutely to the opposite end of the room from where the card room door was. 'Tell me all about the other attractive men you wicked things have in your sights.' There could not have been a better choice of subject to distract them. In a ruffle of gorgeous plumage the group settled down in their chairs again.

'*Well,*' Therese began conspiratorially, 'have you met Lord Betteridge? Just back from the Congress, and I swear...'

Chapter Five

That had not been so bad, Bel told herself as she was driven home that evening. She had survived meeting Lord Dereham again without betraying herself in front of the sharpest eyes for scandal in town, she had mingled comfortably with any number of old acquaintances and met several congenial new people and she found herself more confident and poised than she had ever been in society before.

Age, she supposed, did have its benefits in bestowing some confidence. One came to realise that not every eye in the room was upon you, that you could make little mistakes without the world coming to an end and there was neither a strict father, nor a critical husband, to remind you constantly how much you needed to improve yourself.

Bel recalled with a smile how last month she had even brazenly broken her last days of mourning and taken herself off to the Prince Regent's reception for the Grand Duchess Eva with the sole intention of getting her Serene Highness to herself to upbraid her for breaking her brother Sebastian's heart.

She had cast every tenet of polite behaviour to the winds when she had done that, and, although she suspected her well-intentioned meddling had actually made things worse for a while between the two lovers, she now had a friend for life in her new sister-in-law.

Lucky things, she mused wistfully. How must it feel to have a man look at you the way Sebastian looked at Eva when he thought himself unobserved, his very soul in his eyes?

'My lady?' They were home, the groom was holding the door of the carriage for her, and had probably been standing there patiently for some minutes.

'Thank you, James.' She gathered up her things and stepped out. Yes, all in all, this evening had been a success and she felt confident about repeating it. Tomorrow night was the Steppingleys' dancing party, an opportunity, she had been informed by Mrs Steppingley that evening, of giving her daughter and her friends some experience before their come-out next Season. Lady Belinda need not fear a juvenile party, she had been assured, her hostess had invited a mixture of *interesting* people and there would be cards for those not wishing to dance.

It would be fun to dance again, although she would avoid the waltz, of course, and perhaps meeting all those interesting people she had been promised would help keep her mind off a certain broad-shouldered gentleman with a sinfully tempting curve to his mobile mouth. If only he did not make her feel so *wicked*.

Philpott glided about in her usual stately fashion, unpinning Bel's hair, locking away her jewellery, stuffing the tissue paper into the toes of her evening slippers before coming back to unfasten her gown.

Bel unclasped the *diamanté* brooch that had been holding the rosebuds in place. They were beginning to lose their firmness, the delicate petals felt like limp velvet under her fingers.

'Will you fetch me a box of salt, please?' she asked the dresser. 'About so big?' She gestured with her hands six inches apart.

'Now, my lady?'

'Yes, please. These are so pretty, I intend to preserve them as a memory of the first social engagement of my new life.'

'Very well, my lady.' Expressionless, Philpott helped her into her robe, handed her the hairbrush and went out. Did she guess the real reason Bel wanted to keep the flowers? If she did, she was far too well trained to let a flicker cross her face.

Bel pulled the bristles through her hair in a steady rhythm, contemplating her aunt's demand that she engage a companion, then shook her head, sending the heavy fall of hair swishing back and forth against the silk of her robe. Privacy was difficult enough with a houseful of servants, let alone with some stranger, obsessed with propriety and convinced her employer required her company at all times.

No, life like this might be a trifle lonely, but she had grown used to that, even when Henry had been alive. In fact, loneliness was a welcome space of peace and privacy. Those things were more important than satisfying the conventions.

The guests at Mrs Steppingley's party proved every bit as entertaining as she had promised. After an hour Bel had met a colonel from one of the Brunswick regiments, a gentleman pursuing researches into hot-air balloons as a means of transport for freight, several charming young girls, wide-eyed with excitement at their first 'proper' dancing party, a poetess and an alarmingly masculine bluestocking who, on hearing who she was, delivered a diatribe on the mistaken opinions of her Aunt Louisa on the evolution of English church architecture.

As Bel was just about capable of differentiating between a font and a water stoop and had not the slightest understanding of the vital importance of rood screens, she was greatly relieved to be rescued by the poetess, Miss Layne, who tactfully removed her with the entirely specious excuse that Bel had promised Miss Layne her escort into the room where the dancing was about to begin.

'Phew! At least Miss Farrington despises dancing, so she will not pursue us in here.' Miss Layne found them seats halfway along the wall and sank down with a hunted look back at the doorway. She fanned herself vigorously, giving Bel a chance to study her. She supposed she must be about forty, a slender woman with soft mouse-brown hair, amused hazel eyes and an air of being interested in everything. 'What a bore she is.' She suddenly whipped a notebook out of her reticule, jotted a note and stuffed it back again.

Bel blinked. 'Inspiration?' she enquired.

'Yes! See that young couple over there, pretending not to look at each other. So sweet, and so gauche. It gave me an idea. I have a fancy to write a really romantic verse story.'

'Will I find your work at Hatchard's?' Bel enquired. 'I am afraid I am very ignorant about poetry. My husband considered it frivolous, so I never used to buy it, although I have to confess to reading my way through Lord Byron's works at the moment.'

'Yes, you will find mine there, I have several volumes in print. But you must allow me to send you one as a gift. Some are frivolous, some are serious. But I see no harm in occasional frivolity—' Miss Layne broke off, her gaze fixed at something over Bel's shoulder. 'And speaking of frivolity, what a very beautiful man. Lord Byron would give his eye teeth for such a hero.'

Bel did not have to turn around to know who it was out of all the handsome men in London at the moment. The very air seemed to carry the awareness of Reynard to her, as intensely as if he was running his hands over her quivering skin.

'Really?' she made herself say lightly, stamping on that unsettling image. 'I am all agog, Miss Layne, I do hope he passes by us so I can see, for I can hardly turn round and stare—'

'Lady Belinda. Madam.' Yes, it was Reynard and her pulse was all over the place. Miss Layne was looking up at him with the air of a lepidopterist who has just found a rare species of butterfly and was wondering where her net had gone. Bel pulled herself together. A surge of lust, for she supposed that was what was afflicting her, was no excuse for a lady to forget her manners.

'Lord Dereham, good evening. Miss Layne, may I introduce Lord Dereham?'

They shook hands. 'Miss Layne—not the author of *Thoughts on an English Riverbank*?'

'Why, yes. It was published at the end of last year,' she explained to Bel. 'You have read it, Lord Dereham?'

'On the eve of the battle of Quatre Bras, Miss Layne. It was a lovely contrast to the scenes around me, and I must thank you for it.'

The poetess beamed up at him. 'I am delighted to have been able to provide a distraction at such a time.'

'More than that: a reminder of what we were fighting for.'

Bel bit her lip at the undercurrent of emotion in the controlled voice, then he was smiling again. 'May I have the honour of a dance, Miss Layne?'

'I do not dance, Lord Dereham, Lady Belinda kindly rescued me from an importunate acquaintance and we took refuge in here.'

'Lady Belinda is a notable rescuer of all her friends,' Reynard observed seriously. 'If you are merely hiding in here and the other gentlemen have not yet found you, then perhaps your dance card has a vacancy for me, Lady Belinda?'

Bel laughed, flipping open the fold of embossed card that hung from a cord around her wrist to show him. 'Quite empty, Lord Dereham. I have been talking too much to look for partners, I fear.' She liked the way he had asked the older woman first instead of simply assuming she would not be dancing. It was thoughtful, but done without the slightest suggestion of patronage.

'May I?' He lifted the card, his fingers brushing against hers. Even through the thickness of two pairs of evening gloves Bel seemed to feel the warmth. She made herself sit still while he took the tiny pencil and stared at the list of dances. The noise of the orchestra carrying out its final tuning faded as she looked at his bent head. She knew what that thick golden hair felt like against her cheek, she knew what it looked like, tousled from sleep, and her free hand strained against her will-power to lift and touch it.

'There. I hope that is acceptable.' He had put down a waltz as well as a country dance. Bel opened her mouth to tell him that she would not be waltzing, then threw her resolution overboard with an almost audible splash. This was Reynard; she wanted to be in his arms and she could admit to herself a disgraceful impulse to make other women envious.

'May I fetch you ladies some lemonade?' They shook their heads with a murmur of thanks. 'Then I will see you for the second country dance, Lady Belinda.'

'That man has lovely manners,' Miss Layne remarked as they watched Reynard's retreating back. 'Oh, good! There is my brother now, I was not certain if he was coming tonight.' She waved and a slender, brown-haired man who was just passing Reynard waved back and began to make his way across to them.

'Kate, fancy finding you in the ballroom!' Mr Layne was considerably younger than his sister, but he had her soft brown hair and quizzical hazel eyes. He smiled at her affectionately and bowed to Bel. 'Ma'am.'

'Lady Belinda, may I introduce my brother, Mr Layne. Patrick, Lady Belinda Felsham.'

Bel shook hands and gestured to the vacant chair beside her. 'Mr Layne?'

'Thank you, Lady Belinda, but I am promised for the next dance. Might I ask if you can spare me one later? Although I expect your card is filled already.'

'Not at all, I would be delighted.' She showed him the virtually empty card and smiled acceptance as he indicated the first waltz.

'Very daring of him,' Miss Layne observed as her

brother went in search of his next partner. 'I do hope he has learned the steps.' They both observed in anxious silence as Mr Layne went down the first measure of the country dance without error. 'Thank goodness. He must have been taking lessons. He has been rather preoccupied learning to manage our uncle's estate for the last two years; I was beginning to despair of him ever getting out into society.'

'And meeting a nice young lady, perhaps?' Bel teased.

'Indeed. Our uncle is Lord Hinckliffe and Patrick is his heir—he is taking that all rather seriously. I was worrying that he would end up an elderly bachelor like our relative at this rate.'

Mr Layne was a long way from that condition, Bel realised a little later, as he swept her competently into the waltz. Far from having to temper her steps to a learner, she found he was testing her own rusty technique to the limit. They were laughing as they whirled to a stop and well on the way to being very well pleased with each other's company. He was coaxing her into allowing him another dance when Bel saw Reynard making his way towards them.

Patrick Layne's voice faded and the air seemed to shimmer as the crowded room became a mere background to the man in front of her. Bel wondered dazedly if she was about to swoon.

She blinked and the illusion of faintness vanished, leaving her startled and confused. It was not simply that Reynard was a handsome, personable man. She had just spent five minutes, very pleasantly, in the arms of another man who could fairly be described in the same way. This was different. This was something she could only try to understand.

With an effort she kept her voice normal as she agreed to dance the cotillion with Mr Layne later in the evening. Then she turned, smiling, to take Reynard's outstretched hand with a sense of surrender that filled her with nervous delight. The deep-sea eyes smiled at her and she stopped fighting the apprehension. A die had been cast; the problem was, she did not know what game they were playing.

The steps of the country dance were intricate enough to keep Bel's full attention on her moves. After the first circle she found herself standing next to her partner. His soft chuckle had her glancing up at him, disconcerted.

'What is it?'

'You are frowning Lady Belinda. If I was a nervous man, I would think I had displeased you; as it is, I am hoping you are concentrating on your steps.'

'I do beg your pardon,' Bel said hastily, then saw the skin at the corner of his eyes crease in amusement. 'Oh! You are teasing me. I was not frowning at all, was I?'

'Not at all,' Ashe confessed. 'But you were concentrating very hard and I was rather hoping for some of the stimulating conversation one usually indulges in during these dances. We are off again.' He took her hand, twirled her and began to promenade down the double line. Army life had allowed for numerous scratch balls in the most unlikely places and with the most unconventional partners. Now he did not even have to think about the steps.

'Unless things have changed a great deal while I have been in mourning,' she retorted, 'that means exchanging platitudes about the music, the temperature and what a crush it is this evening. Surely you do not find that stimulating?'

Ashe steered her into place and grinned. 'It depends on the company. I suspect your view of the social scene may be a little more entertaining than most, Lady Belinda.' He had her attention now; she was not anxious about her steps or smiling over that lad she had just been dancing with. He was conscious of an unfamiliar twinge of jealousy. The young man, whoever he was, had made her laugh, had brought colour to her cheeks and she had seemed very relaxed in his company.

He had nothing to feel jealous about, for heaven's sake. The first time they had met he had embarrassed himself and escaped considerably more lightly than he deserved. The second time had been a mere social exchange, although he had applauded the fierce indignation that had made her defend the wounded soldiers and the quick wits that had provided a plausible excuse for their previous meeting. Now they were nothing more to each other than casual acquaintances.

Only...there were none of his casual acquaintances whose back-door keys were in his possession. His valet had found the key in his pocket and wordlessly placed it on his dressing table amidst the litter of cards and notes. Whenever he picked up his cologne, or replaced his brushes, the metal clinked. There was no excuse for leaving it there. He should have wrapped it up and sent it back with the roses, he knew that. Why he had kept it, why he had not mentioned it, he was carefully not examining.

But Lady Belinda had not asked for the key back. Obviously she had not thought about it, forgotten it, or perhaps she had taken the precaution of having the locks changed. He stepped into the circle and took the hands of the lady opposite, twirled her round and restored her to her new place in the set, watching while Belinda was twirled in her turn.

Not a conventional beauty, Ashe told himself, trying to look at her dispassionately. It was difficult to be objective for some reason. He did his best. Speaking grey eyes, glossy dark hair, those were admirable—but a connoisseur would say her nose was a little too long, her chin rather too decided and her mouth too mobile. He watched it now, intrigued. A polite smile for the man who had just turned her became serious, her full underlip caught between white teeth as she thought about the next moves. Then she gave a secret smile of relief when she remembered what she had to do next.

A dancer moved too energetically, knocking against Belinda, and the smile became a fleeting wince, then she caught his eye and smiled and he found himself smiling back as uninhibitedly as though they were alone on a hillside with no one for miles around. It shook him, and it seemed to have surprised her too, as though she had shared the feeling.

Her expression was serious again in an instant, although he was conscious of her glancing at him sideways from under the sweep of her lashes, a feminine trick that always amused him in other women. Now, he felt the urge to whirl her out of the set, catch her face between his palms and lock eyes with her, to read what was going on in her mind.

Ashe gave himself a brisk mental shake. This was not how he had ever felt about a woman before, and he could not account for it. But then, he knew he was not feeling quite himself somehow. Perhaps he would be back to normal when he had bitten the bullet and gone home for a while.

The lines of dancers were facing each other now, men on one side, women the other. The ladies advanced, bringing them together, so close that the provoking swell of Belinda's breasts was almost against his waistcoat. She glanced up, saw goodness knows what in his expression, blushed and retreated. When it was his turn to come forward she did not raise her eyes to his, suddenly endearingly shy.

It was the effect of living with a dull man, no doubt. She was unused to other men, unused to even the mildest flirtation. It was rare in a married woman to see maturity combined with such an air of innocence. Why that made him feel both aroused and protective, both at the same time, was the mystery.

The music came to a crashing finale, everyone clapped politely and left the floor. Ashe returned Belinda to her seat and nodded coolly to the young man who had been dancing with her earlier, noting his likeness to Miss Layne. Her brother, no doubt. Young whelp, Ashe thought with a sudden burst of irritation, striding off to find his partner for the next dance. London was definitely not what it was.

Chapter Six

'Hmm. His lordship does not like me, I fancy.' Patrick Layne stood to position her chair so that Bel could see the dance floor more easily.

'Why do you say that?' She was pleased with herself for not letting her gaze stray after her partner's retreating back. Miss Layne was chatting to a chaperon on her other side, so no one could overhear their low-voiced exchange.

'If looks could kill, I would be laid out at your feet,' he said dramatically, grinning.

'Why on earth should Lord Dereham take a dislike to you?' Bel demanded, genuinely puzzled.

'Need you ask?' Patrick stooped to pick up the fan that had slipped from her fingers. 'I was waltzing with you, and now I am sitting with you. All his lordship gets is a country dance and the privilege of returning you to my company.'

'But…that would mean he was jealous, and he has not the slightest reason to be.' Bel was aghast that anyone might think such a thing, with its implication that she and Reynard were in some way involved.

Which they were not. Not in the slightest. 'I hardly know him. And in any case, he chose which dances to ask me for, and we have a waltz later.'

She was protesting too much, she saw it in the amused quirk of Mr Layne's mouth. The truth was that he too was flirting with her, in a rather roundabout manner. It was all very disconcerting; somehow she had not expected such a thing when she had contemplated her return to society. As a widow she had imagined her attractiveness to men would automatically have ceased. Apparently she was mistaken.

She was saved from any more badinage by Miss Layne returning her attention to her brother and declaring that she was faint from hunger and he must give them his escort to the supper room. Bel was not feeling particularly like eating, but their departure did at least remove her from the sight of Lord Dereham's elegant progression down the floor with a vivacious redhead.

By the time he came to claim her for their waltz Bel was feeling far from happy. 'What is it, Lady Belinda? Are you cross with me?'

'Cross? No, goodness gracious, of course not.' She was so flurried that he might think it that she was in his arms and waltzing before she could be apprehensive about his touch. 'I very foolishly let myself be persuaded into eating a crab patty I did not really want, I have just had my toes trodden on by a very clumsy young man in the last dance and I am wondering if my ambition to establish myself in London was an awful mistake and I should have stayed in the country where at least I know what I am doing.'

Reynard swept her competently around a corner and

Bel found she had settled into his embrace as though they had danced a hundred times before. For a tall and very masculine man he was surprisingly graceful. Bel had never been quite so masterfully partnered before and she was well aware that for the duration of this dance she was going to go precisely where he intended. She realised that, far from feeling overpowered by this, or resentful, she could relax and simply enjoy the dance, confident that he was in control.

'You are feeling as I do at the moment about London, I think.' He gathered her a little closer as an unskilled young couple blundered past, laughing immoderately at their own clumsiness. 'We have been away, living very different lives. Perhaps it will take a little while to get back into the swing of things.' Somehow he kept her just that little bit closer to his body, although the danger of collision was past.

'Yes, you may well be right. No doubt that is all it is.' Comforted, Bel let herself go as he executed a complicated turn. 'Oh!' Her skirts swung, tangled for a moment in his long legs, and then they were gliding down the floor again. 'You are a very good dancer, Ashe.'

The name was out of her mouth before she realised it. 'I beg your pardon, Reynard, I…'

'But I asked you to use my first name.' She could hear the smile in his voice.

'That does not mean I should do so, however.' Bel fixed her gaze on the top button of his waistcoat, which seemed the safest place to look.

'I like it when you do. Do not stop.' His voice was a coaxing rumble close to her ear. Far too close.

'That is all the more reason for not using it!' Bel's

vehement retort make him chuckle. 'Do not laugh at me,' she added crossly. 'Just because I try to behave as convention demands, there is no need to mock.'

'I am not mocking,' Ashe said seriously. 'I enjoy being with you, I do not find your modest demeanour at all amusing. But I do relish the serious way you keep reminding yourself to behave. It makes me sense some tendency to mischief beneath that very elegant exterior.'

Bel was not at all sure how to take that, it was a positive layer cake of a remark. There was some flattery, a somewhat backhanded compliment and a strong hint that Ashe would very much enjoy it if she were to give her mischief free rein. With him. It seemed he had seen the new wickedness that lurked within her. She contented herself with a sound which was supposed to be a disdainful *humpf!* and emerged regrettably like a giggle.

The dance ended and she stepped back out of his arms. Ashe bowed slightly, then, as his eyes met hers, she saw in them quite unmistakable desire. It was gone in an instant, his lashes sweeping it away to reveal nothing more than polite admiration. But it had been there, fierce, thrilling and utterly dangerous, and she had recognised it, even though she had never had a man look at her like that in her life before.

The sudden heat she had glimpsed called up an answering warmth in her. The disturbing pulse she was aware of, fluttering low in her belly whenever she was close to him, became insistent, flurrying her. Just that exchange of glances and they were both aware of his desire and her knowledge of it. In her inexperience it seemed incredible that such a thing was possible.

Then her glance flickered lower and hastily away. Her instincts were palpably correct.

The Dowager Duchess of Malmsbury, an outrageous old harridan, had once announced loudly in her hearing that the fashion for skintight, fine-knit, evening knee breeches was excellent as it allowed one to tell precisely what a young man was thinking. Bel had retreated blushing and had hardly dared look at a man below the waist for weeks after that. Now she knew exactly what her Grace had meant and even more exactly what Ashe was thinking about.

'Th…thank you. That was a delightful dance.' She sketched a curtsy and turned to walk off the floor. The sets were already beginning to form for the next dance.

'Lady Belinda?'

'Yes?' She hardly dared turn round. She had fantasised about physical desire. Now she was so acutely aware of it vibrating between them that it terrified her.

'Might I have one word in private?'

'Um. Yes…of course.'

Ashe guided her towards the loggia overlooking the lawns. It had been opened up as a cooling promenade for the dancers, away from the heat of the ballroom. There was nothing to worry about, Bel assured herself. With so many young and inexperienced girls in the company, Mrs Steppingley had made sure all the curtains were pulled back and the arcaded walk was well lit. Several couples were already strolling up and down its marble floor amidst potted palms and baskets of orchids.

'This is most pleasant.' Bel unfurled her spangled fan, realised she was positively flapping it, and began to wave it languidly to and fro. *What is he going to ask me?*

'Indeed, yes.' Ashe took her free hand and placed it

on his forearm. 'I simply wanted to tell you that I should have returned your key, and I did not want to mention it where we might be overheard. I apologise for not having dealt with it sooner.'

'My key.' Bel stared at him blankly. Despite the relative cool of the loggia, she could sense the heat of his body as he walked so close beside her. And surely he could feel the hammering of her pulse where her wrist lay on his forearm? Of course, the key. She made herself say something sensible before he thought her a complete lackwit. 'You overlooked it, no doubt. An easy thing to do under the circumstances.'

'No. I did not forget.' The denial took her completely by surprise. They had reached the end of the arcade and she turned to face him, her back against the balustrade as he stood close in front of her, one arm raised so his hand rested on the column, effectively cutting her off from the rest of the company.

'I do not understand.'

Ashe nodded. 'No, neither do I.' He grimaced. 'It has been lying on my dressing table in full view ever since that day, being pointedly ignored by my valet. I cannot pretend to have forgotten.' He moved away from her as though he was uncomfortable with their conversation and went to lean on the balustrade. Bel glanced down at the strong ungloved hands as they curled over the carved stone, then up at his profile as he looked out over the garden: classical, handsome, unreadable. Vulnerable.

She blinked and looked again. Whatever it was she had glimpsed, it had gone, leaving only a sense of aloofness.

'I will have it sent round tomorrow.' Ashe turned to face her again, his hands at his back bracing him against the stonework, his long, lean body making an elegant black line against the grey background. 'In a package so it is not obvious what it is.'

Thank you, that would be very thoughtful of you. The right words formed in her mind, polite and cool and correct. Bel opened her lips to articulate them. 'Please keep it,' she said.

What? Ashe almost said the word out loud. He must have misheard her. *Keep her door key?* 'I beg your pardon, Lady Belinda. I thought you said—'

'I said, *keep it*. The key.' There was colour flushed across her cheekbones and her eyes were wide, apparently in shocked disbelief at her own words, but Lady Belinda's voice was quite steady. 'You may like to drop in one evening on your way home. For a nightcap.' She might have been inviting him to afternoon tea. He saw her throat work as she swallowed, hardly able to believe what he was hearing, surprised that he could focus on such tiny details while he was being so amazed.

'A nightcap?'

'To drink, I mean.' Ashe nodded, fascinated. 'Not to wear,' she clarified. Belinda's slender fingers flew up to seal in what sounded like a gasp of horrified laughter at the image she had conjured up. Her wide grey eyes became serious again in a second. 'My staff will always be in bed by one. There is no need to knock and, er… disturb anyone. Just let yourself in as you did the other night.'

This was not an hallucination. This was proper, respectable Lady Belinda Felsham, the widow of a man of paralysing respectability, suggesting that he come to her home at one in the morning—for a *nightcap*?

It was not unknown for married ladies or widows to

make it clear to gentlemen that they would not be averse to an *affaire*. It had happened to him in the past on occasion and he was equally skilled at pretending not to understand what was being hinted at, or at taking advantage of the opportunity for some mutual pleasure, depending on how he felt about the lady, and how territorial her husband appeared to be.

But was *this* sheltered lady really suggesting what he thought she was? Perhaps Belinda genuinely expected him to drop in for a glass of brandy and a chat on his way home from the clubs. She did not appear to sleep very well, if it was her habit to be reading on the hearthrug at two in the morning. And she was most certainly inexperienced with men. It must be his own desire for her that was making him believe she was offering her body, not her company.

'Lady Belinda.' He paused to choose his words with care. 'I should point out that however innocent a late-night drink between two friends might be, it would not be seen in that light by a third party. It would be regarded in the worst possible light. It simply is not done.'

'Oh, dear!' Bel regarded him in dismay. 'I am making such a mull of this. You see, I am not in the habit…that is to say, I am not used to inviting gentlemen to… Oh, dear. I should have asked Ther—I mean, a friend—how it is done.'

'How what is done?' Ashe asked bluntly, wondering if there was something wrong with the champagne. He was not accustomed to feeling this light-headed. Not after a mere three glasses of good wine.

'How one asks a man if he will become your lover.'

'Ah.' Ashe took a deep, steadying breath. It occurred to him, distractingly, that the last time he had found it necessary to do so he had been standing up to his ankles in mud, a sword clenched in his fist while the French cavalry had been advancing towards him at a gallop. He was not certain that this was not more terrifying. 'I was not sure that was what you meant.'

'That I was asking if you would be my lover?' She repeated the noun as though trying to become used to it. 'Of course, if you do not want to…please, do say so.' It sounded as though she was offering him a plate of macaroons. 'I mean, I would feel awful if you felt you had to say *yes*, just to be polite.'

'Polite? No, politeness is not a consideration, I assure you. Nor, believe me, is desire, or lack of it. I find you highly desirable.' Ashe strained his ears for the sound of footsteps behind them. He had moved into this position for discretion; now they were discussing matters so sensitive they should be at the bottom of the garden, not in the middle of a popular promenade.

'Thank you.' She looked up at him from under her lashes, suddenly shy again.

He found his lips curving into a smile. Belinda was so deliciously serious as she accepted as a compliment what he had intended as a simple statement of fact. She should not have needed telling; he was still chastising himself for his loss of control back there on the dance floor. But the rhythms of the music, the sway of her body in his arms, her trusting surrender to his lead just made him want to sweep her away into a bedchamber and continue to explore those rhythms, that yielding, until they reached the ultimate conclusion.

If only he did not keep getting memory flashes of her lying on that damned bearskin rug, her hair tousled, her feet bare beneath a fluttering silken hem, he would find it easier to control himself. But it seemed he did not need to. It seemed, improbably, that the well-behaved widow of the most boring and conventional man in society wanted to take him to her bed.

'Ashe?' She was biting the fullness of her under lip; the idea of his own teeth just there made his loins throb. 'You are frowning. I should not have asked, should I? I expect men always prefer to do the asking. Only, I did not think that you ever would and I have no idea how to flirt so that you would understand it would be all right.'

He wanted to touch her, lift his hand and touch the smooth curve of her cheek, run the pad of his thumb over the line of the enticing red swell of her mouth, but there were people all around them and preserving her reputation had to be paramount.

Ashe did not answer the anxious questions at once. 'Let us walk. I do not want to attract attention.' He turned, offering her his arm again; after a moment's hesitation she took it. He had thought her almost un- naturally composed, now he could feel the tremor running through her, transmitting itself through silk and broadcloth into him. She was as scared of herself, of what she had just done, as she was of him.

'It is not a question of preference, of the man wanting to ask,' he tried to explain, returning to her anxious question. 'Only, with you, it would never occur to me that the question would meet with anything but a stinging box to my ears. My mild attempts at flirtation so far have not been wildly successful.'

Belinda gave a little gurgle of amusement, but her voice retained its anxiety as she probed. 'So, before, you thought me too respectable for such things, and now you think me—what? All the words are so horrible. The reality of doing this is not at all the fantasy I had of it.'

'I think that you owe no one an explanation of your behaviour other than yourself,' Ashe said, meaning it, trying not to speculate about her fantasies. 'You are not contemplating betraying your marriage vows, you have no children to shelter, no great public position to protect. You are discreet, you have honoured me with your trust—and believe me, I will not betray it. I have no attachments or commitments that I would be breaking. That makes you a private woman with private needs who is able to satisfy them. Nothing more.'

He would never have dreamed he would be having such a measured, serious, discussion with a would-be lover, but it seemed Belinda needed that reasoning. She was not doing it lightly, this was no whim. It made him reassess his opinion of the late Lord Felsham. Had the man been such a superlative lover that his wife was pining for a man in her bed? And yet, if he had not known better, he would have thought her a virgin, her responses were so innocent. The effect of knowing one man only, he supposed.

'Then you will?' she asked, looking up suddenly. 'Be my lover?' The intensity in her eyes, even in the shadow of the loggia, shook him. No, she was no natural lightskirt like her frivolous friends, who were separated from their sisters in the muslin company only by wealth and breeding, not by temperament.

'I would be honoured,' Ashe said, meaning it. That Layne fellow was strolling towards them, a very young blonde chattering animatedly at his side. Time to draw this to a conclusion before anyone commented on how long they had spent together. 'Lady Belinda, may I call tomorrow?' He dropped his voice to a murmur as the other couple came up to them. 'Soon after one.'

Not tonight, then. The strength of her disappointment shook Bel. She was shocked at herself. What had she wanted? That Ashe sweep her up in his arms and take her to bed immediately? Find a bedchamber here and lock the door? *Yes, of course that is what I want!*

'Certainly.' Bel produced her best social smile. 'And that time tomorrow would be most convenient. Thank you, my lord.' With a nod to Patrick Layne and his partner, Ashe was gone, cutting easily through the congestion at the entrance to the loggia.

'Lady Felsham, may I introduce Miss Steppingley?' She dragged her attention back and smiled at the blonde girl. She was very young, very pretty, wide-eyed with shy excitement.

Bel shook hands and listened with half an ear to Miss Steppingley's effusions about how thrilling it was that Mama had held this dance party and was letting her and her cousins attend, even though they were not out until the new Season. She caught Mr Layne's eye and he grinned at her over Miss Steppingley's head, obviously amused by the naïve chatter.

'Shall we go back? I am not sure your mama would wish you to be promenading with a gentleman unchaperoned.' Bel began to stroll towards the ballroom. If Lady Steppingley knew what her guest had just done, she would be far more shocked by her daughter talking to Bel than she would by her walking alone for a little while with the respectable Mr Layne. *I am a scarlet woman,* Bel thought. *Almost.* She shot Mr Layne a look that she hoped indicated that she was not suggesting he was an unsafe companion, and was reassured by a slight nod of his head.

Miss Steppingley soon found a friend to chatter to, leaving Bel alone with him. 'That was probably very wise of you,' he said, following the giggling pair with a tolerant eye. 'She's far too young and trusting to know the ropes yet. Not at all up to snuff. Very dangerous.'

'For her to be with you, Mr Layne? Surely not.'

'For me.' Patrick Layne grinned. 'The next thing you know with girls that age, they have decided that a little mild flirtation behind the potted palm indicates lifelong devotion and you're in Papa's study explaining your intentions.'

'And have you ever been in that position?' Bel looked round the room as though watching the party. Ashe had vanished.

'No, I am glad to say. I prefer ladies closer to my own age.' As she guessed he was twenty-six, her age exactly, Bel wondered if this was another of his indirectly flirtatious remarks.

'There is your sister.' It was better, she decided, to ignore it. Her brain was spinning too much to worry about Mr Layne's intentions. 'I must say goodbye.'

'Do call.' The poetess slipped a card into her hand as Bel explained she was about to leave. 'I would be delighted if you would call and take tea.'

'Thank you.' Bel put it carefully into her reticule. This was precisely what she had hoped for in coming to London, to make new friends, to build a pleasant social life for herself. It was not, whatever she had fantasised, to take a lover. But she had—almost.

If Ashe Reynard had not had too much to drink the other evening, this would not be happening, Bel thought, settling back in the corner of her carriage and ignoring how badly her new evening slippers pinched. But Ashe had ended up on his old, familiar doorstep, and they had met, and something inside her could not stop yearning for him.

She had danced with several attractive gentlemen that evening. Patrick Layne was good looking, good company and, she was certain, discreet. But it would never cross her mind, not for a single moment, that she might want an *affaire* with him.

But with Ashe she had met the man of her fantasies, it was the only explanation. And if she did not follow her instincts now, she would never have the chance, or the courage, again.

Chapter Seven

'**D**id you have a pleasant nap, my lady?' Philpott placed a cup of tea by the bedside and went to draw back the curtains at the window, letting in the late afternoon sunshine.

'No, not really,' Bel said vaguely, pushing her hair back out of her eyes. Philpott, studying her with professional frankness, sniffed.

'You will have bags under your eyes, my lady, if you do not get some sleep. London life does not appear to suit you. You look as though you did not get a wink last night either. You are quite pale.' She leaned closer, frowning, convincing Bel that she must look such a hag that Ashe would retreat in alarm after one look at her.

'Yes, there are smudges under your eyes, my lady, even if there are no bags. Yet.' The dresser turned away, leaving her mistress to digest this ominous lecture, and began to tidy the dressing table. 'Once a lady reaches a certain age, she has to take extra care,' she added. 'In my last position, try what I might, I could not persuade my lady to use Denmark Lotion. And look what happened.'

'What did happen?' Bel slid her arms into her wrapper and got up. Perhaps if she got dressed and had a walk before dinner, she could manage a short sleep after it.

'Crows' feet,' Philpott confided bleakly.

Bel sat on the dressing-table stool and regarded herself in the mirror. Even if the ultimate horror of crows' feet had not yet arrived, she certainly looked like a woman short of sleep. And that was hardly the way to appear to a sophisticated, experienced gentleman who was used, she had no doubt, to lovely, assured and vibrant lovers. Not to inexperienced ones who were too nervous to sleep and consequently were wan and heavy-eyed. To say nothing of utterly ignorant on the subject of pleasuring a man in bed.

The thought of pleasuring Ashe in bed, whatever it involved, had Bel closing her eyes with a breathless sigh of anticipation. Then she opened them again and stared at her pale reflection.

She tried to find consolation in the glossiness of her hair, which she had washed that morning. Philpott began to style it again and Bel was seized with a new worry. How should she dress to receive Ashe? Would he expect her to be in evening dress and for them to have a conversation first? Or would he expect her to be in bed? Or up, but *en négligé*? How on earth was one supposed to know these things? Bel worried, distractedly buffing her nails. There ought to be a book on the subject. Perhaps there was, and she was too ignorant to know how to find it. Poor Lord Dereham.

Ashe slid the key carefully into the lock and eased the back door open. The night was quiet, moonless, and here, at the rear of the house, almost totally dark. As he had passed the front façade on to Half Moon Street he had seen the candlelight flickering through a gap in Belinda's bedchamber curtains. She was awake and waiting for him.

His lips curved in a smile of pleasurable anticipation, unclouded by nothing more than two glasses of claret with his dinner. He had returned to his chambers for a shave and to check there was no last-minute message cancelling their rendezvous and now he was conscious of the steady pulse of his blood, of a certain tightness low in his belly and the slight, pleasurable, *frisson* of nerves.

He expected it before battle, welcomed it to keep him sharp and alert. It amused him to feel it now, before the start of a new *affaire*. It was novel, that feeling in these circumstances, but then Belinda was different somehow. He had never been a careless or thoughtless lover, he reassured himself as he made his way unerringly through the familiar house. But this was important to get right.

He paused halfway up the stairs, frowning into the darkness. Why was that? Then he shrugged. The lady was not going to thank him for keeping her waiting while he brooded on the philosophy of relationships. As soundlessly as he had moved operating behind enemy lines Ashe drifted upstairs, turned right on to the landing and scratched lightly on the door panel.

She opened the door to him on to a room lit by a candelabrum on a side table and another by the bedside. As he stepped inside, Bel closed the door and moved wordlessly to stand by the table. It looked as though she had been sitting there reading.

The flickering light struck rich reflections off her unbound hair, as though amber had been threaded through its brown length. Ashe wanted to lift it, run his fingers through it. *All in good time. Patience: she is worth it.* 'Lady Belinda.'

'My friends call me Bel,' she confided, her voice husky with nerves.

'Bel.' He tried it and smiled, pleased with the sound on his tongue. A small word, but sweet and rounded, like her. 'Lovely. It suits you.' She was wearing a long robe of amber silk tied with ribbons that fluttered as she moved. Under it he could see a nightgown in a deeper hue. With her hair heavy on her shoulders and her bare toes peeping out, she was the woman he remembered from that first night.

Only he did not recall her being this pale, nor her eyes looking so enormous in the oval of her face. Last night, at the dance, she had not seemed so fragile. 'Are you all right, Bel?' He moved to come to her and stopped, his toe stubbing against something. He looked down. Malevolent green-glass eyes glinted up from a massive furry head. His toes were against a set of savage teeth. That ridiculous bear again. 'Good evening, Horace,' he said, sidestepping the thing.

Bel gave a little gasp of laughter. 'I am all right. I am just…nervous, I suppose.'

'So am I,' Ashe said easily, closing the distance between them. Hell, she looked as though she had not slept at all, and the hem of her gown was vibrating as though she was shivering. He had the sudden thought that if he clapped his hands she would faint out of sheer alarm. Now was not the time to stand around talking, she needed sweeping off her feet.

Ashe lifted his hands to her shoulders, feeling the slender bones and his breath hitched in his throat. She stood watching him, grey eyes wide so he saw his own reflection as he lowered his mouth to hers.

The shock jolted through him as their lips touched. What was it? The scent of her, faintly floral, wholly feminine—or the taste of her? Even at that light touch he could sense sweetness. But he had touched his lips to her skin before, held her close. Perhaps that familiarity accounted for the sense of rightness as he angled his mouth to slide questing over hers.

Bel gave a little gasp against his lips, but her hands came up to press against his upper chest as though she did not know whether to hold on or push him away. He let his tongue explore along the seam of her lips, wondering how easily she would open to him, how she would taste as he slid inside. Surely she understood what he was doing, what he wanted? He sucked gently on that deliciously pouting lower lip and felt her jolt of surprise.

It seemed she did not understand. Ashe did not try to force it, but eased the pressure, letting his tongue slide over the swell of her lower lip. Her hands crept up to curve over his shoulders and she moved a little closer. Encouraged, he let his own hands slide down to hold her against him, supple, yielding as she had been in the waltz, letting him lead.

He sucked her lower lip into his own mouth and she came up on tiptoe, pressed against him so that the urge to cup her buttocks and crush her against his swelling groin was almost painful. At last her mouth was opening to his gentle assault. Ashe slid his tongue between her lips, into the warm, moist sweetness and her own tongue moved to touch his in a shyly tentative caress. He did not think he had ever felt anything so touching as that innocently trusting gesture.

It seemed her husband was not a magnificent lover who had left his wife bereft after all. But how could a man be married to Bel and not want to lavish every art of seduction and eroticism upon her? How could she be this innocent?

She was clinging to his shoulders now and he sensed it was only that grip that was keeping her standing. Gently Ashe lifted his mouth and smiled down at her. The colour was animating her face now, a little smile tugged at the corner of her mouth. Already it seemed fuller, more swollen from his assiduous kisses.

'Hello,' he murmured, as though she had been away.

'Hello.' Her lashes fluttered down to hide her eyes and he opened his hands to release her. Those frivolous ribbons fluttered with the movement and he began to undo the bows, slowly, indulgently, letting the sensual slide of the silk satin through his fingers tantalise him with the thought of how her skin would feel when he caressed her.

'I can do that,' she said uncertainly, her hands fluttering above his as he worked with slow concentration.

'I enjoy it. This is a very lovely garment; the colour is perfect against your skin, your hair.' The last bow yielded and the robe fell open to reveal the low-cut neckline of the nightgown. Ashe had seen the lovely swell of her breasts before—this was no lower cut than the fashionable gown she had worn last night, but this time it was for him alone, and he could touch her. Holding his breath, he trailed the back of his fingers across the exposed skin.

Bel gasped, stepped back, but he simply stepped forward, matching her retreat, caught the edges of the robe and pushed it off her shoulders. Long, slim arms, bare now without gloves, the light glinting on her skin, turning it to ivory, and shoulders, naked except for slim ribbon straps, sloping elegantly up to the column of her neck. The pulse there was beating wildly, he could see it, was immeasurably aroused by it. Low down, where he ached for her, his echoing pulse throbbed with urgent need.

'*Belle.*' He gave it a lingering French intonation, laying his fingers gently against the betraying pulse. 'Belle. You are so lovely, so lovely.'

'Should I…should I get into bed?'

He had planned to kiss her almost insensible there where they stood, then scoop her up and enjoy the sight of her sprawled on the deep green satin of the bed cover. But all his instincts told him to go slowly, let her do what seemed comfortable to her. 'If you like.'

She edged backwards, lifted the side of the covers. 'With the candles lit?'

'Why, yes. I want to see you.'

'You do?' She slid into bed and sat watching him, the covers up to her chin.

'Definitely!' Ashe sat down with caution on the delicate bergère armchair, took off his shoes, undid the buckles at the knee of his evening breeches and began to roll down the silk stockings. With his feet bare he stood up and shed his coat, letting it fall with a carelessness that would have wrung a moan from his valet's lips.

As he began to unbutton his waistcoat, Bel stammered, 'What are you doing?'

'Undressing.' He dropped the garment on to the coat and pulled the knot of his neckcloth free.

'But…don't you want to do that in the dressing room?'

Ashe stared at her. 'No. No, I would like to undress here, where I can watch you.'

'Oh.' Bel shut her eyes. 'Oh, dear.'

'Bel.' They stayed shut. 'Bel, I know you have seen a naked man before—'

'No, I have not.'

'What?' Ashe sat down, heedless of the crushed garments on the chair. *No, do not tell me you are a virgin. Please!* You heard about it. Marriages that stayed unconsummated for one reason or another. He had never made love to a virgin in his life, and he was most certainly not going to start now.

'I have never seen a naked man because Henry always used to come to my chamber in his nightgown and then snuff out the candles,' Bel explained prosaically, eyes still screwed firmly shut. Ashe let out a tightly held breath and felt the sweat cooling on his brow.

'And then he would take his nightshirt off?'

'Oh, no. He would get into bed and kiss me on the cheek and then he would…you know.'

'With his nightshirt on?'

'Of course.' Bel opened her eyes cautiously as though expecting to see him standing there indecently naked and rampant. She seemed relieved to find him still in shirt and breeches.

'And you still in your nightgown?' She nodded. 'And then he would make love to you?' Another nod.

'And then he would kiss me on the cheek again and say "Thank you dear. Goodnight", and off he would go until Wednesday. Or Saturday.'

'He would visit your room twice a week on set days?' Ashe knew he was staring, but couldn't help himself. His mouth was probably open. The man must have either had ice water in his veins or have been blind. Or both.

Bel yawned, hugely, clapping both hands over her mouth. 'Oh, I am so sorry. I didn't sleep very well last night.'

Ashe ignored the yawn. 'Forgive me, but may I ask…was your husband a very passionate man? I mean, did you find his lovemaking, er…?'

'Dull. I found it very, very dull. But Henry did not seem to think I ought to be enjoying it, you see. He was always rather apologetic about doing it at all, so I assumed it was expected to be horrid.' Ashe blinked at her frankness. *Poor bloody Henry. You idiot.* 'So I had no idea that there was more to it, or that I might enjoy it. Not for a long while. But then there were things people said—when I stopped being a new bride—and things I read. I guessed that perhaps it can be more than just sticky and boring and embarrassing.'

Bel regarded him hopefully. 'It is, isn't it? More? I mean, I began to feel there was something I *needed*.' She frowned over the word, then gave her head a little shake as though she could not think of a better one.

'Yes. I promise it is. So much more. So much that will satisfy that need.' She looked so fragile, sitting up in that big bed. And so nervous and so tired. 'Bel, you have not considered simply getting married again? It would have been a more conventional way of finding affection. Safer, perhaps.'

'Goodness, no. No, I am *absolutely* determined never to marry again. You do not know what a husband is really going to be like—look at Henry. I mean, he was a decent, honest, respectable man. He was kind. But he was so dull and he made me be dull—yet I never guessed how it would be until I married him.

'And even if he is not dull, a husband rules his wife and now I know what it is like to be able to think for myself I could not bear it. And then, if by some miracle he did *not* try to dominate me—imagine how awful it must be to be married to the sort of man who did not care what you did and positively encouraged you to take lovers. How do you respect a man like that?'

'And unlike a husband, you can change a lover if he does not please you? Like a library book?' Ashe asked, only half-jesting.

'No! You should not treat people like that.' Bel wriggled up against the pillows, forgetting to be shy in her indignation. 'That is why I thought it could only be a daydream, a fantasy. I never intended to take a lover, not really. I had no idea how to find one. And then you came that night and I thought you were attractive. I was tempted, when you woke up on top of me, to say nothing, but to kiss you and see what happened. I did not, of course.' She blushed. 'But I thought you were safe.'

'*Safe?*' Never in his life had Ashe been called safe. *Dangerous flirt* was the term that careful mamas had applied to him in the course of the last Season he had spent in London. *Amorous devil* was the description not a few society ladies had used, not without a secret smile as they said it. But *safe*? He rather thought he had just been insulted. 'I was drunk, for goodness' sake!'

'I think that drink shows what people are really like. It makes bullies worse and cruel people violent. You were gentle and funny and polite. And you seemed to want me, but you did not take advantage of me.'

'I did want you. I do.' And if he did not have her soon

he was going to be in agony. Every word she said made him want her more, made him ache to teach her just how sweet love making could be. There was so much to explore together.

'So you see?' Bel's lips curved into a smile. 'You are safe, and you said you are a rake, so you understand about not wanting entanglements, and I will not have to worry about toying with your affections or breaking your heart or anything like that. But you do want to make love to me—even I can tell that. I quite understand if it is only once—I do not expect I will be any good at it. But then at least I'll know what I have been missing.'

'Close your eyes,' Ashe said, returning that smile. 'I can promise to be safe. And gentle. And to show you what you have been missing. But I am not sure I can promise to be funny, not all the time.'

'All right.' Reassured, still smiling, Bel closed her eyes and waited, trying to follow what Ashe was doing. There was some rustling, then his footsteps padding round to the other side of the bed.

'You close your eyes, too, Horace,' she heard him order, and stifled a gasp of nervous laughter. The covers lifted, cooler air fanned over her body for a moment as the bed dipped with his weight, then she felt the length of him against her side. Long, hard, warm. 'You can look now,' Ashe said as he put an arm under her shoulders and pulled her against him.

'Oh.' Instead of the bare skin she was prepared for, there was the soft linen of a dress shirt. 'I thought…'

'And I thought you might be more comfortable like this for a little while. Now, relax, snuggle up, put your arm here and just lie with me. We do not have to hurry.'

It was not at all what she had expected, but Bel did

as she was told, awkwardly putting her left arm over Ashe's chest and letting herself be gathered in against his ribcage.

He was as big as she remembered, his chest broad as she spanned it, the shoulder her head was cushioned against as solid as only hard-won muscle could make it. Her own breathing was all over the place, Ashe's was steady, deep and easy.

And the scent of him was the same, too, only without the tang of sweat from a hard night's revelry or the strong smell of brandy. There was a hint of a subtle citrus that she guessed was his soap, the laundry smell of clean linen, fresh from the iron, and, underneath it, man. Ashe's own, personal scent, his skin.

Bel rubbed her cheek against his shirt, wishing she could feel the texture of that skin. Their feet touched, bare, and Ashe hooked his right ankle over to capture her feet. It felt secure, warm, as though she was special. Her eyes drifted closed as his hand began to stroke her head. The span of his fingers could have encircled her throat, had wielded a weapon, could master a horse, and yet his touch was so gentle that she sighed with content. The thought drifted through her mind that already he had spent almost as much time in her bed as Henry ever did in one visit.

She had expected almost any emotion, any sensation other than this peaceful drift, this warmth moving gently to the rhythm of his breathing. So peaceful, so safe…

Chapter Eight

'Good morning, my lady. You had a proper night's sleep at last, I am glad to see.'

Bel opened her eyes on to bright sunlight and the sounds of Philpott in the next room briskly organising her wardrobe for the day.

She scrambled up into a sitting position and stared wildly round the room. Where was Ashe? Beside her the bed was neat, the far side tucked in tight as she tugged on the covers. The pillows were smooth. There was no litter of male garments across the floor, her poetry book sat chastely on the table where she had put it last night and the candles had been carefully pinched out, not left to gutter and burn away.

It had all been a dream? It must have been. No man would accept an offer to a lady's bed and then simply cuddle her, make the bed again and silently slip away while she slept. Which meant that she had dreamt a safe ending to her fantasy. Had she even dreamed asking Ashe to be her lover?

Confused, Bel turned to run her hand over the pillow

beside her and saw it. On the embroidered linen was a single blond hair. She picked it up and it curled in her fingers, the one strong filament conjuring up the image of a whole head of hair: golden, thick, curving over-long into his nape.

Ashe was here last night. I did not dream it. And he had come to bed in his shirt because she was shy, and he had let her sleep in his arms because she was tired and he had made the bed, quietly, so as not to disturb her or betray that he had been there. Behind her eyes something prickled. Bel scrubbed the back of her hand across them as her dresser came back into the room, her arms full of petticoats.

'Are you quite well, my lady?' Philpott frowned, anxious. 'You look a trifle emotional.'

'No, I am quite well. My eyes are watering, that is all. Just the after-effects of such a long sleep, I expect.' Ashe had been gentle and kind and tolerant. But he was not going to come back, that was certain. Male pride, she knew from observing every male of her acquaintance, did not take kindly to rejection, and rejection did not come in more comprehensive form than a woman falling asleep in a man's arms when he was intending to make love to her.

She felt fidgety, unsettled and sad. A strange combination of emotions. She was going to have to write and apologise. What on earth could she say to excuse her behaviour? But at least she could do something about the fidgets and perhaps later she would know what to say in her note. And there was that kiss to remember, always.

Bel threw back the covers and went to her little desk in her bare feet. 'I will drive in the park this morning, Philpott. Please have this note taken round to Lady

James Ravenhurst's London residence immediately and tell the footman to wait for the reply.'

There was only one woman in London she felt she could safely be with at the moment without betraying some clue as to her inner turmoil and that was Cousin Elinor. Elinor would not notice anything amiss unless a Greek charioteer drove through Hyde Park, or St Paul's Cathedral sprouted minarets, she was certain of it.

Miss Ravenhurst's note gratefully accepting the offer of a drive and luncheon was returned promptly and Elinor was equally prompt when the barouche drew up outside the house. When Bel thanked her for not keeping the horses standing, she brushed it away with a shake of her head in its plain straw bonnet. 'I did not want to dally, believe me! Mama is sure to have thought of some piece she wants me to transcribe after all and really, this is far too lovely a morning to be shut inside.'

'You help my aunt a great deal with her researches, then? It must be fascinating,' Bel added mendaciously, thinking that, unless Elinor was as committed as her mother, it must actually be quite ghastly.

'It has a certain interest. Anything does if you come to know enough about it.' Elinor folded her hands neatly in her lap, the tight buttoned gloves precisely the wrong shade of tan to go with the mouse-brown skirt and pelisse she wore. Either she was colour blind or her mother insisted she dress to repel men. Knowing Aunt Louisa, Bel strongly suspected the latter.

'Besides,' her cousin added, with the air of making her position quite clear, 'I have to do something with my time. Fortunately there are no elderly aunts who require a companion and I may be thankful that neither Simon nor Anne expect me to dance attention on their offspring. I am not at all good with children and I make a dreadful aunt. So, if one must be on the shelf, this at least has the advantage of being intellectually stimulating.'

It was the longest speech Bel had ever heard Elinor make, and certainly the first time she had ever volunteered her thoughts on her own situation. 'I do not understand why you should be on the shelf,' she ventured, choosing her words with caution. 'You are very pretty, well connected...'

'I am too tall and I have red hair,' Elinor contradicted. 'You are lucky, Cousin Belinda, you are one of the brown-haired Ravenhursts. I am one of the redheads.'

'Auburn,' Bel corrected. 'It is lovely, like conkers.' Poor Elinor. At least, whatever other problems she had, Bel had never been made to feel plain. 'Cousin Theophilus has much redder hair than you do.'

Elinor smiled. 'You are very kind, but I know I have no charm and *that* is essential to attract gentlemen. I am too practical, I expect. And I have not met Cousin Theophilus for years: Mama says he is a loose fish and a wastrel. Where are we going to drive?' She craned around inelegantly to see where they had got to, one hand firmly clamped on the crown of her awful hat. 'Hyde Park?'

'I thought so. And then shall we go to Gunter's for ices?' Eating ice cream in the morning was decidedly self-indulgent, but she felt she needed it.

The carriage made several turns, Bel pointing out the exotic sight of a lady with a pair of elegant long-haired hounds on a leash. Elinor twisted again in her seat to watch them, unconcerned about creasing her gown. 'I think those are saluki hounds, from Arabia. Cousin Belinda…' she frowned as she turned back '…there is a man following us in a curricle.'

'How can you tell? The streets are jammed.'

'I saw the curricle behind you when you picked me up, and he was there again when I looked to see where we were and now he is still behind us. He is driving a striking pair of match greys—I cannot be mistaken.'

'I expect he is going to the park as we are and our ways just happen to coincide.' Elinor looked dubious, but Bel was not going to scramble about in the carriage, peering out at the traffic behind them. 'Why should anyone want to follow us? I do believe you are a secret novel reader, Cousin! I can assure you, I am not being pursued by a wicked duke for some evil end. Perhaps he is after you.'

Elinor blushed so furiously at the suggestion of novel reading that Bel decided that not only must she consume the productions of the Minerva Press avidly, but that Aunt Louisa had no idea and would not approve. 'I have just borrowed *The Abbess of Voltiera* from the circulating library, if you would like to have it as I finish each volume,' she offered. 'It is quite blood curdling.'

'That would be very nice,' Elinor said primly as they entered the park. 'Oh look, there's a gentleman waving to you. See? On that horse close to the grove of chestnuts.'

Ashe. Bel followed the direction of her cousin's gaze and saw Mr Layne approaching them on a good-looking bay hack. 'Pull up,' she called to the coachman as her treacherous pulse returned to normal. 'Mr Layne, good

morning. Cousin Elinor, may I make known to you Mr
Layne, the brother of the renowned poetess? Mr Layne,
my cousin, Miss Ravenhurst.'

He brought his horse alongside the carriage and
leaned down to shake hands. 'A lovely morning for a
drive, is it not?'

'Delightful,' Elinor agreed. 'Are you also a poet, Mr
Layne?'

'Not at all, I fear. I can hardly rhyme moon and
spoon.' Patrick laughed, shaking his head in self-dep-
recation. 'All the talent in the family is with my sister.
I manage my uncle's estates.'

'That requires talent also,' Elinor observed.

Now he would be perfect for her, Bel thought,
suddenly struck as she watched them chatting easily. Mr
Layne showed no sign of alarm at either Elinor's
despised auburn hair, nor her appalling dress sense. He
was a young man with his way to make in the world and,
with her connections and excellent common sense, she
was just the sort of woman to…

'Oh, look, Cousin Belinda, that man who was following us has just driven past.' Elinor pointed.

'What?' Mr Layne stood in his stirrups to observe the
rear of the curricle that was sweeping away down the
carriage drive. 'Has someone been annoying you ladies?
Shall I catch up to him and demand his business?'

'No! I am certain it was just coincidence that he was
behind us for such a way. Please, do not concern
yourself Mr Layne. See—he has gone now.'

'Then let me ride beside you as escort in case he
comes back.' He reined back to one side and matched
his pace to the barouche as it moved off, keeping far
enough away so as not to appear to be with them.

'A very gentlemanlike young man, I think,' Bel observed quietly.

'Indeed, he is.' Elinor glanced sideways to observe Mr Layne from under the brim of her bonnet. 'You are fortunate in your admirers, Cousin.'

'Goodness, he is no such thing. I must tell you, Elinor, I am firmly resolved against a second marriage and to encourage anyone to have expectations—not that Mr Layne has any, I am sure—would be most unfair.' No more husbands. And no lover either. Bel repressed a wistful sigh. There was no point in repining; she had daringly given herself an opportunity and it was all her fault it had ended as it had. Lord Dereham could not have acted more chivalrously, poor man.

They trotted along as far as the Knightsbridge gate without further incident. When they reached it Mr Layne came up and touched his hat. 'Your mysterious follower has gone, it seems, ma'am.'

'I am sure it was simply a coincidence, but thank you for your escort. We are going to Gunter's for some refreshment—would you care to join us?' Bel had hoped for some peace and quiet with Elinor to recover the tone of her mind a little, but she had the notion that perhaps she could matchmake here. After all, she had never heard her cousin utter a single opinion about a man before.

'Thank you, but I regret that I have an appointment shortly. Do enjoy your ices, ladies.'

Bel and Elinor watched him canter away, Elinor's face unreadable. *Bother*—perhaps she was indifferent after all.

'Gunter's next, please,' Bel called up to the coachman and settled back against the squabs. Rescuing Elinor from Aunt Louisa was a worthwhile project, she felt. But how to get her into new clothes? She was never going to attract gentlemen dressed like that, even the amiable Mr Layne. This needed some planning. 'I am so pleased you could drive with me,' she remarked as they turned into Charles Street. 'Do you think Aunt Louisa would spare you again?'

'I should think so.' An unexpected twinkle showed in her cousin's green eyes. 'I am sure she would think it a sacrifice well worth while if I can provide some chaperonage for you.'

They were still smiling over plans for further expeditions as they walked into the confectioner's, securing a place in a corner with a good view of the room. Elinor ordered a vanilla ice and chocolate, and, despite her resolution to have only a small lemon ice and a cup of tea, Bel succumbed to the same choices.

'It is delicious if you chase a spoonful of ice with a sip of chocolate,' Bel was observing when Elinor sat bolt upright and said in a penetrating whisper, strongly reminiscent of her mother,

'It's that man again!'

'What man?' Bel had her back to the door.

'The one who was following us into the park. He is coming over, the presumptuous wretch. Oh, dear, and I do not have a hatpin!'

'We are in the middle of Gunter's, Elinor, nothing can happen to us here, you have no need to spear him—'

'Lady Felsham, good morning.'

Bel dropped her spoon into the saucer with a clatter. 'Lord Dereham!' It was Ashe, standing there, large as life, smiling blandly as though he had not seen her since the dancing party. Elinor cleared her throat and Bel realised she was gaping at him in complete shock. *Please*, she prayed, *please don't let me be blushing like a peony.* 'Good morning. May I introduce my cousin, Miss Ravenhurst? Elinor, Lord Dereham.' They shook hands. 'Will you join us?' *He is here, he is smiling, he has forgiven me...*

Elinor's eyebrows rose as Ashe took the third seat at their small round table and clicked his fingers for the waiter. Her lips narrowed. 'Do you know, my lord, I am convinced that I have seen you before today, several times. In fact, I could have sworn you were following us.'

Bel tried to kick her under the table, missed and made contact with Ashe's ankle. It was a very small table. 'Oh, yes,' Ashe admitted, wincing. 'I followed you into Hyde Park. Amazing how easy it is to bump into acquaintances, even at this time of year.' He smiled. 'I would have stopped to chat, but you were talking to Mr Layne and I did not want to interrupt.'

'How fortunate you were able to find us here then,' Elinor observed severely, obviously not believing a word of it. Bel shook her head at her slightly. This was not the time for her cousin to take her pretend role as chaperon so seriously.

'Was it not?' Ashe beamed at her as the waiter produced a pot of coffee for him. 'I could have sent a note, of course, but I wanted to make sure that the problem Lady Felsham is having with the plumbing is now corrected. I could send my own man round if it is not.' Elinor was looking baffled. 'Lady Felsham bought her house from me,' he explained. 'I feel responsible for the problem she is having with it.'

'Oh. I see.' Elinor took a sip of chocolate and subsided, obviously disappointed that this was neither a Gothic horror story nor a case of over-amorous pursuit for her to foil.

'Or I could have called later, but I am going to be visiting old Mr Horace this evening. Do you know him?'

'Old Mr Horace?' Did he mean what he appeared to mean? Bel opened her mouth, shut it rapidly and tried to get her tumbling thoughts into some sort of order. 'The, um...northern gentleman? The one with the snowy white hair and the problem with his teeth?' Ashe nodded. 'And you are going to visit him again?' Another nod. 'That is very kind of you, Lord Dereham. I had understood that your previous experiences with the old gentleman were not encouraging.'

'He is somewhat eccentric,' Ashe agreed. 'And a very poor conversationalist. But I derive a great deal of, um...*satisfaction* from the relationship. And hope to obtain more.'

Now she *must* be blushing. How could he be so brazen? But it seemed that *she* was forgiven for falling asleep: she just hoped that he would not be disappointed tonight. She was very certain that she would not be.

'Virtue,' Elinor pronounced piously, 'is its own reward.' She looked somewhat taken aback when both of her companions collapsed into peels of laughter.

Bel sat in front of her dressing table mirror, brushing her hair. It shone in the candle light, picking up the auburn highlights that all the Ravenhursts had in their hair, even if they were not redheads like Elinor and their cousin Theophilus.

She was quite pleased with her appearance tonight, she concluded dispassionately, studying her reflection.

That was a good thing, considering that she had spent the whole evening fretting over it. The good night's sleep and the fresh air that morning had restored her colour and the smudges had gone from under her eyes. Around her on the stool pooled the silken folds of a new aquamarine nightgown with ribbon ties on the shoulders and at the bosom and not a great deal of substance to its layers of skirt. As for the bodice, Bel was careful not to breathe too deeply. Ashe, she was hopeful, would like it.

She twiddled the earrings in her ears and then removed them, her fingers hesitating over her jewel box before lifting a long, thin, gold chain. She fastened it, observing the way it slithered down into the valley between her breasts. Was she trying too hard? What would he expect? She bit her lip in indecision, then touched a tiny dab of jasmine scent where the chain vanished into shadowed curves.

There. Enough. When she found out what pleased Ashe, then she could be more daring. The thought of what that voyage of discovery might entail sent a shiver up and down her spine as the landing clock chimed the three-quarter hour. Soon he would be here.

The minutes dragged as she sat waiting, elegantly disposed in the armchair, her volume of Byron open and unread in her lap. When the scratch on the door came she was so tense that the book fell to the carpet as she jerked upright and she was scrabbling on the floor behind the bed for it when the door opened and she heard Ashe come in.

'Hello, Horace old chap. Where has Bel gone?'

'Here.' She popped up from the other side of the bed, painfully aware that her hard-won pose of seductive so-phistication was completely ruined. 'I dropped my book.'

'Not playing hide and seek, then?' Ashe smiled. 'A pity—I can think of some entertaining forfeits.'

Bel felt hopelessly gauche. Ashe seemed to regard this lovemaking thing, which she had always assumed was a rather serious business, as a game, as fun. 'I am sorry about last night,' she said, eager to get that over with. 'I was so nervous I could not sleep the night before and then when you were so gentle and soothing I could not help myself drifting off. You must have been so angry with me. It is very kind of you to come back.'

'Don't apologise, Bel,' Ashe said shortly, something very like the anger she feared flickering in his eyes. 'Don't you dare. Do you think I would expect you to make love when you were tired and apprehensive? I am not your husband, I do not expect anything as my due. We give each other only what we are able to, what we want to. Do you understand?'

'Yes,' Bel lied, unable to believe it. Men made demands in bed, women obeyed them, that was the way things were. The only difference was that some men made those demands more nicely than others and would take the trouble to ensure the woman enjoyed the experience.

He smiled, the warmth chasing away the spark of anger. 'Tell me what you would like? Shall we read poetry together?'

'I would like you to kiss me,' she said, boldness masking the fact she could not stand the tension of waiting any longer. He was probably teasing about the poetry in any case.

'Very well, my lady. I feel a trifle overdressed.' Ashe had come in pantaloons and long-tailed coat, not in the formality of knee breeches. As she watched, he heeled off his shoes and shed coat and waistcoat on to a chair, then turned and held out his arms.

Bel walked into them, sliding her palms up his chest, feeling the heat under the fine cotton, catching her breath as they passed over his nipples, hardening under her touch. As she looked up, his lids lowered in sensual pleasure and his arms came round her.

Chapter Nine

The caress of Ashe's mouth was as gentle as it had been the first time he had kissed her, but this time it was surprisingly undemanding. Gradually Bel began to feel impatient with the respectful slide of closed lips over hers. She wanted his heat again, the taste of him, the hard thrust of his tongue, the indecent way he had sucked her lip between his.

Greatly daring, she parted her lips and ran her own tongue along the join of his, feeling them curve into a smile before he opened to her. Hazily Bel was aware that he had lured her into taking the initiative, but she was too engrossed in exploration now to feel resentful at his tactics.

She let her tongue slide languorously over his, then answered a sudden thrust with one of her own, duelling, teasing and being teased while the taste and the scent and the feel of him swept over her, until she felt she was melting into his body.

Ashe lowered his hands until they cupped her buttocks and pulled her up against him so she could feel the hard ridge of his erection against the curve of her stomach. It was a blatantly sexual display of desire and the intensity of the response it provoked in her was outrageous. She wanted him, now, desperately.

Heat seemed to pool low inside her, and she wriggled against him, seeking relief for the ache that was building, just where he pressed. Arousal, desire, sheer physical yearning—all the things she had not realised existed, had now only hazily began to suspect, could be hers with this man.

Shockingly she felt Ashe grow harder as she clung close, and deep in his throat he growled softly, the sound vibrating against her lips, a masculine signal of need that should have terrified her. Instead she felt powerful, amazed that she could have this effect upon him despite her ignorance and his experience.

Bel slid her fingers between their bodies and began to unbutton his shirt. Impatient with the mother-of-pearl buttons, she tugged and pulled and then, as her fingertips met skin and the rasp of hair, she froze. 'Go on,' he said huskily in her ear. 'Touch me Bel. I want your hands on me.'

'I do not know what to do,' she whispered. But it seemed her hands did know, sliding under the parted front of the shirt. She felt the tickle of hair on her palms and then hot, satiny skin as they slid over his ribs. Back to the centre, then down over ridges of muscle to the flatness of his stomach where the hair seemed to focus. Her thumb found his navel and dipped in, wiggled experimentally, provoking a gasp of laughter.

He was moving his hips against her as he held her, signalling his need, yet he controlled it for her. It seemed impossible that this big, powerful man would let her explore like this, would seem content for her to set the pace.

Ashe lowered his face into the angle of her neck and began to lick slowly up until the tip of his tongue found her ear. The caress brought back memories of lying crushed beneath him on the floor, his mouth hot and moist as he explored her, and all she could think about was feeling his body over hers again, his heart against hers, his mouth taking hers.

Bel's fingers slipped lower, into the waistband of Ashe's trousers where the tantalising trail of dark hair vanished. '*Yes*. Bel, yes.' The fastenings were tight; he sucked in his breath so she could twist her fingers round and open them, then her hand was curling round the hard, hot, terrifying length of him. A moment later and she was on her back on the bed, Ashe was shedding the remains of his clothes and she was staring wide-eyed at the first naked man she had ever seen in the flesh.

And what flesh. Bel swallowed. He was beautifully made, the candlelight flickering over smooth muscle and long limbs and... Suddenly she was nervous, her eyes closed tight. She was very aware of how flimsy her own garment was, how she must look to him, sprawled wantonly on the bed.

'It's all right, Bel, don't be frightened.' His weight dipped the bed beside her and Ashe began to stroke her quivering body, his hand running softly over the fine silk. It whispered against her skin. 'I won't do anything until you want me to, I promise.'

'I do want you to. To do everything. Anything. But I do not know what those things are that I want.' Bel opened her eyes and smiled ruefully. 'That is what is so scary.'

'Then, Bel, let's find them together.' He smiled back, then bent to kiss her breast just where the edge of the nightgown ended. '*Belle, bella, bellissima.*' His lips fastened over one nipple and he began to suck it gently through the gossamer fabric, sending shock waves of sensation through her. She writhed, gasped, clutched his head, uncertain whether she wanted him to stop at once or never stop at all. It seemed he intended never to stop. Perhaps she would simply die of the sensation. Tongue, teeth, lips combined to send her into a fever, reduced her to a helpless, panting puddle of longing and desire.

Just when she was certain she could bear it no longer she felt his hand caress up under her skirts, his fingers slide into the secret folds that were hot and wet for him, slip between them to find the entrance to her body and then, as she arched in shock against his mouth, into the heat. Bel sensed her muscles clasp around the intrusion as his thumb found the single aching focus of her straining body and she felt his weight over her, his mouth on hers as she screamed in agonised delight and collapsed, shuddering, under him.

She wondered hazily if she had lost consciousness for, as she regained her senses enough to differentiate between the parts of her own body and his, she found the nightgown was gone and she was moulded, flesh to flesh, heartbeat to heartbeat with Ashe.

'Let me take you, *Belle*,' he murmured and surged into her on one powerful thrust. Always before she had lain rigid under such an onslaught, enduring the mean-ingless, effortful, mercifully short male striving towards release. Only now Ashe seemed quite as concerned to bring her to that peak of ecstasy again as to reach his own, and it seemed that the beautiful body dominating hers was quite capable of going on for as long as it took. She wanted it to last for ever because it was so wonderful, and yet to be over at once, because she wanted to share that storm of completion with him.

She felt the tension twisting into unimaginable heights, felt a change in his body, heard his breath rasp in his throat and curled her legs around his hips, pulling him in. 'Ashe! Ashe, please…' He gave one more thrust as she lost herself, then she was conscious—just—of him leaving her, holding her tight, gasping into her hair as they fell together, down into darkness.

Ashe rolled on to his back, bringing Bel with him to lie cradled against his chest in the curve of his arm. She gave a soft whimper of pleasure and snuggled close as his groping hand found the corner of the sheet and pulled it over their damp bodies.

He gazed up at the underside of the curtains as he let the aftershocks of their lovemaking shudder through his body. It had been beyond anything he had imagined and he could not understand why. Bel was lovely, sweet, eager. But she had come to him completely untutored and repressed—as close to a virgin as a woman could be after sleeping with a man. She had none of the tricks to pleasure him his mistresses had known—and yet the tentative wonder of her hands on his body, the awe in her eyes, the total trust with which she had given herself to him were powerfully erotic. And humbling, he realised.

'Bel?'

'Mmm?' She snuggled in closer, rubbed her cheek against his pectorals and found his nipple with her lips. 'Mmm.'

'Stop it, wicked woman. Let a man catch his breath.' She released the tense flesh and he saw her ear go pink at what she must have thought was a reproof. 'I like it too much,' he explained, mentally cursing her husband again, and she relaxed. 'Are you—are you all right?'

He had expected her to be shy at the question, to answer hesitantly. Instead she wriggled up until she was sitting, her knees curved into his hips, and smiled at him, the sheet pooling around her. Glowing, that was the only way to describe her. Her skin was flushed pink, deeper across her breasts. Her hair tumbled wantonly around her shoulders and her eyes, fixed on him, were wide and wondering. 'All right?' She shook her head, the curling locks shifting in the candlelight. 'That phrase hardly seems adequate. I had no idea it was like that. Is it always like that?'

It seemed he had not disappointed her. Ashe felt himself relax. He had not been conscious of a tension, but now he saw what a responsibility he had accepted and how hurt Bel could have been if she had chosen a man who did not live up to the trust she had placed in him.

'I find it hard to believe that it would ever be like that for me again,' he said seriously. 'It can be as good—it will be—but that was special.'

'Oh.' Bel considered this, equally serious. 'But I did not know what I was doing.'

'You didn't need to; you did what came naturally and that was…wonderful.'

'Oh,' she said again, dropping her lashes. 'May we do it again? Soon? I mean, of course, when it is a con- venient evening for you.'

'It is very convenient now,' he said smiling.

'But—' She glanced down to where her wriggling had pulled the sheet away from his loins, and her mouth opened slightly in surprise as her gaze had the pre- dictable effect on him.

'You see what you can do just by looking? If you would like to explore,' Ashe suggested, lifting her hand and placing it on the flat plane of his stomach, 'we can see just how soon that convenient moment will arrive.'

Bel was woken by the pressure of Ashe's lips against her temple. 'Sweetheart, I must go now. What do you want to do about the bed?'

She struggled back to consciousness through what seemed to be a drift of rose petals, swansdown and fluffy clouds and found him sitting on the edge of the bed, fully dressed and smiling at her. 'What time is it?'

'Four.' It was not a dream this time either, then. He had been there, he had made love to her—*three times*—he seemed pleased with her and she, she was still floating. *Three times, each time different, each time blissful...* 'The bed?' he prompted, grinning at her befuddlement.

Bel pushed back her hair with both hands and looked around at the tangle of bedclothes and the tumbled pillows. 'We will never make it look as it did before,' she concluded. 'If you can arrange the covers so it looks as though I was restless and pushed them right off, and pass me that copy of Byron...' She heaped up the pillows and snuggled back into them, half-sitting, half-lying, then remembered her nightgown, found it on the floor and dragged it on. 'There. I could not sleep, sat up half the night reading and fell asleep with my book.'

Ashe straightened up from arranging the covers artistically and grinned at her. 'Very convincing. But I think next time I had better wake up in time to make the bed—or we strip it first.' He came round to the side of the bed, then bent and kissed her. Bel put up a hand, cupping his stubble-shadowed cheek and enjoyed the rasp of whiskers as she rubbed gently.

'Thank you,' she whispered. *Next time, there is going to be a next time.*

'No, *ma belle*, thank *you*.' Then he was gone, shoes in hand, slipping out of the room. The door snicked shut and she was alone. Bel tossed the volume of poetry carelessly on the covers as though it had fallen from her hand, reached out to pinch the wick of the remaining candle and lay back against the heaped pillows.

Her body thrummed, lighter than air, yet so heavily relaxed it felt she might sink through the mattress. She felt wonderful, although she knew that in the morning she was going to be stiff and perhaps a little sore. It had been a miracle. Ashe had been a miracle. Bel's lids drooped. As sleep took her again she thought hazily, *This is so perfect. So perfect...*

Bel floated, blissful, through the next morning. The fluffy pink clouds still enveloped her, the sun shone, just for her, the birds were singing, just because Ashe had made love to her. At lunchtime she received a bouquet of yellow roses with a note that said simply, 'One? A.' and rushed out to purchase two new nightgowns, a pair of utterly frivolous backless boudoir slippers, a cut-glass vase for the roses and pink silk stockings. She then went and took refuge in Ackermann's, browsing through the latest fashion plates until her maid was nodding with boredom and she could hand a note and a coin to the doorman without being noticed.

'Please see this is delivered,' she said brightly, without any appearance of secrecy. 'I should have left it with my footman and quite forgot.'

The man touched his hat respectfully and snapped his fingers for an errand boy. The note, hurried away in the lad's firm grip said only, 'Yes. B.'

She, Bel Cambourn, respectable widow, was having an *affaire*. She had a lover. She was living out her fantasy and it was utterly perfect. Bel drifted round the end of a rack of maps, wondering vaguely whether she was going to exist in this happy blur for the duration of the affair or whether it would wear off. There were doubtless all kinds of things she should be doing, calls she should make, business she should attend to, but she could not concentrate on a single thing other than the image of Ashe, nakedly magnificent—

'Ouch!' The pained voice was familiar.

She found herself almost nose to nose with her Cousin Elinor, who had been browsing through a stack of small classical prints. Elinor's right foot was under Bel's left. She hastily removed it and apologised for her abstraction.

'I have decided to create a print room in my small closet,' Elinor explained, once they had finished apologising to each other for not looking where they were going. 'I think I have enough now. Do you?' She regarded a pile of prints doubtfully.

'How big is the room? I would take a few more if I were you. And you will need borders,' Bel pointed out, wrenching her mind away from erotic thoughts. 'I did the same thing at Felsham Hall and bought everything here. They sell borders by the yard.' She picked up the top print, discovered it was a scantily clad Roman athlete with a physique almost as good as Ashe's and hastily returned it to the pile. Ashe did not have a fig leaf.

Elinor had found a shop assistant while Bel was re-covering her composure and he returned with a selection of borders for the ladies to chose from. 'You look very well, Cousin.' Elinor glanced up from fitting a length of black-and-white paper against a print of the Forum. 'Excited,' she added, rejecting that border and trying another.

'I do? Oh.' Bel bit her lip; she had no idea that her inner state would be obvious. 'How?'

'Your colour is better and—I do not know quite how to describe it—you are glowing somehow.' Elinor put her head on one side and frowned at her cousin.

'It's the lovely weather, and I am enjoying being back in London. I did a lot of shopping this morning.' Although shopping was not a reason for excitement that Elinor would recognise.

'I wish I could have come with you.' Unaware she had startled her cousin, Elinor made a decision on the borders and handed her choice to the assistant.

'Really?' Thank goodness, her cousin was taking an interest in clothes at last.

'Yes, I need some stout walking shoes, some large handkerchiefs and tooth powder,' Elinor said prosaically, dashing Bel's hopes of fashionable frivolity. 'Mama is meeting me with the carriage—would you care for a lift home?'

Bel sat on one of the stools at the green-draped counter. 'No, thank you, I will walk, I need the exercise.' If truth were told, she was more than a little stiff from last night's exertions and would have welcomed the ride, but the thought of enduring Aunt Louisa's close scrutiny was too alarming. If Elinor could tell something was changed, Aunt Louisa most certainly could.

She walked out with Elinor, the porter hastening behind with the packed prints. Sure enough, drawn up at the kerb side in front of the shop, was Aunt Louisa's carriage with the top down, and there, walking towards her along the pavement, a willowy lady on his arm, was Ashe.

'Belinda!' Aunt Louisa.

'Lady Belinda.' Ashe. 'Miss Ravenhurst.'

'Lord Dereham.' That was Elinor. Her mama, startled by the novelty of her daughter addressing a man in the street, turned with majestic slowness and raised her eyeglass. Ashe bowed gracefully.

'Lady James, Lady Belinda, Miss Ravenhurst.' Ashe raised his hat. 'Are you acquainted with Lady Pamela Darlington?'

'No, I am not. Good afternoon, Lady Pamela.' Bel shook hands with a politeness she was far from feeling. What she did feel, shockingly, was the urge to push Lady Pamela into the nearby horse trough. The pink clouds of happiness vanished.

'Ha! I remember you.' Aunt Louisa was regarding the very lovely young woman severely.

Bel found she could not speak. Lady Pamela was pretty, beautifully dressed, totally confident. She shook hands with Lady James without showing any alarm at her ferocious scowl, smiled at Elinor and Bel and chatted pleasantly while, all the time, keeping her hand firmly on Ashe's arm. From time to time she glanced up at him with a proprietorial little smile that widened as he smiled back. He had all the hallmarks of a man receiving the attentions of a lovely woman, damn him, Bel thought savagely, smiling until her cheeks ached. Behind Lady Pamela stood a maid and a footman laden with packages.

Bel did not know where to look. She did not dare meet Ashe's eye, terrified of showing some emotion her aunt could read. With her insides churning with what she had not the slightest difficulty in recognising as violent and quite unreasonable jealousy, she did not want to look at Lady Pamela and all the time she knew that simply by standing there, dumbstruck and awkward, she risked making herself conspicuous.

'We have been purchasing prints for a print room,' she said suddenly, into a lull in the conversation. Lady Pamela smoothed an invisible thread off Ashe's sleeve with a little pout of concentration on her face. Bel gritted her teeth.

'How very artistic of you, Lady Belinda,' Ashe remarked, the first words he had addressed to her since his greeting.

'Miss Ravenhurst is the artistic one, my lord, I am merely helping her choose some images,' Bel replied, her lips stiff. She made herself meet his eyes. There was not the slightest sign in his expression of anything other than good-mannered interest in what she was saying. How could that be? Bel had felt it would be obvious to everyone who passed—let alone her aunt— that the two of them were lovers; she felt as though it must be emblazoned across her face. But no one seemed in any way suspicious and all Aunt Louisa's attention appeared to be focused upon Lady Pamela and Ashe.

And just what was he doing with the lovely Lady Pamela? Why were they smiling at each other like that? Pamela was hanging on to his arm in a manner that was positively clinging and Ashe was doing nothing to distance himself. He seemed to know her well. Very well.

'Belinda!' She jumped. Aunt Louisa was gesturing

to the open carriage door and the groom waiting patiently beside it.

'No, thank you, Aunt, I will walk back, I have my maid with me.'

'Join us, Lady Belinda,' Ashe suggested, proffering his other arm. Lady Pamela's smiling lips compressed into a thin line. 'We are going to Hatchard's bookshop, so I imagine our ways lie together.'

'Thank you, no, my lord,' she said coolly. 'I have more than enough foolish romance to be going on with, just at the present, without buying any to read.' She bowed slightly to Lady Pamela, smiled at her relatives and set off briskly westwards.

'My lady?' Millie scurried to keep up. 'Are you all right, my lady?'

'Yes, of course I am.' Bel blew her nose fiercely but slowed her pace for the girl's shorter legs. The smoke and the dust must have got into her eyes, there was no other explanation for the way they were watering.

How could Ashe be so…? She wrestled for the word. Deceitful. That was it, horrid as it was. He had told her he had no attachments, no commitments, yet there he was, strolling along, giving every indication that he was on the very best of terms with one of the most eligible young ladies in the Marriage Mart. And that was a highly risky thing to be doing if a man was not serious. It led to gossip at best and to interviews with enraged fathers at worst.

If she had known he was on the look-out for a bride, nothing would have led her to make her outrageous proposition, Bel thought angrily, the low heels of her shoes clicking on the pavement with the force of her steps. He had only needed to pretend to misunderstand her, as he had done at first, and there the matter would have ended. She would have been embarrassed, yet probably relieved once she had time to think things over, and Ashe would have neatly extricated himself from a tricky encounter, as doubtless he had many a time before.

But he had not extricated himself, and she had slept with him. They had made love and while it probably meant nothing to him, Bel told herself, piling on the misery, she was never going to be the same again.

Half an hour ago she had thought her life was perfect. *Perfect.*

Chapter Ten

'It is very nice, my lady. Will you be going in to see if they have it in a different colour?'

'What?' Bel found she was standing in front of a milliner's shop, regarding a hat on a stand, and Millie was waiting patiently at her side.

'You said it was perfect, my lady. But I don't think you usually wear that shade of blue, do you, ma'am?'

Now she was talking to herself. Bel took a long, steadying breath. She was a grown-up woman, if a naïve and inexperienced one. Now she knew about Lady Pamela Ashe would not come to her again, not after having found himself in public between his lover and the object of his more permanent attentions. One just had to put it all down to experience. And at least she had experienced physical pleasure. She knew what all the fuss was about now.

All she had to do was to stop aching with desire for Ashe. Surely that would happen naturally after a few days? One simply could not exist as she was now, feeling like this, not without going mad.

Bel pushed open the shop door and stepped in. Shopping as a cure for misery was shallow, but she did not care. Tomorrow she would find something worthwhile to do. Today she was going to buy a hat.

The soothing qualities of a new hat, even an outrageously frivolous one that an unmarried girl like Lady Pamela would not be allowed to wear, were predictably short lived. Bel knew perfectly well that she could shop until she dropped, dance her slippers through, read the most frivolous journals and gossip until she was hoarse—but the empty ache would still be there. It did not help to tell herself that by the very nature of their relationship there could be no emotional commitment. Ashe had made none. What she felt now was too close to that for either safety or comfort—perhaps it was better that it was ending now.

Bel found herself at half past midnight unable to sleep again. She sat up in bed, her arms wrapped round her knees, her books discarded on the table and tried to think.

She was twenty-six. She was never going to marry again and she would never dare entangle herself with another man. That left a considerable number of years stretching into the future to be filled with something other than domestic duties or passion. Bel knew that while she was perfectly intelligent she would never be a bluestocking like her cousin, so retreating into some form of intellectual study was out of the question. Parties and shopping were fun, but hardly the basis of a fulfilling life.

Which left good works. Bel contemplated the idea. When she had been married she had undertaken charitable activities on the estate and in the surrounding parishes as a matter of course, but now there was no estate to provide her with a ready-made supply of children to educate, elderly and infirm persons to support or fathers of large families to find work for. She was going to have to find a cause of her own.

Throwing back the covers, Bel slid out of bed and padded across to the table, the voluminous skirts of the plain cotton nightgown she had chosen flapping about her ankles. She found paper and ink and settled down to make a list of causes. It would need to be something engrossing and worthwhile—she was not going to play with this like so many society ladies did.

Children, widows, animals, the elderly, she wrote, biting the end of her quill. *Education? Employ...*

The door opened. Bel swung round on her chair and stared. *'Ashe?'*

'You were expecting someone else, Bel, my sweet?' He strolled in and dropped his hat and gloves on a chair. Tonight he was elegant in evening dress. 'Lord, my great-aunt's parties are a bore, bless her. I love the old darling, but her entourage of geriatric swains is quite another matter. I have just sat through at least six elderly gentlemen telling me how Wellington should have deployed his troops at Waterloo and one who was confused enough to think he had been at Quatre Bras personally.'

'I was not expecting *you*,' Bel said, her pen dropping unheeded and spattering ink spots across her list.

'Why not?' Ashe shed his jacket and waistcoat and began to deconstruct his elaborate neckcloth. 'You sent me a reply to my note.' He walked towards her, the ends in his hands, then stopped, frowning. 'Aren't you well, sweetheart? Do you have a headache? I'll go, of course.'

'No, I do not have a headache and I am quite well. Don't *sweetheart* me.' Bel stood up and saw his expression change as he took in the exceedingly chaste nightgown and the sharp tone of her voice. 'And I replied to your note *before* I saw you with Lady Pamela. If I had had any notion that you were involved with someone else, I would never have embarked on this…liaison.'

He looked as tempting as sin itself standing there, those gorgeous blue eyes fixed intently on her, the thick gilt of his hair slightly tousled, the neck of his shirt open just enough to give her a glimpse of the skin beneath. And that was precisely what Ashe was: sin. Highly experienced, completely unprincipled sin.

'Lady Pamela? You think I am in some way committed to Lady Pamela Darlington?'

'Yes, Lady Pamela. Is there anyone else I have missed? So far she is the only one I have seen hanging on your arm, exchanging little smiles with you, generally behaving as though she has proprietorial rights over you and getting doting looks in return. And as Lady Pamela is a well-bred, single young lady and the leading light of this year's Marriage Mart, there is but one conclusion to be drawn from such behaviour.'

'You are jealous.' Ashe said it with a hint of a smile. She glared and the smile vanished. 'But that's ridiculous Bel.'

Bel took two rapid steps forward and jabbed him in the chest with one sharp finger. Ashe swayed backwards a trifle, but did not retreat. 'Yes, I am jealous, and do not tell me I have no right to be because I know that perfectly well. But don't you dare tell me I am being ridiculous either; you told me you had no commitments and I would not have dreamed of…of…' she waved a hand towards the bed '…*that* if I had known.'

'Ah.' Bel narrowed her eyes at him. He did not look the slightest bit chastened, not the remotest bit guilty. 'I have known Lady Pamela since she was six. She is a minx and as much of a hussy as a well-bred girl can be and, despite her father's adamant refusal to consider the suit, she is head over heels in love with a very good friend of mine.'

'That makes it worse!'

'Head over heels,' Ashe persisted, removing himself to the relative safety of the fireside. 'And set on persuading me to invite both him and her to a house party.'

'Which house party?'

'The one she expects me to host for the sole purpose of allowing her and George to moon about in the shrubbery out of sight of her chaperon.'

'If that is the case, why was she spreading herself all over you like butter?' Bel demanded, provoking a grin from Ashe at her language.

'Because she is one of the prettiest girls in London, used to being the acknowledged star in any firmament and, when she comes face to face with another lovely woman, her instincts are to lay claim to any male in the vicinity between the ages of sixteen and seventy. I happened to be handy.'

'Oh.' Bel swallowed, clenching her hands. *Lovely woman? Her?* 'I have made a fool of myself, haven't I?'

'A bit.' He smiled affectionately. 'I suppose I helped. But, given the basilisk eye of your Aunt Ravenhurst, I thought it best to play up to Pamela and to treat you with polite indifference.' Bel bit her lip and focused her gaze on the point where his shirt opened over golden skin. 'Were you truly jealous? That is very flattering.'

'Flattering? It was horrible. Jealousy was a thoroughly reprehensible reaction in the first place, and I know I have absolutely no right to feel it. I felt mean and miserable.' Bel sifted through her emotions, then added honestly, 'But it hurt, and I do not like you telling me I am being ridiculous.'

'I am sorry.' Ashe stepped over Horace and gathered her in against his chest. Bel gave a little sigh and clung to as much of him as she could get her arms around. 'I forget you are very new to these intrigues. It is not in your nature to dissemble, but we cannot afford to look at each other and have our closeness show, you know that.'

'I know.' Bel nodded, rubbing her cheek against the warmth of his shirt front. 'It is all right now.' She had dissembled for all the years of her marriage, feigning interest and obedience. But that was a very different thing to hiding desire and the intimate knowledge of another person.

'I am not sure that it is all right,' Ashe said gravely, running his hands up and down her back. 'What on earth are you wearing, Bel? I thought I had strayed into a nunnery.'

'I did not think you would be coming and this is the most boringly respectable nightgown I have. I didn't want to think about you, you see.'

He gave a snort of laughter and stepped back to study her. Then he frowned. 'We have a problem. You want to make love, I imagine, but I am very much afraid that garment has killed my passion quite dead, which was obviously the intention of the designer. There is only one thing for it, unless you wish me to leave or to spend the night reading poetry with you.'

'What?' Bel enquired, heat pooling inside her. Ashe was teasing her, of course. No man wearing thin skin-tight knit breeches could pretend he was not aroused when he was.

'You will just have to seduce me.' He looked rueful.

'Seduce you?' Bel heard her voice squeak. *Me? How?*

'Yes, seduce me. On the bearskin rug, I think. The novelty will, perhaps, arouse my jaded appetites.' Ashe leaned negligently against the bedpost and waited for her reaction.

Jaded appetites, indeed! This was a game. Bel suppressed her immediate reaction, which was to blush and stammer that she did not know how. He probably expected her to do that, but she would not. The sight of him, elegant and hard and all of him—every inch—hers, made her blood sing and her breath come short. She wanted him desperately, she wanted to learn more about lovemaking, she wanted to please him, and herself.

'Very well, but you must promise to do as I say,' she ordered boldly. She waited for his nod, noticing with interest the effect her agreement had on him. The pulse under the sharp line of his jaw was very visible, the skin at the base of his throat was flushed and his pupils had begun to dilate, turning the deep sea blue a darker, stormier purple.

Very deliberately Bel undid the top two buttons on her nightgown, but that was all. Then she folded her arms, knowing the action pushed up her breasts, and stood there, considering. If Ashe thought she was going to drape herself all over him like a cat begging for caresses, he was mistaken. 'Take off your shirt.'

He pulled it over his head, giving her a view of the

muscles of his back rippling as he bent right over, then stretched upright, magnificently unselfconscious. Bel stood looking, studying the way his muscles strapped over his ribs, the way his chest hair changed texture as it narrowed down towards his navel. She saw his nipples harden under the caress of her gaze. Power. Such power.

'And now the rest of your clothes,' she said, making her voice indifferent. He kept his eyes locked with hers as he undressed and Bel toyed with one more button on her gown. He was so beautiful she found it desperately hard to keep her hands off him. Her own nipples were peaking painfully against the thick cotton, her breasts ached into heaviness; the intensity of his gaze seemed to bore through her to hit at the base of her spine.

'Now lie down,' she ordered, gesturing towards the thick white fur at her feet. *Seduce him? As if he needs it! If he becomes any more aroused, I will refuse to believe it physically possible.*

Ashe stretched out on the great pelt of fur, a magnificent barbarian in his shameless nudity. He moved sensuously on it, his broad shoulders shrugging into the softness, the movement of his hips a demonstration of lithe masculinity.

'Am I arousing your interest yet?' Bel enquired huskily.

'Mmm? This is very comfortable, I may go to sleep.' He was watching her like a hawk from beneath hooded lids, his very focus a contradiction to his words.

Bel moved to stand at his feet and let her gaze wander up the length of him from the high arches, up the straight shin bones, up the trained muscles of his thighs, up—lingeringly—past the slim hips. She let her tongue tip run over her lower lip and saw him shift restlessly as she did so. Bel stepped forward so her feet were either side of Ashe's knees and started to undo the rest of her buttons.

Despite the expression of languid uninterest he was maintaining the heavy lids rose, dragged up to follow her slowly moving hands. Bel fought her own eagerness as she made herself free each button with finicking care until the entire gown to below her waist was open. Then she shrugged one shoulder free. Ashe's tongue slid between his lips and she saw his hands fist into the fur at his sides. Another shoulder, then she let go and the entire garment slipped down to pool around her feet.

She kicked it aside as Ashe came up on to his elbows. 'No, my lord, I am sorry if you are bored, but I must insist you lie down. Do try to sleep if you wish.'

He fell back with a growl as Bel knelt, her knees either side of his hips. The power of what she was doing felt incredible. It was like sitting astride a thoroughbred horse; she could feel the leashed strength beneath her, knew she could not control it, that only his will was keeping him tame, biddable to her.

Her hand slipped between her thighs, found him, hot, hard, impossibly aroused, and positioned herself. 'Now,' she whispered and slowly sank down, taking him within her, stroking every inch of him with her heat and her slickness and her desire.

He growled, reached for her and she caught his wrists, leaning into him so she pressed them to the ground on either side of his head and the tips of her breasts caressed his chest. 'Awake yet?' she teased, her lips hovering an inch above his.

'Ride me.' And he surged up against her. Bel heard herself cry out, knew her body was responding, plunging, demanding, but it all became a blur, a wonderful, intense, heated blur with the only reality the deep blue-black eyes holding hers, the beat of his pulse under her fingers, the musk of their lovemaking as potent as drugged incense in her nostrils.

Ashe bucked beneath her, then she was beneath him, her own wrists trapped, and she cried out again and again as she fell into a whirlpool of velvet darkness and he finally left her body.

Some incalculable time later Bel felt Ashe roll away from her and reached for him. He was back in a moment, carrying pillows and the bedcover. 'I like it on this fur. Here, these will make us more comfortable and preserve your chaste bed from disturbance.'

Bel snuggled up against his chest again. Horace's soft fur was warm and sensual beneath her, Ashe's body was hot and smooth under her hand. 'This is nice.' *This is Heaven.*

'You are addictive Bel,' Ashe said ruefully, gathering her snugly against himself. Other women had curled against him like this, but none had ever seemed to fit so well. 'But I am going to have to leave you for a few days.'

'Leave? Why?' Bel wriggled free and sat up, shaking her head at her own vehemence. 'No, I am sorry, I did not mean to sound so demanding, or to pry. Will you be away long?'

'Ten days, perhaps.' He reached up and traced a finger round the curve of her jaw, enjoying the way she turned her head into his hand for more caresses. Bel was so sweet, so formal somehow—when she wasn't in the throes of passion. She had even managed to be jealous in a polite manner. Ashe could recall mistresses and lovers who would have thrown ornaments at his head for less provocation than he had given her that morning. 'I am going home. I should have gone at once, but somehow—' How to explain to her?

'Somehow what you had just experienced abroad was too raw?' Bel suggested.

'Yes.' She understood what he sometimes had difficulty articulating to himself. Ashe lifted her hand and kissed the knuckles, then turned them against his cheek. 'Exactly. But if I stay away any longer, they will start worrying that I am hiding something after all.'

'And you can make arrangements for the house party you are going to give,' Bel suggested slyly.

'I had no intention of doing any such thing, although if you would come to it, I might be persuaded to change my mind.'

Bel looked deliciously ruffled by the suggestion. 'I could not bear to be so close to you and have to behave properly all the time.'

'Who said anything about behaving? That is the whole point of house parties—camouflage for misbehaviour.'

'I…I find I am shocked.' She shook her head in wonderment at her own reaction. 'How very hypocritical of me!'

'You are not being uniquely wicked in taking a lover, you know, *ma belle*, other people have liaisons too.' But in a way she was unique, Ashe realised. Bel would not move from him to another lover when this was over. This was an experience for her that she would sample because she had needed so badly to understand physical love, then put aside, never to be repeated.

'What are you frowning about?' She reached out and massaged the crease between his brows with the pads of two fingers. Ashe fought not to close his eyes and simply purr.

'I'm not sure,' he confessed, smiling at her anxiety. But he knew, all the same. He did not want to envisage life without Bel, he did not want to imagine her alone, chaste, unkissed and uncaressed and he could not imagine having another woman in her place, in his arms. But *affaires* ran their course, it would happen one day and they would move on. He would find someone else.

'Tell me about your home,' she suggested, snuggling down again, her hand drifting slowly up and down his chest in a way that predicted any conversation would be short.

'Coppergate? Well, it is in Hertfordshire, out beyond St Albans in the hills. It was built in the seventeenth century by a Mr Copper, a merchant who made his fortune, bought by my ancestor when Mr Copper's luck ran out and it has been with us ever since. There is a lake…'

Chapter Eleven

The lake was still as a reflecting mirror under the August sunshine as Ashe tooled the team through the gates and up the long curving sweep of carriage drive towards the old house.

Home. And by some miracle he was approaching it unscathed, with all his limbs intact and not even a romantic scar for his sisters to exclaim over. No scars that showed on the outside at least and those that were hidden were far from romantic. But the nightmares were fewer now and he no longer woke confused about where he was, worrying that he had fallen asleep on duty. Bel had helped, he realised. He did not have to talk about it to her, but whenever the subject had come up, her empathy soothed him.

Ashe rolled stiff shoulders to ease them, finding the very thought of Bel relaxed him, even if it provoked an uncomfortable physical reaction. He was going to miss her in so many ways. The curricle rounded a stand of ancient beech trees and there was the house, low, rambling and—thanks to Mr Copper's original design and Ashe's ancestors' numerous additions—without any outstanding architectural merit whatsoever. But he loved it, even if he found it hard to stay there for long.

The front door opened as his wheels crunched to a halt on the gravel and there was a flash of white fabric. For a moment he saw Bel standing there, her arms held out to him. Then the vision shifted and blurred and it was Katy, his youngest sister, running down the steps to meet him, her blonde curls flying, skirts hiked up. 'Ashe! You are home!'

'As you see.' He grinned at her, jumping down from the curricle to return her enthusiastic hug. That image of Bel was disconcerting, but he did not want to explore why his mind was playing such tricks on him.

The sound of footsteps behind him made him turn, his arm still round Katy's shoulders, everything else forgotten as his mother, Frederica and Anna came to join the reunion. 'You know I'm all right,' he protested, as they patted and stroked him, trying to make himself heard over the babble of excited voices. 'You got all my letters, I know you did, for you answered them all.'

'Yes, dearest.' Lady Dereham smiled happily. 'You are such a good correspondent; we heard that you were safe almost as soon as the newspapers were reporting the outcome of the battle, so our minds were set at rest much earlier than many families, I am sure. And so many thoughtful letters telling us where you were and when you would be home.'

'Why didn't you come at once?' Katy demanded as they walked up the steps, his two elder sisters still inclined to stroke his sleeves as he walked, as though to reassure themselves he really was there in the flesh.

'Because Ashe had business to attend to, you know

he explained that,' Frederica reproved her. 'And he probably needed a rest before you start bombarding him with questions. Look at poor Philip Carr over at Longmere Hall—the wretched man has had to escape back to town under the pretext of consulting a physician, just because his family would not stop talking at him.'

'Carr's hurt?' Ashe stopped on the top step. *Not another one, not another friend maimed.* 'I had not heard.'

'Only a flesh wound in his thigh, apparently.' Lady Dereham urged him into the hallway. 'He should have stayed in London on his way through, but his mama descended and bore him off and then wondered why he was so taciturn. It has healed cleanly, although he is still limping very badly.'

'My lord, may I say on behalf of the entire staff how happy we are at your safe return?' It was Wrighton, the butler, allowing himself a rare smile as he took Ashe's hat and gloves. 'The household feels the honour of serving a Waterloo hero most keenly, my lord.'

Ashe bit back the retort that he was no damned hero, he was just fortunate to be alive to be fawned over, unlike many men far more worthy of that title. There was no way to say it without upsetting people. He would simply have to adopt an air of manly reticence and hope they would take the hint and stop talking about the damned battle.

'Thank you, Wrighton. I am delighted to be back.'

The arrival of Race and the carriage with his baggage effectively distracted Wrighton and his footmen and allowed Ashe to escape into the drawing room. Behind him he heard his mother ordering *tea and Cook's special lemon drop scones his lordship likes so much.* 'I will be pounds overweight,' he grumbled affectionately as his sisters pressed him down into his usual chair, fussing as though he, and not the unfortunate Mr Carr, was wounded.

'We want to make a fuss of you.' Anna, the elder and most level-headed of his sisters, smiled affectionately as she sat down. 'You must allow us that indulgence, you know. In return, we promise not to plague you with questions about the army.'

'Very well, I consent to being spoiled.' It seemed strange to be spending so much time with women. First the attention he and the other returning officers received from society ladies, then the time with Bel and now he was the focus of four women's world. 'You will have to civilise me again, I expect—I have been in rough male company for too long.'

They sat around him in an attentive semi-circle and he made himself concentrate, think what would please them to talk about. But first he wanted to find out about them. 'Tell me what you have all been up to.'

'I have a new governess.' Katy, predictably, was first to speak. At twelve years old—going on twenty, as her older sisters were known to remark in exasperation— she had no reticence and complete self-confidence. Worryingly she also looked like being the prettiest of the three with hair as blonde and eyes as blue as her brother's. Ashe shuddered at the thought of policing her come-out. 'Her name is Miss Lucas and she is very nice.' That presumably meant she let Katy do what she wanted. 'And I need a new pony, I have quite outgrown dear Bunting, so Mama is driving him in the dog cart.'

'I have been taking dancing lessons with the Rector's daughters.' That was Frederica, seventeen, with a face that everyone described as *sweet* and mouse-brown hair.

'And helping Mr Barrington with the estate books. It is very interesting and he says my arithmetic is exemplary.'

Barrington was the new estate manager, appointed by Ashe on his last furlough. Young, keen, well favoured and hard-working, he had seemed just the man to leave in charge of the estate. He was also the younger son of a respectable gentry family. Now Ashe caught a glimpse of a frown between his mother's brows and glanced sharply at Frederica. *Too young and good looking to have introduced into a household of susceptible young ladies?*

'And I am coming out next Season,' Anna pronounced. 'But you knew that, of course.' She was calm, elegant and usually described as handsome, with honey-blonde hair and blue eyes. She smiled at her mother conspiratorially. 'And I expect I am going to be a great expense to you, Ashe dearest, for Mama and I have very long shopping lists.'

'I suppose that means we need to set the town house in order,' he said, teasing her by looking solemn when all along he had known it was going to be needed. 'Did I tell you I sold the Half Moon Street property?' It was like touching a sore tooth with his tongue; he wanted them to ask who had bought it so he could have the pleasure of talking about Bel.

'Yes dear, you did. Are your chambers comfortable at the Albany?' Mama was giving him no opportunity to indulge.

'Perfectly, thank you. When will you need the town house ready?'

'There is no need for you to do anything, dear.' Lady Dereham lifted the teapot and began to pour. 'We will come up in January and start ordering gowns and planning parties then. I will bring most of the staff from here, if you would not dislike that.'

'Whatever suits.' Ashe accepted a cup of tea. He had no intention of rusticating in the country any longer than he had to, so he had no need for the servants. 'But the place is sadly in need of a new touch; I think we should not leave it until you come up after Christmas. I will write to Grimball and have him make a complete survey and do any repairs, then if you come up to town later this month before you go down to Brighton you can decide what redecoration you would like and he can have that done over the winter.'

'Redecoration? Are you sure? Is that not rather extravagant?'

'With three sisters to come out?' Ashe smiled. 'I am sure it will be an investment.'

He was rewarded by a trio of grateful smiles. Even Anna clapped her hands in delight.

'It is the first week of August now,' Frederica calculated. 'Only two or three weeks and we will be in London!' Watching her, Ashe saw the pleasure falter and she became sombre. Damnation, she was thinking she would be parted from Barrington. Just how far had this gone?

'Think of the ballroom done out in blue silk to match my eyes.' Katy sighed. Her sisters rolled theirs in unison. 'And my bedroom needs new curtains.'

'Shh!' Frederica ordered. 'Stop plaguing Ashe with such nonsense. Blue silk will have faded long before you get your come out, you precocious child!'

Katy subsided mutinously.

'Only, I did wonder…' Lady Dereham completely ignored her bickering daughters, fiddled with the cake slice, then made rather a business of cutting the almond tart.

'Yes, Mama?' Ashe found he was reaching for a third lemon scone and put his plate down firmly.

'I thought perhaps I should be putting the Dower House to rights.'

'Why now? Are any of the elderly aunts in need of it?' But she was right, it did not do to let a house stand empty and neglected and it must be all of three years since Grandmama had died. 'I suppose we could bring it back into use and invite some of them to stay there.'

'No, not the aunts, I think they are all quite content where they are. It was just that I did wonder—now you are back and out of the army and settled—if next Season you would be looking for a wife?'

'A wife?' Ashe regarded his mother blankly. Throughout his childhood she had exhibited the maternal witchcraft of knowing exactly what was on his conscience. It seemed the knack had not deserted her. 'How did you kn…I mean, what on earth would I want a wife for?'

Even well-behaved Anna giggled at that. 'For all the usual reasons Dereham,' his mother said tartly. Lord, he was in trouble if she was using his title.

What did I almost say? How did you know? *Is that what just came out of my mouth without apparently passing through my brain?* Ashe closed his eyes. An image of Bel sitting by the fireplace, just where his mother was now, filled his imagination. The apparition lifted the teapot, smiled at him and began to pour. He opened his eyes hastily. *No! I do not want to get married.* Bel *does not want to get married to me, or to anyone else, come to that. I am* not *in love with her. She is my mistress; a man does not marry his mistress.*

'I meant,' he said, getting his tongue and his brain lined up again, 'I meant, what would I need a wife for *now*?' Damn it, he could command a company of soldiers, he could fight the French, he could manage a great estate—when he felt like it. Why did he feel completely helpless and at bay when confronted by the women of his own family with *that* look in their eyes?

'You need an heir, unless you want Cousin Adrian— who has the wits of a gnat—in your shoes,' Lady Dereham retorted. 'I need to be able to concentrate on launching your three sisters into society—and I would welcome some mature feminine assistance with that, let me tell you—and finally it is about time you took an interest in this house and this estate and put your own mark upon it. And a wife will help you do that.' She wagged the cake slice at him. 'You are not getting any younger, Reynard.'

'I am thirty,' Ashe said, stung.

'Exactly my point.'

The words came out again, apparently bypassing the conscious part of his brain, apparently from some well of certainty deep inside his mind. 'I will marry when I fall in love, and not before.'

'In love?' Lady Dereham regarded her son with well-bred horror. 'In *love*? That is no criterion for a good marriage, Reynard. Heaven knows who you might fall in love with! Men fall in love with dairymaids, but they do not marry them—not men in your position, at least.'

'I consider it a perfectly reasonable criterion,' Ashe said firmly, deciding that a protest that he had never so much looked at a dairymaid in that, or any other, light was a waste of time. Marrying for love had never occurred to him until a minute ago; up until then he would have agreed with his mother.

Marriage demanded a well-dowered young woman of suitable family, modest habits, intelligence and good health. One assessed which of the available ladies on the Marriage Mart fulfilled these requirements, selected from amongst them the one for whom one felt the greatest liking and respect, and proposed. Short of a Royal princess, there were few females who would consider the Viscount Dereham anything short of a brilliant catch, and he knew it.

'And what will you say if your sisters come to you with some unsuitable man in tow and demand to marry for love, might I ask?' his outraged parent demanded.

'I will trust their judgement.' Ashe was conscious of three wide-eyed, open-mouthed faces staring at him.

'Oh,' breathed Frederica softly. 'Oh, Ashe.'

Oh, Ashe, indeed! She is in love with Barrington and I have just walked straight into that!

'As soon as they reach the age of twenty-one,' Ashe added hastily. 'Unless the man they love also meets the usual criteria of acceptability.'

'Oh,' Frederica said again, flatly.

'That's all right,' Katy announced smugly. 'I intend falling in love with a duke. You will have to approve of him, Ashe, won't you?'

'Which duke?' Ashe asked, diverted and rapidly running the available candidates under review. 'I do not think there are any available.'

'I have six years,' his baby sister informed him smugly. 'One is sure to die and have a young heir, or be widowed or something in that time.'

'Why a duke?'

Katy proceeded to count off points on her fingers. 'They are all rich. I would like being called your Grace and I would outrank Lucy Thorage.'

'She might marry one too,' Ashe pointed out, fascinated and alarmed in equal measure.

'I am prettier,' his sister pointed out, incontrovertibly.

'If you do not wish to go to bed now without your dinner, Katherine Henrietta Reynard,' said her mother awfully, 'you will be quiet and behave like a lady.'

'Yes, Mama.' Katy subsided, leaving Ashe the uncomfortable focus of attention again.

'And what are you going to do to find this paragon?' Lady Dereham enquired. 'Wait for her to appear like a princess in a fairy tale?'

A princess on a white bear who will carry me off to Paradise... But that was Bel. I am not going to have that sort of luck twice.

'I shall do my duty escorting you and Anna next Season. Perhaps I will find her there.'

'I sincerely hope so.' His mother regarded him anxiously. 'I worry about you. You do seem different somehow, dear.'

'Poor Ashe has been through a terrible experience.' Anna leapt to his defence. 'Of course he seems a little altered. Several weeks here at Coppergate with us and he will be his old self again.'

Several weeks in the country? No, ten days at most, and then back to London, back to Bel. Back to uncomplicated bliss.

Ashe spent the next day riding around the estate with Barrington, trying to size up the man, not as an estate manager, for he had already done that and was satisfied, but as a husband for his sister. He would do, he thought grudgingly. A far from brilliant match, but a kind, decent, loving husband was more important for sensitive Frederica than some cold and suitable society marriage.

She would be well dowered. An intelligent, hard-working man like Barrington could build on that foundation to give them a good life. There were a few years before he need worry too much—more than enough time to see if this attachment of his sister's lasted and whether it was returned.

'What do you think of the Wilstone estate?' he asked, an idea coming to him as they reined in to inspect the effects of liming on a stubbornly sour field.

'That was a good purchase, my lord,' Barrington said judiciously. 'Needs work, of course, it had been neglected, but in time it could be very productive. There are fine stands of timber and it borders the new canal—I think you could build wharfs there, a timber yard. It would repay the investment with all the building going on in London. But I had thought you were intending to sell it on.'

'No. I think we will keep it.' The idea was taking more concrete shape as the estate manager talked. 'Make it a special project, Barrington; give it, say, three years and see what you can make of it.'

'What about the house?' Barrington looked interested. 'Sell and just keep the land? The last owner neglected it badly, what with all his debts and so forth. But it is quite sound—just shabby.'

'No, don't sell it. Get it into order. I'll give you a free hand—think what you'd like if it was yours, but stay within the income from the lands.' They moved off, satisfied with the state of the field, the expression on the steward's face showing he was already thinking about the prospect of reviving the rundown estate that Ashe had bought as a speculation the year before. Ashe waited a few minutes, then added, as if the idea had just come to him, 'See if my sister would like to help with the house.'

'Miss Frederica?'

'Yes,' Ashe agreed. 'Frederica.'

If things worked out, then he would give Frederica the estate as part of her dowry and if Barrington couldn't manage to found his fortune from there, then he was not the man Ashe thought him.

'Thank you, my lord, I will get right on to it.'

'Reynard,' Ashe corrected, a warm feeling blossoming inside as he contemplated the possible outcome of his matchmaking. All this talk of love—he must be getting soft. 'But don't neglect everything else,' he added severely, wiping the grin off the younger man's face.

'No, of course not, my...Reynard.'

Hopefully that would take care of Frederica. Anna, he had no doubt, would sail serenely into society and find herself an eminently suitable beau without his help, and as for Katy—well, there were at least four years before he had to face that nightmare, and perhaps one could hire Bow Street Runners as chaperons.

Bel could advise him; he would enjoy talking to her about his sisters. She would take an interest. He could imagine her grey eyes lighting up at the thought of all the alarming things women appeared to find so fascinating: shopping, gossip, matchmaking. But he was trying to matchmake now himself—what had come over him?

'...coppicing?'

'Hmm?' Damn, he was daydreaming. His hack was

standing next to Barrington's and the man had apparently been holding forth for some time about the overgrown woodland in front of them.

'Absolutely,' Ashe said firmly. 'I quite agree it is the best thing.'

'Which? Clear felling and replanting or coppicing?'

Damn again, the man must think him quite buffleheaded. 'Coppice,' he decided at random, finding he was staring into the dense thicket and assessing it as cover for marksmen. Or you could put a field gun just there and cover the whole of the little valley, sweep it with grapeshot. He shivered. No. No more fighting, no more violence, no more gripping a sweaty palm around the butt of a pistol and waiting for death. Peace, growing things, love. That must be it, he was feeling dynastic as a result of seeing all that death and destruction.

Chapter Twelve

'Where to next?' Ashe stretched, standing in the stirrups, suddenly aware of the warmth of the sun on his back, the scent of flowers and hay, the sheer delight of the English countryside in summer. For the first time in a very long time—other than when he was making love to Bel—he was aware of his body and of feeling pleasure in it and its reaction to everyday things.

'The Home Farm?' Barrington suggested. 'I need to talk to you about reroofing the long barn.'

'Race?' Ashe did not wait for a reply, but turned the gelding's head towards home, conscious of the power gathering itself between his thighs, of the muscled curve of the animal's neck as it strained against the bit. 'Get up!' As the hooves beat a tattoo along the packed chalk of the track, Barrington's dapple grey thundering behind, he found himself wondering if Bel would enjoy this, whether she enjoyed the countryside, whether he could, after all, hold a house party and invite her.

He beat his estate manager into the yard by a length

and reined in, laughing. 'I'm thinking of holding a house party, Barrington. What do you think?'

'Lady Dereham would be delighted, I image,' the other man responded, swinging down out of the saddle and looping his reins through a ring on the wall.

Yes, she would and there was the rub. It was madness to contemplate bringing Bel here. He could not hope to hide their relationship from close scrutiny by his family, especially as his mother would probably consider her a most eligible candidate for his hand. And besides, they were due to go down to Brighton soon. It would cause endless speculation if he reversed those plans.

Sobered, he put his hands in the small of his back and craned to study the sagging ridgeline of the barn roof. 'Before Christmas, perhaps. This roof, now, is in a poor state,' he commented. 'It'll either have to be done now, quickly, before we want to bring the harvest in or it'll have to wait the winter out.'

It would surprise Bel if she could see him now, standing in a farmyard and worrying about barn roofs and the harvest. What was she doing? he wondered.

Bel was, for once, not thinking about Ashe. She stood in the middle of Madame Laurent's elegant dress shop and sighed in exasperation. 'But don't you *want* a new gown Elinor?'

'I do not *need* one.' Elinor set her mouth stubbornly. 'We came to shop for you, not for me. What use do I have for a full dress outfit? I never get invited to that sort of occasion.'

'Then buy a half-dress ensemble and work up to it! Something that is not fawn or beige or taupe for a change.'

'They are practical colours,' Elinor said calmly.

'Not for evening wear.'

'I do not need evening wear.'

They were going around in circles. Madame Laurent had tactfully withdrawn her assistants to the back of the shop when it was obvious that a fullscale debate was about to ensue between one of her most favoured new clients and her drab companion.

'How are you ever going to meet men if you do not attend evening functions?' Bel asked in a whisper, driven to a frankness she had intended to avoid.

'I meet men at lectures and during the day on business. I meet quite enough of them for my purposes—which do not include marriage!'

'Don't you want to get married?' Bel exclaimed, keeping her voice down with difficulty.

'No. I do not. And you don't either, you say, so why are you trying to persuade me?'

'Because I do not think you are happy at your mother's beck and call and, just because my marriage left me disinclined to repeat the experiment, there is no reason why you should not find a husband you could like.'

What was the matter with her? She wanted to matchmake, to set to couples—yet Elinor was quite correct, she most certainly did not want to remarry herself. But, of course, she had the best of both worlds: the freedom of a widow and the attentions of a lover.

'I am sorry,' she said pacifically. 'I am getting carried away. Perhaps a husband is a step too far. But I am so fond of you and I hate to see you wasting your looks so. Why not wear colours that suit you? Clear greens, ambers, strong, rich browns. Red, even.' It seemed outrageous that her cousin with her striking colouring should look so drab. 'Madame?'

'Your ladyship?' The modiste hurried forward from the rear of the shop.

'What do you have that would set off my cousin's colouring and that would be suitable for a nice, practical walking dress?'

'I have the very thing my lady, newly come in. Paulette, the ruby twill and the emerald broadcloth.'

Elinor rolled her eyes. 'I have better things to do with my pin money.'

'To please me?' Bel tried again. *And Mr Layne, perhaps.* She was not going to give up hope. He was not boring, his temper appeared lively yet equitable and he was intelligent and hardworking. Perfect.

So perfect, in fact, that Bel was conscious that, if it were not for Ashe, she might feel a fluttering of her own pulse at any attention from Patrick Layne. As it was, she could indulge in a little harmless, and probably futile, matchmaking and enjoy his company, quite unruffled.

Bel managed to persuade Elinor into a walking dress and a carriage dress and even a new pelisse to go with either. Both were rigorously plain, but a least none of the garments were dun-coloured.

'Where to now?' Elinor asked patiently, evidently resigning herself to a further round of shopping.

'Hookham's Library.' Bel's driver raised his whip in acknowledgment and the ladies settling back on the cream squabs. 'I hope that is all right with you?' Elinor nodded, no doubt relieved to be back on safe and familiar ground again. 'I would like some new novels, but I mainly want to find some directories which will tell me about charitable institutions.'

'You wish to contribute?'

'Well, yes, if you mean money. But I want to do

more than that, I want to do something practical to help. I feel I live such a frivolous life now I have no responsibilities to the estate. The dilemma is, I cannot choose what type of good cause I wish to support, let alone which one. You would think it would be easy, but there are so many, all no doubt deserving in their way.'

They were still comparing the merits of various types of charity as the barouche swung into Bond Street and began to draw up outside the circulating library. The crowd on the pavement seemed strangely animated, then Bel saw that the porters who opened doors and ushered in customers were attempting to drive away a pair of men in stained uniforms. Both were on crutches, one with the lower part of his right-hand trouser leg pinned up, the other dragging a useless limb.

'On your way,' the head porter was ordering. 'This is a respectable establishment. We don't want the likes of you begging here.'

'Outrageous!' Bel jumped from the carriage without waiting for the steps to be put down and marched up to the group before the doors.

'Just what I said myself, ma'am.' The porter turned a harassed face to her, grateful for the apparent support. 'You go inside, ma'am, quick as you can, we'll soon move them on, never you fear.'

'No—*you* are outrageous, you heartless, ignorant man,' Bel snapped. 'What do you mean, *the likes of you*? These men have been wounded in the service of their country; how dare you insult and abuse them!'

The burly man gaped at her, his glossy tall hat askew from the scuffle. 'Ma'am, this is *Bond Street*.'

'Exactly so. And the reason we are not speaking

French in it or on our way to the guillotine is because
of men like these, you ignorant bully.'

'You should be ashamed of yourself,' Elinor chimed
in from beside Bel, brandishing her parasol belliger-
ently.

Bel turned her elegant shoulder on the spluttering
head porter and smiled at the two soldiers. 'Here, please
take this.' She took a folded five-pound note from her
purse and handed it to the one with the amputated leg.
'Where do you sleep?'

The man with the dragging leg made a choking
sound and she realised he had a badly healed wound on
his neck; it must have affected his throat or mouth. 'No,
do not try to talk. Elinor, what money have you? They
must go and find a doctor at once.'

Her cousin was already pressing a note into the first
man's hand. He found his voice. 'God bless you ladies.'

'Where do you sleep?' she repeated her question and
the man shrugged.

'Where we can, ma'am. Down in Seven Dials
mostly, there's dossing kens to be had there for coppers.'

Goodness knows what a dossing ken was, but if this
accommodation was in Seven Dials, one of the most no-
torious slums in London, then it was the worst possible
place for two men in their condition.

'Get into the carriage.' Bel made up her mind suddenly.

'Bel!' Elinor gasped.

'Oh, yes, I am sorry, I should have thought. You had
better take the carriage and my footman as escort, Aunt
Louisa would not approve. I will take them in a hackney.'

'Never mind Mama! What are you going to do
with them?'

'Look after them, of course.' Bel turned back to the

men who were staring at her as they might a carnival freak. 'I have room in the loft over my stables. It is dry and clean and you can bathe, eat and my doctor will tend to you. Will you come with me?'

'Bel, you cannot! You have no idea of their character...'

'I have James here.' She gestured towards the alarmed-looking footman who was trying to interject with protests about what Mr Hedges would say.

'He'll have my guts for garters, my lady...'

Both women ignored him. 'You won't have a footman if you send him with me in the carriage,' Elinor said practically. 'Oh, very well, I will come with you. I agree, something must be done, we cannot leave them here at the mercy of such bigots as this.' With a glare at the flustered doorman, Elinor climbed back into the barouche and gestured to the soldiers to join her.

'Come on,' Bel urged them. 'If you can face the French, you can cope with two English ladies.'

'Yes, ma'am.' She received a smart salute and a grin from the one with a voice and a lopsided smile from his companion.

'Well, give these men a hand up, James,' Bel ordered.

Her vocal soldier informed Bel that they were Jem Brown and Charlie Lewin of the 14th Battalion. 'The Buckinghamshires ma'am,' Brown explained. Lewin had been hit in the neck at Quatre Bras, the day before Waterloo, but the wound had not seemed serious at first, until he had been wounded at Waterloo. 'Lying out for twenty-four hours in the mud with your leg shattered doesn't do much for your wounds, though, ma'am,' his friend explained. 'I had it easier; a ball carried mine off nice and neat.'

Bel swallowed hard, wondering what Aunt Louisa

was going to say if she returned Elinor in a fainting condition, but her cousin was made of sterner stuff than that. 'A doctor is the priority, then,' she said firmly. 'And to send out for supplies of bandages, gauze and salves.'

They drove round to the mews and Bel sent James running for Hedges and the other footman while her coachman and groom helped the men down. She expected opposition from the butler. Hedges marched into the yard, his face grim, then stood assessing the two men through narrowed eyes. They met his scrutiny with more calm than Bel would have predicted. Hedges grunted. 'I reckon they'll do, my lady. Come on, lads, help them up to the hay loft.'

He watched them struggling up the stairs and turned to Bel. 'I had a nephew, wounded badly at Salamanca. Died later on, after he'd come home, but at least it was in his mother's arms, warm and comfortable and with those he loved all around. If he'd had no family to go to, he'd have ended up like those two, and it don't bear thinking about.' His mouth worked for a moment as though something else was going to burst out, then he was composed again, his face expressionless.

Bel stood back while Hedges organised the staff, sent for the doctor and had the footmen running for hot water and tubs. 'First thing, get you clean,' she heard him ordering from the loft. 'Look at the state of you! I'm not having you on her ladyship's premises in that state, even if it is only the hay loft. Then you'll be fit to see the doctor. And then you can eat.'

When the butler came down to the yard again his face was grim. 'National disgrace it is, the way the army treats its men. They do it better in the navy, that's for

sure.' He looked up at the long loft, then back to Bel.
'How many more of them have you got, ladies?'

'Just the two,' Elinor said faintly as Mrs Hedges
appeared, the kitchen maid at her heels.

'How many more can we take?' Bel asked.

'Up there, my lady? Half a dozen or so.'

'Well, Elinor,' Bel said with a rueful smile, 'It
seems I did not have to look far—my charity has
found me.'

Ashe remained in Hertfordshire for ten days, surprised at how content he found himself, getting to
know the workings of the estate in far greater detail
than he had ever done while his father was alive, or
while old Simmons, the previous estate manager, had
been in charge.

John Barrington was a stimulating companion to
work with, his family stopped their overt fussing after
a day or two and the sun shone. If it were not for missing
Bel, he could have rusticated happily until the start of
the hunting season.

But miss her he did, and not, as he had expected, just
in his bed. There was that, of course, and on several occasions he had tossed and turned, failing to sleep until
he had given up, gone out and swum in the lake in the
moonlight. That was some help, until his over-active
imagination produced the picture of Bel in there with
him, her skin pearly in the silver light, slipping like a
fish through the cool water as he dived after her, his
hands skimming over her sleek curves.

Ashe missed talking to her. That was the shock. He
had not realised just how much time they had spent
talking, exchanging opinions and confidences without

really being aware of it. He knew she disliked striped fabrics, ormolu and the fad for the Egyptian style and was entirely in agreement with her. He knew she preferred opera to drama and chamber music to orchestral and that there they disagreed. He knew she would like a dog, but not a cat, and that she would rather ride than drive and he had no preferences as far as equestrian exercise was concerned but admitted to a weakness for cats about the house.

Bel declared herself a Whig not a Tory, but expressed distrust of most politicians and was very clear that she preferred short sermons on Sunday, which meant that she would be at odds with several of their neighbours and bored by the Rector. And at that point he realised he was again imagining her at Coppergate, gave himself a brisk mental talking-to and went to discuss pigsty design with the Home Farm stockman.

But despite his attempts at self-control, Ashe was conscious of his heart beating faster as he sifted through the pile of letters, bills and notes that Race retrieved from the Albany porter's lodge when they arrived back in London. He had written three days ago to tell them to forward on nothing more to Hertfordshire, so there was a considerable stack to flick through.

Yet there was no cryptic little note signed B, to greet him, hinting at a time for their reunion, despite his having sent a letter, ostensibly enquiring if she had any further problems with the house, as he would be able to call any day after this date. Disappointed, Ashe poured himself a glass of Madeira and began to work systematically through the pile, tossing the bills aside to deal with later. He had had almost two weeks of paying careful attention to accounts; he was in no rush to immerse himself in them here yet a while.

Invitations, advertisements, solicitations from tradesmen, more invitations… He opened one letter, addressed in a clear black hand that looked vaguely familiar, and found it was from Bel. Not a hastily scrawled, secretive note, but bold as brass, a formal invitation to take tea tomorrow at three o'clock.

Ashe folded the invitation and sat, absently tapping it against his lips as he tried to divine its meaning. Was Bel about to give him his *congé*? Or was she becoming much bolder, entertaining him openly in front of her staff? Or…what?

He unfolded the paper and scrutinised it again. No, surely not his dismissal; the tone, although completely harmless if anyone else happened to see it, was warm.

There was the familiar tightening in his loins as he thought of her, but overriding even that, the desire just to see her, to hold her, to talk. What had she been doing? What would she think of how he had spent the past days? He would welcome her opinion about the actions he had taken to advance Frederica's romance, his ideas for the town house.

'My lord?'

'Eh?' Race was standing by his side, looking faintly martyred. Presumably he had been speaking for some time. 'Sorry, Race, did you say something?'

'I enquired which garments you would wish me to put out for this evening, my lord.'

'I'm going to White's, I think, so the usual for that. And for tomorrow afternoon, those new kerseymere pantaloons and the dark blue superfine swallowtail coat.'

'Indeed, my lord. Most suitable to the occasion, if I may say so.' Race produced a discreet smirk and took himself off before Ashe could retaliate. It really was almost impossible to hide anything from your valet.

Chapter Thirteen

At three on Tuesday afternoon Ashe walked up the steps to what had once been his own familiar front door, knocked and was admitted by Hedges. The butler regarded him with more approval than might be expected, given that on the occasion of their last meeting in Half Moon Street he had been hideously hung over and in the wrong bed.

'Good afternoon, my lord. Lady Belinda is in the drawing room.'

Ashe handed his hat and gloves to a footman, the butler opened the door, announced 'Lord Dereham, my lady', ushered him through and closed it behind him with a soft click.

Bel came towards him, her hand held out, her smiling lips parted as though to speak. He did not give her the chance. His coat was off, thrown to one side as he took two urgent strides across the room, then she was tight in his arms, his mouth crushing down on hers, every soft curve pressed against him as he drank in the taste and the scent of her like a parched man.

She writhed in his arms, inflaming him further; her hands were clenched against his chest, beating a tattoo of desperation every bit as urgent as his. Her mouth was open, working under his searching lips as he swept her further into the room, past the knot of chairs around the hearth and towards the sofa. All he had to do was to get there, although the urge simply to drag her to the floor was overwhelming.

One hand slid down to cup the delicious peach-curve of her buttock; she was so tense, quivering with an excitement that matched his own, struggling in his embrace. They were almost there, almost at the sofa. Out of the corner of his eye, Ashe glimpsed the tea tray on a low table, swerved to avoid it, swept the honey-sweet moistness of Bel's mouth with his tongue—and froze.

The tea tray was laden with cups and plates and more cakes than two people could eat in a week. The realisation sunk in as Bel's teeth closed on his tongue in a sharp bite that had him freeing her with a yelp of pain. From behind him a voice like thunder said, 'Unhand her, you libertine!'

Bel staggered back from Ashe's arms, panting from her struggles to free herself. His appalled expression contrasted with the outrage on her aunt's face as Lady James surged to her feet from the depths of the wing armchair, reticule clenched in one mittened hand, intent on saving her niece from masculine assault.

To an onlooker it would have seemed highly amusing, a farce of the first order; all Bel could feel was a sick apprehension. There was absolutely no way this could be explained away, no way that she was not now exposed, before her own aunt, as a loose woman.

'Explain yourself, sir!' Ashe turned slowly to face Aunt Louisa. Her face, as she recognised him, was a picture of shocked disbelief. 'Lord Dereham! What is the meaning of this outrage?'

'Lady James. I can explain—'

'I would like to hear you try, sir!'

Bel groped for the high curved end of the sofa and held on to it. Explain? How could he possibly explain that away? How on earth had it happened? She had felt so safe, so happy, and now, in a few seconds, it was tumbling around her ears. She swayed, dizzy, convinced that every ounce of blood had drained out of her face. The back of Ashe's neck was red, but his voice was steady as he faced the outraged widow.

'The force of my ardour—'

'Hah! Is that what you call it, you libertine?'

'—for Lady Belinda,' he continued steadily, 'deceived me into believing that my feelings were reciprocated, and, in coming here today with the intention of proposing marriage, I—'

'What?' The question was out of Bel's mouth before she could stop herself. Neither of the other two answered her, or even appeared to remember that she was standing there.

'In short, ma'am, the novelty of finding myself, as I thought, alone with Lady Belinda so inflamed my passions that I threw caution to the winds and seized her, wishing to press my suit with more zeal than, I know, is proper.'

'Proper, indeed! You were about to ravish the poor child upon the sofa, sir. That is not zeal, that is not ardour, that is the action of a ravening beast! You are half-dressed—'

'Will someone please listen to me?' Despairing of

either of them attending to her, Bel poked Ashe in the ribs so that he half-turned towards her. His neckcloth was askew, his shirt half-untucked and his coat gone.

'Lord Dereham,' she said, with as much steadiness as she could command, shock at his words overriding even her shamed confusion, 'I do not believe that I have, on the few occasions we have met, given you any indication that your suit would be acceptable to me.'

'I agree, ma'am,' Ashe responded with equal control. 'Nothing you have said to me could be construed as encouragement for me, or any other man, to make you an offer of marriage.'

'Then why—?'

'You must forgive the ardour of a man seized with feelings too strong to be denied. I had hoped to persuade you.' Ashe had shifted so that Aunt Louisa could not see his face. His intense expression urged her to agree. His lips moved. Bel strained to read them. *Say yes, for goodness' sake, Bel.*

Yes? Marry him? Bel was aware that her mouth was opening and shutting like a carp in a pond and that nothing was coming out.

'Well, you have achieved your aim, young man,' Aunt Louisa said wrathfully. 'Because you are most certainly going to have to marry my niece after this exhibition of unbridled lust.'

'No!' The word burst out of her tight throat. 'No, I am not going to marry him.' With denial came a kind of awful calm.

'Of course you must, you foolish gel! Your reputation is at stake.'

'You must. Bel…Lady Belinda… Think of the scandal.'

'Considering that my aunt is the sole witness of this débâcle, and knowing that she has only my interests at heart, I fail to see where the scandal is going to come from, my lord,' Bel said frostily. Over his shoulder her aunt moved and Bel caught a glimpse of herself in the mirror. Her mouth was swollen with Ashe's kisses, her hair was half-down and the pretty fichu she had arranged at her throat was a wreck. 'Oh, my God! Look at me.'

'Lady Belinda.' Ashe raised his voice over her gasp of horror and Aunt Louisa's furious mutterings. 'Please listen to me…'

Bel slapped his face.

She did it without thinking, her hand flashing out in a reflex that dismayed her almost as much as it must have shocked him. 'How dare you?' she whispered. 'How dare you talk about marriage? How dare you try to force me into something I am resolved never to do?'

There was a silence as they stared into each other's faces. Bel could feel the heat and sting of tears and fought them back. Ashe's eyes were dark with what she could only assume was thwarted anger at her refusal to bow to the conventions and satisfy what his masculine code of honour told him he must do. And the marks of her fingers branded his cheek, to her shame.

From the hallway there was the murmur of voices, the sound of the front door closing. The drawing room door began to open. The three of them, united suddenly, stared at each other. Then Bel spun round on her heel and ran for the door at the other end, the one that opened on to the service passage. As she whisked through it she heard Hedges announcing,

'Lady Wallace, Lady Maude Templeton, Miss Ravenhurst, the Reverend Makepeace, my lady.'

How Ashe and Aunt Louisa were going to explain his presence in her drawing room in his shirtsleeves she had no idea, and, she told herself furiously as she wrenched open the back door that led into her tiny garden, she did not care either.

It was not so much a garden, more of a court, the width of the house and a few yards deep, paved and with tubs of shrubs and flowering plants set about it. But, despite its modest size, in the afternoon it caught the sun and was a pleasant place to sit. Bel remembered too late as she ran down the six steps into it that she had urged her loft-full of soldiers to take the air there whenever they chose: today it seemed they had taken advantage of the offer.

She stood and regarded them, five of the eight who now occupied the loft, brought in over several days by Brown whom she had sent out in a hackney to scour the streets. He had recovered quickly with good food and medical attention, but his friend Lewin was still very poorly and confined to his bed.

They got to their feet with varying degrees of ease and stared at her mutely. Then Brown took a step forward. 'What's the matter, ma'am?' His big fists clenched. 'Who's touched you? You tell me, I'll sort them out.' The group at his back growled agreement.

Bel pushed pins back into her hair with hands that shook. 'No one. I…I had a stupid argument with a friend. I am upset… I am sorry, I forgot you might be here.'

'We'll go, ma'am, let you have your garden back for a quiet sit, don't you fret.' The others began to shift towards the gate, uneasy, she realised, that she was less than poised, less than completely in control. Probably, she thought with a flash of desperate humour, they were afraid she was going to weep.

'No, please, don't go. Stay and I will sit out here too. Tell me how everyone is doing.' Bel forced a smile and saw them begin to relax.

'Well, ma'am, Lewin's sitting up and seems to be getting his appetite back, leastways, for Mrs Hedges's soup. And Jock here…' he tipped his head towards the taciturn Scot with an eye patch who seemed to be resigned to never being addressed by his real name '…his foot's a lot better. And I found two more lads this morning, the doctor's looking at them now.' He talked on, marshalling and presenting his facts efficiently. Bel found herself wondering why he had not become a sergeant, he seemed to have the requisite qualities. She must ask Ashe about how that worked. If they ever spoke to each other again.

Ashe shot one glance down the length of the room to where his coat lay crumpled on a chair where he had thrown it. The door was already opening—he could never make it in time, and besides, the marks of Bel's hand on his face must be crimson.

This entire ghastly episode was like a farce, he thought, despairing for a second before military training kicked in. *Think, improvise, survive.* If this was a farce, then salvation might lay in making it even more of one.

'Scream,' he ordered brusquely, lifting Lady James bodily and standing her on top of a side chair. 'And stay there.' She gave a muffled shriek and waved her arms for balance. As the sound of the entering guests' chatting reached him, Ashe dived under the *chaise*, the poker snatched from the hearth in his hand.

The door closed, the animated conversation petered to a halt. Obviously the new arrivals had taken in the scene. 'Damnation!' he exclaimed, wriggling right back out again and getting to his feet in front of two young ladies, one formidable matron and a rector. 'I do beg your pardon, please excuse my language.'

'Lord Dereham!' Lady James glared down at him from her precarious perch on the chair. 'This is an outrage!'

'I am sorry, ma'am, but it escaped into a hole in the skirting—too fast for me. There was no need to slap me, Lady James,' he added reproachfully. 'I only lifted you up in case it tried to run up your skirts.

'A very large rat.' The bemused guests gaped at him as he set the poker back in the hearth and offered a hand to Lady James, who accepted it with a glare and allowed him to help her down.

'You are a very ingenious young man, are you not?' she asked grimly, settling back in the chair with an awful dignity.

'Taking off my coat in an attempt to throw it over the creature?' Ashe snatched gratefully at an explanation for his missing clothing. 'Ingenious, perhaps, but it was a poorly executed manoeuvre, I am afraid; I missed it by feet.'

'Your coat, my lord.' Hedges approached with the garment, well shaken out. 'I will send for a rat catcher directly. Shall I bring the tea now, my lady, or should I wait upon the return of Lady Belinda?'

Lady James folded her lips, stared arctically at Ashe and then appeared to realise that she had to give him some help for Bel's sake. 'Please bring it in at once, Hedges.' She turned a thin smile on the guests. 'My niece spilt milk on her skirts, jumping clear of the rodent. She retired in some confusion to change.' She gestured to the seats around the tea table. 'Please, everyone, do sit down, I am sure she will not be long. Lady Wallace, how fortunate you were able to come this afternoon, I had feared you might not be back from Exeter in time…'

'If you will excuse me, I will just go and wash my hands.' Ashe took himself off through the door while the others settled down to greetings and exclamations about Lady James's adventure. 'Where is Lady Belinda?' he demanded of Hedges the moment the door closed.

'In the garden, I believe, my lord.' The butler assessed his appearance with professional detachment. 'If you would care to step into the dining room, I will bring some warm water and a towel. Your lordship may also wish to adjust your neckcloth, which is a trifle disarrayed.'

He reappeared as promised a few minutes later, his face a perfect blank. 'Should I send for a rat catcher immediately, my lord?'

'No, you should not, as you very well know, Hedges.' Punching the smug butler, who was now so expressionless as to make it quite clear he had a very good idea about the truth of the situation, would relieve his feelings but could only make matters worse.

Ashe soaped his hands vigorously, his emotions churning. *I asked her to marry me. Why did she slap me? Didn't she believe I meant it? Of course I have to offer for her now.* He used the towel, then tugged his neckcloth back into some semblance of order. Brummell would have had kittens at the sight of it.

'As you say, my lord. I should perhaps mention that Lady Belinda appeared a trifle distressed when she passed me.'

A small understatement, he imagined. His cheek was

still stinging like the devil. 'She is not the only one,' Ashe retorted grimly.

'My lord—there is something you should know... The garden—'

'Later, Hedges,' Ashe threw back over his shoulder as he strode down the hall. *I have got a marriage proposal to get right first.*

Ashe flung open the door into the tiny garden and stopped dead on the top step. He had expected Bel to be pacing furiously, or to be in tears in one of the arbours. What he had not expected was to find her surrounded by a motley group of men in what appeared to be the ragged remnants of British army uniforms, incongruous amidst the topiary and the tubs of bright blooms.

'What the devil?' Had they broken in, intent on burglary, and found Bel, alone and defenceless? His eyes swept over them, assessing, calculating odds. There were five of them, standing close around her. As he stared they closed in tighter with the air of a pack of dogs guarding a bone. Then he realised that not only did Bel not appear at all alarmed, but they were looking at him with deep suspicion, as though he were the threat to her, not them.

The big man on crutches standing closest to Bel glanced down at her, as though for confirmation, then back up at Ashe. 'Is this the *friend* who upset you, ma'am? Because if it is, we'll sort him out for you.'

'This is Lord Dereham,' she said hastily. 'Major Dereham. I do not need any protection from him, I assure you.'

'Major? Stand up straight, lads!' The group shuffled to attention and he saw all of them were wounded, more or less seriously, and that their uniforms, although tattered, were clean and darned.

'No need for the rank. Not any longer, I'm a civilian now,' Ashe said pleasantly, coming down the steps. He swept the group with his eyes as he did so, keeping his weight on the balls of his feet, still not trusting the situation. 'You are all acquaintances of Lady Belinda?'

'Aye, we are that. And I know you, Major, I saw you at Waterloo, just before the end.' The broad Scottish accent drew Ashe's attention.

'Did you now?'

'I did, and I'm fair dumfoonert to see you standing here now, all in one piece, sir, and that's the truth. Seeing what you were doing at the time. Aye, bludy brave, it was.'

He did not want to get into reminiscences of that last, all out, charge, certainly not now. 'I have been more fortunate than you and your friends, by the look of it. And you are here because—?' His eyes locked with the big man who still had his shoulder turned in a way that shielded Bel from Ashe.

'They live here, all of them,' Bel said firmly, stepping out from amongst the men. Most people would not notice anything wrong now, but Ashe could see the tension in her, the rigidity of her shoulders, the bruised look in her eyes. He had improvised as best he could, but she had not escaped that scene unscathed. What was her old dragon of an aunt going to do now? He realised Bel was still explaining about the soldiers and pulled his attention back to listen. '…in the mews. There are eight of them at the moment.'

'So that is why you invited me here?' It was beginning to make sense. Bel was collecting wounded veterans from somewhere and wanted advice on what to do with them.

'Exactly,' she said briskly, turning back to the small group. 'I must go back inside; let Mrs Hedges know if you need anything. I will come down this evening.'

They were treating her with respect, Ashe saw, scanning their faces covertly as they watched her make her way to the steps. Wherever they had come from, and whatever their stories, they did not appear to be intent on taking advantage of her. With a nod Ashe followed Bel, closing the door to leave them alone in the empty hallway.

'Bel—'

'How *could* you, Ashe?' she demanded, her voice shaking with barely suppressed anger.

'I did not know anyone else was there,' he began, but she shook her head impatiently, dismissing the explanation.

'No, not that, I realise you thought we were alone. But how could you ask me to marry you? I thought I could trust you.'

'Damn it, Belinda—' Ashe kept his voice down from a roar with an effort that hurt his throat '—of course you can trust me! And trust me to do the right thing, I hope—'

'Poppycock,' she said baldly, 'You are just like all the rest of them.'

Bemused and affronted, Ashe stepped in front of Bel as she stalked down the passage towards the front hall. 'Bel, my honour demands that I marry you.'

'So that is all right, is it? I marry you, honour satisfied?'

'Yes.'

'No. No, no, a thousand times *no*. It takes two to marry, my lord, and if I ever should again—which I very much doubt—it will not be because it is necessary to save some man's honour.'

'I see. So I am just *some man* to you. Do I have that correctly?'

For a moment Ashe though she was going to either slap him again or storm off. Bel stopped in front of the dining-room door and looked at him from under levelled brows. 'No, you are not, and you very well know it. You are the man I am having an affair with and now I have no idea what to do about you.'

Chapter Fourteen

They could not stand there in the hall glaring at each other, Bel realised. There were more practical and immediate things to think about than her sense of betrayal.

'What happened after I left?' she demanded, pushing Ashe into the dining room in front of her. 'How did you explain being half-dressed?' Was she ruined? Bel closed the door and leaned back against it. What had the other guests seen—and what on earth had Aunt Louisa said?

Ashe gave her a long look, then summarised as concisely as an officer delivering a report. 'I pretended a large rat had run in, causing you to spill the milk over your gown and flee. I lifted your aunt on to a chair to lend credence to that story and explained that this had caused her to slap my face. I said I had then ripped off my coat to try to throw over the creature. I missed, so I said, and had dived after it under the *chaise* with the poker just as the other guests were announced.'

'You are very facile with your explanations,' Bel said tightly, feeling the shock begin to ebb and the anger to build in its place. Inventions came so easily to Ashe, it seemed. He would say whatever he had to, make any claim in order to smooth the way. She knew she should be grateful for his ingenuity, but the emotion proved elusive.

'It seemed to cover all the angles of the situation; there was not much time before they came in to think of anything else.'

'And your explanation to my aunt while I was there? Did that, too, cover all the angles?'

'Apparently not.' Ashe lifted his hand to his bruised cheek and smiled ruefully.

'*Indeed* not,' she snapped. 'I cannot talk to you now. I must go back and you can follow me in a few minutes. I need have no anxieties that you will not be able to behave as though we are the merest acquaintances, I trust?'

'No, I believe I can manage that.' Ashe sounded cool now, his eyes hard.

Damn him! Bel thought as she whisked out of the door and into the drawing room. *He puts me in this impossible position and then is angry when I am not grateful to him for condescending to offer marriage…*

'Good afternoon! I am so sorry I was not here when you arrived, what a ridiculous situation!' Bel fixed a warm social smile on her lips and went to shake hands with Lady Wallace and the Reverend Makepeace. 'Aunt Louisa, I do apologise, leaving you to cope, but I really cannot bear the creatures and I am afraid I panicked… Lady Maude, Cousin Elinor.'

They settled down again, shifting positions to give her room on the *chaise* next to Lady Maude who was, so rumour had it, engaged to Bel and Elinor's cousin Gareth Morant, Earl of Standon. If it was true, the pair were not hastening to announce the fact. Lady Maude was wealthy and intelligent as well as possessing a wide range of influential acquaintances.

'Where is Lord Dereham?' Bel asked brightly as her aunt passed her a cup of tea.

'Putting himself to rights, having dived under the *chaise* with a poker in pursuit of the rat.' Lady James's expression defied anyone to elaborate on the matter.

'Delicious! I do wish I had been here to see it, don't you, Miss Ravenhurst?' Lady Maude, who had a reputation for being both fast and unconventional, seemed immune to the atmosphere or to hints. Or perhaps she delighted in gossip. Bel did not know her well enough to judge. 'Lord Dereham gallantly attacking the creature in a state of undress! Really, when he emerged from beneath the sofa in his shirtsleeves, clutching that poker—I declare I was quite overwhelmed.'

'Most diverting, indeed,' Elinor agreed repressively, glancing from her mother's stony face to Bel's carefully smiling countenance. 'But I do hope his lordship is not detained too long; I am most interested to find out what he recommends for our soldiers.'

'Mr Makepeace also has experience in this field,' Lady Wallace intervened, with a stately inclination of her head towards the middle-aged cleric who was consuming buttered toast in silence. 'Which is why I suggested he should join our little group.'

'Indeed, ma'am.' He put down his plate and regarded them dubiously. 'I have, as you say, experience in this field, and I will do my best to assist, but I must confess that ex-soldiers are not the most amenable recipients of charity and good works. Most are, to put it kindly, ignorant and wilfully independent, however bad their case is.'

'Independence is to be applauded, surely?' Bel interjected. 'And *charity* is not at all what I had in mind. These men—most of them, at least—ought to be able to earn their own living, once they have had the chance to recover from their injuries. I want to give them medical assistance and a safe, decent place to live while they look around them for work. That is not charity, simply a helping hand. Who, however respectable, can hope to find employment when ill, filthy and dressed in rags?'

'Bravo, Lady Felsham. Who indeed?' Ashe had come into the room without her noticing. 'I would suggest that what is needed is a lodging house of sorts. One where we can control who resides there and provide medical assistance and food and clothing. Then we can assess who is fit for what occupation.'

'That sounds ideal.' Bel smiled with real gratitude, then felt her expression turn stiff as she caught Ashe's eye. 'Where would you suggest?'

'I own a warehouse at the back of Oxford Street,' Ashe offered. 'It will need cleaning, fitting out and so on—but the location is central. I am more than willing to donate that to the cause.'

'An excellent suggestion, Lord Dereham.' Lady Wallace beamed at him. 'I will undertake to supply bed linen and mattresses.'

'And I know of a manufacturer of beds for work-houses,' the reverend offered, apparently unoffended by Bel's rejection of his earlier opinions.

'I will pay for the cleaning and decorating,' she added, trying not to think about Ashe sitting so near. It was the practicalities of assisting the soldiers that were important, she told herself firmly. Her personal life must wait. 'And fitting out a kitchen. But we are going to need more assistance with furnishings, food, clothes—we cannot do it all ourselves if this is to grow and help more than a handful of men.'

'If we draw up a list of possible supporters, I will write to them.' Elinor reached for the notebook she had put beside her plate. 'I can draft a letter and see if it meets with your approval.'

'I think we should hold a subscription dance.' Lady Maude, who had been sitting silently listening, suddenly joined in. 'Papa has put our ballroom in order for next Season, I am sure he will not mind. I will organise it; I am very good at organising balls.' She smiled with all the confidence of a young lady whose father doted upon her, then turned her long-lashed green eyes on Ashe. 'You would support a ball, would you not, Lord Dereham?'

'Only if you will dance with me, Lady Maude,' Ashe rejoined smoothly, earning himself a dimpling smile from Maude and a cool stare from Bel.

They spent a further hour exchanging ideas while Elinor competently made notes, which she promised to copy out and send to each of them, and Bel fought to maintain her composure under her aunt's severe scrutiny and Ashe's carefully maintained distance. She wanted to shout and throw things—a desire she had never experienced in her life before; she wanted Ashe to go away and never come near her again and she wanted to throw herself into his arms and beg him to make love to her.

At least when Ashe had asked her to marry him, he had never mentioned the one word that he might have expected would persuade her to reconsider marriage: love. But of course he did not feel that, and had been too honest to pretend it, even though that would have been the icing on the cake of his careful fabrication to deceive Aunt Louisa.

Bel stared into the tea leaves in the bottom of her cup and wished she had the power to read them. Even if it were, impossibly, true that Ashe felt like that about her, she did not want the burden of being loved and she could not return such an emotion, ever.

Her guests left at last, all except Ashe, who hung back in the hallway, talking to Hedges and discussing going down to the mews to meet the men, and Aunt Louisa and Elinor.

'Belinda, a word with you, if you please.' Lady James closed her eyeglass with a snap and replaced it in her reticule. 'Elinor, kindly wait for me in the carriage. And shut the door behind you on your way out.'

'Yes, Mama.' Her cousin raised one quizzical eyebrow at Bel, as if to say, *Why are you in disgrace?*, and obediently went out.

'Well, Belinda? What, exactly, is your relationship with that man?' Lady James seated herself firmly in Bel's favourite armchair. 'The truth this time, if you please, not Reynard's work of fiction.'

'There is nothing I wish to discuss, Aunt.' Bel made herself sink down gracefully into the chair opposite. 'You heard me reject Lord Dereham's proposal—there is nothing to add to what I said then.'

'Reject it! Hah! Why should you reject it, you totty-headed girl? That man's the best catch you're ever likely to make. Title, money, connections, fine war record and a fine pair of shoulders to him.'

'I have no wish to remarry, Aunt. If Lord Dereham asks me again, I shall continue to refuse.'

Lady James stared at her beadily. 'Are you lovers?'

Bel knew she was blushing. But then, any respectable lady would blush at being accused of having a lover. 'As I said, I do not intend discussing such things, Aunt.'

'Hmm.' Her formidable relative eyed her with something like respect. 'Well, can't say I blame you if you are; he's a handsome fellow and he'll do you a damn sight more good between the sheets than that dull ninnyhammer you married. But that's a risky path, taking a lover; better to be wed if you want a man in your bed.' She ignored her niece's dropped jaw and swept on. 'Does he love you?'

'Certainly not. And I do not want to be loved and I am not in love with him.' *I was simply swept up into some ridiculous fairy tale where I could defy convention, take a handsome lover and get away with it unscathed. Well, I know better now.* The fluffy pink clouds of her happiness were tattered wisps now, blowing in the wind.

'Then be careful how you go on with him, my girl. If you lose your reputation, it won't matter whether you've been in his bed or not, you'll be treated as though you have.'

'Yes, Aunt Louisa.'

It was excellent advice, and she knew it. This was the end of her blissful fantasy and she had to make sure Ashe understood that.

'Where is Lord Dereham?' she asked Hedges after he showed Lady James out.

'Down with the men looking at the loft, my lady.'

'Please ask him if he will join me in the garden after he has finished.' Bel found herself a seat under the arbour well away from the house windows and waited.

She had thought that some moments of quiet reflection would allow her to get her emotions under control and to be able to speak to Ashe with composure. She had not expected that by the time he reappeared, some twenty minutes later, she would be even less poised.

'*Belle.*' He stood looking down at her, his smile rueful. 'We have had an exciting afternoon, have we not?'

'That is not how I would characterise it,' she retorted. 'How *could* you?'

'I told you, I thought the room was empty. I had not seen you for days—I missed you.' Ashe put one hand against the frame of the arbour and looked down at her. 'May I sit?'

'No, you may not. And I do not mean you kissing me. You know I mean you proposing.'

'What else could I possibly do? I had compromised you in front of one of your relatives.'

'You were quick thinking, I will say that for you! But once I had refused, once Aunt had heard your story about being overcome by passion—not that she believes a word of it—why on earth did you persist? You know my feelings about marriage.'

Ashe stared at her. 'You must see I had no alternative, under the circumstances. I have compromised you; the honourable action is quite clear, even if you do not agree with it.' His blue eyes were narrowed as he frowned at her, puzzled, she supposed, that her vehemence persisted after the first shock was over. He looked harder, older, more dangerous than the teasing, flirtatious man she was used to. She had seen it with the soldiers; now he was looking at her in the same way, assessing a problem. She was the problem.

'But you do not mean it—do you? You do not wish

to marry me. It is not as though you love me, is it?' It felt so dangerous, uttering that word, but the question just slipped from her.

Bel expected either an avowal—which she would not believe—or a denial, which she would. 'I do not know,' he said slowly, startling her. 'I had not thought about it before, but now you ask…I must admit to feeling quite sanguine about the thought of marriage to you.'

Ignoring her refusal to let him sit, he dropped into the seat next to her, trapping her between the woven greenery of the side of the arbour and the length of his body. He picked up her left hand and began to play with her fingers, his concentration focused on them. 'I missed you, Bel.'

'I missed you too.' It was foolish to try to deny it. Her heart was thudding uncomfortably and she felt a trifle sick. The repetitive brush of his fingers made it hard to concentrate. 'But that does not mean I love you.'

'Why should me wondering about it make you so angry?' Ashe asked, abruptly dropping her hand and looking into her eyes.

That had been what she had been trying to work out, and becoming so muddled about. 'It sounds like emotional blackmail,' she said at last.

'I see.'

'And I had told you I would never marry again. You knew that when I asked you to be my lover that I did not intend it to be anything more.'

'I know.' He caught her hand again, turned it over in his big one and began to rub his thumb against the tender skin of her palm. 'I believe you.'

'You made me feel as though I was responsible for putting you in a position where you were honour-bound to offer for me. You made me feel as though I had been trying to trap you. I was an idiot to even mention love just now. I am not in love with you—I did not ask because I wanted to hear you say *yes*.'

'Ah.' The pressure of his thumb grew more, making her fingers curl around it reflexively.

'I do wish you would say something—not just *Ah* and *I see* and *I know*.' Bel knew she was sounding irritable, knew that what she really wanted was a magnificent row to clear the air. And then for Ashe to take her in his arms and tell her it was all perfectly fine and they could go on being lovers, without any strings attached, as though nothing had happened.

'Very well.' Ashe released her hand and stood up. 'While I was away I kept thinking about you, imagining you in my home, wondering what you would think about things, what you would say about the everyday problems and decisions. I found I was visualising you as my wife. Is that love? I do not know, I have never been in love. I am trying to be truthful with you.'

'Oh.'

'And I did not want to think about marriage, if you want the complete, unvarnished truth. It was most uncomfortable.'

Oh. That is truthful indeed. No attempts at flattery or evasion there!

'I want my independence, my freedom, just as you want yours.'

'Of course,' Bel agreed brightly. That was exactly how she wanted him to feel. Of course it was.

'But there it was, this thought that kept intruding when my guard was down, this picture of you in my home.' Ashe frowned down at an inoffensive rose, then began to pull off its petals. 'I felt…different and I could not understand it. Then, when I held you in my arms again, when I realised we had been seen, compromised—I felt relief. I did not have to make a choice or a decision and neither did you. We would have to marry.'

How honest. And how thoroughly deflating. Bel knew she was being hypocritical—she had been flattered by the idea that Ashe was in love with her, even as she did not want him to feel like that.

'Well, we don't have to. Aunt Louisa warned me to be discreet, that is all. I was amazed—I had expected her to announce she would write to my brothers.'

'She is a woman of the world.' Ashe shrugged, dismissing her aunt. 'Very well. We will be discreet. No more kissing except behind a closed bedchamber door, I promise.'

'No. No more kissing at all.' Bel stood up, found her legs were shaking and took hold of the arbour frame. 'We must end our *affaire*. Now.'

'You are punishing me for my carelessness, in effect?' Ashe said slowly. 'There is no good reason why we should cease to be lovers, Bel.'

'I am punishing myself.' Bel felt a kind of bitter cold inside her, but she pressed on. 'I was a naïve fool. I thought I could take a lover, live out my fantasy and there would be no risk, no…effect. But there is a risk, and there is an effect. You speak of love and indecision…'

'I speak of real life and real emotions.' He sounded detached. Looking at him, Bel thought she had never seen him look so handsome, so severe. 'Reality is uncertain and messy, my sweet.'

'Yes,' she agreed. That was certainly true.

'We are real people, Bel. There is always the risk that things will change, that what seems safe will fail to be.'

'I will not take that risk; it is not in my nature to be reckless, I see that now. Ashe, I am grateful—'

'No!' His rare temper flared like a coal dropping into oil. One moment he had been detached, faintly ironic and standing a yard away; the next Bel was jerked towards him, mere inches from eyes like ice and the hard, set lines of his face. 'Don't you dare be grateful, Bel Cambourn. Don't you dare be one of those needy women who beg. You made a decision—a scandalous one—and you had the nerve and the courage to follow it through. We came together as equals, you and I. I may have been able to show you something you had not experienced before, but you gave me the privilege of your trust. You owe me nothing, I owe you nothing. Do you understand?'

'Yes, Ashe,' she managed as he let her go and she swayed, off balance. Bel reached out a hand and steadied herself with a touch on his arm. It was like iron with the tension of his temper. 'You will still help with the soldiers?'

'Bel's battalion?' Ashe's smile was wry. 'Yes, of course. Do you think I am going to storm off in a temper and leave them? I have a duty to them, and I thank you for showing me a way to fulfil it.' Relieved, Bel lifted her hand. 'Listen, Bel, we have had a near miss; you are very angry, very shaken. We will not end this *affaire* now, but we will not come together again, alone, for—say—two weeks. That will allow us to calm down. If then you still want to end it, so be it.'

'Yes,' she said shakily. 'Yes, I agree to that. But you

must promise not to speak again about love and marriage—I want neither from you.'

'I promise.' Ashe lifted her hand and kissed her fingertips. 'But tell me one thing though, before we part. You are not refusing me because of any other man?'

'I told you not.' She stared at him, perplexed. 'I swear there is no one else. And I meant what I said—I am not contemplating marriage—not to you, not to anyone.'

Chapter Fifteen

Why had he asked that? Ashe wondered, staring into Bel's wide and puzzled eyes. Was it that it was easier to accept her refusal of his proposal if she loved another man? But he was making no sense. This was Bel: painfully honest, frank, honourable. She would have told him at once if there was someone else, not fallen back on saying she did not want to wed again.

And why should her refusal hurt? It was his pride and his honour, that was all. He had told himself, over and over at Coppergate, that he did not want to marry yet. It was just that she was so very different from any other woman he had ever met and certainly from any other lover. Her innocence made him feel protective, and that was what he was mistaking for love.

'Love is not something one is ever in doubt about, is it?' he asked lightly.

'I imagine not.' She seemed to be trying to match his tone. 'From everything one reads, it comes like a *coup de foudre*. One can hardly mistake it, surely?'

'No, surely not,' Ashe agreed, curiously relieved. It

was this strange back-to-front relationship that confused him. Normally one would meet a respectable woman like Bel, fall for her, marry her and *then* make love to her. The lovemaking would be the culmination of the emotion. Because she was not a lightskirt, he was unconsciously expecting the love.

Relieved by this rationalization, Ashe smiled at her and saw the answering curl of her lips. But her eyes were still as shadowed as his mood. There was never going to be anyone like Bel, ever again, and this ending—if that is what it would prove to be—had come too soon, too suddenly for him to take it in his stride.

'Are you going to be all right?' he asked.

'Of course.' Her chin went up and her back straightened, the almost imperceptible droop in her shoulders vanishing. 'I expect it will be a trifle awkward when we meet in society, but I am sure I will manage. Do you intend to stay in town long this time?'

'Long enough to see your soldiers established in their new home. My family is coming up later this month to decide what they want done to ready the town house for my eldest sister's come-out next Season, and then I expect I will escort them down to Brighton.'

Ashe fought the urge to sit down and tell Bel all about his sisters, his suspicions about Frederica's feelings for Barrington, his worries about Katy, his hopes for Anna. He must learn to keep his distance from her, emotional as well as physical, while she made up her mind about their relationship.

'You are a good brother,' Bel said lightly, leading the way back to the steps. She held out her hand. 'With your plans for Brighton we would be separated soon for some time in any case. Goodbye, Ashe.'

'Goodbye, Bel.' It was more than a form of words—this could be a very final farewell and they both knew it. The next time they met it would be Lord Dereham and Lady Belinda again, perhaps for ever.

He took both her hands in his, feeling the narrow bones, the long, clever fingers, the warmth, the tremor of her pulse. He held them for a long moment, then bent and touched his lips to hers. They seemed, despite the deliberate lightness of the contact, to cling, seeking her sweetness, the taste of her. He felt more than heard her sharp intake of breath and released her.

'Goodbye, *ma belle*.' Then he made himself stride up the steps and through the doorway without looking back.

It is over. She could not let herself believe that in a week or so they could come together again, that they could be lovers once more. There had been such an innocence about their relationship, such a simplicity that she knew they would never be able to find it again.

Yes. It was over. Bel stood in the garden, staring up at the door for a long moment, then gave herself a little shake. *That's all right, then.* She had come out of her scandalous experiment unscathed. She knew all about physical love now; thanks to Aunt Louisa's astonishing forbearance, she had escaped any consequences of her rashness and she and Ashe had parted as friends.

Her mourning was over, her foolish daydreams and yearnings had been more than satisfactorily fulfilled and she had a purpose in life that was worthwhile and demanding. Really, one could not be happier, Bel told herself, climbing the steps and letting herself into the house. She was exactly what she had set out to be: an independent woman in charge of her own life, her own destiny.

'My lady?' Hedges materialised from the shadows of the front hall. 'Is everything all right?'

'Perfect,' Bel assured him with a smile. 'Things could not be better.'

'As you say, my lady.' Something akin to sympathy showed fleetingly on the well-schooled countenance and Bel felt a stab of pain, the sensation that a curtain had flicked back to reveal something unpleasant behind it. Something she did not want to know was there.

'I do say,' she said firmly. 'How are our soldiers?'

'All doing well. I venture to say we will have no trouble finding more men in need once we have the warehouse that I understand his lordship is providing.'

'Indeed.' Bel turned briskly to the drawing room. 'I can see I have much to do and lists to make, Hedges; I shall get on with it.'

There was a little pile of invitations on top of her appointments book, neglected while she had been preoccupied with Ashe. Bel opened the book and found herself flicking back to the page where she had slipped his card, the one that had come with those first roses. She picked it up, fretting at the thickness of the gilt-edged pasteboard with her fingertips, then suddenly decisive, tore it across, twice, and dropped the pieces into the little basket that served as the waste container under her desk.

She fanned out the invitations, dipped her pen in the standish and began to write. Time to get out into the world again, time to move on.

Lady Belinda Felsham thanks Lady Cardew for her kind… A tear dropped on to the last word, blurring it, soaking into the paper. Bel screwed up the sheet, found her handkerchief and blew her nose with more force than elegance. *Lady Belinda...*

Lady Cardew's musicale was delightful. Bel circulated, exchanging gossip against a background of chamber music. Where she could, she steered the conversation to her soldiers and their needs, ruthlessly jotting down the slightest hint of a promise of help on her ivory tablets.

'Thank you so much, Lord Stonehaven,' she said to the elderly peer, who had just found himself promising a weekly contribution to food and fuel costs. 'I should have known you would be so generous.' She dimpled prettily at him, knowing the effect a little harmless flirtation had upon certain old gentlemen.

He was beaming at her as she turned away, only to find herself face to face with Patrick Layne. 'Mr Layne, good evening. What a long time it seems since we last met. Is Miss Layne here, too?' She had neglected her friends in her preoccupation with Ashe, Bel thought guiltily.

'My sister is interrogating a composer on the subject of setting lyric verse.' Mr Layne grimaced. 'I escaped. And whose fault is it, might I ask, that we have not met lately, Lady Belinda? I swear you have been positively reclusive these past days.'

'I have a new project; let me tell you about it.' Belinda tucked her hand through his proffered arm and allowed herself to be guided through the guests towards the champagne buffet.

Patrick listened patiently as she explained, in more detail than she had to anyone else, all about her soldiers and why she felt so strongly about them. He listened, she realised, with complete focus and intensity, leading her on to explain more and more.

'I believe you,' he said, laughingly dodging one particularly expressive sweep of her arm as she tried to describe the size of the warehouse Ashe had donated. 'It sounds as though you need lumber to make room dividers in all that space. May I contribute that?'

'You may indeed!' Bel beamed in delight. 'How generous of you. Will you join our committee?'

'I would be honoured.' Patrick took two glasses of champagne from the footman and presented one to Bel, raising his own in a mock-toast. 'To your new venture and its hardworking committee.'

She touched her glass to his, laughing up at him. 'How do you know they are hardworking, Mr Layne?'

'Because I fear you will prove to be a hard taskmistress, Lady Belinda,' he teased.

'Nonsense, you are teasing me, Mr Layne. I believe one of my faults is that I am not forceful enough.' *But I was when I wanted Ashe*, she thought. Now, after it was all over, she could not believe she had been so brassy, so daring in asking for what she had wanted. It was as though he had bewitched her, she thought, wondering when the spell was going to wear off.

'I wish you would call me Patrick,' Mr Layne said, reminding her that this was quite another man at her side. He was so nice, just right for Elinor. 'And I believe you would be a positive Joan of Arc in pursuit of what you thought was right, however reticent you may be about your own desires.'

Bel felt her cheeks reddening at the perfectly innocent remark. It heaped coals upon her own awareness of how wanton she had been in pursuit of those desires. Her companion looked at her quizzically, obviously wondering what he had said to make her colour up so.

'Patrick, I—' Bel put her free hand on his arm, lost for words.

'Good evening, Lady Belinda, Mr Layne.' It was Ashe. His eyes flickered briefly to Belinda's hand and she made herself leave it where it was for a moment before removing it and sketching a curtsy. 'You remain in town, Layne?'

'As you see, Reynard. At Lady Belinda's beck and call.'

'Mr Layne is kindly contributing to fitting out the warehouse,' Bel intervened hastily, before Patrick made things any worse. 'I have invited him to join the committee.'

'Then we will doubtless see more of each other.' How Ashe managed to make that sound like a threat while speaking perfectly pleasantly and smiling, Bel had no idea. It appeared to be a masculine talent, for Patrick smiled back just as smoothly.

'I look forward to it.'

Bel supposed she should be flattered that their hackles were up over her—if that was what it was—but, given that Ashe was no longer her lover and Patrick had no reason to claim any rights whatsoever, she could only feel vaguely apprehensive.

'Miss Layne is here this evening also.' Bel snatched at a different subject. 'Lord Dereham admires your sister's writing very much,' she added to Patrick. 'I understand Miss Layne is contemplating some lyric verse.'

'I shall seek her out.' Ashe bowed and strolled away, apparently unconcerned about two pairs of eyes fixed on his back.

'My cousin Miss Ravenhurst is also on the committee,' Bel informed Patrick, wrenching her gaze and her mind away from broad, well-tailored shoulders and the memory of just how they looked with no tailoring at all. 'You met her in the park the other week.'

'So I did. I look forward to meeting her again.' Good, he looked quite pleased at the news; Bel had hoped for a spark of interest and was encouraged. Now all she had to do was to make sure Elinor came to their next meeting wearing one of her new gowns. It was a pity that her cousin's natural charm and intelligence were not enough, but Bel very much feared that even the most perceptive gentleman needed help to see past dun-coloured gowns and hideous bonnets.

'Are you well, Lord Dereham?' Ashe regarded Miss Layne with some surprise. It was a blunt query from a single lady to a gentleman. The poetess merely smiled at him maternally, waiting for an answer, her mittened hands folded neatly at the waist of her very elegant gown.

'Quite well, I thank you.' She merely pursed her lips and regarded him sceptically. 'Why? Do I seem pale to you?'

'You do not look as though you have been sleeping well.' Miss Layne smiled. 'You must forgive me, but when a gentleman has dark shadows under his eyes and spends time discussing lyric poetry with a spinster ten years his senior when the room is filled with a bevy of delightful young ladies, one does wonder if the poor man is ailing.'

Ashe thought fleetingly that Miss Layne would get on well with his mother. 'I have merely been burning the candle at both ends, ma'am, which accounts for the shadows. As for the young ladies—you must believe me when I tell you that I value intelligent conversation and elegant sophistication above giggles and naïve banality.'

'I am flattered, Lord Dereham, but surely there is at least one young lady who can supply both intelligence and elegance.' Miss Layne nodded towards her brother who had paused near the chamber orchestra, his head bent to listen to what Bel was saying.

Ashe reminded himself, for the second time that evening, that he had no right to feel possessive about Bel, that Patrick Layne was an apparently perfectly decent man and she could do a lot worse in either a friend or a lover. None of that stopped him wanting to land Layne a facer.

'Lady Belinda seems more than happy with her present conversation.' He made himself speak lightly. Bel laid a hand on Layne's arm and laughed up at him. The smile froze in place on Ashe's lips.

'Yes, they make a handsome couple,' Miss Layne remarked. 'But I fancy Lady Belinda is rather too complicated for my brother.'

'Complicated? Bel? In what way?' *Oh, God...*

Miss Layne showed no sign of noticing his slip with Bel's name. 'Patrick needs a nice girl who will adore him; he is quite conventional at heart, bless him. Lady Belinda needs a man who wants a partner and who will help her find her wings. She needs a man who can think in more than straight lines.'

'Wings?' Ashe watched as Bel dragged an amused Patrick Layne over to talk to three elderly ladies. He strongly suspected that she had sized up the effect a well-favoured young man would have on them and was even now extracting promises of money with the aid of her new ally.

'She has already found her feet, and I do not think that she is going to be happy with simply being a pedestrian in life now,' Miss Layne said drily. 'Something has changed in her over the past few weeks; I suspect that the real Belinda Cambourn is emerging for the first time since before she married.'

A man who can think in more than straight lines. Ashe pondered the poetess's words as she took out one of her endless supply of notebooks and jotted down an impression. Well, that ruled him out. He seemed incapable of thinking about anything except in a *very* straight line—one that led right back to Bel. He had given them two weeks to reconsider their relationship, but a chill doubt was forming inside him that Bel had already decided that it was irretrievably over.

Knowing that he should not, he read Miss Layne's neat notes upside down as she paused, nibbling the end of her tiny pencil and gazed up at the ceiling. *Wings. Birds? No, hackneyed. Icarus? Falling or soaring?*

He had an unpleasant feeling that for the first time in an *affaire* he had come out of it with scars. He was Icarus, with his wings scorched, and Bel, so far as he could see, was happily soaring off, flaunting her bright plumage in the sunshine.

But why was he scorched? Surely he hadn't fallen in love with her after all? Surely he would know if he had? *Hell.* How his mother would laugh now if she could see him, her unimpressionable son, unable to think about anything but a woman—and a woman who didn't want the eligible Lord Dereham at that. What he needed was a nice, uncomplicated encounter with a thoroughly wicked professional to get this nonsense out of his head, and his loins.

'Reynard!' The voice behind him had him turning, very slowly, on his heel. It could not be. It was.

'Mother. And Anna.' He had a certain reputation for *sang froid* to maintain. His family did not make it easy. 'I am delighted to see you, of course.' *Liar.* 'But what the dev…what on earth are you doing here? I was not expecting you in town for at least another fortnight.'

'I started writing to friends to say we would be here later this month and Leticia Cardew wrote back to say what a pity we would miss her *musicale*, so here we are. I did not want to trouble you about the town house, so I have brought most of the staff up with me.' Lady Dereham smiled fondly at her son. 'And what were you doing, standing there like a pillar of salt, might I ask?'

Thinking about love, sex and marriage. 'Discussing poetry,' Ashe said, regretting the ending of the medieval tradition of sending interfering mothers off to nunneries, something several early Reynards had resorted to in the past. 'May I introduce my mother and my elder sister to you, Miss Layne?' The poetess started, removed her gaze from the painted roundels of flitting cherubs on the ceiling and extended a hand.

The ladies exchanged greetings. 'But I love your work,' Anna exclaimed. 'Might I ask where you found the inspiration for the rustic romance in *Hedgerows and Pasture*?'

'I brought your sister here to begin to get used to chatting to young men in company before the Season starts,' Lady Dereham complained, *sotto voce*, as she drew Ashe to one side. 'Not to fill her head with poetry in the company of middle-aged spinsters!'

'Miss Layne has a handsome younger brother,' Ashe suggested blandly.

'Excellent.' His mother unfurled her fan and plied it

vigorously. 'Now, I shall not need your escort, dear, not for the few weeks we will be in town. I intend only accepting the sort of invitations where I can take Anna, and possibly Frederica, with little fuss. Not full-dress occasions, naturally.'

'None of those in any case, not at this time of year, although there's more company than usual up.' Ashe scanned the crowd to see if he could spot Bel. There she was, talking animatedly to an officer in regimentals. He steered his mother in the opposite direction towards the buffet. 'Frederica, too?'

'Yes,' Lady Dereham said with a touch of steel in her voice. 'I thought it best to remove her from Coppergate and give her thoughts a different direction.'

'From what?'

'From your estate manager! Really, Reynard, I realise that men do not think about these things, but you have positively thrown them together with the predictable result that she fancies herself in love with the man.'

'What is wrong with that?' Ashe asked provocatively, feeling more than a little fellow feeling for his middle sister.

'I want her to make a good marriage.'

'I want her to be happy,' he countered.

'I declare, Reynard,' his mother said with a snap, 'if I did not know better, I would think you were suffering from a broken heart and have some romantic notion of fostering love matches as a result.'

'Not at all,' he was goaded to retort. 'But I am certainly coming round to thinking of Cousin Adrian as my heir with some affection if finding a wife is to be so hedged around with calculation. I will call tomorrow morning, Mama, and see in what way I can assist you. Now, I regret I have a commitment elsewhere.'

He strode off through the crowd to find his hostess and make his graceful excuses. And then, he thought grimly, he would take himself off to the salon of one or other of the Fashionable Impures who would be holding court amidst champagne and candlelight and light-hearted banter and banish all this nonsense about romance from his mind.

Chapter Sixteen

~~~

She had never been aware of her body before, Bel realised as she strolled along the winding paths in the shade of the elms in Green Park. Not truly aware. She had thought about it when she was not feeling well, or when shoes pinched or she had eaten too much. But most of the time it was just there. Now it had become a constant part of her consciousness. She was far more sensitive to heat and to cold, to the touch of the different fabrics she wore, to the warmth of sun on her skin or the breeze against her cheek.

There was the compulsion to take off her gloves and stroke the textured bark on the trees as she wandered past, to pet a cat for the sinuous silk of its fur, to brush her hair for long minutes past the regulation one hundred strokes at bedtime.

And the smell of things, even smells that were not so pleasant—surely she had not been so sensitive to those either? After almost ten days she had learned not to mope, thinking of Ashe. She had taught herself not to save up titbits of news or silly ideas to share with him.

She could almost get through a whole day—if she did not see him—and not feel as though there was a hollow inside her, waiting to be filled with his company.

But she could not stop dreaming about him—hot, fevered dreams and languid tender ones—and waking in the morning restless and yearning. And even when willpower, breakfast and the business of the day got those feelings under control, there was still this enhanced sensual awareness, Ashe's legacy to her.

And it was a legacy, she was beginning to accept that. She had said nothing to him, but she was certain she was not going to resume their relationship. It was as though the flash of courage that had fuelled her proposition to him had flickered out. Or was it simply that common sense and her sense of propriety had reasserted itself? She should have felt relief at the decision, but all she could feel was a nagging sense of loss.

Bel walked slowly, studying the way the grass grew thick and soft in the shade, seeing each blade, smelling the freshness of it, even as the heat of the day built. She was not looking where she was going, but then neither was the child who was walking backwards down the same path, vehemently disputing something with her older companions who were walking more slowly several yards behind. They came together with a painful thump and the child landed up on the ground.

'Are you all right?' Concerned, Bel bent down and offered her hand. Ocean-blue eyes stared back at her from under a tumble of long blonde hair, then the child's mouth curved up into an irresistible, all-too-familiar smile that took Bel's breath. She was a miniature, feminine version of Ashe. His daughter? Even as the girl put her hands into Bel's and scrambled to her feet, she realised that this child was perhaps twelve, a little too old—unless Lord Dereham had begun on a career of precocious sin at an alarmingly early age. She must be his sister.

'Thank you, ma'am. I do beg your pardon.' The child bobbed a respectful curtsy. 'I was not looking where I was going; I hope I did not hurt you.' She ignored the two young women hurrying towards them and added, 'I am Katherine Reynard, ma'am.'

'Katy!' The taller of the two young women reached them, her slightly younger and shorter companion at her heels. 'Ma'am, I can only apologise for my harum-scarum sister! I trust you are not hurt, or your gown damaged?' Despite the anxiety on the smooth oval of her face, Bel could see that this sister too was an uncommonly handsome girl.

'Not at all, although I believe Miss Katherine might find she has a bruise or two. Neither of us was paying attention to where we were walking, I am afraid.' The third girl arrived and smiled shyly. Not a beauty, this one, with her mousey hair and her rather indeterminate nose. But her expression was sweet and the anxious affection with which she was running her hands over her younger sister to check for injury, touching. 'I am Lady Belinda Felsham,' she added, holding out her hand to the older girl.

Ashe had not spoken much about his family, and she had not probed, feeling reticent in case he thought she was overly curious about his domestic situation. She recalled him saying he had three sisters, but that was all.

'I am Anna Reynard, this is my sister Frederica and you have already met Katy.' Miss Reynard directed a rueful smile at her sister, who was submitting to having her bonnet straightened and her skirts brushed. 'We have been in London a full week and still we are giving the impression of being complete country bumpkins.'

'I believe you must be relatives of Lord Dereham,' Bel said, turning her steps to stroll with them, Katy's hand trapped firmly in Frederica's.

'You know our brother?'

'We have been engaged on the same committee for some charitable work,' Bel explained. It was dangerously pleasant to speak about Ashe. 'I have started a scheme to give medical aid and temporary shelter to soldiers who have returned from the continent wounded and without families to go to.'

'Oh, yes, I can see that Ashe would be concerned to help with that,' Anna said, her face serious. 'What happens to them when they leave your care?'

'One or two who had a skill and were only lightly wounded have gone back to trades already, but I am not sure what we are going to do with many of them.' That was the biggest worry. Bel had no intention of making work, or fobbing the men off with something that did not have any hope of lasting. 'As they recover their strength, I am sure they will start to think of ideas for themselves.'

'Ashe always says that the army is like a family,' Anna mused. 'He found it difficult to adjust, coming home—I am sure men for whom the life was everything are going to find it much harder.'

'Ashe is very different now,' Katy interrupted. 'Mama says she doesn't know what has come over him.'

'Katy!' her sisters chorused. Bel had the impression that this cry of dismay was a frequent occurrence.

'Well, he is,' Katy persisted. 'Look at the way he is

throwing Frederica together with Mr Barrington.' Frederica went scarlet.

'*Katy!*' Anna said sternly. 'Little pitchers with big eyes and ears and even bigger mouths get to sit in the corner at home and not come out with the grown ups. You should not be talking about such things.' She smiled an apology at Bel. 'Perhaps you have younger brothers or sisters, Lady Belinda?'

'No, none.' Bel laughed, then lowered her voice. 'I find your sister refreshingly frank, Miss Reynard.'

'She is certainly that, I fear!'

'Are you in town for long?' Bel enquired. Ashe had said something about readying the town house for them and then escorting them down to Brighton, but she had been so upset at the time she could not be certain.

'We will go down to Brighton with our brother in a week or so, after Mama has decided what she wants done to the house. I am coming out next Season, you see.'

'You are not out yet?' Bel was surprised, then realised that Miss Reynard's calm air made her seem a little older than she was.

'Mama is allowing Frederica and me to attend small parties now,' Anna explained.

'Then you could come to a picnic I am organising to raise money for the soldiers next Tuesday?' Bel found she was anxious to see more of the Reynard sisters. 'Your brother will be there, so I hope your mother would not mind. No doubt Lord Dereham has already arranged for you all to come? And Miss Katherine would enjoy it as well, I am sure—there will be other young people, it is all quite informal. I am asking for pledges to our funds with acceptances.'

Bel raised her parasol against the sunlight as they

stepped out of the shade. 'I believe it will be a very pleasant day—Lady Rushbrook is lending her ornamental gardens near Richmond. There is a lake, floral walks, a bowling green and an archery lawn and the weather seems set fine.'

The sisters agreed with enthusiasm. Anna, predictably organised, had remembered to carry some of their mother's London cards with her, so she was able to exchange one with Bel in form and they parted with mutual expressions of anticipation.

Bel stood looking after the three sisters as they made their way up towards Piccadilly, Katy already skipping ahead now the pressure of keeping company manners was off. How nice they seemed, how close and affectionate. And how much they looked like Ashe, Katy in particular. Bel thought wistfully of a child like her, Ashe's child.

'Children?' she said out loud, earning herself a very strange look from a passing governess with two small charges at her side. Children? But she had never thought of them except as a very vague concept. She had certainly never imagined Henry's children, but now, here she was, thinking yearningly of Ashe's! That was a ridiculous indulgence for a woman who had no wish to remarry.

Flustered, Bel turned on her heel and began to walk briskly towards Fortnum's. She had a long list of items to order for the picnic and a bill for unsatisfactory anchovies to dispute.

Ashe, already feeling harassed by the conflict between his agent's advice on the need to treat the woodworm in the ballroom panelling before doing anything else in the room and his mother's insistence that she wanted to see the effect of painting the pale green woodwork cream before she went off to Brighton, was not best pleased to find himself besieged by all three sisters wanting to discuss Lady Felsham's picnic.

'In a moment—Katy, you are going to get paint on your skirts if you stand over there—Mama, I really think we should allow Mr Grimball to try the wood treatment first. Yes, I do know who you mean, Frederica, of course; Lady Belinda's charity is deserving of support, certainly, but I doubt Mama wants—Katy!'

By the time he had rescued the painter from his sister and despatched her upstairs to change her dress, his other sisters had already told their mother about meeting Lady Belinda and the plans for the picnic.

'Why should you assume I would not want to go, Reynard?' she enquired. 'Thank you, Mr Grimball, if you think it best, the wood treatment first and then the cream paint with the mouldings picked out as we discussed.' Lady Dereham led the way back to the small drawing room, the first room to have been put back into order as a sitting room for the ladies. 'Is this the current Lady Felsham or the widow of the late viscount?'

'The widow,' Ashe said shortly, pretending to be engrossed in the colour samples for the hangings.

'I cannot recall her at all. *He* was the most complete bore, famous for it. He once talked to me about drains for twenty minutes at a levée, and of course I could not escape for we were all standing around waiting to be presented.'

'Felsham caught a chill inspecting drains, that is what carried him off.'

'One is tempted to say it was a judgement, poor

man! I am not surprised his widow has turned to good works, it must seem like a riot of pleasure after life with Henry Cambourn.'

'She appears very competent,' Ashe said dispassionately, flattening every iota of emotion out of his voice.

'She is very pretty,' Frederica remarked. 'And her walking dress was so well cut! I mean to look in *La Belle Assemblée*, for I am certain I saw the very same thing in there. It had a pink satin spencer and a pink-and-rose-striped scarf with lace trim. And the skirt was white muslin, Mama, with folded bands at the hem.'

'It sounds delightful. Very tasteful.' Ashe was conscious of his mother's eyes on him. He had obviously overdone the indifference. 'Your praise of the lady seems somewhat lukewarm, my dear. Merely *very competent*?'

'I hardly notice fashion.' Ashe walked to the window to hold up a sample to the light.

'You notice pretty women, though,' Frederica observed pertly. 'I for one am looking forward to this picnic.'

'It was kind of you to invite my family to the picnic.' Ashe accepted a cup of tea from Bel in her drawing room, taking advantage of a moment to speak to her apart from the rest of the committee.

'If I had known they were in London already, I would have sent a card earlier. Although presumably, as a member of the committee yourself, you were already arranging for them to attend.' She was looking particularly lovely that afternoon, he thought, calmly organising tea for the committee as they stood chatting before gathering round the table to finalise arrangements for the picnic.

'Is that one of Mrs Bell's designs?' he asked abruptly. Bel turned from the tea tray, the flounced hem of her afternoon dress whispering against his ankles. It was in the popular Elizabethan style, he decided, with full gathered sleeves of white muslin emerging from a bodice of striped blue silk. Her face was framed by a pretty stand-up collar, its edges pinked into sharp points.

Ashe found himself staring at the shadows it made on her throat and how the sheen of the simple string of pearls echoed the texture of her skin. Only a little while ago he had been able to bend his head and touch his lips to the pulse that beat just there…

'As it happens, it is. How strange—I would not have expected you to be an authority on ladies' fashions.' Bel reached for a teaspoon, then turned to regard him with a cool gaze. 'Or perhaps I am mistaken and you shop there frequently.'

'No.' That was not true. In the time before Bel he would accompany his latest *chère amie* and indulge her with new gowns as a matter of course. He knew where all the leading modistes were and which would serve their frailer sisters and which would not. The thought recalled his uncomfortable evening after he left Lady Cardew's party.

He had taken a hackney cab and gone straight to the first house on his list, had been halfway up the front steps and had stopped. He could not do it. The memory of Bel's shy passion, the scent of her skin, the generous innocence of her response all contrasted so sharply with the sophisticated, perfumed, commercial pleasures that lay through that door that for a moment he felt a disgust that was almost physical.

He had talked himself into a less dramatic and more

reasonable frame of mind soon enough, but even so he had walked the hot, dark streets aimlessly for two hours before returning to his own bed and a long, restless, frustrated night.

'My sisters read *La Belle Assemblée*,' he explained and the suspicion in Bel's face vanished. 'And all the other fashionable journals as well, for that matter. I was treated to a description of your elegant walking dress after you encountered them in the park.'

'They are very charming. I was particularly taken with Miss Katherine.'

Ashe grimaced. 'She terrifies me. Can you imagine what a nightmare it will be for her chaperon when she comes out? And I pity the poor young men. Mind you, she is determined to marry a duke, so most of them will be safe.'

Bel gave a gurgle of laughter that sent a rush of pure lust shivering through him. Every time he believed himself safe, started to think that they really could just be friends and that in time he would become interested in other women again, she said or did something that transfixed him with the desire to sweep her up in his arms and make love to her, there and then.

A glance around the drawing room, the scene of the last time he had yielded to that impulse, had a sobering effect. To bolster it Ashe collected a second cup and carried it across to Lady James, who was already ensconced in her place at the head of the table. The charity might have been her niece's idea, but there was never any doubt who was in the chair at meetings.

'Thank you, Reynard.' She fixed him with a beady eye. 'I hear your mother is in town.'

'Yes, ma'am.'

'I'll see her the day after tomorrow at this picnic nonsense that Bel is organising. Haven't spoken to her in an age. Brought all your sisters up, has she?'

'Yes, ma'am.'

Lady James's thin lips twitched. 'You don't fool me with your meek *yes, ma'am*. Wishing me at the devil, aren't you?'

'Yes, ma'am,' Ashe responded with a perfectly straight face and took himself off to the foot of the table to discuss the progress of the carpentry work with Patrick Layne. Behind him he heard a rich chuckle. She was a battleaxe, but she was a loyal one, supporting Bel and not letting a hint of what she had seen in this very room escape her.

'Do we need another carpenter on the job?' he asked the other man, trying to ignore the memory of those last, heated moments Bel had been in his arms. Working with Layne was helping to damp down the spark of antagonism between them. It also helped, Ashe realised, that it was a while since he had seen Bel and Layne in a social setting. He was not certain how well his tolerance would hold up to seeing her whirling around in Layne's embrace in a waltz.

'No, it will be finished by the end of the week. Some of the men are helping—I have hopes they may get offers from the craftsmen we are using.'

'Order, ladies and gentlemen!' Lady James rang her teaspoon against her cup. 'Take your places, it is time we began our meeting.'

'…so you can see, the finances are in a very healthy state,' the Reverend Makepeace, in his office as treasurer, closed the ledger and sat back. A murmur of pleased comment broke out around the table and Lady James rapped upon it for attention.

'I believe that concludes our business for the day.'

Bel stood up, glad to be able to move around after an hour of sitting opposite Ashe. Most of the time she simply did not know where to look, for every time she glanced across the table his blue eyes were resting on her, his expression unreadable. Then she would look away, gaze about the room until she felt she must look shifty. Finally she compromised by looking firmly at her notebook and jotting things down, quite superfluously, for Elinor was making her usual competent record.

As the others broke up into smaller groups, she found Ashe at her side. 'May I collect you tomorrow in my carriage for the drive to Richmond? My sisters would enjoy travelling with you and my mother would be delighted to meet you.'

'I…' How could he do it? Bel was certain that anyone could tell they had been lovers, just by seeing them together, yet Ashe appeared quite comfortable at the thought of spending an hour with her under the no doubt intent scrutiny of his mother. 'Thank you, but I am going early, with Miss Ravenhurst, to help organise things.'

'Of course, I should have realised. We will see you there, then.'

'Goodbye, Lady Belinda. I will call for you at eight as agreed, shall I?' It was Patrick Layne, hat in hand, about to take his leave.

'Yes, thank you…' Ashe, standing just behind Mr Layne, raised one sardonic eyebrow and walked out. Bel felt the colour come up under her skin as though she had been caught out in a lie. He must have thought she was using her cousin as an excuse. 'It is very kind of you to take *all three* of us,' she said clearly, but Ashe was into the hall and out of earshot.

'Not at all.' Patrick shook hands and departed, leaving Elinor and her mother alone with Bel.

'That young man pursuing you, Belinda?' Lady James enquired.

'Mr Layne? Goodness me, no.' With any luck he was making subtle advances to Elinor, although she could wish he was rather more bold about it. Still, offering a lift to Lady James was proof enough of devotion, she supposed.

Elinor, looking more than usually expressionless, gathered up her notes and stood patiently waiting for her mother. If only she showed some emotion over the man! Still, Bel consoled herself, she had bullied her cousin into buying a very pleasant afternoon gown, had lent her her own best parasol, and if she did not manage to throw Elinor and Mr Layne together in some romantic spot, then she would be disappointed indeed.

And perhaps if she achieved that, Ashe would stop regarding her as though he thought she was chasing Patrick herself. And he had no right to care about that at all, no more than she would have if she found him flirting with a pretty girl.

Chapter Seventeen

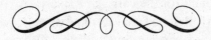

Bel took her disorganised thoughts down to the mews. At least there she could have conversations uncomplicated by emotion, misunderstanding or conventional expectations.

Jem Brown was sitting on the mounting block, his crutch propped up beside him and the *Morning Chronicle* open in his hands. Bel had not realised he could read.

'Good day, my lady.' He tossed away the paper and reached for his crutch.

'No, please, don't stand up.' Bel gestured towards the newspaper. 'Is there anything interesting today? I have not yet had the chance to read it.'

'I wasn't reading the news, ma'am. I was scanning the advertisements.' Brown stuck his hat on the back of his head and gathered up the sheet.

'For work?' One of the grooms emerged from the stables with a wooden chair, dusted it down with his blue-and-white spotted kerchief and set it by the mounting block. 'Thank you, how kind.' Bel settled herself down.

'In a manner of speaking, ma'am. The thing is...' Brown scratched his chin meditatively '...there's a lot of us and what is needed, to my way of thinking, is a way of settling several at once. And there's something in here that's given me an idea like.'

'Go on,' Bel urged.

'See here, ma'am.' He folded the paper and handed it to her. 'Third column on the back page, just below the advertisement for the carriage horses.'

'An inn?' Bel read it and looked up at Brown. The big man endured her scrutiny stolidly. 'Where's St Lawrence?'

'Just inland from Ramsgate, on the Canterbury road. Couldn't be better placed for all the trade to and from the port. And it's a big inn, judging by what it says about the stabling.'

'You want to buy an inn?' Bel queried. 'Do you know anything about running one?'

'If I can run a platoon, I can run an inn,' Brown said. 'I was a sergeant once.' So she had not been wrong, Brown did have the capacity to lead. Bel raised an interrogative eyebrow. 'Swore at a lieutenant, stupid young bu—sprig, and lost my stripes. I can manage it, do the books, keep order. We've got men here who can cook, look after horses, run the cellars. I reckon a place this size—' he tapped the advertisement '—could take twelve of us, one way and another.'

'It would take all the funds and more,' Bel said thoughtfully. It did sound a good idea.

'I know that, ma'am. And I reckon you'll need those funds for more lads in any case. I was wondering if one of your rich friends would lend us the money and we'll pay it back in a few years, regular like.'

'That is an idea, certainly. But I think we ought to look at the place first, don't you, Brown? Get someone to check through the books, see what would need to be done. It may need a lot of money investing.'

'Lewin could do the books, ma'am. He was a book keeper before he joined up.' Bel's astonishment must have showed, because Brown grinned and explained. 'Got himself in a bit of bother with his employer's wife and the army sounded like the healthy option. He doesn't seem so much now, what with his voice and everything getting him down, but he's a bright lad.'

'I'll think about it,' Bel said, getting up from the hard chair. 'And you make a list of all the jobs the men could fill and we'll talk about it after the picnic.'

She walked slowly back up through the garden to the house, mentally reviewing her investments. What would be a reasonable price for an inn and could she afford it? What would Henry have said if he had guessed his wife would ever contemplate buying an inn? Bel laughed out loud, startling the footman on duty in the hall. She could always call it the Felsham Arms.

'This is going to be a complete success.' Elinor leant on the balustrade of the upper terrace two days later and surveyed the closely scythed lawns sweeping down to the lake edge. 'Virtually everyone who accepted seems to have turned up—almost two hundred people!'

'And it feels as though I have shaken every one of them by the hand personally,' Bel said with feeling. The committee members had shared out the meeting and greeting between them and now were circulating, making sure the guests were all enjoying themselves and, with varying degrees of subtlety, working on extracting even more funds.

'Mama is outrageous.' Elinor's tone was dispassionate as she looked for her parent. 'See, she has cornered Uncle Augustus and Aunt Sylvia now.' On the lower terrace below them Lady James was lecturing Augustus Ravenhurst, Bishop of Wessex and his poker-faced wife.

'So she is. I haven't seen Theophilus, have you?' Bel craned to look for the Bishop's only son. With his red hair Theo was usually easy to spot.

'It's an age since I met him—not since I was about ten, I imagine. Mama says he is a scapegrace and a limb of Satan and will not know him.' Elinor twirled the parasol Bel had lent her.

'Poor Theo! He is not as bad as that, and, quite frankly, if Aunt Sylvia was my mama, I would probably turn to wild dissipation in reaction.' When in fact she had managed to behave outrageously with no excuse whatsoever. 'There are Lord Dereham's sisters—that must be their mother, don't you think?'

'Lord Dereham is not with them.' How Elinor managed to insinuate a question into that bland observation, Bel had no idea. If her cousin expected her to express an interest in Ashe's whereabouts, she was not going to oblige her.

'No, he is not. Shall we go down and I will introduce you to them?'

They met the Reynard family at the foot of the terrace steps and between them Anna and Bel performed introductions. Anna began to stroll with Elinor while Frederica lagged behind to look at the progress of a croquet match and Katy skipped along between her mother and Bel.

'I understand my son is an enthusiastic supporter of your charity, Lady Belinda.'

'Yes. He understands the soldiers and they respect him, which is such an asset in the work we are trying to do.'

'I imagine it is. I must admit I was surprised to find him absorbed in charitable work. He has always taken care of our dependents and tenants, of course, but this is rather different. Do tell me, Lady Belinda, how exactly Reynard came to be involved?'

Bel felt herself go hot and cold all over, then told herself it was simply her guilty conscience and Lady Dereham was making conversation, not probing for signs of immorality.

'We met because of my purchasing Lord Dereham's house in Half Moon Street and he told me a little about his military background. When I decided to help the men, he seemed the obvious person to advise us.'

'He discussed his army career with you?' Lady Dereham's fine-drawn brows shot up. 'You have succeeded in gaining his confidence to a greater extent than his sisters and I have, in that case.'

'No doubt he is reticent for fear of distressing you, ma'am,' Bel suggested. 'His experiences must have been harrowing.'

'No doubt.' Bel braced herself for further questions and then relaxed as Ashe's mother enquired, 'Do you stay in London throughout the summer, Lady Belinda?'

'I had intended to,' Bel admitted. 'But now I think I might go down to Margate for a while.'

'Margate? Surely Brighton is more select?'

'So I believe, but at this late stage I am sure I will never secure eligible accommodations in Brighton, and what Margate lacks in royal patronage, I believe it makes up for in the excellence of its sea bathing.' Bel did not think that revealing her intention to inspect an inn with an intention to purchase it would be considered quite the thing. It was not exactly trade, under the circumstances, but it was close enough to be considered shocking, she had no doubt.

Since Brown had shown her the advertisement Bel had made some enquiries of her own and come to the conclusion that Ramsgate might be a little too cosmopolitan and busy, but that a trip to nearby Margate would serve the purpose just as well. Now, talking to Ashe's mother, her resolve hardened; it would be a change of scene and it would remove her completely from all risk of encountering Ashe himself until this foolish yearning for him died down.

She and Elinor parted from the Reynards at the end of the terrace. 'If you will excuse us, we must go and circulate and see if there are any other guests who might be persuaded into taking a more active interest in our cause. If we do not meet again, Lady Dereham, I do trust you have a very pleasant stay in Brighton.'

Bel steered her cousin towards the edge of the lake where Mr Layne was standing beside a vast weeping ash watching the half-dozen or so rowing boats that were dotting the still surface. She had a plan and kept an eye on his broad-brimmed straw hat as they navigated through several brief conversations and two firm promises of help before they reached the water's edge.

'Mr Layne!' He turned and raised his hat. 'Can you row?'

'Why, yes, quite well, I flatter myself. Would you ladies like me to take you out?'

It was even easier than she had expected. 'Yes, please!'

Elinor looked less than entranced at the idea, but permitted herself to be handed down by Patrick and seated while he balanced the small boat. 'I'll untie the rope, shall I?' Bel offered, contriving to both loosen the knot and give the vessel a push as she did so. 'Oh, how clumsy of me! Never mind…' she waved them on as Patrick would have paddled closer '…you go without me; now I see it rock, perhaps I would not like it after all.'

There, now if he has any gumption at all he will contrive to make the best of such privacy, Bel thought smugly, strolling along the narrow strip of bank between the weeping boughs of the tree and the water and watching as Patrick rowed towards the centre of the lake. Elinor had unfurled her parasol and was sitting back, so hopefully that meant she had relaxed somewhat.

Bel paused, finding herself in an unexpectedly quiet and private spot, unable to see the grounds at all and visible only from the boats scattered across the lake. It was pleasant not to have to make conversation for a while and she could puzzle over why the encounter with Lady Dereham had so disconcerted her. For it had, despite the innocuous words they had exchanged. There had been something in the older woman's eyes when she had commented upon Ashe confiding in Bel. And surely there had been something besides polite chitchat in her question about Bel's plans for the summer? Had Lady Dereham wanted her to be in her son's vicinity— or as far away as possible?

She lifted a hand to shade her eyes as she scanned the lake for Patrick and Elinor, but the boats were all too far out now to tell which was which. 'It is very pretty out there,' she commented to a duck that had paddled up, hopeful of a crumb. 'It should be romantic enough for anyone.'

'Nonsense. It might if either of them had the slightest interest in each other.' The voice, so unexpected, made her jump, staring wildly at the duck as though it had spoken. Her foot slipped on the dry grass and she lurched as an arm came from behind her, encircled her waist and lifted her back through the screen of trailing leaves, under the canopy of the tree.

'Ashe!' He set her on her feet, but his arm remained around her waist, holding her close. Bel pressed one hand to her breast, feeling her heart thudding. At his touch every one of the feelings she had been so rigorously suppressing came flooding back. 'You scared the wits out of me—I thought it was the duck talking.'

Ashe, as far as she could see in the deep shade, looked less than delighted to be mistaken for poultry. The old weeping ash enclosed them totally. It was like being inside a giant green parasol with the light filtered through the leaves and only the occasional small gap allowing sunbeams to penetrate. Outside she could hear the loud buzz of conversation, the distant strains of the orchestra on the upper terrace and occasional shrieks of laughter from playing children. Inside they were in a private world of their own.

'I would suggest that you will hear more sense from me than you will from that duck,' Ashe remarked as a plaintive quack from outside marked the creature's disappointment at her disappearance.

'I have no idea what you are talking about,' Bel said stiffly, furious with herself at her reaction to him and her desire to take the short step closer that would bring her right into his arms. The pulse in her neck was racing and quite another, shameful, pulse of arousal quivered into life.

'Your delusion that you can matchmake between Layne and your cousin. She is not remotely interested and he, as is quite apparent to everyone else, is dangling after you.'

'He is not,' Bel retorted furiously. *Patrick? Dangling after me?* 'And that is a horrid expression. *Dangling* indeed!'

Is he? She had acknowledged Patrick Layne's attraction and had dismissed it because she had no desire for anyone but Ashe. But that had been when she and Ashe were lovers. And now? Was Patrick really attracted to her? If he was, why did she not feel happy about it? He was a handsome, kind, intelligent man. *And I am free*, a little voice said inside her head.

'Bel? What is wrong?' Ashe tipped up her chin, turning her face so a shaft of sunlight from above fell across her features. 'There are tears in your eyes.'

'There are no such things.' She swallowed what felt horribly like a sob. 'I have the sun in my eyes, that is all.' *I am free, and I do not want to be.*

'Nonsense.' He gathered her efficiently into the white linen waistcoat he was wearing under his pale tan coat. The broad brim of his fine straw hat bumped against the edge of her bonnet and he took it off, tossing it to one side before tackling the primrose satin ribbons under her chin. 'This is a very pretty piece of frippery, but I believe we can dispense with it.' The bonnet slid down her back to the grass. 'Now, then. Do you want Patrick Layne?'

'No.' Bel put every ounce of sincerity into the

denial. 'Of course I do not. He is a very pleasant man, but that is all.'

'Excellent. Because I still want you Bel. Very much. And it is a trifle disconcerting wondering what deep game you are playing with the poor man.'

'I am not playing any game.' Bel sighed. 'I just want to rescue Elinor from Aunt Louisa and I thought they would suit.'

'Even though you do not think marriage is a good thing?'

'It is not for me, but that is not to say it might be perfectly all right for someone else. And Elinor—'

'Elinor is an intellectual. She needs someone who can match her in that, not a respectable, conventional chap like Layne. Have you got any bachelor intellectuals up your sleeve?'

'None. And you are quite right, I should not matchmake.'

'There's nothing wrong with it in principle—I am in trouble with my mother for matchmaking for Frederica.'

'You are?' Bel gazed up at him, fascinated, her own preoccupations momentarily forgotten. 'With whom?'

'Our estate manager. I think he'll do, and she fancies herself in love with him, but he'll need to prove himself.'

'Goodness, how very kind of you.'

Ashe shrugged. 'I want them all to be happy.'

'And what about you?' Bel murmured.

'I would rather like to be happy too.' Ashe's smile was crooked. 'It is two weeks, Bel—will you come back to me again?'

'Is that why you were following me? To ask that?'

She wanted him, badly, so badly she had no idea whether she could trust her own judgement or not.

'No, this was a coincidence. I came in here for some solitude, to think. A weeping ash—rather apt, don't you think?'

'You are not weeping,' Bel pointed out, the pattering of her pulse making it hard to think clearly.

'No, not yet. I have missed you very much, though.'

'We have met, quite often,' she pointed out, trying to be reasonable and rational. His fingertips, which had been under her chin, slid round to cup the back of her head. Reasonable and rational thought became harder.

'That is not what I mean.'

'You have missed making love?'

'So much that I ache. And I have missed talking to you alone. I have missed your company, *ma belle*.'

'You must not call me that.' She heard the betraying shake in her voice and fought not to move her head against the warm support of his palm.

'No? You have not missed me at all?'

'Of course I have. I have missed talking to you, I have missed making love with you and I have told myself it is right that it has ended and I will miss you less with time. It will become easier.' She saw from his expression that he did not believe it and knew that her own certainty was less than complete. 'Besides,' she added briskly, trying to tell herself that this was not something she should mind, 'you are a man—it is easy for you to find consolation elsewhere, at least for your physical needs.'

'You would think so,' Ashe said. 'But I find that I cannot bring myself to seek that…consolation, however much I need it.'

'Oh.' Bel found she could not meet his eyes, could not look into his face, which he was keeping so carefully neutral without a hint of need or entreaty showing. 'I must choose, then?'

'Yes, because I have chosen, but it needs both of us. I want you for my lover, Bel, you and no one else, but I am not going to persuade you or coerce you or seduce you.'

She had been standing with her hands clasped to her bosom as though that would still the pounding of her heart. Now, seemingly of their own accord, they reached out and flattened themselves against the smooth linen of his summer waistcoat.

Under her palm the thud of his heart seemed uneven, as she had never felt it. Her eyes fixed on the back of her hands as she let them slide up, under the lapels of his coat, up until they encircled his neck and her gaze rose to his mouth. He licked his lips, a sudden, uncharacteristically uncertain gesture and she rose up on tiptoe and pressed her mouth to his, heat to heat, need to need.

'Aah.' He sighed against her lips and was still, his arms holding her just as she was for a long, aching moment. Then he pulled her in hard, his mouth claiming hers, claiming her again, his tongue sweeping in to remind her—as if she could have forgotten—of the taste of him, of the passion of him, of what his body and hers meant together.

Yes, she said in her mind as her fingers laced up into his hair, the elegant strength of his skull familiar to her touch. *Yes, this is my man.* Ashe's hands slid down her back, lifting against him, reminding her, as though she needed it, of how his body, roused, felt against hers. He was hard with his need for her, she ached with hers for him. *Tonight, oh, yes, tonight.*

The pressure of his mouth on hers was savage with a need that she responded to shamelessly, unafraid, triumphant that he wanted her like this, above all others.

Mine. My man, my lover, my love…

My love. The thought lanced through her like a lightning strike and she trembled in his arms. *I love him.* It changed everything. It changed her world for ever. It was the end.

Chapter Eighteen

I love you. It was a disaster. Bel freed Ashe's head, put her hands on his shoulders and pushed, dragging her mouth from his.

'Bel? What is wrong?' He sounded as shaken as she felt.

'I cannot. I… This is all wrong. Ashe, I cannot be your lover again.'

'I do not understand.' He stood there in the green shade, inches from her, their arms still around each other, their breath mingling. 'How can you say that? When you kiss me—'

I do not understand either, but I love you and I cannot do this. Not if you do not love me. Not when I want you for ever.

'I cannot explain,' Bel whispered. 'But I cannot be with you any longer. Ashe, I am sorry—'

There were no words. Her tongue dry and clumsy, Bel wrenched herself out of his encircling arms, snatched up her hat and stumbled through the screen of leaves to the lake edge. Out of the strange green shade and into the fresh air she felt as though she had woken from a weird dream.

Reality. She had to pull herself together and be seen. As one of the hostesses, there was no hiding. It was the work of a moment to jam her hat back on her head and tie the ribbons, to smooth down her skirts and to walk briskly along to where the lawn opened out again.

Seconds, and she was back in the midst of the party, smiling and nodding, stopping to scoop up an escaping toddler and return him to his flustered nursemaid. She did not dare look behind her to see if Ashe had come out too or whether he was recovering from her outburst in privacy.

Things were suddenly very clear. Painful, but clear… Bel tried to think, heard her name, stopped. 'Lady St Andrews, good afternoon. Lovely, is it not? We are so lucky to have such fine weather.' An exchange of bows, smiles, on to the next group. 'Mrs Truscott, thank you so much for your kind donation. Yes, such a worthy cause…'

She loved Ashe. No wonder she recoiled now from the thought of simply being his lover. It had been one thing when all she felt for him was liking, attraction and respect. She could share how she felt with him and be honest. An equal. But she could not tell him she loved him, or he would think she expected him to marry her. And snatched nights of lovemaking were no longer enough, not when she yearned for a lifetime together. And not when she could not trust herself not to speak her feelings in the throes of passion.

Bel found herself next to an unoccupied Gothic bench and sank down on it, her fingers twitching her skirts into order without conscious thought. What a blind fool she had been, to imagine that just because her marriage to Henry had been dull, loveless, pointless, that therefore she could never find a man with whom it would be wonderful. And she could hardly tell Ashe now that she had changed her mind, and why—not after protesting so vehemently that she would never marry again.

He had asked her to marry him because he had compromised her and because, she supposed, he was aware that soon he must find himself a wife to carry on his line and share his life. If he had loved her, surely that was the time to tell her? Ashe was no coward, he would not hesitate for fear of a rebuff. Instead, when he had mentioned love, it was to make it more than clear he neither felt it nor understood it.

'Belinda.'

'Aunt Sylvia, Uncle Augustus.' Bel jumped to her feet. 'I am so sorry, I was just resting…'

The Bishop regarded her with stern benevolence, his wife simply sternly. But then she rarely approved of anyone. 'Is your brother back from his honeymoon yet?'

'No, not yet. Sebastian and the Grand Duchess will remain in Maubourg for the summer in any case,' Bel explained. She was sure Lord Augustus did not approve of Sebastian's marriage, but it was difficult for such a pillar of the Establishment to criticise a nephew's connection to a member of the ruling house of an allied state. 'I have not seen Cousin Theo here today. Is he well?'

'Theophilus has departed on the Grand Tour,' his mother said repressively. 'It is to be hoped that a prolonged period of study of the great antiquarian sights will enable him to fix his mind upon a suitable future career.' Her expression implied a grim disbelief that he would do any such thing.

Given that Theo was wild to a fault, it was hard to imagine what that career might be. Certainly not the church! 'His languages are good, are they not?' Bel offered. 'Perhaps the diplomatic service?'

That earned her a frosty stare from her aunt. Oh, well, at least poor Theo was having a holiday; she very much doubted that he was applying himself to serious study.

'Are you remaining in London throughout the summer, Belinda?' The question was not accompanied by an invitation to stay at the Bishop's Palace, much to Bel's relief.

'I am going to Margate, Uncle, for the sea bathing.'

'Not by yourself, I trust?'

'Goodness no, with Cousin Elinor.' Bel crossed her fingers. Elinor was probably not speaking to her after being cast adrift on the lake with Patrick Layne.

After a short lecture on the perils of the unsuitable company to be found at seaside resorts and a warning about the moral inadmissibility of sea bathing on a Sunday, her uncle and aunt moved on, leaving Bel wishing she had a fan with her. What was the time? She glanced up at the clock tower over the stables: only half past two. It would be hours before she could go home and have some peace in which to contemplate a lifetime without the man she loved.

There was Ashe to avoid, Elinor to placate and Patrick Layne to evade also, if what Ashe thought was true. Then there were the endless encounters with the guests and potential donors to endure with a smiling face, alert for every opportunity to secure support.

'There you are!' It was Elinor, alone and none too pleased with her cousin if her thinned lips and aggressively tilted parasol were anything to go by. The hem of her pretty new dress was wet. 'I never want to be that close to a duck again! What on earth did you think—?'

'I am sorry.' Bel spoke before her cousin could manage another word. 'I thought you and Mr Layne might find you would suit if I threw you together. I was wrong.'

The wind taken out of her sails by this frank acknowledgement, Elinor sat down beside her and adjusted her parasol so that it shaded them both. 'Well, I never thought you would give up on the matchmaking just like that. You do realise that Mr Layne's interests lie elsewhere, don't you?'

'You mean with me? Yes, Ashe told me so. I had no idea.'

Elinor's strong dark brows rose. '*Ashe*, is it?'

There was no one close by. Suddenly the strain of keeping it all locked inside was too much. 'Yes. Elinor, I love him.' Said out loud, it was terrifying.

'But that is wonderful.' Elinor beamed at her. 'I do wish you both happy!'

'He does not love me.' It hurt to say it. Bel licked her lips and swallowed, terrified she might cry, here, where everyone could see her. She sucked in her stomach, straightened her back and sat up, deportment-class poised, focusing everything on presenting a tranquil face.

'Oh. But surely—I have seen the way he looks at you.'

'Lord Dereham desires me. It is not at all the same thing, believe me.'

'And?' Elinor prompted, her head cocked on one side like an inquisitive sparrow. Bel could feel the colour flooding her cheeks. 'Bel—you haven't? You and he are not…'

'Yes, we were.' It was highly improper to say any of

this to an unmarried young woman, but Elinor, at twenty-four, was hardly just out of the schoolroom. And Bel knew she could trust her. 'But not any more.'

'Why ever not?' Elinor was shockingly unshocked. She frowned in thought as though Bel's words were some obscure Greek text, then her brow cleared. 'I see. You have realised you love him and to continue as his lover is too painful when what you want is to be wed. He does not love you, but if you tell him how you feel he will be honour bound to offer for you and that would be intolerable.'

'You understand so clearly?' How did Elinor, who was apparently immune to thoughts of love, fathom that? Presumably by applying the same clear-eyed analysis that she used on ancient texts. 'I have been so confused, and then I realised how I felt about him and it was awful.'

'You *are* rather close to it. For someone not emotionally involved it is a simple matter of logic,' Elinor said tactfully. 'What are you going to do now? I can quite see how you would shrink from allowing him to glimpse your feelings.'

'I am going to run away to Margate. Will you come too?' Bel began to explain about the inn at St Lawrence's. 'We could take Brown and Lewin with us, along with a maid for the two of us, and a footman would be handy, I think. We could go down by river on the Margate packet. I am sure the boat journey will be more pleasant than the route by coach, and probably easier for the men than being shut up in a carriage for hours.' She watched Elinor anxiously. 'Would Aunt Louisa mind, do you think?'

'She is going to stay with Aunt and Uncle Augustus

for two weeks with the intention of subjecting Uncle's restoration proposals for the cathedral to the strictest scrutiny; believe me, she will not need me and I will be only too happy to escape the Palace.' Elinor slid her hand into Bel's lax one and gave it a squeeze. 'We will run away together and go dipping in the sea and be so shocking as to inspect inns with Brown and Lewin and take a subscription to the circulating library and read all the newest sensation novels and eat ice cream every day.'

The prospect of such mildly wicked entertainment made Bel smile faintly. 'And forget about men?'

'I do not have one to forget, but for you I doubt it will be that easy, not if you love Lord Dereham,' Elinor said frankly. 'I don't pretend to understand love, but I expect you will mope a little; I won't mind that, you mope as much as you like and I will read.'

'Oh, bless you.' The thought of uncomplicated feminine company was heaven. She made herself sit up straight and release Elinor's hand, doing her best to present a smiling face to the passers-by. 'Miss Layne!' Oh, dear, that was perhaps one female friend she did not want to have to talk to just at the moment. What if Patrick had said something about her to his sister, or she had guessed her brother might be harbouring a liking for Bel?

'What an interesting party this is.' Elinor moved along the seat to make space between herself and Bel and the poetess sat down. She was without a parasol and the tip of her nose was red with the sun, but she had her notebook open in her hand and Bel could see it was full of scribblings. 'I have lost my sunshade somewhere.' She flapped a hand vaguely. 'But I have so many notes. Have you seen Patrick, Lady Belinda?'

'He kindly took me out on the lake,' Elinor interjected, 'but I have not seen him for perhaps half an hour.' She must have decided that it would be a good idea to steer the conversation away from him, for she added chattily, 'Cousin Belinda and I were just making plans for a trip to Margate. We think we will go down on one of the packets; it will be quite an adventure.'

'What an excellent idea.' Miss Layne appeared quite struck by the notion. 'I was only saying to Patrick that I would like to go to the seaside now it is getting so hot, but that I find Brighton rather trying with so many of the Regent's cronies everywhere you go. I shall find him and suggest we follow your example.' She got to her feet and shut her notebook with a snap. 'When will you be going?'

'I...er...it is not yet quite decided,' Bel groped for an answer that did not sound discourteous. 'I have not yet secured accommodations.'

'Do, please, let me know as soon as it is settled. It will be so pleasant to have acquaintances there.' Miss Layne beamed at them and hurried off.

'Oh, dear, I had no idea she would take me up so!' Elinor said in dismay. 'And Mr Layne is certain to accompany her. We can hardly change our plans now.'

'Never mind.' It had been too good to be true, Bel thought. A fantasy of untroubled escape just as her love affair had been a fantasy of uncomplicated pleasure. 'It will give me the opportunity to make clear to Mr Layne that I cannot return his regard, I suppose.'

A perusal of the guidebooks at the library revealed that the Royal Hotel was considered to be the most eligible lodging. *'For neatness, comfort and luxury, the Royal Hotel will not suffer in comparison with any house in the country,'* Elinor read out. Bel, determined to fix her mind upon practical matters, conjured up a smile and hid her yawns behind the packet company's literature. Insomnia was claiming her nights again and she was doggedly ploughing her way through everything Lord Byron had written, trying to distract her mind from a flesh-and-blood man with the highly coloured adventures of the poet's heroes.

Confirmation of a suite being set aside for their convenience came by return, and Brown and Lewin assured Bel that they were more than capable of finding lodgings for themselves in the town once they arrived.

'I have tickets for the packet.' Bel opened a package delivered as she and Elinor sat at breakfast the day after Lady James had departed for her ecclesiastical holiday. She had left her daughter in Half Moon Street with a stack of reading matter, most of which Elinor ruthlessly stowed in a cupboard.

'I am taking nothing but frivolity and guidebooks,' she pronounced. 'When do we sail?'

'Tomorrow morning at seven.' Bel scrutinised the accompanying pamphlet. 'We leave from Ralph's Quay near Billingsgate and we should arrive in Margate at about three or four in the afternoon, depending on the wind.'

'There is a letter from Miss Layne.' Elinor flattened out the sheet. 'She says she had secured rooms at Wright's York Hotel on Marine Parade and leaves this morning. She and Mr Layne look forward to meeting us there...she will review all the subscription rooms to ascertain which is best in advance of our arrival.'

'At least they will not be in the same hotel, so it will be less difficult to avoid Mr Layne. If it were not for the awkwardness of that, I would be glad to have their company.' Bel said, turning over the remains of her post.

Nothing from Ashe, of course. Why should she expect it? She had thrown herself into his arms and then rebuffed him without explanation; the man would have to be a saint to overlook that, and, whatever else Ashe was, he was not a saint. The recollection of just how unsaintly Ashe could be burned through her like a draught of strong wine.

'What is that rueful smile about?' Elinor paused with a piece of bread and jam halfway to her lips. 'Mr Layne? You simply have to continue as before, only this time pretending you do not notice his partiality. Either he will take the hint or he will make a declaration.'

'I do not like to think I could hurt him,' Bel said, suddenly worried. 'It never occurred to me that he might feel like that about me until Ashe pointed it out. You do not think he feels strongly, do you?'

Elinor shrugged in a thoroughly unladylike manner. 'I have no experience of such matters—but you most certainly have not been encouraging him.'

'True.' Comforted, Bel wiped her fingers and gathered up the papers that strewed the breakfast table. 'There is a lot to do, and not much time. Certainly no time to sit around brooding about men. I think we had better make a list and divide things up between us.'

It had not occurred to Bel to spend her guineas on a private stateroom for the space of a few hours' voyage on a fine August day. The deck of the packet boat was spacious and tidy, with benches for those who wished to sit, and between them Brown, Lewin and Peter, the footman Aunt Louisa had left with Elinor, soon had their baggage piled up and securely corded under a tarpaulin.

Elinor, her bonnet inelegantly tied on with a shawl against sea breezes, was guarding a large picnic hamper. Bel strolled up and down the deck with Millie, the maid's eyes wide with the adventure of her first trip outside London, at her side. She surveyed her little party with proprietorial pride, just as Peter turned an unpleasant shade of green and rushed to the side to be comprehensively sick.

'We have not cast off yet!' Bel said with exasperated sympathy. 'Elinor, do you have anything we can dose him with?'

'I've just the thing, ma'am.' Brown produced a flask from under his greatcoat and hauled the unfortunate footman upright. Lewin pressed a blue-spotted handkerchief into Peter's hands. 'Come along, cully, we'll soon put the roses back in your cheeks,' Brown promised. 'Here you go, down the pointed end where the breeze is good and fresh.'

Bel watched the three of them passing the flask around. 'They'll have him as drunk as a lord by the time we get there,' she prophesied, then grinned, suddenly carefree at the thought of their unconventional day's holiday. 'What would your mama say if she could see us now?' she said to Elinor who was watching, wide-eyed, as a cit in a startlingly striped waistcoat pushed his wife, vast in pink bombazine, up the gangplank. Her shrieks of terror competed with the circling gulls.

'She would say that we had taken leave of our senses,' her cousin replied with a grin, jamming her hat down with one hand. 'Fun, isn't it?'

'Yes.' Bel smiled back. *I wonder what Ashe is doing.*

Chapter Nineteen

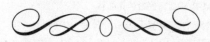

'I regret to say that Lady Belinda is not at home, my lord,' Hedges said.

'Then please give her my card and tell her I called. When do you expect that she will be returned?' Ashe reached into his breast pocket for his card case. There was something particularly expressionless about Bel's butler this morning. Almost disapproving, which was ridiculous. It was not Hedges's place to disapprove of him—unless whatever it was that had led to Bel's strange mood four days ago was infecting him also.

It had been hard to wait, to brood on what had happened in that dreamlike green space. In a moment Bel had turned from a passionate wanton in his arms to a stranger, rejecting him, spurning the kisses she had incited only seconds before. Ashe had paced the floor of his bedchamber, had sat silent and uncommunicative in his clubs, had thrown away good hands because he was not concentrating on play, and still he did not know what had happened.

It had hardly been something he had said—his mouth

had been on hers from the moment she had melted into his arms. So it had to be something in her head, something that had changed for Bel. And now her butler, who had always seemed to regard him with as much approval as such an individual ever showed, was fixing him with a chilly stare.

'Her ladyship is out of town, my lord.'

'Indeed? Where has she gone?'

'I could not say, my lord.'

Of course he could, Ashe thought, regarding the man through narrowed eyes. He could, but he would not. And that could only be because Bel had instructed the butler not to tell him. Hence Hedges's air of disapproval; it would be enough to be told her ladyship did not want her whereabouts communicated to Lord Dereham for that to be taken as an indication that he had upset her.

His fingers closed around the coins in his pocket, then relaxed. Hedges was not the sort of upper servant who would accept a guinea or two to flout his mistress's instructions.

'Yes, I am sure that is the case.' Ashe allowed the edge of his temper to show. 'Are you forwarding her correspondence to her ladyship?'

'I have specific instructions as to which items to forward, my lord.' He realised suddenly that Hedges was enjoying this as little as he was.

'Her ladyship is well, I trust?'

There was an hesitation, the merest flicker of the studiedly blank expression. 'Her ladyship enjoys her usual good health. If there is nothing else, my lord?'

'No, thank you, Hedges.' Ashe turned and walked slowly down the steps as the door closed behind him.

Her customary good health, but not, he would guess, *her customary good spirits*. And what was the matter with him? Moping because, for once, a mistress had taken the initiative and ended a relationship?

Yes, that for sure. He could identify the coiling strands of wounded pride and frustrated passion knotting in his stomach. But there was something else. He wanted Bel, all of Bel, not just her body. His feet carried him around the curve of Half Moon Street and into the turmoil of Piccadilly. Ashe stared at it as though seeing it through glass a foot thick. What was he doing here? This was unreal, irrelevant, unimportant. He shook his head, trying to clear it, then set off up the slope towards the Albany. What he wanted—no, needed—to do must wait until nightfall.

Distantly a clock struck two. Under his hand the key turned in the lock and the garden door swung open on to darkness. Ashe eased off his shoes and padded along the corridor, into the hall and up the stairs to Bel's bedchamber. Around him the house breathed in its sleep, timber softly creaking, clocks ticking, the soundless pad of the kitchen cat's hunting footsteps.

It held people, sleeping, but it did not hold Bel. He could feel her absence as a physical thing as he opened the door to what had once been his room, the long-familiar embossing of the door handle reassuring to his hand.

Inside the faint light from the street picked up the great white fur sprawled before the cold hearth, the glint of glass eyes in the head turned snarling towards him.

'Hello, Horace.' Ashe shrugged out of his coat and

folded down cross-legged on to the thick fur. It yielded beneath him and he flattened his palms at his sides, letting his fingers thread into the pelt. The faint smell as he disturbed it was of dusty old fur, of wood ash and of Bel.

Ashe allowed his shoulders to relax and drop, lifted his hands to his knees and let them rest, palm up, cupped. He felt his breathing slow and his mind clear. Long ago, at school, he had learned this from a fellow pupil, the son of a maharajah, sent to the cold, harsh world of an English education. Ashe had befriended the slender, golden-skinned, terrified boy and had marvelled at his poise and his resilience as he adapted to this hostile new world.

And in return for Ashe's cutting tongue and ready fists, both deployed in his defence, his new friend had taught him a secret. He could not remember now what this strange weapon of the mind was called, only that he had used it before battle, when his father had died so suddenly and when Katy had been taken dangerously ill with a fever and the whole family despaired for her life. It left him focused and strong and calm. Now he turned it inwards to try to read his own heart.

The clocks in the house struck and tinkled and chimed the quarters as Ashe sat there, his eyes wide open on to the darkness, his fingers sliding from his knees to mesh in the thick fur. When five clear chimes reached him, each as distinct as a hammer blow, the answer came with them, the words, clear on his lips. 'I love her.'

The relief of understanding his own feelings washed through him, breaking his calm, and Ashe jerked to his feet and began to pace. He had been right when he had said to Bel that surely love was something you recognised when you felt it. The moment he had stopped fighting against it, it claimed him.

Bel had come to fill his mind, his thoughts, his dreams. She had slipped in there without him being conscious of it, driving away his nightmares of battle, replacing them with the sweetness of her, the ache of needing her.

The sheer physicality of this new emotion surprised him. He wanted to shout, to run, to ride at the gallop to wherever Bel was, take her in his arms and shower her with kisses.

But the woman he loved did not want his kisses any more, she was not in love with him and she did not want to marry him.

Ashe found himself by the fur again and sat down abruptly, the burst of energy vanishing as fast as it had seized him. Bel had rejected him and she had fled from him—why, he had no idea. He needed to find her and then, assuming he managed that, he must persuade her to marry him.

Damn it, he thought with a flash of anger, he was eligible enough. Once his mother began to whisper that he was in the market for a wife, every single lady under the age of thirty would be trotted out for his inspection. But he wanted none of them. He wanted the one single lady in society who did not want marriage—or, it seemed, him.

Simply proposing was not going to do the trick, she would just refuse. If he made a declaration of love, she would counter with her accusation of emotional black-mail. So he would have to court her, something he had never had to do before with any woman, and he had to do it without making her feel trapped. Before he had met Bel, Ashe would have accepted quite easily the proposition that he could make a lady fall in love with him if he exerted himself enough. Now that smug masculine confidence deserted him and in its place was a growing chill, the thought of what his life would be like without her now that he knew that he loved her.

'One battle at a time,' he murmured to Horace, pulling the moth-eaten ear nearest to him. 'I've got to find her first.'

The effect of a virtually sleepless night and the pressing request from Lady Dereham to join her and her daughters at the breakfast table in the town house, at an hour which he stigmatised to his valet as the *crack of dawn*, had Ashe stifling his yawns and gazing with unfocused eyes at the back page of *The Times*.

Around him his sisters prattled happily of their plans for the seaside while his mother slit the wafers on her morning's correspondence. 'Excellent!' He glanced up to see she was scanning some missive or another and went back to his sightless contemplation of an advertisement for a new three-volume work on Classical mythology, a subject in which he had no interest whatsoever.

'Reynard!' From the tone, she had obviously already addressed him. Ashe forced his mind back to the present and away from plans to hire Bow Street Runners to check at every tollgate out of London for sightings of Bel's carriage.

'Mama?' He folded the news sheet neatly beside his plate and assumed an expression of filial attentiveness.

'I have here confirmation from the best hotel in Margate that I have secured their most superior apartments for three weeks. I shall write and cancel Brighton immediately.'

'Margate? But, Mama, the shops…' Frederica wailed.

'But the parties at the Castle Inn…' That was Anna.

'I wanted to drive a donkey cart again,' Katy said mulishly.

'I have been worried for some time about the tone of some members of society one finds at Brighton at this time of year,' Lady Dereham pronounced. 'Too many rakes and beaux. And the sea bathing at Margate is much superior, the beach is sand and the bay well sheltered.'

'This is rather sudden, is it not, Mama?' Ashe asked, frowning at her. There was something that did not quite ring true about his mother's explanations.

'I have been thinking about it ever since Lady Belinda Felsham told me she was going there.' She paused and studied Ashe. 'Your mouth is open, dear.'

He shut it with a snap. 'Be…Lady Belinda has gone to Margate?' *It is going to be this simple to find her?*

'Yes, with her cousin and the Laynes, I believe,' his mother said tranquilly. He almost took her tone at its face value, then something in the closeness with which she was watching him caught his attention. This was nothing to do with dubious company at Brighton—Lady Belinda had caught his mother's eye as a suitable bride. He frowned, deliberately, and saw the anxiety in her eyes.

'Do you still wish me to accompany you?' Ashe let a faint tinge of reluctance colour his voice. 'I had made plans to meet a number of friends in Brighton. I suppose I could go there and travel round the coast once or twice to see you.' To have discovered Bel's whereabouts so easily was a miracle, but he had no intention of letting his mother guess he had already lost his heart. This wooing was going to need subtlety, not the intervention of well-meaning relatives.

'I am sorry to disrupt your plans, dear,' Lady Dereham said hastily, 'but I really do feel I would need you more than ever in a strange resort.'

Ashe pursed his lips and regarded the four pairs of eyes fixed on his face. It was cruel to tease them, and, if they could only guess, he was within an inch of leaping to his feet and hugging his mother out of sheer gratitude. 'In that case, of course I will accompany you,' he said, smiling, and trying to ignore the sensation in the pit of his stomach that was warning him that it was only the easy part out of the way. Now he had to woo his reluctant love.

'Do you intend to dip?' Miss Layne viewed the ranks of bathing machines drawn up on the sweep of golden tan sand below the Marine Parade dubiously.

The two parties had exchanged notes the night before and had met by agreement outside one of the numerous establishments advertising steam and vapour baths, warm saltwater baths and attended dipping from the shelter of a bathing machine.

'I *think* so.' Elinor, equally dubious, watched a female bather, clad head to foot in fashionable attire, being helped up the steps into a bathing machine. The horse was harnessed to the shafts and a muscular woman kilted up her skirts and hauled herself up on to the seat beside the driver. The vehicle set off down the beach and into the mild surf. Once the water was up to the base of the compartment, the driver slid down, unhitched the horse and rode it back up, ready for the next customer.

'What is she doing now?' Miss Layne enquired, raising her eyeglass in an effort to see better. 'Patrick, you have a telescope.'

'And I am certainly not going to deploy it upon a bathing machine occupied by a female,' he said with a grin. 'What sort of fellow do you take me for? Do you want me escorted off by the beadle?'

'I only want to see what is happening,' his sister protested. 'Oh, look, the woman is letting down the hood.' Sure enough, a great canvas awning was falling down to shield the entrance into the machine and covering an area of sea quite one hundred feet square, by Bel's estimation.

'There is enough space to swim in,' she said thoughtfully. The idea of being forcibly dunked by one of the large dippers was not appealing, but she could swim quite well and the thought of doing so in the sea was very tempting.

'It all looks far too cold and exposed for my liking.' Miss Layne shivered. 'I intend to take one of the warm water baths. What about you, Patrick?'

'Oh, I shall swim,' he said. 'Without the assistance of one of the dippers, I might add. Shall I go and find out what is the best time to come back this afternoon?'

'If you would, dear. I shall go and put my name down for a warm bath.'

'Please, add mine,' Elinor added hastily. 'The more I think about it, the less I fancy all that cold water.'

Bel adjusted her parasol to shield her cheeks from the sun and sat down upon one of the benches that lined the Marine Parade. The scene on the beach below was sufficiently engrossing to while away any amount of time, and beyond the bay there were the comings and goings at the pier to add animation.

Behind her a chattering group of washerwomen strode up the hill, their baskets overflowing with towels from the various bathing establishments and sweating porters in their white smocks struggled with the luggage from the packet boats and hoys newly tied up.

She eyed the ladies timorously walking out to the bathing machines, studying their complex bathing costumes. Her own, an elaborate confection of pink and green fabric, had fluttering green zigzag trim at the hem and neck, which she suspected was supposed to be seaweed. The only relevance it had to bathing, as far as she could make out, was that it was cotton and would therefore dry easily, and fastened at the front, which would make it easy to undress to reveal the utilitarian flannel garment beneath in which she was supposed to take to the waters. Bel had no intention of trying to swim in that. Thanks to the all-covering hoods, invented fifty years before by the enterprising Mr Beale, she could disport herself naked in perfect modesty, just as that worthy Quaker had intended.

And as the men still did, she thought, rather naughtily letting her gaze stray along the beach to where the men's machines were drawn up. Gentlemen were strolling down to those in light cotton trousers and shirts, straw hats tipped negligently over their brows. As she watched, a tall figure came into view, raised his hat in response to a greeting from a fellow bather and the breath caught in her throat. Blond hair glinted in the sunshine and no one else, surely, moved with quite that long-limbed elegance?

'Ashe?' Her fingers clenched around the iron rail

and she gave a little gasp of pain as the rough, rusty surface cut into her thin cotton gloves. He had followed her here? Somehow, despite the fact that she had told her staff to refuse to say where she had gone, he had found her. Bel sat quite still, the joy bubbling within her, as she watched him swing up easily into the bathing machine and disappear inside the wooden cabin.

'Bel? We are ready to go now.' Elinor and the Laynes stood beside her, eager to be off on the next part of their morning's exploration. 'We are going to take out subscriptions at the lending library, don't you remember?'

'Oh. Yes, of course. Only it is so lovely here, I think I will just sit a little and take in the air. You register my name for me, please, Elinor.' Ashe cared for her—there was no other explanation for the fact that he had abandoned his family party and come here. 'It is quite all right,' she said, urging a dubious Elinor to follow the Laynes towards the High Street. 'I will be quite safe— look how many respectable families there are here.'

Ashe's bathing machine began to move, down to the sea. In her mind's eye she could imagine him in the dark space, stripping off his clothes, bracing himself with those long, muscular legs against the sway of the vehicle, stepping out into the light under the canvas and…

'There are, indeed,' Elinor exclaimed with a laugh. 'Look who is walking down the hill towards us—Lady Dereham and all three girls.'

'*What?*' Bel swung round as Elinor waved and Katy ran to meet her.

'Good morning, Miss Ravenhurst, Lady Belinda! Isn't this exciting? I was disappointed about Brighton, but this will be just as good and Frederica is taking me bathing tomorrow!'

'Yes, very exciting,' Bel agreed, the backwash of disappointment leaving her queasy with reaction. Ashe hadn't come for her after all, he had come with his family. He had no idea she was here. She made herself stand up as Lady Dereham and her two elder daughters reached her and shook hands, finding a bright social smile from somewhere. 'What a surprise, I thought you were fixed upon Brighton this summer.'

'And you are all here together?' Elinor asked, earning her Bel's undying gratitude.

'Yes, indeed. Reynard had gone sea bathing.'

'No doubt he was surprised I had recommended Margate,' Bel remarked idly.

'I did not mention that you had done so.' Lady Dereham watched her daughters petting a small dog another promenader had at the end of a green cord. 'Although I am sure your opinion would have weighed with him if I had needed to use any persuasion.'

So Ashe had no idea that she was there. The last trickle of hope ebbed away. After the way she had reacted at the picnic, she should have had no hope that he would have any interest in her any more and yet some foolish part of her heart held on to the dream that he did care for her, more than as a lover and a friend.

The awning at the seaward end of his bathing machine unfurled itself to the waves. Bel dragged her gaze away and fiddled unnecessarily with her parasol. 'I am afraid we must catch up with our friends the Laynes, but I am sure we will meet again, Lady Dereham.'

'You have gone very pale,' Elinor observed as they walked up the gentle hill towards the circulating library. 'Was it a very great shock to discover Lord Dereham is here?'

'I thought—just for a moment—that he had sought me out and followed me,' Bel confessed. 'Such foolishness, after the way I snubbed his advances. Why should he?' Elinor opened her mouth to respond. 'That was a rhetorical question,' Bel added with a glimmer of a smile as they reached the door of the library and Patrick Layne came to open it for them. 'I know the answer perfectly well.'

Chapter Twenty

Ashe eased his shoulders more comfortably against the stack of casks and watched the entrance to the Royal Hotel with the same stoical patience he had exhibited for the past hour. Surely Bel had to come out some time? Luncheon was long over, the sun was shining, the crowds were promenading. One did not come to a seaside resort to sit inside one's hotel.

Unless, of course, meeting his mother and sisters had made her keep to her room to avoid seeing him. But that was not like Bel, he told himself. She had too much pride to skulk. If she did not want to see him, she was more than capable of sweeping past him with her nose in the air. He just wished he had a rational plan for courting her.

That damned Patrick Layne was here with his feet well and truly under the table, whatever his sister said about his lack of suitability for Bel. His unpredictable love was upset and who knows what she might do, who she might turn to? If he caught that man pressing his attentions on her... Ashe grimaced and relaxed his hands that had balled into fists. If Bel wanted Layne's attentions, then who was he to stand in her way? He was her discarded lover, not her husband and not her betrothed. He had no rights.

The doorman at the Royal hurried into the street, bowing and scraping as Bel, Elinor and their maid came out. Ashe straightened up, keeping in the shadows, his eyes hungry on Bel's face. She was wearing an expression that he knew signified embarrassment and determination. When he dragged his eyes from her face to look at the whole of her, he saw why and could not repress a smile.

It was a puzzle why otherwise rational females should find sea bathing an excuse to wear quite ludicrous garments, but they did and it appeared that his love was not immune from this form of lunacy, even if she had the taste to be highly dubious about the result.

Falling in behind the three women at a discreet distance, Ashe was able to admire the froth of seaweed-green pinked ruffles around the hem of the garment, the lurid green and white peppermint stripes of Bel's canvas half-boots and the plume of feathers that threatened to dislodge the utterly impractical bonnet which crowned her head. Under this rig she was doubtless clad in an all-covering flannel shift to preserve her from the gaze of any lecherous crabs or lobsters that came within range.

Ashe grinned as he walked, his mood lifting as he imagined Bel being ruthlessly dunked by one of the muscular female dippers whose job it was to ensure their shrinking charges received the regulation three total immersions that medical opinion had decided was the best for health. She would emerge from the experience shaken and probably grateful for a nice cup of hot chocolate and an ice provided by a friend. He would be careful to behave in a completely neutral manner, do nothing to alarm her, appear delighted that she was so comprehensively chaperoned. Do everything, in effect, to try to stop her associating him with naked, uninhibited, physical passion.

Bel waved to Elinor and the maid and descended the steps to the beach. The other two women walked on to the entrance to the warm baths together and vanished inside. Ashe hitched one hip on the balustrade and waited until at length Bel reappeared on the beach below in vigorous discussion with a stalwart dipping woman. She appeared to be refusing something, then the woman helped her up the steps into a bathing machine and walked back up the sand. The driver backed a horse into the shafts and the machine set off down the beach.

She was going to go in without a dipper, relying, as he had earlier, on raising the little flag on top of the machine when she wanted the driver to return. Ashe found he was running down the steps without consciously making a plan.

'Sir? Looking to go in again, sir?' It was the proprietor who had rented out the machine he had used that morning.

'Yes,' Ashe nodded. 'Straight away, if you please.'

The door closed, leaving Bel in near darkness. Light filtered through cracks in the wooden walls of the hut on wheels in which she was enclosed and she wondered why no one had thought to put windows in the roof. She reached out her hands and found she could just touch the planks on either side. Beneath her feet what felt like wet carpet squelched. With a lurch the vehicle began to move and Bel sat down hard on the narrow wooden seat that ran front to back. Above her head there was a shelf for her outer clothes and for the pile of towels that were provided as part of the fee of one shilling. She had saved three pence by not taking a dipper's services, although she had tipped the woman for helping her in and explaining the limited facilities.

The machine lurched again and there was a strange slapping noise, which Bel realised was the waves splashing up under the floor. Hastily she took off her bonnet, laid it on the shelf and began to unbutton her gown. At least it was easy to get out of, leaving her in the sack-like grey flannel bathing shift. She eased off her half-boots and stockings and stood up uneasily on the cold and sodden carpet while she stacked everything carefully away.

The machine stopped. There was movement outside, then a rattle and a flap and the driver shouted, 'All set!' Bel waited a moment, then lifted the bar on the door and peeped out, blinking in the brightly lit space. All around was the white canvas hood of the bathing machine, at her feet the green water, swelling up to splash her feet as she hesitated at the top of the steps. Below, the sand shimmered in shafts of sunlight and a shoal of tiny fish flashed across the space and were gone.

From outside she could hear the screech of gulls, the shouts of excited children, the cries of the sailors manning the vessels further out in the bay, but here, in her own little sea world, all was tranquil.

Bel dipped a cautious toe in the water that was chuckling and splashing over the top step. It was cold, but only, she guessed, in contrast to her warm feet. Sunlight reflected on the ridged sand, sparkling off a shell as she gazed down, mesmerised. The skirts of the flannel shift flapped around her calves and, impatient, she pulled it off over her head and tossed it on to the bench.

Walk down the steps or jump? Bel took a deep breath and jumped, plunging under the water, then coming up with a shriek that was half-shock, half childlike delight to be in the sea. She found she could stand on the bottom, her shoulders out of the water. Between her toes the sand sifted delightfully and she wriggled them, scaring the inquisitive little fish as she pushed back the soaking mane of hair from her face.

It felt quite different from the still, greenish waters of the lake where she had learned to swim. This water was vibrant, shimmering, alive with wavelets, and her whole body came to life with the sensual caress. Bel kicked off and swam up to the edge of the canvas, then turning, back across the width, delighting in the buoyancy of the salt water.

She stood, running her hands down her body, shivering with the sensual freedom of being naked in this translucent world. But already the restriction of the enclosure was frustrating her—she wanted to swim free, watch the horizon. Daring, Bel ducked her head under the water and opened her eyes. For a moment it stung and the image blurred, then she could see all round her own bathing machine for yards on all sides. Dare she swim under the awning's edge and pop her head up like a seal in open water?

No, of course not, it was a scandalous thought. Bel dived again and lifted a shell from the sand. Increasingly confident, she swam as far under the water as the awning, then under it, then with a panicky flick of her feet, turned and hastened back into her safe cocoon.

There was another shell. She dived for that, then hung in the water with it clenched in her fist as she tried to make sense of the dark shape she could see coming towards her. That had not been there before—a seal? A shark? Bel surfaced, spluttering and paddled back to the steps in a panicky flurry of foam just as the shape slipped under the edge of the awning and surfaced. Not a fish, not a sea mammal. A man.

'Ashe!' Without thought Bel tumbled down the steps and into his arms. He was naked, sleek with water, his hair otter-dark, his skin cool over the hard heat beneath. Bel wrapped her arms around as much of him as she could and clung. 'Ashe—oh, but I have missed you.'

'How can you complain about missing me, you ran away,' he countered reasonably, lifting her under her arms so that she slid up his chest. 'Put your legs round my waist.' It was an utterly indecent position and one that demonstrated clearly that cold sea water had no effect at all on the evidence of how much he had missed her.

Something—common sense, she supposed—struggled to make itself heard. 'This is so wicked!'

'Pleasantly wicked?'

'Yes,' Bel confessed, blissfully overwhelmed by the shock and the sensation of wet, naked man holding her so close. 'Oh, Ashe, I do—' She almost blurted it out, the way she felt about him. Bel smothered her own words against his mouth, losing herself in the heat and the demand of his possession, rubbing her body shamelessly against his, all her reservations about making love with him again swept away. Vaguely she was aware that she was going to regret this later, but now she did not care.

Ashe lifted her again, wriggled his hips and slid into her in one smooth thrust, making her gasp at the heat of him filling her. 'Lie back and float,' he commanded, letting her go, and she did, her legs holding her tight to him, the bobbing movement of the swell sending *frisson* after *frisson* of pleasure shooting through her as their joined bodies rocked. Bel closed her eyes as he began to run his hands over her breasts, teasing the nipples under the water so they peaked as hard as tiny beach pebbles between his tormenting fingertips. It felt as though they were making love in the clouds, almost weightless, flying.

All the sensations were subtly different, she could not relate anything her body was feeling to what she had experienced before. Adrift, yet anchored, ecstatic yet fearful, Bel opened her eyes to find his on her face, wide and blue, darker than the sea, deeper than the sea, drowning her. 'Ashe!'

I love you! He wanted to shout it; instead, he took Bel by the shoulders and hauled her back desperately against him, murmuring the words over and over into her mouth as she opened for him, letting him feast on the salty tang of her lips as he lost himself in her. His hands were cupped around her hips, holding her as he braced his feet on the firm sand and began to thrust. He was not going to be able to hold on for long, he needed her too much. The thought came like a lightning flash behind his closed lids: *Don't withdraw, get her with child, she will have to marry you then.* He fought it, knowing it was wrong, wanting nothing more in the world than Bel, blossoming with their child.

Bel was clinging to him as if for life itself, her mouth free of his now, her lips roaming frantically over his neck, his shoulder, wherever she could reach, her breath gasping as he plunged into her, deeper than he had ever been. He felt the pleasure take her, throw her over the edge beyond reason as her head fell back on a sobbing cry and with an effort he did not know he was capable of, Ashe lifted her away from him, holding her tight as he shook with the force of his own release.

'Oh,' she murmured softly against his neck as he forced his shaking legs to walk to the steps, climb them and sit down at the top, holding her.

He felt like a sea god, like Neptune on his throne with a nymph in his arms, capable of anything, lord of all he surveyed. 'Oh,' Bel said again. 'That was so…so…' Ashe rested his cheek on her hair as he thought of some of the adjectives. *Wonderful, blissful, astonishing, perfect.* Whatever had been wrong at the picnic was now all right again.

'I was never going to do that again,' she said ruefully, her breath fanning warm on his wet chest, shattering his new-found security.

'Why not?' He knew he sounded harsh, did not care.

'It is wrong,' she said sadly, slipping out of his grasp and down into the water, hanging there, her hair fanning out around her, her eyes solemn on his face. His own mermaid.

'Why? Why now is it wrong and before it was not? Explain to me. What has changed, Bel?'

'I have changed.' A shoal of fish darted across the space behind her, a flash of silver that drew his eyes from her for a moment. When he looked back, she was rubbing her hand across her eyes.

'Bel? Are you crying?' Ashe pushed off the steps and stood beside her. What cause had she to weep? It was his heart that she was breaking. He lifted his hand and brushed the back of it across her cheek, the feeling of tenderness for her struggling with the urge to shake her until she explained, told him she loved him.

'No, just salt in my eyes.' She turned her cheek against his hand for a moment. She was a very poor liar, Ashe thought. 'I must go and get dressed. We should not be here like this.'

'In my arms just now you were like molten silver. It hurts you to turn me away—you want to cry. Just now I felt what you felt and it was not wrong, Bel.' She glanced up, the reflection of his desperation stamped on her face.

'It is wrong in my heart,' she said and reached up to him, pulling his head down to hers, finding his mouth with desperate lips. She kissed and clung as he fought to be gentle, not to ravage her mouth with the love and frustration and incomprehension that was filling him. She pulled back, her mouth a whisper from his and murmured something, so softly that all he could sense was the movement of her lips. What had she said? *This is breaking my heart?*

'Go now.' She stepped back, her cold hands pushing against his chest. She was shivering now, from chill or emotion he had no idea, but he could not let her stand here like this while he struggled to understand.

'Yes, I will go.' Ashe made himself smile, saw the answering curve of her lips as she tried to send him reassurance. Which of them was reassuring the other, and what about? he wondered bitterly, with one long last look at her before he dived under the edge of the awning and kicked hard in the direction of his own bathing machine.

He surfaced, tossing his hair back from his face and climbed into the cabin of the machine, reaching for a towel and rubbing with painful vigour over his salty wet skin, haunted by the thought of Bel drying herself alone, just a few yards away.

Ashe had no difficulty cataloguing the emotions that were warring within him. Hurt masculine pride, frustrated love, baffled incomprehension were uppermost. He dismissed the first, despising himself for it, absorbed the aching hurt of the second and wrestled with the third as he dragged his thin cotton trousers on over still-damp skin.

If he had done something to hurt her, she would have told him so, she would certainly not have gone into his arms with that uncomplicated passion he had just experienced. If there was another man, she would have told him that too—and she certainly would not have allowed him to so much as kiss her cheek. And she was unhappy, so unhappy. Yet that was the one thing she would not explain.

Ashe tied his neckcloth in a slipshod knot and dragged on his coat, then reached out and pulled on the cord that would raise the flag to summon the horse and driver. Something was stirring inside him; then he realised what it was—hope. If Bel was unhappy, it was because she did not want to renounce him. Something was making her do it, not her own inclinations. All he had to do was to find out what—or who—was behind this and then his way would be clear.

Ashe stood in the doorway as the sound of the horse splashing through the water reached him and the driver began to haul up the awning. He shut the door and perched on the outside bench as the animal was backed into the shafts. The flag was up on Bel's bathing machine too. *I am going to marry you, Belinda Cambourn*, he vowed silently, as the machine lurched back to shore. *Court you, win you, wed you.*

Chapter Twenty-One

She had three choices, Bel told herself as she sat giving a good imitation of a woman deeply engrossed in Ackermann's *Repository of Arts, Literature and Fashions &c*. Distracted for a moment, she wondered what the *&c* covered, then flattened the journal open at the section of 'General Observations on Fashions and Dress'. A lady might be excused for sitting in Garner's reading rooms staring at that for quite some time.

Three choices. She could flee back to London, either dragging poor Elinor with her or leaving her with Miss Layne. On the face of it, that was the easy thing to do, for it would remove her completely from Ashe and she had proved only yesterday that she was completely incapable of behaving with any restraint or sense the moment he touched her.

On the other hand, it was cowardly to run away and most unfair on her cousin and on Brown and Lewin, who were expecting her to go and look at their inn that afternoon. And how would she ever learn to live without Ashe if she could not confront this?

Or she could stay here in Margate and do everything possible to avoid seeing him. Which would involve dodging round like a criminal and giving offence to Lady Dereham and her daughters.

Or she could steel herself to meeting him socially, act as though there was nothing but acquaintance and their mutual interest in the wounded soldiers between them. Which would be so hard when she feared that her love must show in her eyes every time she looked at him, and her hand was trembling even now, just thinking about him. She must compose herself, think of light subjects for conversation, prepare her defences thoroughly.

'Good morning, Lady Belinda.' The journal fell from her hands to the floor and Miss Katy Reynard hastened to pick it up and smooth the crumpled pages. 'I do beg your pardon, I made you jump. There, I do not think the fashion plates are damaged.'

'Thank you.' Bel accepted it back and fixed the smile on her lips before she looked beyond the girl. The entire Reynard family was there. So much for preparation. She rose to shake hands with Lady Dereham and the two elder sisters. 'Good morning, you find me very reprehensibly immersed in the latest fashions.'

'That I confess is our intention also,' Lady Dereham admitted. 'At least, to provide ourselves with some light reading of various sorts. We are taking a foot tour of the town to view all its amenities and for Reynard to call at the bank.'

Bel made herself look beyond the ladies to where Ashe was standing, a folded newspaper in one hand, his hat in the other. He bowed gravely and she inclined her head. *There, that was easy. I did not faint, nor fly into his arms and no one has remarked upon any peculiarity in our manner.* Then she met his eyes and read neither desire nor anger, but something new, intense and strange. The pulse in her throat fluttered and she looked away hastily.

'Have you seen the sea view from here? It is very fine.' Frederica, who was perusing a copy of the *New Margate Guide*, unwittingly came to her rescue, pointing from the window. 'There are the towers of Reculver church, see? There is such a romantic story here about how they came to be built.' She began to read as her brother came to stand next to Bel.

'Lady Belinda. We are taking a carriage for a drive along the coast to Broadstairs this afternoon. Would you care to join us?'

'How kind of you to ask. But I have an engagement this afternoon—perhaps some other time?' Bel looked down and saw the journal was crumpled in her grip. Now she would have to buy it. 'Oh, dear, look at that,' she said, trying to flatten it again, making a business of it to draw those steady blue eyes away from her face for a few moments of relief.

'Allow me.' Ashe took it and strode off to the counter.

'Lord Dereham!' He was already paying. 'Thank you, but that is very extravagant.'

'Four shillings? Merely the cost of four uses of a bathing machine—without an attendant,' he observed blandly as she twitched the neat parcel from his grip. 'Now tell me, where are you going this afternoon? Is Layne escorting you?'

What was that? A flicker of jealousy? 'No,' Bel responded with composure, deciding to use shock tactics. 'I am meeting Brown and Lewin in a public house.'

'Brown and—' He frowned. 'Two of your soldiers? The big one who growls if anyone comes near you and his friend with the damaged throat?' She nodded. Of course he would remember; a good officer knew the names of all his men. 'What are you up to, Be…Lady Belinda?'

'Brown found details of an inn for sale in St Lawrence, on the London road out of Ramsgate. He thinks it might be suitable for quite a number of the men to run together.'

She had expected that she would have to persuade the others on the committee that this was a good idea, but not, apparently, Ashe. He was nodding. 'A good idea. They know horses, they know how to work as a team, some of them will be able to cook and all of them will know about beer.'

Bel felt her spirits lift at his response and found herself smiling. 'Brown can run it, he was a sergeant.'

'I thought he might have been. What did he do?'

'Swore at a young lieutenant—he would not say any more.'

Ashe grinned. 'I would have liked to have seen that—he strikes me as a man who does not suffer fools gladly. And how much is it? Can we afford it?'

'I intend purchasing it myself, as an investment.' Bel found that she was tensed for his response and her chin was up. 'If it is suitable, of course. Lewin was a book keeper, he is checking the records.'

'You have it all worked out,' Ashe said. His tone was pleasant, but there was an edge under the words. 'You did not see fit to consult the rest of the committee? Or perhaps that is why Layne is here.'

'No, I shall look at it first. I found myself wanting

to leave London and this seemed as good a destination and reason as any,' Bel responded. There must have been something in her voice, for she saw Lady Dereham glance in her direction. 'Miss Layne heard we were coming down and found the idea attractive,' she added with a completely contrived smile.

'I will accompany you,' Ashe said abruptly.

'You are already committed to your family for this afternoon,' Bel pointed out, strolling nearer to the others who were grouped around Frederica, reading aloud from the guidebook about the ruined church at Reculver.

'...*we recollect the pious labours of those ladies who raised these sacred fanes in commemoration of their escape from a watery grave, and as landmarks to the adventurous mariner, whereby he may avoid those dangerous shallows which wrecked their brittle barque.* And it is about to fall into the sea, along with the remains of a Roman fortress,' she added.

'Nothing endures for ever,' her mother observed. 'Reynard?'

'I was going to ask if you would mind very much if we changed our drive to tomorrow, Mama. The weather seems set fair for several days and I find that Lady Belinda has located a suitable source of employment for some of our soldiers and has an appointment to view it this afternoon. I do not feel she should be doing so unescorted.'

'But of course.' Lady Dereham smiled approval. 'I have not the slightest objection and, naturally, Lady Belinda should be escorted.'

'I would not dream of disrupting your plans,' Bel protested, vaguely aware of someone else approaching their group but too concerned with not finding herself tête-à-tête with Ashe for an afternoon to look. 'I will have my cousin's company and two of the soldiers…'

'May I be of service? Good morning.' It was Patrick Layne, smiling, bowing, shaking hands. 'I could not but help overhear—are these our soldiers you speak of, Lady Belinda?'

She did not want him either. Bel bit down on a sharp request that the men simply leave her alone, and explained all over again about the inn. Hopefully it would shock Lady Dereham that Bel should involve herself in such a thing and she would cease to urge Ashe to accompany her.

'What a good idea,' Ashe's mother said warmly, dashing that hope. 'But you must certainly have a gentleman's escort.'

'She has it,' Ashe said. Bel thought she could detect teeth being gritted.

'But you have your delightful family to look after,' Patrick intervened. 'My sister has made it very clear to me that she is spending the entire day immersed in her latest poem, so I am entirely at your disposal, Lady Belinda.'

'As am I,' Ashe said. It was less a grit, more of a snarl this time.

'Perhaps you should both come.' Elinor appeared, somewhat dusty, from the depths of the book stacks. 'Good morning, everyone, do excuse me, but I have just discovered an excellent antiquities section including a book my mother has been anxious to acquire and I was quite absorbed.' She beamed equally upon the men. 'After all, there are two ladies to escort.'

'There, now,' Lady Dereham said peaceably, 'that solves that. I am more than happy for you to take my barouche, Reynard.'

'I have found a pamphlet of walks in the vicinity,' Anna added. 'There is one to a delightful-sounding pleasure gardens just a mile and a half away, called Dandelion of all things! Shall we go there this afternoon, Mama?'

The Reynards made plans and polite conversation with Patrick while Bel bit her lip and restrained herself from taking Elinor by the elbow, marching her off and demanding just what she thought she was doing, saddling her with two antagonistic men. And what was Ashe about? She had expected almost anything other than this degree of attentiveness in full view of his family. It was almost as if he were paying court to her.

Which was ridiculous. Bel studied him from beneath her lashes as he chatted easily with Elinor, drawing her out and making her laugh. He turned his head suddenly and caught her watching him. One eyebrow rose inter-rogatively and she made herself stare haughtily back—which was a mistake. Ashe smiled and her heart stuttered in her chest, then he was serious again, listen-ing to her cousin. He knew she would not be his lover again, he knew she did not want to marry again. No, she corrected herself, he *thought* he knew she did not want to marry again. Which was, unless she was prepared to risk her pride and her dignity and what remained of her battered heart, how things would remain. For ever.

'If you will excuse me, I must go and do some shopping. Cousin Elinor, would you prefer me to leave Millie with you, or the footman?'

Ashe made himself stand, as though simply waiting for Miss Ravenhurst to turn her attention back to him. He kept his eyes on her face and did not indulge in the luxury of watching Bel as she walked away.

'What exactly are you up to, Miss Ravenhurst?' he enquired softly as Elinor turned back to him. The redhead coloured up, but she maintained her composure.

'Up to, my lord? I am afraid I do not follow you.'

'Why are you encouraging Layne to dangle after your cousin?' He watched the other man warily, but he was helping Katy focus the reading-room telescope on the end of the harbour wall and appeared quite unconscious of being under scrutiny.

'Perhaps I wanted his company myself, my lord,' Elinor suggested outrageously. 'I doubt if my cousin will object if I flirt with him all afternoon.'

'I have observed Lady Belinda's previous efforts to pair you off with Layne, Miss Ravenhurst—you are not going to convince me that you are angling for his attentions.'

'And if you have observed so much, Lord Dereham, you should realise that Belinda is not angling for them either.' She regarded him shrewdly, an uncomfortable echo of her formidable mother in her expression. 'There is no need to be jealous, you know.'

'*Jealous?*' Ashe just managed to articulate the word in a hiss, not a bellow. 'Of course I am not jealous. I simply do not trust the fellow's intentions.'

'I believe them to be completely honourable,' Elinor countered with an earnestness that Ashe suspected was deliberately provocative, 'but it is very kind of you to take such an interest.'

Ashe regarded his tormentor in fulminating silence for a long moment. 'Do I need to tell you, Miss Ravenhurst, that my feelings towards your cousin are not those of kindness?'

'No, Lord Dereham, you do not. I imagine they swing rather wildly between an urge to strangle her and a quite different emotion altogether. Unfortunately, I am not sure if Belinda realises that and, although I am not at all experienced with this sort of thing, you do appear to be making something of a mull of bringing it to her attention.'

Amusement twinkled in her greenish eyes and through his irritation he thought that, animated like this, she was far from the dowdy bluestocking everyone dismissed her as. 'And now you would like to strangle me too, so I will run away.' Her smile was pure provocation. 'If it is convenient, could you call at two?'

She took his curt nod for agreement and took her leave of the Reynards, pausing to confirm the time for the afternoon's expedition with Patrick Layne.

Ashe sat down and snapped open the *Morning Chronicle* as an effective barrier to think behind. How was he going to find some decent privacy to court Bel if his entire family and that damned Layne fellow kept intruding at every turn? He was certainly not going to find it traipsing round every nook and cranny of an inn in company with two ex-soldiers, a bluestocking and a decent fellow whose eye he would very much like to black.

'How interesting,' Elinor observed, as the barouche came to the crossroads in the centre of the village of St Lawrence. 'The church tower is of Saxon origin.' She consulted the guide book again. 'This appears to be quite accurate—so often they confuse late Saxon with early Norman, you know.'

Her cousin had maintained a flow of informative chat

for the entire journey. Bel, who would normally have been bored to death by talk of Saxon towers, ancient seats and the remains of Elizabethan warning beacons, had been grateful for the necessity placed on the two men to respond appropriately to Elinor's flow of antiquarian information. Ashe and Patrick had settled down diagonally opposite each other with polite enquiries and smiles that she would have trusted about as far as she would have trusted those of a brace of crocodiles.

Now, at least, she could see their destination. 'Look, there it is—the Kentish Samson.'

The creaking and faded inn sign showed a huge man rending a thick cable apart with his bare hands. 'Richard Joy,' Elinor informed them helpfully. 'He lived here in the last century and was famed for his strength.'

'Which is more than can be said for the structure named after him.' Ashe eyed it critically as they drew up in the inn yard. Shutters hung off their hinges, stable doors stood open on to dirty, empty stalls and the yard itself did not appear to have been swept for a year.

'It may not be structural,' Patrick countered, standing to help Bel down as the groom folded down the steps. 'Do mind where you put your feet.'

'Half the window frames look rotten,' Ashe observed, handing Elinor out.

'But the roof line is perfectly sound,' Patrick responded, apparently intent on making Ashe sound negative. He took Bel's arm and pointed upwards. 'See? The ridge line is quite straight, which is a good sign, and there are few slipped tiles.' Having secured her arm, he tucked her hand firmly under his forearm and walked towards the back door. Conscious of Ashe's gaze on them, Bel forced a smile and left her hand where it was. She supposed she should feel flattered that Ashe was so hostile, but as he seemed more motivated by antagonism to Patrick than affection for her, she was not much encouraged.

'My lady.' It was, thank goodness, Brown with Lewin hopping on his crutch behind him. The ex-sergeant kept his voice down, waiting for Ashe and Elinor to join them. 'It looks good—needs some work—but the books seem honest and if it was fettled up right I reckon it'd be a little gold mine.'

'You had better show us round then, Sergeant,' Ashe said, earning himself a sharp look from the big man.

'I don't rightly hold any claim to that rank now, Major.'

'Nor I to mine. Very well, Mr Brown, let us go and see if you have found yourself an inn to run,' Ashe returned, assisting Elinor over a puddle.

They spent an hour poking through the place from attics to cellars, dogged by the owner, anxiously twisting his hands into his stained apron. 'It's a good place,' he whined, 'only since my wife died I don't seem to be able to get a grip on it like I used to.'

'Since she ran off with that Sergeant of Marines you mean, Tom Hatchett,' one of the men in the bar shouted unkindly. 'Sooner you sells it and we get a landlord who can keep a sweet barrel of Kentish ale, the happier we'll all be.'

'Let's have a look at the books,' Ashe said, seconded by Elinor, a notebook ready in her hands. They followed the landlord and Brown and Lewin into the inner parlour, leaving Bel with Patrick in the bar.

'Outside, I think,' he said, holding the door for her. 'This isn't a place for a lady, although I think we could get the carriage trade in once it was done up.'

'Yes, I think so too. I really feel quite optimistic about it.' At least something was going well. She could quite see that Brown's claim that a successful inn could employ a dozen men was no exaggeration.

'Reynard is not so confident,' Patrick observed, holding a door open for her. Bel stepped through into what appeared to be a harness room, now more a haven for spiders and rubbish.

'I think he is merely sceptical. He does not want me making a poor investment.' Bel lifted an empty sack to see what lay beneath, then dropped it again with a grimace as thick rolls of dust fell to the floor.

'He seems most protective of you.' Patrick came fully into the room behind her, his body blocking out the light. 'Lady Belinda…Belinda. I must ask you, what is Dereham to you?'

'Nothing—other than a friend and a fellow committee member.' She should enquire haughtily what right he had to ask, she realised as soon as she began to speak. It seemed her guilty conscience about Ashe would be her undoing.

'I am glad to hear you say it, although I doubt that is how he sees himself.' Patrick sounded more serious than she was used to hearing him.

'What right have you…?' Bel began, but he moved closer, holding up a hand to silence her.

'You will forgive me if I observe that you have spent some energy on matchmaking between me and Miss Ravenhurst.'

'Yes. I am sorry, that was foolish of me, I just thought that perhaps you would suit—' She broke off and regarded him ruefully. 'But you would not, would you?'

'No, Belinda, we would not. Miss Ravenhurst is an

admirable young lady, both intelligent and amiable, but I am attracted to quite another woman you see.'

'You are?' *Oh, Lord, he is going to make a declaration.*

'Belinda, have you no idea how I feel about you?' His brown eyes were earnest as he reached out and caught her hand in his. Bel tugged, but he held her firm, pulling her towards him so that her captured hand was pressed to his breast.

'No,' she lied. Ashe had warned her, but she had not taken him seriously, knowing that Patrick was wrong for her; she still could not believe he thought they were suited. 'No, I had no idea. Mr Layne, I truly value you as a friend, but I could never regard you in any other light, believe me…'

'Just try to think of me in that other light.' He secured her other hand. Trapped between his body, which suddenly seemed much larger than she had thought, and the metal saddle racks and wooden boxes, Bel found she had nowhere to go. 'Bel, I cannot offer you a title, but I can offer you my devotion and my—'

'No!' She pushed against his chest. 'Mr Layne… Patrick, I am of course honoured by your regard, but I am certain that we would not suit.'

'Let me show you how suited we could be, Belinda.' And he bent his head to kiss her.

Chapter Twenty-Two

P atrick's attempt at a kiss would have been more successful if Bel had not ducked her head at the last
moment, fetching him a nasty blow on the bridge of his
nose from the high poke of her straw bonnet.

'Hell!' He staggered back, clutching his face with
one hand, the other still clasping her wrist, and came up
hard against Ashe, who was striding into the harness
room.

'Hell indeed,' he said grimly, taking Layne by the
shoulder and turning him, the other hand already
clenched into a formidable fist.

'Ashe!' Bel, propelled by the force of Patrick's turn,
spun with him, landing against Ashe's chest as the other
man released her. 'Ashe, stop it.'

She stood between the two men as they glared at
each other. Patrick's hat was off and a darkening weal
cut across the bridge of his nose. Ashe was poised on
the balls of his feet as though ready to spring.

'Did he hurt you?' he demanded.

'No, of course not. I turned suddenly and caught

him a glancing blow with my bonnet brim. Really, my lord—'

'And your wrist?' Ashe seized her right hand and lifted it. In the gap between her cuff and the edge of her light summer glove the skin was reddened.

'Mr Layne caught at it instinctively to save his balance when I knocked into him,' she improvised. 'And then you jerked him out of there at such speed I was dragged too.' Bel tried to interpose herself between Ashe and Patrick and found herself bundled very firmly to one side.

'There is no need to lie for me, Lady Belinda,' Patrick said with cold dignity. 'My lord, I was making Lady Belinda a declaration when you intruded. I must request you to retire, you are embarrassing her ladyship.'

'Embarrassing her more than you making her a declaration in a filthy hovel? One that she finds so distasteful that she tries to break your nose for you? One that she must be restrained to hear, you bastard?'

'Really, my lord, I must protest. The intemperance of your language before a lady is completely unacceptable. The force of my ardour—'

The echo of Ashe's words when Aunt Louisa had caught them in the drawing room was too much for Bel's overstretched nerves. She gave a gasp of shocked laughter, then clapped her hands to her mouth as Elinor, followed by the two soldiers, the landlord and several interested customers, spilled out into the yard.

'You can take this for your ardour,' Ashe said grimly, punching Patrick square on the jaw. He went down in an ungainly tangle of limbs, but got to his feet gamely, his fists clenched.

'Here, gentlemen, not in front of the ladies!' It was

Brown, nimble now on his crutches, swinging his formidable bulk between the two men.

'You will meet me for this,' Patrick said fiercely.

'Damn it, *you* will meet *me* for the insult to Lady Belinda.' Ashe glared back at him.

'You cannot meet anyone,' Elinor declared coolly, in a voice of flattening common sense as she came to take Bel's arm. 'You have no seconds. It would be most irregular.'

Ashe turned to look at her, a glimmer of a smile just touching his mouth as she met his hot blue stare with unflappable calm. 'Thank you for that observation, Miss Ravenhurst. Brown, Lewin, you will have to stand for us.'

'Aye, well, there's no one else. I've seen these affairs before,' Brown observed. 'And it's the challenged party what gets to choose the weapons. You've challenged each other so we need to sort that out first.' He frowned, then fished in his pocket and drew out a heavy coach wheel, tossing the penny coin to Ashe, who caught it one handed. 'And you lot!' He raised his voice to a bellow. 'Get out of here and mind your own affairs.'

The spectators shuffled off reluctantly as Ashe balanced the coin on his bent thumb, said 'Call', and sent it flying upwards.

'Heads.'

They all bent to observe it as it lay on the filthy cobbles, King George's fleshy profile uppermost. 'I choose pistols,' Patrick said. 'If we have any.'

'I have a pair. Tomorrow at six on the cliffs?' Ashe asked.

'Right.' Patrick nodded.

Bel looked from one man to the other. They did not

seem unduly hostile now, it was incomprehensible. 'Stop it,' she said, finding her voice again. 'This is madness.' She might as well not have spoken.

'Good day, Lady Belinda. I will hire a gig to return to Margate.' Patrick Layne bowed punctiliously and strode out of the yard.

'Right.' Ashe tugged his glove back more firmly over his knuckles. 'Have we finished looking at this place?' Bel and Elinor exchanged incredulous glances. 'It looks good to me. If you do not wish to purchase it, Lady Belinda, I certainly will, if Brown and Lewin feel it matches their needs.'

'Aye, my lord, it does that, I thank you.'

'Very well.' Ashe reached into the breast of his coat and produced his pocket book. There was an exchange of something that crackled. 'Tell him to take it off the market and my man of business will be in touch with him directly.'

'I want to buy it,' Bel said flatly as they got back into the carriage.

'You will surely not wish to be involved in negotiations. Let my man handle it, we can discuss who makes the purchase later.' Ashe settled himself opposite the ladies, as at ease as a man who had just spent an hour strolling round the garden, not one who had been involved in fisticuffs ending in a challenge.

'And you will stop this duel nonsense,' she began.

Ashe raised one brow. 'Certainly not, and I will not discuss it further.'

Bel opened her mouth and received a sharp jab in the ribs from Elinor. Her cousin was doubtless right. Expecting a man to take a sensible view of an affair of honour was like expecting the sun not to rise in the morning. She held her peace as they travelled in silence back to the resort, her brain spinning with fruitless ideas for stopping it.

She dismounted at the hotel with a stiff nod to Ashe and swept inside and up to their suite, Elinor hastening behind her.

'How do we stop them?' she demanded the moment the door was closed. 'Tell Lady Dereham and Miss Layne?'

'They will not be able to do anything.' Elinor frowned. 'And we will be worrying them, for I doubt the men will tell them.'

'No doubt they intend just to leave a letter with directions on where to find their respective wills.' Bel felt savage. 'And if one of them kills the other, then the survivor will have to flee abroad. They have probably got Brown reserving a hoy at Ramsgate against just such a contingency.'

'Well, it is illegal,' Elinor said thoughtfully. 'We could inform the magistrates. After all, we know where and we know when.'

'So we do.' Bel jumped up and kissed her. 'That is brilliant! Should we do it now?'

'No, later this evening,' Elinor decided. She hesitated. 'You do still love him, don't you?'

'Ashe? Oh, yes. So much. I thought he had followed me here, but of course, he had not. We…met while we were swimming.' Elinor's mouth formed a perfect O of shocked surprise. 'I should never have…not again…and afterwards I told him that. If he had felt anything for me other than physical desire, surely he would have said so then?'

'I have absolutely no idea, I am glad to say,' her

cousin retorted with some asperity. 'I knew I was right to resolve upon a single life.'

'I ought to wish I had never embarked upon the affair,' Bel said painfully. 'But I cannot. It is breaking my heart and yet I cannot wish I did not love him.'

Ashe stood on the cliff top, watching a fishing smack making its way towards a small buoy that bobbed scarlet and black against the grey morning sea. The sky was lightly overcast with cloud, the wind still cool up here on the sheep-cropped turf.

A few yards away Layne stood likewise, affecting an interest in the seascape while Brown and Lewin loaded the pistols. At the edge of the road, against a distorted clump of trees, the doctor's closed carriage lurked, far enough away to give some credence to the tale he would tell of just passing by when he heard a shot. If there was a death or a serious injury today the doctor could be incriminated if it were proven he knew about the duel beforehand.

Ashe pushed the flicker of speculation about Layne's intentions, and his skill with a pistol, to the back of his mind. It was better to starve the imagination in situations like this. He touched his thumbs and forefingers together and began to discipline his breathing, wishing for the comfortable white pelt of the bearskin rug beneath him as he strove for balance and focus.

'Right, then.' Brown had reached his side unnoticed. 'Here's your pistol, Major.' He hesitated. 'Lady Belinda's going to be mad as a wet cat if we bring you back with a hole in you.'

'She won't blame you,' Ashe said with a grim smile. 'She knows exactly whose fault this is.' He walked towards Layne, bowed as they met, then turned on his heel to stand back to back with the other man.

'Walk,' called Brown and he began to pace. 'Stop. Turn. Take aim.'

Ashe lifted the pistol, his arm straight, his body turned to offer the smallest target to Layne's bullet. The tiny black mouth of the other pistol leered at him as he took his aim.

'Stop in the name of the law!' The shout had them all turning. Ashe threw up his pistol hand so the weapon was pointing skywards and saw Layne do the same as the gig bounced towards them over the hummocks, two red-faced men in bag-wigs glowering at them.

'How the hell—' Layne began.

'Look behind them,' Ashe said grimly as a second gig, driven by Miss Ravenhurst, swung off the road in the magistrates' wake. Bel spilled out of the vehicle as it came to a halt and ran, stumbling, across to him, her skirts kilted up to scandalous heights. Ashe lowered his hand and fired into the ground, hearing the echoing bark of Layne's safety shot.

'Gentlemen,' he could hear Layne saying fluently, 'we are merely rabbit shooting, you have obviously been sadly misinformed if you feared something else was afoot.'

'Rabbits, my eye, sir! With Dr Lambert's carriage—'

'What carriage?' enquired Layne coolly, gazing around. 'I greatly regret that you have been led on a wild goose chase, your worships.'

'Just get out of our parish next time you want to shoot rabbits,' the stouter magistrate ordered, heaving himself back into the gig. 'Madam,' he said with dignity to Bel who had arrived breathless on the scene, 'I bid you good day.'

'What do you mean, Mr Manningtree—*next time*?' she demanded. 'You have stopped them.' Her bonnet was hanging down her back by its ribbons, her slippers were grass stained and her muslin skirts creased and rumpled from where she had screwed them up as she ran. Ashe wanted to shake her until her teeth rattled.

'Madam, this is a *duel*,' the thinner one explained, glaring at Ashe in such a way that made him sorry for any poacher who came up in front of this bench. 'Once *gentlemen* have resolved on this course, they will not be deterred unless one of them apologises—or is dead. Our sole concern is that they do not continue within our jurisdiction. Good morning to you.'

'Ashe, no!' She turned to him, her mouth trembling. 'This is finished now, surely. Tell me you are not going to persist with this idiocy.'

'Not even if you hound us out of Kent, Bel,' he said. His anger with her was still hot, but he wanted to take her in his arms and kiss her until those lips were trembling with desire and passion and not fear for him. 'You will just have to let us get on with it.'

He expected—feared—her tears. He had not expected anger, but that was what lit up her eyes. She marched up to him, so close that their toes bumped, grabbed him by the biceps and shook him. Ashe rocked back on his heels a little, braced for a slap, but all she said, her voice intent and shaking, was, 'You and your damnable honour. You will break my heart, Ashe Reynard, won't you? But, of course, this is more important. Off you go and kill each other.'

Break my heart? 'Bel?' But she was gone, running across to where her cousin waited, her white face turned to them, her hands on the reins of the hired gig. A slow, incredulous smile spread across his face.

'There is nothing we can do?' Elinor demanded as she steered the sluggish pony back down the hill to the seafront. 'They will just go somewhere else?'

'That is what Ashe says. That is what the magistrates said—all they wanted was to chase them away so they did it in another parish, can you believe! Why could they not have arrested them?'

'Arrest a viscount? With no actual shots fired? I doubt they have the courage.' Elinor sighed. 'All we can do is wait. Shall I have tea sent to our room?'

'We cannot watch for them to return if we wait up there.' Bel went into the public drawing room, which was set out with groups of *chaises* and armchairs. A number of formidable dowagers had staked out a claim to the best viewpoints to observe and criticise the passing throng.

'Here, these seats by the window.'

'That is where Lady Throckington and her companion always sit,' Elinor protested.

'She will just have to sit somewhere else today.' Bel sat in a chair overlooking the Marine Parade and facing the way they had entered the town. 'Here, you face in the opposite direction in case they circle around.' She hitched her chair closer to the glass.

'Bel, you will be visible from outside.' Elinor twitched a curtain across to provide some sort of screen. 'We are not the men in the Bond Street coffee-house windows, you know!'

Ninety minutes and two pots of tea later they were still sitting there. Lady Throckington had arrived, glared, and retired defeated by Bel's flat refusal to be shamed into moving. She sat in the next group of chairs along and fixed the two younger women with a basilisk stare while carrying out a loud and rather one-sided conversation with her companion on the manner and morals of today's generation.

Bel, who had hardly noticed her, was beginning to feel desperate. Surely they should be back by now? Surely such a delay meant that one of them was wounded, at the very least? Her imagination filled with horrid pictures of Ashe white, dead, on the green grass. Of Ashe, Patrick's blood still staining his hands, running for a boat and exile. Of…

'Miss Ravenhurst?'

'What? There is a mistake, it must be a message for me.' Bel swung round to find one of the pageboys holding out a salver with a sealed note upon it.

'No mistake. It is addressed to me.' Elinor picked it up and slit the seal.

'I was to wait for a reply, if you please, ma'am.'

'What is it?' Bel demanded, her heart in her throat.

'Oh, nothing of any moment.' Elinor frowned down at it. 'I wonder what to do for the best.' That appeared to be a rhetorical question, for she stood up. 'I will not be long—will you wait here?'

'Yes, of course—but, Elinor, I need you with me.'

'Of course. Truly, you will not be alone long. Now, where is the nearest writing desk?'

Biting her lips, Bel turned from watching her cousin's retreating back and fixed her eyes on the road. Had she missed them? Surely Brown and Lewin would come and tell her if the worst had happened? The minutes ticked by and still Elinor did not return.

Then there was a movement beside her and she half-turned, her eyes still fixed on the street. 'Where on earth have you been—*Ashe*!'

'May I sit down?' He placed his hat on a chair, propped his cane against it and sat, one leg elegantly crossed over the other, an immaculately groomed figure in pantaloons and Hessian boots, his coat of superfine fitting to a nicety, his linen crisp.

The room swam around her. Ashe was alive. He was here and not dead, not heading out of Ramsgate harbour.

'You stopped and *changed*?' she demanded, relief fuelling her fury. Lady Throckington raised her quizzing glass and Bel dropped her voice to an enraged hiss. 'You knew I would be frantic and you stopped to *change*?' Then thought became easier and she gasped, 'You haven't been wounded?'

'No. And neither has Layne. We both deloped.'

'So neither of you ever had the slightest intention of killing each other?'

'Don't sound so cross about it Bel, I thought that was what you wanted. No, no coffee, thank you.' The waiter bowed and took himself off.

'Of course that is what I wanted—but why have you had to go through this farce? I have been worried to distraction.' Her eyes searched his face anxiously, the way he was sitting. He truly did appear to be unharmed.

'Because it was a matter of honour,' Ashe said quietly, watching her face. 'And that is how matters of honour are settled—or a gentleman has no honour.'

'But you *like* Patrick,' she puzzled. 'You did not truly believe he would hurt me—or you would not have deloped. You did not mean to kill him.'

Her voice had risen again, heads turned as her words

became audible. 'I do disagree with *killing animals* for sport,' Bel said clearly and faces turned away.

'Once I had hit him there was no going back.' Ashe leaned forwards so they could continue their conversation more quietly.

'Then you should have apologised.'

'But I wanted to hit him,' he admitted ruefully. 'And I enjoyed it.'

'Why are you here?' Suddenly she was finding his closeness almost unbearable. She wanted to be in his arms and that was impossible. She wanted to speak openly to him, but that too was impossible. He had frightened her almost out of her wits and for that she wanted to hit him. Hard. Bel contented herself with a frosty stare.

'Because I want to know what you meant by what you said on the cliff top,' Ashe said softly, leaning forward, his clasped hands between his knees, so close that she could feel his breath. 'You said "you will break my heart". What did you mean, Bel?'

'I…' Had she really said that? She had thought the words were only in her mind. 'I meant it would be so terrible to have to tell your family that you had been killed, or had to flee abroad, all because of me.'

'Little liar,' he said amiably, his tone belying the intensity in the dark blue eyes. They were the colour of storm sea again: deep, dangerous, intense. 'You will tell me what you meant. The truth now, Bel.'

'That is what I meant,' she lied, looking around her for Elinor and some rescue. 'Where has Elinor got to?'

'She has gone to the library to meet Miss Layne and then they will have luncheon.'

'But she knows I was frantic! ̵ ̵
leave me?'

'Because I told her to.' Bel sat stunned by her cousin's desertion. 'She knew we were both all right. I told her in my note that I wished to speak with you alone. At length.' There was no mistaking what he meant by that. Bel could feel the heat building inside her, treacherous, betraying, weakening.

'We have said all there is to say.'

'No we have not. Bel, you will tell me what you meant. Come, let us go up to your suite.'

She gasped. 'No! Of course we cannot, that is scandalous!' The quizzing glasses swung round again. 'The price of French silk,' she extemporised wildly. 'Quite scandalous.'

Ashe appeared unconscious of the fact that they were in a public place. 'Oh, I think we can, Bel. You see, we need to talk and it is going to be the sort of conversation we need to have naked.'

'Na—' Bel slapped her hand over her mouth before she could say it. 'No. I will sit here all day if need be.'

'So be it.' Ashe sighed and sat back, beginning to tug at the fingers of his right glove. 'I have never thought of myself as an exhibitionist, but if that is what you want…'

'You cannot mean to sit there and take off all your clothes,' Bel whispered. 'I refuse to believe it.'

'I will have to stand up to remove my pantaloons,' Ashe said thoughtfully, finishing tugging each finger and pulling off the glove. He tossed it on to the table and began on the other. Slowly. 'And then I will have to stand up to undress you…'

Bel pursed her lips and sat bolt upright in her chair, staring out of the window. He did not mean it. He could not possibly mean it.

The second glove landed on the tea table with a soft

leathery sound. Out of the corner of her eye Bel could see Ashe's long fingers begin to toy with the top button of his coat.

Lady Throckington's quizzing glass was trained on his profile. 'A handsome young man that,' she informed her companion loudly with all the outrageous frankness of women of her age and class. 'Boxes, I have no doubt. Strips well, I should imagine.'

The companion, no doubt inured to an employer who was not above ogling good-looking footmen, did not respond. The tips of Ashe's ears went pink. But the button was undone. He moved on to the next one.

'Well, Bel, that old trout will appreciate the scene, even if you do not.'

'You would not dare.'

Ashe smiled, a slow, sensual smile that made every cell in her body remember how that mouth felt on her skin, how those long, clever fingers could drive her to madness.

'Try me.'

Chapter Twenty-Three

His coat undone, Ashe began on the buttons of his waistcoat. Frantically Bel counted them. Four. *One... two...*

'I am going.' She put her hands on the arms of the chair and started to stand.

'With me?'

'No.'

'If you set foot in that lobby, still refusing to take me to your room, I will pick you up and carry you.' Bel sat down.

Three.

'You do not know which one is mine.'

'Second floor front, first door on the left. The key is in my pocket. Which reminds me, I must take it out against the moment when I have no pockets about my person.'

Four.

'Where did you get it?'

'Cousin Elinor, of course.' Ashe pulled the ends of his neckcloth free. 'I will do this, Bel. I never make threats, only promises.' He started to unwind the long white muslin strip. Lady Throckington's mouth dropped open.

'Very well,' Bel capitulated. Anything rather than a scene in here. Once she was in the lobby, she could run. He could hardly snatch her in the street. 'You must tie it again,' she hissed as he sat back with a grin.

Ashe stuffed the ends unceremoniously back into his shirt and stood up, offering her his hand. Bel ignored it, stood up and swept across the room, knowing her cheeks were scarlet. As she passed Lady Throckington's table the old woman gave a cackle of laughter, but she kept her eyes straight ahead.

The lobby was, unfortunately, empty. Bel had hoped for a crowd of people to dart between. She feinted towards the stairs, then spun round and dashed for the street door. Ashe caught her before she was halfway to it, one long arm lashed around her waist, then she was thrown over his shoulder like a sack of grain.

'Ough!' Breathless, her head spinning, Bel kicked, but Ashe's arm was firm, clamping her in place as he started to climb—and then she was too afraid of being dropped to fight. 'Just you wait until I am on my feet,' she threatened, her mouth muffled against the back of his coat.

No response. There was an awkward moment while he shuffled his hand into his pocket for the key, then he had shouldered the door open and they were inside.

Bel staggered as Ashe set her down, too dizzy while the blood went back towards her feet to do more than grip the bedpost. He was locking the door, she saw, then he threw the key out of the window with a flick of his wrist.

'How are we going to get out now?' Bel demanded.

'When we are ready—eventually—we will ring and someone will come and I will explain through the door that unfortunately I have lost the key.' Her eyes fixed on the bell pull, but he was there before her, tossing it up so that it caught high on the edge of the ornate mirror over the fireplace. She was trapped.

'Very well.' Bel walked stiff legged to the nearest chair and sat down. 'You have gone your length, I imagine.' Her heart was pounding. If he tried to make love to her again, how was she ever going to say no? She wanted him so much. So very much. Beyond all sense. 'What do you wish to say to me?'

'Tell me what you meant on the cliff top.' Ashe shrugged out of coat and waistcoat together and pulled his loose neckcloth free.

'Stop taking your clothes off,' she said shakily. 'You distract me.'

'Tell me the truth and I will stop.'

Bel searched wildly for something convincing, something that was not *I love you*.

'I am fond of you, you know that. I did not wish you hurt or in trouble.'

'I am fond of a number of people,' he countered, tossing the neckcloth aside and beginning on his shirt buttons. 'It does not break my heart if something untoward happens to them.' The fine white linen landed on the floor and he sat to tug at his Hessian boots.

'I told you I do not wish to marry again,' Bel said desperately. 'If I tell you what I meant, you will think me a hypocrite.'

Ashe pulled off both boots and sat, his head lowered as he dealt with his stockings. 'Try me,' he said at length, looking up at her.

'If I tell you, you must not think I mean to go back on what I said about us being lovers.'

'Go on.' At least he was not removing his pantaloons, she thought with shaky relief. She would lose all power of coherent thought if he did that. It was bad enough to see him sitting there, the clear marine light bathing his naked torso, highlighting the flat planes of muscle, the gilding of hair across his chest, the strong column of his neck. She dropped her gaze and the long-boned feet, flexing in the carpet, were just as distracting.

'I love you,' she said as though admitting to a charge in court.

'Bel!' He was on his knees at her side, her hands caught in his. It was too much, he was too close. She could smell him, the heat of him, and if she leant forward, just a little, she would be able to rest her forehead on his shoulder, kiss the satin skin over that hard muscle, taste the male saltiness of his flesh.

'I am very sorry,' she apologised. 'Right at the beginning, I told you that I was not—at least, I hope I made it clear that I was not looking for anything but a physical relationship. An *affaire*.'

'Yes, I was quite clear about that,' he agreed. 'Look at me, Bel.'

'No.' She shook her head. Their hands were entwined together in an elaborate love knot, her white fingers lost and enlaced in his long, strong brown ones. 'I was angry when you proposed after Aunt found us together. I hated the thought that you would be trapped into such a thing for convention, for honour.'

'And I made a mull of things, speculating about love,' he said musingly. 'I have always wanted to be honest with you, Bel. I would not have been honest if I had told you then that I loved you.'

The little glimmer of foolish hope flickered and went out. 'No, of course, I quite understand.'

'Because I did not understand what I felt. Then.' Her head came up as though he had put his hand under her chin and lifted. So close, she could see the dark flecks in his eyes, the sprinkling of darker lashes in amongst the honey blond. So close, she could drown in those eyes. 'What happened under the ash tree, Bel?'

'I realised I loved you,' she faltered. Ashe released one hand and brought it up to cup her cheek, stopping her turning her head away from him. *Go on*, his eyes said. 'And that I could no longer be your lover, because that would not be honest, not if I wanted something from you that I could not have, something that you could not give.'

'And you chide me for placing honour high?' She shook her head, puzzled. 'That is honour of a high order, Bel.' His lips found hers in a gentle salute, then he sat back on his heels, her hand still enveloped in his.

'Don't pity me.' She tried to keep her voice strong.

'I do not pity you, Bel. Do you know what I did when you vanished from London?'

Ashe watched her shake her head, her wide, strained eyes fixed on his face. She had not slept all last night worrying about him, he could see. He fought the urge to stroke away the shadows under them. 'I went to Half Moon Street and Hedges would not tell me where you were. I expected to be irritated by that, to feel frustration because I could not find you. Instead I felt lost. I felt incomplete, unable to settle or to focus. I did not understand it. I am perfectly aware of what sexual frustration feels like—you had inflicted that on me for a fortnight past.' Bel blushed deliciously and something hot and dark and possessive stirred inside him.

'No, this was something new. So I let myself into the house that night and I went to your bedroom and I sat on the bearskin rug and I thought about you. About us. In the dark, all night. And with the morning light I knew why I felt like that, Bel. I love you.'

'Oh.' Her lips parted on a soft gasp of surprise and Ashe waited, schooling himself into patience while he read on her face the questions chasing the joy into puzzlement. 'You said nothing?'

'I had to find you first. That at least was the easy part. I was planning to employ Runners—I had all kinds of stratagems and I needed none of them. Mama announced calmly at breakfast that we were all going to Margate because that nice Lady Belinda mentioned it.'

'She thinks I am nice?' Bel queried, momentarily distracted.

'She thinks you would be the perfect daughter-in-law, I can tell.' He smiled lovingly at her. 'But that can wait. I resolved to court you as though we had never been lovers, to start again. That lasted just as long as it took to see you enter that bathing machine. I wanted you with every bone in my body and I simply could not resist.'

'Neither could I,' she admitted shakily, reaching out her hand as though to lay it on his chest and then snatching it back.

'And then you were so upset, so adamant that we must never do that again. I knew something was wrong, but I could not understand what. I resolved to go back to courting you while I tried to understand, or you could come to trust me enough to tell me.'

'I trust you,' Bel said fiercely. 'I trust you as I trust nothing else in my life.' And this time she did touch him, laying her hand over his heart, her bare palm hot and strong against the beat of his love.

'I knew there was something wrong. But if I told you I loved you, you would throw emotional blackmail in my face as you had before. And I want to marry you, Bel. I want this to be for ever. I want to have children with you and grow old with you. I had to work out why you fled from me even though in my arms you were fire and passion and utter abandon.'

'Marriage?' The clear grey eyes held his, full of hope and anxiety and questions.

'I know you do not want to marry again, Bel. I will give you as long as you need if you will only think about it. I promise I will give you all the freedom you want.'

'I want nothing more than to be married to you.' The intensity of her happiness steadied her voice. 'I had no idea that feelings like this existed. I had no idea that I could ever want to belong to someone as utterly as I want to belong to you. Ashe, the day I met your sisters for the first time, before I knew who they were, I thought that Katy must be your daughter, until I worked out that the ages were wrong. I spent the day in a daze, thinking about having your children.' She smiled tenderly at him and he realised he must be staring at her like a besotted idiot. He did not care. 'And yet I didn't realise I was in love with you then,' she added. 'I think that should have been a clue.'

Ashe felt like Joshua blowing the trumpet before the gates of Jericho and then being stunned that the walls fell so easily. He should have had more faith. 'I love you.

You love me. We want to get married. If I get a licence, can we be married here? Do you mind or do you want to go back to London and do it all properly?' He felt like Joshua and he felt about seventeen again and he felt like fainting from sheer happiness. Which was impossible because what he wanted to do next was pick Bel up, lay her on that big bed and…

'May we be married from your home—from Coppergate? I want to be part of it, I want all your people around us so I can start to be part of its life. Ashe…' she stroked her hand down his chest, making him catch his breath painfully '…you have been reluctant to go home before now. Can we make it ours, together?'

'Oh, God, yes.' The breath sighed out of him as he realised why he had not felt comfortable there. It was still his parent's home and it would never be his until he brought his own bride to it. No wonder he had seen Bel everywhere he looked. Deep inside him something had known instinctively that she was the one for him. He should have listened to his heart.

'Only, it will not take too long to make the preparations, will it?' she asked anxiously. 'I wonder if Sebastian and Eva can come from Maubourg in time? I had a letter from Maubourg just before I left London and they are thinking about coming back soon.'

'We will make it as soon as you want. As soon as your family can be with us,' he assured her. Anything for Bel—he would beard the Archbishop in his palace if that was what it took. He sat looking at her, stunned that she was really his, almost afraid to touch her, the awe of it paralysing him.

Bel saw the change in Ashe and did not know whether to cry or give thanks. He had realised she was his and now he was about to set her on a pedestal, honourably determined to be the perfect gentleman.

'Ashe,' she began, letting her hand slide slowly downwards until his nipple was between her fingers. She squeezed gently. He closed his eyes. Better. 'I do not want to spend a month or so pretending that this is a suitable society marriage and that I have nothing on my mind beyond buying my trousseau. I have bought one trousseau and very boring it is.'

She lifted her other hand, bringing his with it, and bit on the knuckle of his index finger. He gasped, his eyes still closed.

'What I want is for us to make love, now, this minute and on every possible occasion. And I want to feel you inside me, not being careful, not careful at all. I want you to take me, fill me—' his eyes opened, dark as the depths and he pulled her hard into his arms '—complete me. And,' she added with a shaky smile because he was going to kiss her in a moment and it was going to be wonderful, 'we could make a start on the family.'

'Bel—' he stood and scooped her up in his arms, strode across the room and set her on her feet beside the bed '—do you realise we do not have to worry about the state we leave the bed in any longer?'

Doubt flickered through her and he laughed. 'You are just going to have to be the scandal of Margate, because I intend to demolish this bed this afternoon.'

'Oh, yes, please,' she breathed as he began to unfasten her gown. It slithered to the floor and she kicked it away, heeling off her slippers with scant regard to their fragile kid. Her petticoats and chemise followed the gown, leaving her in stockings and garters and a blush.

'Hmm,' he hummed appreciatively. 'How very pretty.' To her surprise he turned her so that she faced the bed and pushed gently until her hands rested on the counterpane. 'Oh, yes, so pretty.' His caress slid down her back, over the swell of her buttocks and he moved in close, nudging her legs apart with his knee.

Bel shivered with a mixture of shyness and wicked erotic delight. What was Ashe going to do? It did not matter, it was Ashe and he loved her and she wanted to please him. Instinctively she pushed backwards, finding the curve of her buttocks cradled against his loins. So hot, so ready for her. His hand slipped between her thighs from the back as the other one began to caress her breasts, cupping them, stroking them as he nuzzled the nape of her neck.

She was utterly open to him. 'I can't touch you,' she protested, the words breaking off on a moan as his clever fingers slid into her, filling her and tormenting her with the promise of what would follow. 'You will, *ma belle*,' Ashe promised, huskily against her nape as his other hand tormented her aching nipples into points of aching desire.

His fingers slid out of her and he surged against her, filling her more than she had ever imagined possible. With a cry Bel braced herself on her arms, her head thrown back into the angle of his neck, as his mouth worked up and down the tender flesh, driving her into screaming, shameless, writhing ecstasy.

'I love you.' His voice was a claiming in her ears as his body drove hers harder and harder to where she wanted to be.

'Ashe, please…' She did not know what more she wanted, what more she could endure.

'Yes,' he said, stroking hard into the heart of her, his hand slipping round to find the aching point of need and touching, touching until she was almost, desperately, there. 'Now, Bel?'

'Yes,' she sobbed and he took her over into bliss, into fire and light and almost unbearable pleasure and he was still with her, inside her, completing her as his voice cracked on a cry that was her name and she felt, for the first time, his love shuddering to fulfilment within her.

'I love you.' Bel woke and stirred lazily, stretching against the long, hot body beside her and remembering—Ashe telling her he loved her, Ashe murmuring words of love after his body had shown her over and over the truth of it.

'I love you too,' she whispered, mouthing the words against sweat-filmed skin. Ashe tasted delicious. Salt and male and sex and satisfied desire. Her body ached with the delicious fulfilment of their love-making and yet, deep inside, something stirred. Something wicked and needy and dark and sensual. 'Have we quite wrecked this bed yet?' she murmured, working her way up with nibbles and licks towards his ear lobe.

'Not quite,' he answered, rearing up on his elbows to survey the tangled sheets.

'Oh, good.' Bel settled down against his chest, wondering which of the infinitely delicious fantasies she had in her mind they could try next. Or which of Ashe's.

'But I suppose we have a lifetime of beds to wreck,' he said thoughtfully. 'Should we go and tell our family and friends the good news?'

'In a minute,' Bel agreed, sliding down the bed on a voyage of discovery.

'All right,' Ashe said, his diction somewhat muffled by a gasp as he grabbed for the bed head. 'In about an hour.'

* * * * *

MILLS & BOON®

Let us take you back in time with our Medieval Brides...

The Novice Bride – Carol Townend

The Dumont Bride – Terri Brisbin

The Lord's Forced Bride – Anne Herries

The Warrior's Princess Bride – Meriel Fuller

The Overlord's Bride – Margaret Moore

Templar Knight, Forbidden Bride – Lynna Banning

Order yours at
www.millsandboon.co.uk/medievalbrides

MILLS & BOON®

Why shop at millsandboon.co.uk?

Each year, thousands of romance readers find their perfect read at millsandboon.co.uk. That's because we're passionate about bringing you the very best romantic fiction. Here are some of the advantages of shopping at www.millsandboon.co.uk:

* **Get new books first**—you'll be able to buy your favourite books one month before they hit the shops

* **Get exclusive discounts**—you'll also be able to buy our specially created monthly collections, with up to 50% off the RRP

* **Find your favourite authors**—latest news, interviews and new releases for all your favourite authors and series on our website, plus ideas for what to try next

* **Join in**—once you've bought your favourite books, don't forget to register with us to rate, review and join in the discussions

Visit **www.millsandboon.co.uk**
for all this and more today!